Praise for the David Slaton Novels

"Highly reminiscent of Rober̲t L̲u̲d̲l̲u̲m̲... son Bourne series!" ...d Hagberg,
...ing author

"Sure to e... d Robert Ludlum . . . ... Greaney,
...*Times* bestselling author,
on *Assassin's Run*

"A must-read for anyone looking for the next great assassin saga." —*Kirkus Reviews* on *Assassin's Game*

"The action-filled, high-octane thriller that you have been waiting for. Ward Larsen delivers enough page-turning suspense and globe-spanning action for ten novels." —William Martin,
New York Times bestselling author,
on *Assassin's Silence*

"A superbly written story." —Larry Bond,
New York Times bestselling author,
on *Assassin's Game*

"Slaton is the perfect assassin, and this is the perfect action-adventure thriller." —*Booklist* (starred review)
on *Assassin's Silence*

"A stunning thriller, one that ranks right up there with *The Day of the Jackal*. Frankly, this is the best nail-biting suspense novel I've read in years." —Stephen Coonts,
New York Times bestselling author,
on *Assassin's Game*

"Sharp as a dagger and swift as a sudden blow, *Assassin's Game* is a first-rate thriller with a plot that grabs you hard and won't let go." —Ralph Peters,
New York Times bestselling author,
on *Assassin's Game*

* Published by Forge Books

ASSASSIN'S REVENGE

WARD LARSEN

A TOM DOHERTY ASSOCIATES BOOK
NEW YORK

This is a work of fiction. All of the characters, organizations, and events portrayed in this novel are either products of the author's imagination or are used fictitiously.

ASSASSIN'S REVENGE

Copyright © 2019 by Ward Larsen

All rights reserved.

A Forge Book
Published by Tom Doherty Associates
120 Broadway
New York, NY 10271

www.tor-forge.com

Forge® is a registered trademark of Macmillan Publishing Group, LLC.

ISBN 978-0-7653-9155-1

Our books may be purchased in bulk for promotional, educational, or business use. Please contact your local bookseller or the Macmillan Corporate and Premium Sales Department at 1-800-221-7945, extension 5442, or by email at MacmillanSpecialMarkets@macmillan.com.

First Edition: August 2019
First Mass Market Edition: August 2020

Printed in the United States of America

0 9 8 7 6 5 4 3 2 1

To Herbert D. Kelleher
A man who had more friends
than anyone I've ever known

ASSASSIN'S
REVENGE

ONE

The F/A-18F Super Hornet threaded between hills at less than three hundred feet. Had it been daytime, the craggy terrain would have been a blur, trees and rock rushing past like a *Star Wars* jump to light speed. As it was, on a clear half-moon night, the hills were no more than fleeting glimpses of shadow in the periphery.

It was enough to hold the attention of both the jet's occupants.

The pilot, Commander Dan "Gonno" Rhea, was navigating using the thermographic display from their latest and greatest gadget, a forward-looking infrared pod that gave a righteous picture for hand-flying the jet at MSA—minimum sane altitude. He took particular care not to stroke the afterburner. They were flying single ship, and completely unannounced, deep inside North Korean airspace. That being the case, he had no desire to advertise their presence with thirty-foot-long plumes of fire from the twin exhaust cans. Along the same lines, he was careful not to break the sound barrier and throw a sonic boom across the countryside. That would be like ringing the doorbell on air defense networks which had so far remained quiet. The fact that Rhea was committing every synapse to flying his jet was probably just as well—his egress back over the border could prove even more problematic.

"Sir, are you sure about this?" he asked again through the intercom.

"Never more sure in my life," came the response from the back seat.

Rhea had always thought himself unflappable—as Navy pilots tended to be. Yet this present situation, to put it mildly, had his full and undivided attention. What mystified him was the guy in back. Rhea was sure he wasn't an aviator, yet he seemed infused with a surreal calmness. His voice was more level now than when they'd been standing next to the briefing room coffee pot. His words were perfectly focused, his responses clear and succinct. Whoever and whatever he was . . . the guy was in a zone.

Commander Rhea didn't even know how to address his stand-in weapons system operator. As far as he knew, the man wasn't a military officer. But he definitely had clout—more than any admiral Rhea had ever seen. The air wing commander had given explicit orders: *Give him anything he wants.* Emphasis on *anything.* Unfortunately, what he wanted—and hadn't mentioned until after they were airborne—seemed like a death wish.

Rhea wished he had more time to think about it. More time to weigh the risk-reward balance of a maneuver that was going to put his career on a fast track: whether it was to aviation legend or Leavenworth he had no idea. But then, it was probably for the best—in the dead of night, at two hundred feet above the ground and 550 knots, there was no time to dwell on his next fitness report.

He couldn't avert his eyes from the terrain display for more than a second. He stole the occasional glance at the map. A momentary cross-check of airspeed and the time-to-target clock. He'd given up trying to talk his nugget backseater out of what they were about to do. That had been settled definitively ten minutes earlier. Rhea's eyes flicked again disbelievingly to the standby compass on the far right side of his instrument panel—it was no longer functional, a bullet hole dead center.

"Ninety seconds," Rhea announced. "We're gonna pop-up now, slow to the speed we briefed."

"Do what you have to, Commander."

"Double-check that lever."

A pause. "NORM position confirmed."

"Okay," Rhea said, because what else could he say? "Thirty seconds." He pulled the throttles to idle, and the aircraft began to decelerate. Rhea pulled back, the G-forces increasing smoothly until the jet was established in a twenty-degree climb. The deceleration became more pronounced, the airspeed tape winding down as if falling off a cliff. The sudden slowdown caused a slight uptick in the computed arrival time as the nav computer corrected for the lower speed.

"Last chance to change your mind . . ." Rhea said, more a comment than any kind of advice.

For the first time there was no reply from the back seat. Rhea didn't know what to make of that. He'd only met the man a few hours ago. He was slightly on the tall side, in very good shape. Sandy hair and unusual gray eyes, a five-day beard to suggest he was either trying for the chic rough-hewn look, or that grooming had become secondary in recent days. Rhea would have bet his pension on the latter. The man's English was effortless, but there was a hint of an accent Rhea couldn't quite place. Yet he always found himself coming back to the eyes—they held a surreal intensity. Rhea had the feeling that every word he'd spoken in his quick-fire preflight briefing had been recorded on some kind of hard drive in the guy's head. Oxygen mask, fast pants, parachute procedures—every detail, notched word for word.

Gotta be a snake-eater or a spook, he decided. *Maybe both.*

Commander Rhea had seen a lot in his fifteen years in the Navy. Plenty of combat during cruises to the Gulf and Med, two spins through TOPGUN, one as a student, another as an instructor. He'd strafed ISIS strongholds and dodged surface-to-air missiles. But he'd never done anything as dodgy as this. Never heard anyone *think* about performing such a move. Not over open ocean or a desert training ground. *Sure as hell not over North freaking Korea.* The maneuver wasn't in any NATOPS manual. Not really. Then again, as a graduate of TOPGUN, he did see one parallel. It made Rhea think of the tables for a JDAM precision bomb, or maybe a Maverick missile. He was making a weapon delivery of sorts.

"Yeah," he whispered to himself, "that's exactly what it is."

"What?" said the backseater.

"Nothing." The radar altimeter was passing three thousand feet, airspeed falling through two fifty. Rhea checked the timer, began to trim forward with his thumb. "Ten seconds. Remember the position—spine straight, look forward."

"Got it."

"And by the way . . . best of luck, Killer."

"Thanks. And thanks for getting me this far."

Rhea glanced at the bullet hole in his compass. "Two . . . one . . . *go!*"

David Slaton, who was already gripping the yellow handle between his thighs, pulled it sharply upward and hung on for dear life.

TWO

Having committed fourteen years of his life to safeguarding the most prized weapons in the Korean People's Army, Captain Jung Dong-hwan found it disquieting to stand looking at an open bunker door.

The lighting inside the underground chasm was typically poor. A snaking series of overhead bulbs ran along the ceiling, the wire-encased fixtures dim on the best of days and subject to the power outages that were endemic across North Korea. Tonight, however, the usual deficiencies had been compounded by the visitors who'd taken over the place—a group of men, dressed in simple workers' coveralls, had severed the light string near the entrance, leaving a fifty-foot tract of darkness as the only connection to the outer world.

Jung strained to see through the open entrance, searching for the benevolent glow of the partial moon. At least the open door gave ventilation, he reasoned, the usual stagnant air stirred ever so slightly by a cool evening breeze. His musings were interrupted by a barked command.

"Outside!"

He turned to see his colonel's stony face—he was jabbing a finger toward the exit.

"Yes, Colonel."

Jung turned to his senior NCO, Sergeant Kim, tapped him on the shoulder, and together they began walking.

That their commander was here at three in the morning was notable in itself. The regiment's mission was to guard a network of eighteen similar bunkers spread across the nearby hills. The colonel, however, rarely ventured into the field, preferring the warmth of the headquarters complex—thirty miles away at Panghyon airfield. Jung typically saw his commander once each week, when he traveled to headquarters for the regular Tuesday-morning staff meeting. To the best of Jung's knowledge, the colonel had never set foot in this particular tunnel.

It was called Bunker 814. The question of whether there could possibly be 813 other such fortifications in the network run by the People's Strategic Rocket Forces—or for that matter, a thousand or two thousand—was something he and Sergeant Kim had often debated. It seemed incomprehensible that so many tunnels might be carved into the northern hills. Then again, there was no denying the government's emphasis over the last twenty years. Jung couldn't remember the last time he'd seen a road or a power line built whose primary purpose was not military. He knew bunkers like 814 were carved into countless mountainsides, burrowed into valleys, and that all of it was connected by thousands of miles of roads and tunnels. Whatever the true scope of the project might be, there was no denying it was a shell game of the grandest proportions.

Jung hoped the imperialists would someday see the folly of their ways. His countrymen were starving, disease running rampant, all thanks to the aggression of America and its deranged leaders. As was often made clear by Chairman Kwon, a strong nuclear capability was of paramount importance. Indeed, as Jung's colonel so regularly attested, it was the only thing that stood between peace and invasion. He felt pride that Bunker 814 was doing its part.

With their boots crunching over the gravel, the two men passed through the massive main doors. Jung had always thought they looked like something from a bank vault, two great slabs of meter-thick steel. When fully open, as they were now, the tunnel was wide enough to receive a Rodong missile transporter. For years the trucks had come and gone on a regular basis, at least one arriving each week. They typically stayed between two and ten days, the duration of their visits ostensibly a strategic decision, although Jung had come to suspect it might have less to do with any military scheme than the availability of diesel fuel on a given day. At the height of last summer, however, things had changed. The regular visits of ballistic missiles to Bunker 814 came to an abrupt halt. What arrived in their place was a mystery, and a matter of quiet speculation within the unit.

Jung reached the tunnel entrance with Kim at his shoulder, and they were met by a cold and clear night. Dim moonlight filtered through the camouflage netting overhead, and the air seemed alive, chill and fresh compared to the sulfuric humidity of the tunnel.

By design, there were few external traces of the bunker's existence. Drilled deep into the mountain, the entrance was camouflaged by plastic trees and vegetation. A two-hundred-meter gravel access road weaved through dense forest, the canopy of which was augmented by more netting. That road connected to a nearby paved artery that was opened sporadically to commercial traffic. Sergeant Kim insisted the Americans' satellites could not be so easily fooled, and Jung thought he might be right.

Kim was a technically gifted young man, and until last year had been posted near the DMZ. The unspoken assumption was that such individuals had great insights into the outside world. Internet connectivity in North Korea was strictly forbidden, but those who lived close to the southern border, and who dared defy the prohibition, found ways to connect. A friend with a smartphone or tablet computer, a hijacked signal. Rumor had it the South Koreans encouraged such connections, and Jung didn't doubt it. He also believed what he read in Workers' Party communiqués: that the South fabricated incomprehensible achievements in industry, commerce, and sport, all while erasing news of rampant unrest. Drug use, pornography, greed—as he'd been told since he was a child, these were the enduring products of capitalism.

Jung led his second to a small rock outcropping and paused there.

"Where have the others gone?" Sergeant Kim asked, his eyes searching. The rest of Jung's unit, a contingent of sixteen men, had been ordered outside an hour earlier when the visiting team had taken over.

"I don't know—I thought they would be here."

"Might they have been sent home?"

Jung shook his head. "I never heard the bus," he said, referring to the rattletrap shuttle that at the end of every shift transferred crews to their barracks fifteen miles away. "Anyway, someone would have told me if our watch was standing down."

"Perhaps we should ask what is happening."

He frowned at his senior NCO. Sergeant Kim had a habit of making such suggestions, and Jung took it as a critique of his own decisiveness.

"All will become clear. You heard the colonel—our orders are to assist these men in every way."

"But when they leave . . . there will be no one to secure the bunker. How can we manage without our men?"

Jung didn't respond.

Kim looked at him tentatively. "Do you think they might be closing 814?"

The question *had* crossed Jung's mind. And how could it not given what they'd seen? He and Kim had both been on duty that warm night six months ago when a new consignment arrived and was put in their custody. It rode in on the biggest forklift either of them had ever seen—carried on twin prongs, an off-white steel container that was the length of a small car, but narrow and peculiarly shaped with bulges on either end. Based on how the forklift strained and swayed with every turn, it was also tremendously heavy, giving the sum impression of a giant barbell. Together, he and Sergeant Kim had watched it disappear into Shaft 3, going so deep that the sound of the forklift's engine ultimately faded to nothing.

Jung had never ventured inside that passage, either before or after the delivery—it had always been off-limits. Yet according to the site map—which, as shift commander, it was his duty to commit to memory—Shaft 3 was the deepest in the complex, over twice the length of any other. For reasons never explained, the Rodongs were prohibited from using it. The passage had remained dormant as long as anyone could remember, and until that night had fallen to little more than a curiosity. Jung assumed the shaft suffered from either instability or flooding, which he knew from his headquarters meetings was a problem at some of the other complexes.

The arrival of the big cask put that notion to rest. And whatever it was, the container had become a permanent fixture. Jung and his men were briefed that what lay down Shaft 3 was highly radioactive—perhaps because it was, or perhaps to tamp down any thoughts of a closer inspection. They'd also been ordered in strictest terms to not speak of its presence. As far as Jung knew, those warnings had been heeded. He himself had not gone near Shaft 3 since the mystery container arrived, and he could honestly say he'd never heard rumors that any of his men had done so. More curiously, since that balmy summer day, the visits of the Rodong transporters had ceased completely.

"I am glad they're taking it away," said Kim. He was looking at a sturdy flatbed trailer sitting in wait. It had brought in another big forklift, which was presumably now retrieving the container. Three men stood guard next to the truck, compact semiautomatics slung across their chests. Jung had glimpsed at least two others at the top of the road.

"I too am glad," Jung replied. "I didn't like so many inspections."

Since the cask's arrival, teams from headquarters had been coming on a stepped-up schedule, often unannounced, to inspect 814. They scrutinized security measures and interrogated Jung and his men. Notably, however, not a single inspector had ever ventured into Shaft 3 for a direct look at whatever they were guarding. Like any company-grade officer in the Korean People's Army, Jung knew being in the spotlight had little upside. He'd always answered the inspectors' questions truthfully, happy he had nothing to hide. Even so, he'd never been able to shake the unease that whatever lay in Shaft 3 was going to have a bearing on his career. Jung knew it had to be extremely valuable—more so, apparently, than mobile ballistic missiles fitted with nuclear warheads.

"Do you think we have done something wrong?" Kim asked. "What if the inspectors reported our work as being deficient?"

"No. If that were true, they would not remove this thing. It would be far easier to replace us with another brigade."

The two exchanged an uncomfortable glance. Before either could speak again, a distant rumble stirred from the tunnel. Like a cough from the throat of some waking beast, the reverberation grew. As the forklift neared the tunnel mouth, Jung felt its arrival more than he heard it—the ground trembled beneath his feet.

Finally the container emerged. With the forklift not yet in view, it seemed to levitate through the great steel doors. It looked much as Jung remembered. Under the forklift's floodlights, he noticed the white outer shell had gone to a dull gray, a result of the dust that accumulated on everything placed in the tunnel for any length of time. As before, he had the impression of a great leaden barbell, an image amplified as every movement was translated to the machine behind.

Yet for all its ponderous appearance, there seemed something strangely innocuous about the outer shell. In spite of the briefings they'd had, Jung saw no radiation labels or stenciled warnings. Were he to see such a container traveling down a road on a truck, he would presume it to hold fertilizer or some kind of industrial solvent.

More armed men emerged from the tunnel in the forklift's dusty wake. Like the others, they were dressed in simple coveralls—a uniform of sorts, but lacking any rank or insignia. They were followed by Jung's colonel. Everyone watched in silence as the cask was loaded. The trailer groaned beneath the container's weight. Once it settled completely, a pair of men began securing heavy tie-down cables. The forklift disappeared up the road, where Jung assumed another trailer was waiting. There also had to be a troop carrier or bus for the visiting contingent.

The truck fired to life and began crawling up the access road. It was then, as he watched the mysterious cask disappear down a tunnel of wintering trees, and as the moon fell obscured by a passing cloud, that Jung was struck by what was missing. A number of the visiting squad, probably a half dozen, were no longer in sight. He wondered if they'd departed with his own men, whom he'd still seen no sign of since coming outside.

Once the big truck was gone, the commander of the visiting detail appeared from the tunnel. A round-faced man with severe black eyes, he pulled Jung's colonel aside. He'd said his name was Park, and in spite of the fact that he wore civilian clothes, Jung had heard one of his own men address him as "General." This seemed odd—every general Jung had ever seen wore their hard-earned stars like a second skin. Whatever he was, Jung saw clearly the deference his own colonel paid the man. The two locked in a private conference, Jung's commander nodding as Park spoke. At the end he bowed tamely, which for a full colonel in the Strategic Rocket Forces was saying something.

The colonel motioned toward Jung and Kim. "Come back inside," he ordered.

Jung quick-stepped toward the entrance, his sergeant following. He noticed a man from the visiting contingent falling in behind them. He was average in height but extremely muscular, and his close-cropped black hair had a strangely angular part across the top of his scalp. Like most of the others, he carried a compact semiautomatic across his chest. Another man, carrying a spool of wire and a crate, took up the rear.

They were all passing through the blast doors when Jung heard a distinct crackle in the distance. He saw his colonel, who was in front with General Park, glance once over his shoulder.

Jung knew what he was thinking. As army officers, they'd all been to the firing range a hundred times, and so they knew the sound of distant gunfire. It began as an extended barrage, multiple guns on full automatic shattering the calm night like so many strings of firecrackers. Next came a series of distinct single-round *pops*. Jung exchanged a look with Kim. His normally steady second was clearly unnerved. He found himself tallying the single shots. Seven . . . eight . . .

When the count reached sixteen, Jung found himself holding his breath. Hoping they would continue. He heard nothing but five sets of boots crunching over gravel.

Ten paces inside the bunker, General Park suddenly pushed Jung's colonel against the curved stone wall. The big man behind them shuffled to one side and raised his weapon.

"What are you doing?" the colonel demanded in his brusque commander's tone—the one Jung knew all too well. Raising his arm, he stepped toward Park as if preparing to dress down a slack cadet in a formation. The muscular man intervened, unleashing a burst with his weapon that struck the colonel squarely in the chest. He seemed to vibrate from the impacts, then fell face-down in the dirt, his arm raised in eternal protest.

Jung took a step back, stunned. In the final seconds of his life, he wished he had the courage of Sergeant Kim. Without hesitation, Kim rushed the gunman. He didn't cover half the gap before he was cut down in a hail. The sounds of the shots reverberated like thunder in the tunnel.

Jung stood frozen. He looked at the round-faced general, and saw not a trace of mercy in his oil-black eyes. In his final moments, Jung thought of a son he would never see again. Of a dear wife who had been sleeping gently when he'd left home four days ago. He closed his eyes, and felt a surprising moment of tranquility.

Smoke from the machine pistol was still swirling toward the roof of the tunnel when the great blast doors were run closed. Ten minutes later, a large and carefully crafted explosion brought the complete collapse of the outer tunnel.

And with that, the darkness inside Bunker 814 was made final.

THREE

"Gone," David Slaton repeated, staring at the empty slip where his boat and family had been two hours ago. "I can see that, but where did they go?"

The Scotsman on the cabin cruiser in the adjacent berth, a lanky ginger-haired man, was coiling a line near the stern. He stood framed by one of the most recognizable backdrops on earth—less than a mile distant, the iconic sentinel that was the Rock of Gibraltar. "I couldn't say," he replied. "I was below when they left. I presumed you were with your wife and lad."

"No, I don't know where they went."

When he'd first seen the empty slip, Slaton's concern was muted, recalling what the dockmaster had told them when they'd arrived. *We're busy this time of year, but I have a slip that isn't reserved for the next four nights. If you stay longer than that I may have to move you.*

Slaton walked his eyes up and down the piers, then out across a forest of masts and rigging. It was an expansive marina, but his wife and son had to be here somewhere. He pulled his burner phone from his pocket. He and Christine each carried one when they were apart, the sacrosanct rule of their irregular lifestyle. He saw no missed calls. Slaton tried her number. With each unanswered ring his unease rose a notch. After ten he killed the call. As a matter of security, they never left voice mails.

"So you were below deck when they pulled out?" he asked.

"Aye. I heard the engine, saw the cabin easing back," the Scot attested. "I did go above a few minutes later and caught a glimpse of a mast rounding the breakwater—mind you, I can't say it was your boat."

"The *breakwater*?" Slaton repeated.

His discomfort went to full-on alarm. He squared his shoulders, set down the two canvas sea bags he was carrying. They contained his morning's work: a flush motor for the head, expendables for the engine, a few provisions from a nearby grocery. Less conventionally, they held two fresh burner phones, still in their blister packaging, a modest brick of cash, and a gallon of black paint to be used in their monthly alteration of the boat's name—the necessary evils of life on the run. Slaton looked seaward for the first time that day. He scanned what little he could see of the choppy bay for the forty-four-foot Antares catamaran they called home. He didn't see its distinctive shape.

"I talked to your wife last night," the Scot said. "She mentioned you'd been working on the reefing gear. I told her she should give it a trial before settin' out to sea. Perhaps that's where she's gone."

"No, she wouldn't have done it without me."

His vagabond neighbor nodded, either to say he understood or that he wasn't going to argue the point. "Sorry I can't be more help," he said, disappearing into the cabin of his boat.

Slaton was sure Christine wouldn't have gone out with Davy only to check new rigging. He wished it were so simple.

Old impulses took hold. He scanned the parking lot for unremarkable vehicles. The wharves for people who didn't fit in. Marinas were, by definition, transient places, and so on the height of midmorning there was no shortage of either. He found himself scouring distant rooftops and windows. On their first day here, he'd noted cameras at the head of every pier, part of a security system to keep a record of comings and goings. He wondered where the control center was. Inside the nicely furnished marina office? Or perhaps at the headquarters of some security company in a faceless building across town? He should have already known that. Should have worked it out ahead of time. The all-too-familiar recriminations began to percolate.

He studied the slip where *Sirius* had been moored. Her original name was *Windsom*, but a regular change had proved a necessary accommodation—in the age of shared data, the names of vessels could be tracked from port to port all too easily. So their nautical home had acquired a rotating identity, much like the names they themselves used through expertly forged passports. He and Christine had chosen the name *Sirius* on a cold night, somewhere south of Sicily, as the two of them lay splayed on the afterdeck gazing at constellations with a superb bottle of wine. Next month they would choose something new. Perhaps *Hydra* or *Auriga*.

Next month . . .

He studied the immediate dock area, but it gave up nothing. He saw no scuff marks from boots, no empty equipment carts or abandoned lines. Slaton was well schooled in the art of not leaving traces. Ten years in the employ of Mossad, as an assassin no less, instilled the art of coming and going invisibly as a kind of second nature. Unfortunately, dealing with the aftermath of that existence was equally well practiced. Killing wasn't the kind of job one walked away from easily. Targeted organizations reappeared, bent on settling scores. There were visitations from the friends and family of his victims, no allowance given for how deserving the dearly departed might have been. How many missions, long thought finished, had already risen from the dead like operational zombies?

"I don't expect they'll be out long." The Scotsman was back on deck, his voice disrupting Slaton's scattershot thoughts.

"What?"

The man pointed across the bay, toward Algeciras and the brown hills at the foot of the Iberian Peninsula. The skies above were nearly black, thick with the promise of rain and wind.

"A gust front," said the Scot. "I've been watching it on my radar. She'll sweep through fast, but it'll be a wicked thirty minutes."

For Slaton, a patch of rough weather barely registered. "Yeah, I'm sure they'll be back before it hits. Tell me, how long ago did they leave?"

"I remember it being near the top of the hour."

Slaton checked his watch, ran the math. *Sirius* had been gone roughly forty-five minutes. In that amount of time a sailboat could only go so far. Ten miles tops in the current wind, even with the help of the motor. Probably closer to five. He saw two immediate options. The first was a fast climb up the Rock of Gibraltar. As had been the case for millennia, it offered a commanding view of the surrounding waters. From there he could survey the sea in every direction: across the bay to Spain, south to Morocco, and on the east the boundless Mediterranean. From that high ground, with a set of binoculars, he was certain he could spot *Sirius*. But that was all he could do, and *seeing* his family wasn't enough. His second option lay bobbing aimlessly behind the Scotsman's boat: a twelve-foot inflatable with a good-sized outboard.

Slaton crafted the most carefree tone he could muster. One that was completely at odds with the churn in his gut. "I've got a favor to ask . . ."

Five minutes later Slaton was steering the little inflatable through the gap in the twin breakwaters. The seas met him firmly, a steadfast swell driven by the storm reaching across the bay. His first turn, south toward open water, was a precaution against the most trying scenario: if *Sirius* had taken that tack, she might soon be lost. Any other course would keep her in the bay, a contained search box Slaton was sure he could manage.

He pushed the runabout to nearly twenty knots, the bow launching over the crest of every wave and battering down the backside. Within minutes his street clothes were drenched in cold spray. He used a sodden shirtsleeve to wipe the brine from his eyes.

Where the bay widened to meet the sea, he turned east and kept that heading long enough to get a good look around Gibraltar's southern tip. He saw no sign of *Sirius*' intimately familiar shape. Certain he'd reached a point beyond which she could have sailed in an hour, Slaton reversed course toward the

Atlantic. He went through the same drill to eliminate a westerly departure. Currents in the narrow passage ran rampant, and rising winds added to the turbulence. He saw great tankers and merchant ships, most anchored close to shore, but a few under way. A British Navy frigate plowed past indifferently, the Union Jack snapping smartly astern. Nowhere did he see the silhouette of an Antares 44 catamaran.

With comforting logic, he reasoned that *Sirius* had to be somewhere inside the bay—thirty square miles of sea, more or less, along with a handful of marinas and coves. It would be no small feat to search, but far less daunting than all the world's oceans.

The storm was closing in. A shelf of clouds, as black as night, seeming to tumble over itself, rolling like the top of a breaking wave. The first raindrops were heavy, great pellets of water slapping his face. He imagined how Christine might be handling *Sirius* at that moment. She would have the storm jib raised, the main reefed in, and was probably making for sheltered waters—if she wasn't there already.

He scanned back toward the marina, then the mole near the tiny airport. Might the Scot have been wrong? What if *Sirius* hadn't left the harbor at all? What if she was snug in a new slip, riding out the blow. He imagined Christine at the stove preparing lunch, wondering where her husband had gotten off to. Imagined Davy sitting on the floor sorting plastic dinosaurs. He again used a sleeve to wipe the rain from his eyes—the distracting images went with it.

At the mouth of the bay Slaton decided to veer east. By concentrating on the shores closer to Gibraltar, he would keep the storm at bay a bit longer. He was almost abeam the great rock itself when a shape appeared on the northern horizon. It came like an apparition, a hazy silhouette materializing out of the heaviest downpour. Slaton first saw no more than a sleek hull and mast. Then the cabin gained definition, and finally the appendages. Antennas, solar panels, dodgers—the kind of intimate seafaring details that set any two boats apart.

There was no doubt—he was looking at *Sirius*.

Slaton pushed the outboard's steering arm to the right and twisted the throttle wide open.

FOUR

From a mile away Slaton knew something was wrong.

The first thing he noticed was that their dinghy, which should have been tethered to *Sirius'* stern, was nowhere in sight. The sails remained stowed, yet one blue cover had come loose and was flapping in the wind—a sloppy display of seamanship Christine would never have tolerated. He saw no anchor line, and the engine exhaust appeared quiet. The boat was simply adrift, forsaken to the coming squall. None of those details alone were damning, but together they reinforced the most glaring inconsistency—there was no sign of Christine or Davy on deck.

Slaton reckoned the nearest shore to be half a mile distant. There were no other boats nearby. The city carried on without remark, lost in its self-centered turmoil and oblivious to a lone catamaran bobbing offshore. When he was a hundred yards from *Sirius*, Slaton had to make a decision. If he throttled back now it would provide a stealthier approach. Yet it would also take two minutes longer. It was the easiest choice he'd faced all day.

He kept the little inflatable running at full speed,

and reached *Sirius'* stern in a shower of whitewater and noise. He killed the engine at the last instant, letting momentum carry the last few yards. In those interminable seconds, as he edged closer, impatience took hold. Slaton moved to the bow, alert and ready, straining to see inside the cabin. He saw no movement. With the motor silenced, the white noise of rain on the sea predominated. Whatever resonance might have been added by the distant city was driven away by the gathering wind.

The dinghy was coasting toward the swim platform on *Sirius'* stern. From there, an integral set of steps led up to the main deck. Slaton was picking up the bow painter, taking in every nuance before him, when it struck him that he ought to be armed. He saw two immediate possibilities: a wooden paddle and a small mushroom anchor. He chose the anchor. It was not much larger than his fist, but the dense mass was undeniably comforting.

The inflatable's bow nudged the platform and Slaton leapt aboard. He wrapped the painter once around a cleat, his senses reaching for any sight or sound. A gust of wind rushed through the rigging, stays and shrouds humming like the strings of a cello. He would later critique his next moves, realizing he should have been more cautious. In that moment, however, and in a behavior that was entirely uncharacteristic, Slaton let emotion overcome reason.

He rushed headlong over the aft deck, past the helm, and burst into the main cabin. He saw no sign of his family. Hope fading, he checked each of the three staterooms, every closet and compartment. Each step came quicker, each breath more shallow. He called out their names, more in torment than hope. Only the pelting rain answered, drumming over fiberglass and canvas in an unrelenting din.

With a mounting sense of dread, he pulled out his burner phone and tried Christine's number again. Still no answer. It occurred to him that he didn't hear her phone ringing in their stateroom. He rushed to the bedside drawer, where she usually kept it, and confirmed it was gone. In that awful moment, he couldn't decide if a missing phone was good or bad. He saw an unmade bed, a toothbrush on the sink. Everything around him became noise, an avalanche of information that somehow crushed any logical process. After a brief hesitation, he checked the opposing nightstand—his side of the bed—where the only weapon they kept on board, a 9mm Beretta, should have been. That too was gone.

Slaton staggered back to the main cabin. In the center he stopped cold and spun a full circle.

He grasped for some reasonable scenario to fit what he saw, if only to suppress the building madness. Was it possible someone had tried to steal *Sirius* while Christine and Davy were ashore, then abandoned their plan? He looked around and saw a laptop computer, a high-end sat-phone, a rack of valuable nav gear. Not plausible. Could Christine have motored into the bay for some reason, then returned to shore using the dinghy after *Sirius* had somehow fallen disabled? It hardly made sense. It was a sailboat after all, and his wife was a seasoned captain. Just to be sure he went to the helm and cranked the engine. It fired right to life. He gave the wheel a half turn. The rudder felt free, nothing jammed or frozen.

He was grasping for miracles. Coming up empty. More wild theories raged, and he jettisoned them as quickly as they came. There was simply no possible solution that didn't fail on one count: Christine wasn't answering her burner. That was the death knell to anything innocent. Their phones were an absolute, the last-ditch tether that always connected them.

Never to be broken.

Surrendering to reality, Slaton climbed back out on deck. He made a despondent survey of the sea all around. Rain was coming in torrents now on the squall's leading edge. The entire hemisphere to the northeast was obscured, and elsewhere he saw only featureless sea.

It was a rainy day on the Bay of Gibraltar.

In the city nearby, business as usual.

On the docks, a day to stay below with a cup of coffee.

And for Slaton: it was the day his wife and son went missing.

FIVE

Earlier that same morning, long before Slaton stood drifting on a catamaran near the western terminus of the Mediterranean, five men had set out across the arid reaches of central Turkey. It was a region where the passage of small groups had fallen to a cliché. War refugees, asylum seekers, economic migrants. As contrasting as their motivations were, all had one thing in common: a desperate urge to leave the ravaged homelands of their ancestors. Indeed, the region once referred to as "the cradle of civilization" had, in little more than a generation, become something nearer its grave.

The five travelers began their journey, in the faint predawn light, when a pair of guards at the Suruç refugee camp turned their heads right on schedule. As jailbreaks went, it was hardly notable. The camp's security had gone lax as the war in Syria abated. There had never been strict confinement, and no one could say whether the original half-hearted curfew was aimed at keeping local thieves and smugglers out or refugees in. Whatever the intent, everyone still went through the motions: the gates were locked each night from midnight to six in the morning.

Slack as the watch might be, the leader of the group of five was a thorough man. The day before he had given inducements to the guards to turn a blind eye. The night shift commander had in fact been left slack-jawed, knowing the man had overpaid severely. The desired effect, however, was had: the departure of the small band, who had arrived at the camp separately over the course of the last week, caused barely a ripple in the cool morning air.

After clearing the main gate, the faux refugees rendezvoused in a derelict rooming house a mere hundred paces to the north. Three top-floor hovels had been procured in advance, and in the tiny shared bathroom each of the five men bathed and shaved their beards. They took turns giving each other haircuts, and later convened for tea at the first café to open. There, at a quiet corner table, the leader went over the plans for the next two days. He mostly addressed contingencies in case their respective travel plans were interrupted, but there were also subtle critiques—like the suggestion that two of the men get some sun to cover the lighter skin where their beards had been shaved away. He reiterated the need to avoid Turkish police checkpoints, and even more importantly, those of local militias in the villages—both had elements who preyed on refugees, and who would gladly lock a man up for no cause but to see how much money his family could wire.

After tea, they split up and entered the souk that had risen in the camp's shadow. It was a busy and nervous place. Overhead a riotous tangle of phone and power lines webbed between buildings like a living thing. At its peak population, the Suruç camp had hosted eight thousand refugees—Syrian mostly, with a few Iraqis, Afghans, and Somalis thrown in the mix. At the height of the war, vendors with push-carts had done a brisk business with the guards, and a better one with the constant flow of transients suffering worn shoes and empty bellies.

Now, with the conflict winding down, there were fewer merchants, but enough that each of the five men had no trouble acquiring a new wardrobe in something near their size. As the leader had instructed, they kept to Western clothing, all of it gently used: denim and khaki pants, light jackets, casual shirts. They sported the emblems of European football clubs and famous Italian designers. By the time they walked away from the souk, with the sun nearing its midday peak, the five men were fully transformed—at a glance, indistinguishable among the hundreds of thousands of exiles who'd passed through in recent years.

Yet there were subtle differences from the usual human flotsam. Chief among them was in their pockets. Each man carried a passport that was perfectly legitimate, albeit originally drafted in the name of another. The documents had been acquired by one of two methods: either appropriated from foreign ISIS fighters who'd joined the war and perished, or confiscated from locals during the course of the caliphate's occupation—an administrative spoil of war. Every passport so obtained was carefully vetted by the caliphate's "record specialists." Those not flagging on terrorist watch lists, not reported as stolen or missing, and issued by a country that didn't employ biometric marker technology were given the highest grade. From that group, it was simply a matter of matching each man to a "donor" whose picture, age, and physical characteristics were a reasonable match.

Each of the bogus refugees also carried a modest sum of cash. This was commonplace for those trying to reach Europe, although the amount involved, type of currency, and denominations had been carefully considered—not too much to draw attention, but enough to bribe a border guard or modify travel plans. Melding into the westbound river of humanity was a necessary diversion, and relatively simple. Yet there was one hidden commonality that distinguished the five from the usual bands of migrants: the highly unusual destination they shared. At the edge of town, they all shook hands and exchanged best wishes before dividing—two groups of two, and one man going solo. The next time they saw one another, God willing, they would be very near the North Korean border.

The two designated martyrs began walking north along the main road. The porosity of the Turkish frontier had long been established, and it was even more sievelike now that things were easing in Syria. After clearing the patrolled areas, the pair shifted to a secondary road and rendezvoused with a prearranged car. The car would take them as far as Istanbul. From there the plan was to split at the airport, one aiming for Doha on Qatar Airways, with a follow-on flight to Beijing. The other would try for the same destination by way of a connection in Frankfurt on Lufthansa. By midday all was going to plan.

The two technicians were close behind. Both were in their early thirties, and because each was vital to the operation—one a bomb-maker, the other as close to a scientist as existed in the caliphate—their travels had been strictly tailored. For the same reason, they had been issued the most convincing documents of the bunch, perfectly valid EU passports, along with the attendant visas to match their itinerary. They began by walking west, and found an SUV waiting in the recesses of a work shed outside the first village. The driver whisked the pair north, and by late that afternoon they arrived at Fatsa, a small fishing village on the hip of the Black Sea. There they took passage on a small fishing boat, a fast run north toward Ukraine. Once ashore, the plan was to cover the remaining ground to Kiev via bus, followed by a nonstop flight on Air China.

They too got off to a good start.

The last man to leave Suruç retained the most freedom of movement. His name was Kasim Boutros, a native of Iraq, and he was the commander of the mission. Since Boutros was firmly established on EU watch lists, and because facial recognition software was increasingly a problem, he began his journey with an easterly vector. He first crossed into Iraq, skirting the Kurdish strongholds with practiced deftness. South of Mosul, he fell back on old Baathist connections. The first of these: an uncle with a taxi.

"It has been a long time," Boutros said.

"Six years, I think," Uncle Hakeem replied. He was leaning on the fender of his beaten Toyota sedan, the bright red paint having gone to dull orange. They bantered for a time about family, a bit more about the war. Preliminaries complete, the pair were soon in their respective seats and heading south, a rooster tail of dust trailing behind.

"The roads in this area are safe now," Hakeem said. "But the Shiite militias have checkpoints outside both Ramadi and Fallujah. They are bastards, each group beholden to their own cleric. The government in Baghdad has no control outside the city."

"Can we get around them?"

Hakeem smiled. "That is how I make my living."

Boutros knew better than to ask for specifics on his uncle's initiatives, and Hakeem returned the favor, not questioning why his nephew needed a surreptitious passage to Baghdad. Even among family, the wary crosscurrents of the new Iraq ran deep.

Hakeem threaded his way expertly through territory that had twice in Boutros' lifetime been the front lines of combat. First the Americans had invaded, and later the Islamic caliphate. As he watched the familiar tawny hills roll past his window, the irony did not escape him that he had served in both conflicts, first as an officer under Saddam, and later in the army of God. That he had been on the losing side in both campaigns seemed predestined.

And here I am once again, he thought. *In that eternal bed of conflict.*

His new mission would be undertaken far from these arid lands. But then, when he'd served under Saddam his expertise had also been utilized elsewhere, far to the south, in surroundings far removed from this land of his youth. It didn't matter. Boutros knew the sands around him remained central to everything. The refrain of his ISIS commanders, of course, never wavered: only when the West was driven clear could the law of Allah return. Boutros had always nodded in agreement, never mentioning the truth of the matter: that his own relationship with Islam was far more indirect.

He doubted anyone really cared. A motivated

soldier was worth his weight in gold. And the source of that motivation?

That, he was sure, could be left for God to judge.

They reached Baghdad in midafternoon, and arrived at the airport uneventfully. There Boutros rendezvoused with one of his old Republican Guard commanders, the sort of man who always seemed to land on his feet, and who'd taken a post as the airfield operations chief. The one-time major had been expecting him, and he already knew where Boutros wanted to go—a tentative passage to Belarus.

They shared the embrace of old comrades, and after a few reminisces, and a bit of cautious fencing about present situations, the ex-major got down to business. "Minsk, is it?"

"A business matter. We all have to get by."

A knowing smile. "You are in luck, my friend. Our airfield is less busy than usual today, but I have found the exact connection you need!"

He pointed to a massive airplane across the tarmac.

"It's very big," Boutros remarked.

"Unfortunately, an Antonov," the major said with some caution.

"Is that a problem?"

"They are safe enough, but have a tendency to break. Once the pilots get her into the air . . . then you will be fine. The better news is that the crew are Kazakhs."

Boutros *was* encouraged. The Kazakhs had long been a rebellious lot, dating back to the sixteenth century when their homeland in Central Asia was overrun, in turn, by the Persians, Mongol hordes, the British Empire, and finally an emergent Russia. It was precisely the kind of history that bred contempt. So too, the kind that fostered bonds amid vanquished brethren.

Boutros was introduced to the captain as the big jet was being loaded with fuel and cargo. They struck up a conversation in English—his grasp of the language was decent, and he knew aircrew were required to speak it. He learned that the man was a vagabond aviator and, more relevantly, a casual Muslim who'd spent the bulk of his life running freight in and out of war zones. Even more encouragingly, he displayed the anti-Russian leanings typical of those born on the shoulders of the Caspian.

They talked an insurgent's shop for nearly half an hour: which shoulder-fired missiles had proved most effective for shooting down Russian airplanes, how many Chechens had volunteered in Syria. At the end, with a guarded rapport established, Boutros showed the captain documents that were perfectly in order. Six thousand U.S. dollars changed hands—terrorist camaraderie went only so far—and he was directed to the great jet's cargo bay.

At the top of the rear cargo ramp he was introduced to his host for the next half day—a taciturn loadmaster whose dominion involved everything aft of the cockpit door.

"Where would you like me to sit?" Boutros asked, once again reverting to English.

The loadmaster said in a gruff voice, "No smoking, no drinking . . . but then, I'm sure I don't have to say this to a soldier of Allah." Clearly the man had been given a briefing. He studied Boutros closely, his dark eyes and stubble-framed lips forming a silent query. Trying to reconcile his new passenger with the standing image of a battle-hardened jihadi.

He was not the first to wonder.

On appearances Boutros was not cut in the typical mold of an Islamist field commander. Rail thin, he was of average height, his face a bit too round for intimidation. Although the loadmaster could not know it, Boutros was not uneducated, amiable when he wanted to be, and a bourbon drinker of some repute. In casual situations he exuded a thoughtful, almost academic nature, notwithstanding that he'd had neither the chance nor the means to attend university. His bookish disposition, however, vanished the moment bullets began flying. What Boutros lacked in size, strength, and gravitas, he more than made up for with a ferocious fighting nature. He'd survived some of the most vicious battles of the caliphate's war, along the way earning more than a few scars and, more critically, the unwavering respect of his men. Most curious of all was that his training in the Iraqi armed forces had nothing to do with desert firefights. It was that special qualification, in concert with his fierce reputation, that had made Boutros the singular choice to lead this mission. A mission that, if successful, could alter the tide of battle for the foundering Islamic State.

"This way," the loadmaster said. He led Boutros to the forward cargo area where a handful of webbed seats lined either sidewall. "Starboard side," the Uzbek said, not gesturing either way.

Boutros veered to his right and took a seat, knowing he'd passed the man's test.

"If you need something, don't call me," the man added. With that, the world's worst flight attendant ambled aft and disappeared behind a stack of crates.

Twenty minutes later the old Antonov was airborne. Boutros sat staring at crates of motor oil and car parts, all of it lashed firmly to the deck. At the last minute a second suspicious passenger had boarded the Antonov, an unsmiling young man who looked more frightened than purposeful, and who'd belted into a seat on the opposite side of the cargo bay.

As the big jet climbed smoothly and turned toward the Zagros Mountains, an ever-thoughtful Boutros found himself ruminating on the chances of success of their mission. Merely getting his squad to the staging point was the first order of battle, and no small task. He'd opted for an admittedly shotgun method of moving his unit, but thought it the best strategy. If he had learned anything as a commander in ISIS, it was that victory and defeat came in degrees, neither absolute a realistic outcome.

He had allowed from the outset that one of his team members might be detained somewhere along the way, either sent back from where they came, or delayed to the point that they would not arrive in Beijing on schedule. The Chinese themselves were not party to the mission, but Boutros had been assured they would not interfere. Someone, apparently, had connections. At a minimum, he prayed the two technicians would get through—if either was delayed, the mission would have to wait. His own presence was also required. The martyrs were less essential—in truth, little more than a convenience.

The airplane jostled under turbulence, and Boutros gripped his seat. As he did, a grim derivative of his commander's calculus lodged in his mind. *On this mission,* he relented, *we must all be prepared for martyrdom.*

SIX

The storm abated quickly, and in less than thirty minutes Slaton had *Sirius* back in the harbor. Her bow split the twin jetties, and soon she was in the slip where she'd begun the morning. The Scotsman next door was nowhere to be seen, which was fine with Slaton—he didn't want to waste time concocting a story about where his family had gone.

While he secured the boat, his eyes kept sweeping the piers and shoreline—dying hope that it was all only some great misunderstanding. He saw people going about their business. Tourists strolling, boat detailers scrubbing, waitresses on the way to the lunch shift. None of them could imagine the crisis he was facing. He briefly weighed playing detective, canvassing the pier to ask if anyone had seen or heard anything suspicious. There was a chance he would uncover leads about what had happened. More likely: he would raise suspicion and waste precious time. Slaton felt a cresting sense of urgency, as if Christine and Davy were slipping farther out of reach every second.

At the very least, he decided he could search the boat. He began by looking for differences from his recollections of that morning. The coffee pot was half full, and an unwashed mug sat in the sink. Toys scattered across the floor suggested Davy had been awake—and that they'd departed without the customary cleanup. With aching vividness, he remembered stealing a glance at them both on his way out. Christine had been rustling in bed, Davy sleeping soundly in the adjacent cabin. Slaton was overcome by the grim notion that it would be his last vision of them.

He pushed the thought away. Beating himself up was a waste of time.

He focused on the electronics suite. Nothing new had been entered into the navigation system—in particular, no course plots to suggest where *Sirius* had been headed. He powered up the sat-phone, which was strictly an emergency backup due to its susceptibility to tracking. Nothing in the call log. He spun a circle in the main salon, and his eyes settled on their laptop. It was right where he'd left it, shut down after acquiring directions for his morning errands.

He was weighing whether to boot it up when the phone in his pocket vibrated. He wrenched the handset clear and saw not an incoming call, but a text. He tapped on the screen, hoping for a message from his wife that would explain everything. What appeared, he would later reflect, was precisely the opposite.

It originated from Christine's phone. Yet the leading line, one word in bold letters, caused his stomach to lurch: *kidon*.

He felt as if the floor beneath him had been pulled away.

It was the term used by Mossad to refer to its assassins.

What Slaton had once been.

His finger hovered over the bubble, ready to call up the full message.

Slaton felt like the frontman on a bomb squad, cutters poised over the final wire. Part of him wanted answers. Another part didn't, fearing what they might be.

He tapped down and the full message flashed to the screen. Slaton was surprised by the compactness of what he saw. There was no salutation, no narrative. Only a short series of bullet instructions.

> Kidon
> Vienna, Wednesday evening, 8:15
> Target photo attached
> Danube Island, north shore semicircle
> Three benches, three trees
> Do what you do best
> After confirmation, expect contact here
>   regarding safe return of family

He tried to hold steady, yet found his free hand clutching the chart table. It was the worst possible scenario, the one from which they'd been running for so long. A living nightmare condensed to a few lines of bland prose.

Christine and Davy had been taken. And for the worst possible reason.

Do what you do best.

That could have only one meaning. Someone knew about his background, and they were compelling him to return to his old life . . . for their own dubious ends. Whoever it was, they were capable enough to find him. Capable enough to seize his family and appropriate their one secure means of communication.

Clearly not secure enough.

Slaton realized he'd let his guard down. His family had been taken, and while the details were unclear, he recognized the hallmarks of a competent operation. The Scotsman, only a few steps away, hadn't noticed anything amiss. Slaton himself saw virtually no trace of how his wife and son had been taken. Nothing at all regarding where they might be now.

Any hope of finding them quickly was lost. They could be a hundred miles away on an airplane. Aboard any of the two dozen freighters he'd seen on the back side of the cape, or even a British Royal Navy frigate. Perhaps they were secreted away in a false compartment in a delivery truck hurtling through Spain. Slaton had seen many such conveyances play out—in truth, he had devised more than his share. Terrorist financiers extracted from Europe. Militant leaders targeted for rendition. By virtue of that experience, he knew there was little chance of intervention. Not when things were planned and executed properly.

And this, by all appearances, was a proper abduction.

The more Slaton thought about it, the more traces he saw of a state-sponsored operation. The execution of a double snatch on foreign soil was no easy thing—allowing that the tiny principality of Gibraltar was itself off the table as a suspect. The naked use of a pirated messaging account suggested a measure of cyber skill. Israel was the most likely suspect, the United States a close second. In recent years he'd had dealings with the intelligence services of both nations. They knew his vulnerabilities, and both had the assets to find him and manage a complex extraction. Yet on another level that didn't make sense. If either of those countries wanted to hasten a prospective target's journey to the afterlife, wouldn't they deal with it directly?

Perhaps.

State-sponsored assassinations were delicate business, and certain targets were untouchable by the usual means—a drone or a Spec Ops strike. For a target that *had* to be kept at arm's length . . . *What better cutout than me?* he thought. An assassin long thought dead. A man without a country. And best of all, a shooter who didn't miss, and who had a knack for disappearing without a trace.

Then Slaton was struck by a more elemental truth: by virtue of his lack of ties to any nation or cause, he was also uniquely expendable.

He readdressed the phone's tiny screen, memorized the instructions word for word. He looked at the unopened photo attachment. Who would it be? he wondered. Someone he knew? A face recognized around the world? A head of state or underworld kingpin? A rogue agent or intelligence chief? Whoever it was, their identity would hopefully provide a hint as to who was coercing him to undertake an assassination.

The idea rose that he might be dealing with an organized crime syndicate, or even some terrorist element. He hoped that wasn't the case, because it implied even greater risk for his wife and son. He stared at the final line of the message, the suggestion of their safe return. Having long lived on the dark side of such bargains, he knew the playbook. Operate by their rules, and there *was* a chance he would see his family again.

The only alternative: to set his own rules.

Slaton considered the location specified in Vienna. He had been there many times, yet saw no particular relevance in either the site or the timing. All the same, he would research both in great detail, hoping for any fingerprint as to who was responsible. The most telling clue, however, remained in hand: the attached photograph. Identify the target, he reasoned, and the patron of his or her demise might become clear.

An old counter-sniper adage came to mind. *Track the prey to find the hunter.*

Slaton tapped down on the screen to find out who he was supposed to kill.

SEVEN

The image that arose was a candid shot, taken in what looked like an office setting. Slaton saw a man in his thirties framed by an empty white board. He had a serious face and dark, almost delicate features. A face, Slaton had the impression, that might once have been prone to smiling, implied by certain lines around the mouth and eyes. Here it seemed captured in reflection, and perhaps a trace of melancholy. The man was small in stature, thinly built, with black hair that fell over his collar in unkempt waves. Unshaven stubble darkened his chin and cheeks. Not a conformist by nature.

He pored over the rest of the photograph for clues. He noticed a pair of glasses on a table, and a pen in the man's hand. Quite deliberately, Slaton closed his eyes, then opened them again and looked at the picture anew—an old shooter's trick to acquire a second "first impression." The more he studied the man, the more he was nagged by a vague notion: this was a face he'd seen before. Distant and indirect, yet someone from his past. He racked his brain, but the identity escaped him.

He wished he had access to cutting-edge facial recognition technology—great strides had been made in recent years, and databases were expanding daily. Unfortunately, that would require going to either the CIA or Mossad for help, either of whom might be responsible for the whole affair. It was an inescapable dilemma. Until he knew more, he had to operate alone, the only files available those banked in his head.

He drew a deep breath and turned away from the phone. His eyes fell to a Lego-block boat on the floor. He and Davy had built it last night, a marathon session to keep his son occupied while Christine mapped out the next leg of their never-ending voyage. When she finished, they'd put Davy to bed and gone over the itinerary. From Gibraltar the plan was to sail southeast, ten days, more or less, and spend a week in the Canary Islands. From there, Cape Verde, followed by a right turn to Brazil. Only a few short hours ago, that had been their near-term life plan.

And now?

He picked up the Lego boat and set it on Davy's bunk. As he did so, a single block detached, falling onto a comforter decorated with whimsical animals. Slaton retrieved the yellow rectangular brick, which they'd declared to be a lifeboat, and carefully reattached it.

Precisely as it had been.

He cleaned the mug in the sink and emptied the coffeemaker. It had nothing to do with housekeeping. Everything to do with imposing order on his thoughts.

Slaton had succumbed to the darkness once before, predating his years with Mossad. That devastation had come when he was twenty years old, still in university and not yet tarnished by intelligence agencies or Special Forces training. Still unknowing of the dark arts he would come to master.

Slaton had married early, a girl who'd swept into his heart like a summer breeze. Two years into that marriage, with graduation pending and a beautiful young daughter named Elise, his world had been up-ended in one terrible moment. The tragedy that stole them from his life could not have been more indiscriminate. Nor could Mossad have been more manipulative in how it leveraged his misfortune.

To this day Slaton remembered the pain, the feeling that his soul had been torn away. Only later would he realize how his grief had made him the perfect recruit. Mossad planted the seeds of revenge, played his psyche brilliantly. With one recurring lie, they had molded him into the most lethal of assassins. Slaton had long done his best to keep that part of his past locked away. On most days he managed it, probably because, after so many turbulent years, he'd recovered some semblance of a normal life. Yet now he felt the blackness coming again. Descending like a crushing weight. The mere thought of losing Christine and Davy awakened demons he'd long thought slayed.

He spun a slow circle in the main salon. He needed to make travel plans, begin his research. Instead he found himself staring at the new curtains on the port window. The carpet was also a recent upgrade, as were the dishes in the cupboard. Christine's campaign to feather their nautical nest. He recalled suffering similar disruptions years ago, in those long-forgotten days. A year of getting junk mail that was jointly addressed. Finding his wife's exercise mat under the bed. He'd left his daughter's clothes in her laundry basket for months, treasuring the last traces of her sweet scent.

He forced his eyes shut, desperate for order. Demanding it. *If I can't act rationally, I can't save them.*

When he opened his eyes again, equilibrium had returned.

He retrieved a screwdriver from a drawer and went aft to the engine compartment. Slaton opened the portside access door and pried loose a panel to reveal a watertight box concealed in the recesses of the bay. It wasn't a particularly stealthy hiding place—nowhere on a forty-four-foot sailboat could be—but it had so far held against a series of lazy customs inspections.

A check of the thread-thin security seal told him the box had been opened—someone, he was sure, had accessed it this morning. He pulled the lid of their get-well kit and took a quick inventory. One stack of five thousand euros in various denominations—there had originally been two—along with a spare smartphone, and two false passports with his picture. Two other passports, high-quality forgeries designed for Christine and Davy, were missing.

He considered the implications. Because half the money and his own documents remained, it followed that Christine had accessed the box. It also suggested, very loosely, that she'd not been under duress at the time. Or were these the very thoughts someone hoped him to have? Someone who could flag and follow the passports, who could track the spare phone?

He pinched the bridge of his nose. How easily the old ways, with their circular logic and storming insecurities, came rushing back.

He pocketed the cash, the phone, and after a brief hesitation, added the false identities. He decided the odds were fair that none of it had been compromised. Either way, there was no time to procure new documents. He needed to travel, needed to move.

One of the passports, a Canadian item, was paired with a driver's license and valid credit card. He had diligently kept it all current—last-ditch insurance against an unforeseen crisis.

Today certainly qualified.

He next addressed the boat. Electronics off, bilge pumps checked, shore power connected. New curtains drawn. He locked the companionway hatch, and as he was stepping to the dock for a final check of the mooring lines, the Scotsman appeared at the gangway next door.

"Looks like you've found your boat!" he said.

Slaton forced a grin that he hoped appeared casual. "It was all a big misunderstanding. We're heading to Spain for a few days—going to do some sightseeing. Would you mind keeping an eye on her?"

"Happy to! I'll be in port another two weeks, then it's off to Greece. You should give me a phone number where I can contact you."

"Actually," Slaton said, "I'm in the process of switching phones. Could you write yours down for me?"

The Scot went below, and moments later came back up with a slip of paper. He handed it over a weathered lifeline.

"Thanks," Slaton said, pocketing the number. "Hopefully I can return the favor someday."

"What goes around comes around," said the Scot.

Slaton nodded pensively, his gray eyes a blank. "Yes . . . I was thinking that very same thing."

EIGHT

Gibraltar's airport was a nominal affair, and resultingly offered few flight options. The most efficient course to reach Austria proved to be a connection in Madrid. Slaton arrived at Vienna International Airport at precisely nine o'clock that evening.

With a small carry-on in hand, he was outside quickly, and his first greeting came from the Austrian winter. Against a temperature near the freezing point and a biting wind, Slaton turned up the collar on his heaviest jacket.

He procured a taxi from the slush-laden curb, and gave the cordial driver the name of a well-known restaurant not far from the Donaustadt district. Slaton had conjured the address after landing using his reserve smartphone, which might or might not be clean. He had no intention of dining at Restaurant Thalassa, but it placed him roughly where he wanted to be. It was his standard practice to give cab drivers a prominent destination. It led to fewer questions, less chance of getting lost, and if the driver were questioned about it later, he would remember the endpoint—providing nothing but a false lead. It was an elementary precaution, and tonight would leave Slaton with little more than a short walk.

The traffic was heavy but moved without pause. As they neared downtown, Slaton had the impression of a city alive, brisk and full of energy. The sidewalks were thick with people bundled against the cold, the adjacent buildings a counterpoint, great slabs of warm light shimmering in the darkness. Slaton had been to Vienna many times in his years with Mossad. He had even spent two years here as a schoolboy. That being the case, his ultimate destination was not unfamiliar. *Danube Island.* The specific point referenced in the message—a semicircle with benches and trees—sounded strikingly ordinary, and he hoped he wouldn't have trouble distinguishing it.

The driver turned west on Handelskai Road, the Danube becoming a constant on the right. The neighborhoods here were among the oldest in the city, and inseparable from the river, every path leading to its banks, every foundation following its contours. On the left was the vaulted cityscape, and to the north, across the river, affluent neighborhoods and business parks reached to the horizon. His eyes were drawn to the waterway, which here fell divided into parallel channels. The northern branch appeared stagnant, while the nearer fork kept the river's flow. Fixed in between them—Danube Island.

The driver veered south into town, and before leaving the riverside, Slaton noted the distinctive curving towers of Vienna International Centre. This was where the U.N. maintained its considerable Austrian presence. Not by coincidence, the nearby office towers housed countless NGOs. Slaton knew this because he'd long ago been part of a Mossad operation that had leased space in one of them, a hard-to-find office on a middling floor. The agency had gone so far as to create a short-lived charitable trust, an initiative ostensibly designed to fight malnourishment in remote Sinai villages, but whose real aim was to effect a meeting between an elusive Libyan militia leader and one standard NATO 7.62mm match-grade round. In the end, three months of work had gone for naught when the Libyan was killed by one of his closest lieutenants.

How distant it all seems now, Slaton thought.

He tracked the driver's progress using the map application on his phone, well aware that mobile position data was a double-edged sword. He was searching ahead, taking in street names and landmarks, when his eye was caught by a photograph attached to the dash: what had to be the driver's wife and two daughters. They were all arm in arm on a couch, laughing at something unseen.

The driver caught him looking. "Iricha and my two girls," he said amiably in the English Slaton had begun.

"They're lovely."

"Indeed. I am a lucky man."

Slaton smiled at the mirror. The driver's eyes smiled back.

The photograph seemed such an ordinary thing. What bankers and accountants tacked on walls next to their diplomas. What waiters and bartenders uploaded to their Facebook pages. Virtually every father in the world had a picture of their child tucked under clear plastic in their wallet.

What kind of man doesn't have a picture of his family somewhere?

Of course he knew the answer.

After two final turns their progress slowed in fast-coagulating traffic. The driver pulled to a stop along a busy curb. "The restaurant is there," he said, pointing to a rust-red awning half a block ahead.

The tiny payment screen told Slaton he owed twenty-six euros. He ignored a credit card swipe and handed thirty euros over the seat. "Is there a hotel nearby?" he asked as the driver took the cash.

"Of course, there are many. I have heard Gasthaus Thaller is nice, and quite reasonable." He gave easy directions.

"Thank you for the recommendation," Slaton said.

The driver handed over an old-fashioned business card with a phone number for Flughafen Taxi. He smiled again. Slaton pocketed the card, bid the man a pleasant evening, and left the warmth of the cab.

He zipped up his jacket and began walking east on Vorgartenstrasse, toward both the restaurant and the rooming house. Only after his taxi was out of sight did he pause on the sidewalk, do a calm about-face, and set out in the opposite direction. With one right turn, the river was ahead of him. Of all the hotels in Vienna, Gasthaus Thaller was the last he would patronize tonight. Nor would Restaurant Thalassa have his company for dinner. And if he needed a ride? In spite of its competent service and smiling drivers, Flughafen Taxi would not get the call.

At a casual pace it took him ten minutes to reach the Danube. Slaton veered onto the pedestrian walkway built into the broad Reichsbrücke Bridge. The ebony water below reflected the city's lights, giving definition to swirling currents and spin-off eddies. At the bridge's halfway point he reversed onto a set of switchback stairs, descending to the tree-lined island that split the two branches of the river. He emerged from the shadows of the overpass, paused briefly, then took up the southward walking path.

He saw no obvious tails. His surveillance detection routes on the streets of Vienna had so far mirrored the precautions of his flight and cab ride— rudimentary at best, and patently overt. Because the park was expansive, and because at this hour there were still a good number of people milling on its trails, even the most stringent defensive protocols could not rule out the chance of surveillance.

Given the method by which he'd been contacted, not to mention the compressed time frame, Slaton thought it very possible that he was under watch. In effect, he had been summoned to this little plot of Europe by persons unknown. His thoughts roved to the negative, and for a moment he imagined himself a slow-moving target in another shooter's gunsight. The chance of such a trap was small, he decided, and anyway, there was nothing to be done about it.

It was simply a risk he had to accept.

Move like what you are . . . an assassin plotting a kill.

He advanced westward down the riverside path, keeping an easy pace. The island was more narrow than he remembered, a common idiosyncrasy of childhood memories. He knew it carried centrally through the river for more than ten miles. The portion he was now strolling was the most frequented, while the extremes on either end were little more than paved trails that drew the odd bicyclist or distance runner. The central gardens were the most popular, built for summer but frequented year-round. He saw a clapboard café and a paddleboat rental shack, and across the waterway, at the foot of the greater park, a disassembled pontoon bridge stood ready to be connected to the island. All of it was stilled now, dusted in snow. Waiting for the season of life.

To his left the river kept its faithful passage, while the water on his right was closer to an elongated lake, currentless and, on this chill night, ice-bound at the edges. He walked west along the shoreward path, his orders echoing in his head.

Danube Island, north shore semicircle
Three benches, three trees

The place where his target would appear in roughly twenty-four hours. A plot of ground Slaton had to find and feel and memorize from every angle. He rarely undertook such surveys under rushed conditions. He preferred to linger and study, to consider variables and make assessments. Unfortunately, on this assignment, he had no such luxury.

He passed a number of people on the trails, couples mostly, and a few singletons walking dogs. His attention was caught by a pair of young boys—twelve, perhaps thirteen years old. They were meandering the greater park to the north, across the lake, and Slaton watched their every move. Kids were invariably local area experts. They knew where to find broken panels on fences, which vacant backyards could be cut through. In this case, he watched them disappear into a small grove of trees. They fell completely out of sight. Probably to smoke a joint, or perhaps share a pint of whiskey.

Noted.

There were overhead lamps at intervals along

the paths, and light from the city cut the gloom between them to something near dusk. After five minutes Slaton encountered a semicircular observation patio that jutted toward the shore on his right. It was backed by a single bench. No trees nearby. He kept going, but sensed he was on the right track. Three minutes later he came upon a second arc of pavement. It was similar in size to the first, but the half-moon of concrete was accented by chords of inset stone that Slaton thought might be Wetterstein limestone—masonry was his subordinate calling. More notably, to his left, along the flat shoreward edge of the path, he saw three empty benches and three leafless trees.

He looked up the trail, wondering if there could be others like it ahead. He decided the possibility had to be ruled out, and continued for another mile. The farther he walked, the more remote things became. Fewer people encountered, more space between lights. Convinced he'd found the right spot, Slaton turned back. When he again reached the half-circle terrace he paused.

He stood in the center and turned 360 degrees. He imagined how the scene might be different tomorrow night. Would there be changes in weather or visibility? Was tomorrow an Austrian holiday of some kind? Across the river to the north he noted a natural amphitheater with a small stage. Could there be an event scheduled for the following evening? A concert or a party? A corporate gathering? All seemed doubtful given the season, yet points worth checking. Discreet variables that could be factored out. He recalled passing a cluster of buildings at the outset of his walk, the small café and a pair of docks backed by boat sheds. All were locked down for the season, but these were the nearest structures, and so they warranted closer inspection.

Absorbing the scene around him, Slaton found his attention drawn northward. His shooter's eye progressed instinctively to areas of high ground and cover, no bias given for what was natural or man-made. As he did so, he was struck by an obvious spectacle: something that made this tiny slab of con-crete and stone different from anyplace else on the thirteen-mile-long island.

There, straight across the river and fixed centrally in Danube Park, was a landmark that stood above all others—quite literally.

The Donauturm.

The Danube Tower.

Slaton remembered touring the tower as a young boy. At over eight hundred feet, it was the tallest structure in Austria. It had been built sometime in the sixties, when giant urban needles topped by rotating restaurants were all the rage. He recalled two high-speed elevators. A harried teacher usher-ing her gaggle of wide-eyed schoolboys inside. He remembered standing on the high observation plat-form and marveling at the spectacle beyond: one of Europe's great cities sprawling before him. He sup-posed little had changed since then, other than a thickening of the city's urban waistline.

He pulled out his smartphone and checked the hours of operation for the Donauturm. It was open nightly until 11:30. A peculiar notion began to settle in Slaton's head. It began as a curiosity, but soon grew and gained definition. Before he knew it, he was succumbing to an outright revelation.

Twelve hours ago, he had received the instruc-tions to an assassination on what he'd thought was his "safe phone." Since then, he'd been operating on the assumption that he was dealing with a state actor. Or at the very least, some established criminal or terrorist organization. Either way, an adversary who would know how assassins operated, and who understood the implicit rules of such contracts.

Now, as he stood staring at the needlelike tower, Slaton realized he'd gotten it all wrong. He wasn't dealing with professionals at all.

He was dealing with amateurs.

On one hand it made tomorrow's job that much easier. On the other—it made the outcome far less predictable.

NINE

If words could have nationalities, *repression* would keep full citizenship in North Korea. A traditionally agrarian society, its people have an extensive history of suffering. While surrounding nations have modernized, the North has lagged at every turn. Foreign invasions, royal assassinations, and outright annexation by neighbors have all laid the pitch.

These epic struggles are largely a misfortune of geography. The upper Korean Peninsula lies doomed in a political no-man's-land, vised between great powers whose strategic turns and shifting alliances are nothing short of tectonic. To the north and west, respectively, are borders with Russia and China, the world's corruption-laden communist champions. Along the 38th parallel it stares down South Korea, Asia's new and full-throttled economic miracle—which from the North's perspective can only be like looking into a mirror to see the beauty that might have been. Across the eastern sea is Japan, the previous generation's powerhouse, and, as oft reminded by the North's leadership, a former colonial master.

Notwithstanding North Korea's troubled pedigree, the bygone ravages inflicted by its neighbors are trivial compared to those more recently endured.

The Kwon dynasty has ruled since the settling of dust after World War II. In that time, slave labor, Soviet-style Gulags, and religious persecution have become the norm. Outside Pyongyang there are few basic services, and years of mismanagement have made famine and malnutrition pervasive—to the point that an entire generation of North Koreans suffer stunted growth. The ruling class is spared hunger, but suffers in its own way, a fitful blend of infighting, purges, and arbitrary executions. Yet if the Kwon dynasty could be distilled to one summing legacy, it would be that after seventy years in power, following Soviet and Japanese domination, not a single living North Korean has a first-hand recollection of living in freedom.

Boutros looked out the window as the small airplane descended. He saw what could only be the Sea of Japan. It looked utterly frigid, slabs of ice lining the shore like so many winter beachgoers. Distant breakers gave the appearance of being tipped in snow before fading into the nothingness of a flat black sea. For a lifelong resident of the Fertile Crescent, it was all strange and mesmerizing. It was also a timely distraction. A rare buoyant moment to lessen the weight on his shoulders.

He pulled his eyes back into the cabin and took stock of his team. *Four out of five,* he thought with satisfaction. *Not bad.*

It had taken the best part of two days for his squad to reach North Korea. But reach it they had. Only one member had failed to complete the journey—Adnan, one of the two martyrs. According to a message he'd been detained in Frankfurt. The authorities had released him after a brief questioning, but he'd missed his connecting flight to Beijing.

Boutros realized that trying to go through Germany was a mistake—they were always such sticklers. But what was done was done. He had no idea if Adnan was still trying to reach China, but it hardly mattered. Sami, the martyr who'd gotten through, was capable enough, and probably the more useful of the two. Even more encouragingly, both technicians had arrived—a sure sign of Allah's blessing. Boutros never doubted that he himself would complete the passage.

Not bad at all.

They'd been collected at the Beijing airport by a taciturn man who spoke tortured English through lemon-sour lips. He claimed his name was Park, and he was certainly North Korean. Boutros guessed him to be an intelligence officer of some manner—and by the clout he'd displayed so far, he had to be high-ranking. His face was round and smooth-skinned, and dark eyes were set behind thick glasses. He had a stocky, squarish build beneath a fur-trimmed hat and high-collared parka. After Boutros and his men had arrived, closely spaced at Beijing's Capital International Airport, they'd waited over an hour for word on Adnan. It was Park who finally received a call detailing Adnan's troubles.

When Boutros mentioned that Adnan wasn't critical to the mission, Park never hesitated. He had whisked them through a series of hallways, somehow bypassing customs. At three security checkpoints their guide flashed his credentials, the guards snapping to attention and waving them onward every time. Boutros knew the Chinese and North Koreans had a close alliance, but he'd been prepared for at least a cursory inspection before departing Beijing.

Next had come a short ride on a shuttle bus to a remote corner of the airport. There Boutros and his squad had been ushered onto a small turboprop. Park complained they were running late—he said they never should have waited for Adnan if he wasn't critical to the mission. The flight across the final border took less than an hour. Now, after transiting the narrow waist of the Korean Peninsula, they were skirting the eastern coastline. Boutros heard the engines throttle back, felt the airplane begin to descend.

He watched through the oval side window, and soon they were skimming low, the trees below seeming close enough to touch. The forest suddenly fell away and a runway appeared. The airplane touched down smoothly, and as it slowed Boutros saw what looked like a military airfield. On a tarmac washed in blowing snow, a small fleet of mismatched aircraft sat parked in a row. He saw one fighter, three transports of various types, and a pair of helicopters. The only commonality between them was the paint scheme—dull gray body, a bold red star on the tail. All looked old enough to have flown in the big war seventy years ago.

The turboprop pulled to a stop, its nose bowing once as if playing to an audience. The engines went quiet, and a short set of stairs were wheeled to the entry door. Park produced a small leather satchel, then led the way outside. At that point, four life-long residents of the Middle East were introduced to true winter. Beneath a steel gray sky that would have done London proud, a harsh wind swept snow sideways. Boutros and his squad walked unsteadily across the ramp, which seemed to undulate under ribbons of snow. The visitors slipped on patches of ice and stuffed their hands deep into the pockets of their light jackets. Park hurried ahead of them. With short quick steps and a satchel looped over his shoulder, he looked like a mailman running behind schedule.

They reached a big sedan, and, after the visitors dropped four pieces of hand luggage into the trunk, everyone bundled inside. Park started the engine, then went back outside and began feverishly scraping snow and ice from the windshield. His breath went to vapor as he worked, clouding in front of his mouth like so many empty speech balloons. He finally got back behind the wheel. Boutros was next to him, the other three bundled in back.

Without a word, Park put the car in gear and steered north along the coast road. Everyone waited for the heater to take hold.

TEN

After an hour Boutros couldn't say where they were. He certainly knew better than to ask. The late-afternoon sun topped the hills to his left, and on the right the Sea of Japan ran defiantly to the horizon. He studied the water with a cautious eye, and thought how different it seemed from the Persian Gulf.

They passed through villages dotted with ramshackle houses, and a few clapboard sheds might have passed for businesses. The people he saw looked weary and beaten, and more than a few appeared to be gathering firewood. Along the two-lane highway, he noted the occasional road sign, although those without pictograms were wholly indecipherable. They had so far encountered three roadblocks, but were waved through each time. Boutros noticed that the soldiers at the checkpoints seemed to have no transportation beyond the odd bicycle. Even ISIS, in its heyday, had managed to supply traffic stops with technicals.

His men conversed occasionally in hushed Arabic—what sounded to Boutros like the musings of tourists on their first overseas trip. With the first part of their journey behind them, things were loosening up.

"Look!" Sami said to Saleem. "What is that?" He was pointing toward a great concrete monument on the shore to the right. It consisted of a thirty-foot-tall concrete fist holding a hammer, and next to that was something akin to a rain gutter—albeit large enough to carry a small ship to sea.

Boutros exchanged a knowing glance with Rafiq. The engineer was the only one among them who'd traveled abroad. He had been born in Syria, and attended university for a time in London, although he'd never graduated. He had also spent a year in Russia, which meant he was well versed in the Brutalist glory of communist architecture.

Park's attention had been stirred. Sami had posed his question in Arabic, yet they were all looking at the monument. "Monument of Victorious Liberation," said Park with no small measure of pride. "A tribute to Chinese soldiers who died in war."

Boutros thought it looked more like a monument to subjugation, hectares of gray concrete brooding over the shoreline, all sharp angles and conquest.

"Do you think such a monument will be built in our honor?" asked Sami, keeping to Arabic.

"Of course," said Saleem. "There have long been plans to build a martyrs' square in the center of the caliphate. God willing, when our lands are restored we will be so remembered."

In the visor mirror Boutros saw Sami beaming. The kid was nineteen, or so he said, from a rough section of Tripoli. He had the smile of a schoolboy but the nerve of a true believer. *The best weapon Allah has ever bestowed upon us*, thought Boutros.

Sami and Saleem were actually cousins, albeit from opposite sides of Libya. As if reflecting that geographic divide, they displayed diametrically opposed personalities. It was a false premise that suicidal jihadists were uniformly taciturn and twitchy young men. Sami had worked as an entertainer at children's parties, and confessed to once being an aspiring comedian. That dream had been curbed two years ago, on the day a rival militia had sent a rocket-propelled grenade through his mother's kitchen window. He'd immediately vowed revenge, but lacking a clear idea of who was responsible, Sami had let God and his ISIS disciples set the course for retaliation. And so they had—owing to Adnan's non-arrival, he was now the lone martyr on their mission.

Saleem, with his sunken cheeks and dark eyes, was a stark contrast to Sami's cheerful visage. Innately grim and purposeful, he had his own foundation in religious-fueled outrage—the loss of two older brothers to an airstrike in Syria. That the bombs could have been dropped by the Russians, Syrians, or even the Americans was immaterial—in his eyes, they were all cut from the same godless lot. Saleem was consumed by anger, and ISIS had been happy to funnel his rage into a relationship with improvised explosives—over time, a calling that came to border on artisanship.

In the greater scheme, of course, backgrounds were secondary. Boutros knew that when the time came for sacrifice, all would be equally committed. For now, he was happy to keep the mood light—no small feat for an ISIS commander guiding his team through the most rigid police state on earth.

"Is the heater working?" asked Saleem. The weather was deteriorating, curtains of cloud seeming to touch the brooding black sea. The temperature, according to the dashboard readout, was −9 Celsius. Well below the freezing point.

"Barely," said Rafiq.

"We need warmer clothes before the next part of our journey," said Boutros in English. They'd all brought jackets from home, but the Arctic wind sweeping off the sea was unlike anything they'd experienced.

"It will be arranged," said Park.

"How long until we reach our destination?" asked Saleem.

Park either didn't hear the question or chose not to answer.

"I think we are close," said Boutros. He had a general idea of where they were headed, but no map, nor any way to fix their present position.

"What will it be like?" asked Sami, switching to Arabic.

"You think I have been here before? Look out the window. It is cold and wet and gray."

"Just like the women!" Rafiq added.

There was laughter among the squad, until Saleem asked, "How long will we stay?"

Boutros could almost feel the light mood seep from the car, as if pulled into the bitter air outside. He was suddenly struck by the precariousness of their situation. North Korea and ISIS, born of wildly different circumstances, had somehow been cast together. He supposed it was inevitable—a strained brotherhood among the world's outcasts. One a hermit kingdom, the other a decimated army of Allah. But together? Soldiers in search of a battle.

"We stop here," Park announced.

Boutros looked ahead and saw a roadblock, two

trucks and a handful of soldiers. One of the soldiers put up his hand in a classic *halt* signal.

"Stay inside," Park ordered. He didn't seem particularly worried.

Park got out, walked toward the guard, and put his credentials on display. The man went to rigid attention, and the ensuing conversation was decidedly one-way.

"Is there a problem?" asked Sami.

"No, it will be fine," Boutros replied. He turned to face his men, his voice going an octave lower. "I have shared few details of our plan with you, but I'm sure you can understand why. If any of us had been captured or interrogated during our travels, it could have jeopardized everything. Believe me when I tell you this—we are pursuing the most important mission our caliphate has ever attempted." He let that sink in for a moment. "We are traveling to a small fishing village. We will stay there one night, perhaps more—things are very dependent on the weather this time of year. Once conditions permit, we will be given a boat carrying almost everything we need for our strike."

"Almost?" queried Saleem.

"We are to be given the components of a very lethal weapon. Most of it is in place, and the rest will be delivered soon."

A clearly doubtful Saleem looked outside and said, "It seems strange that we can find something so important here, in this godforsaken place."

Boutros followed his eyes out the window. Snow rippled over the road in waves. It reminded him of sand undulating across dunes during the haboobs back home. There was something about this landscape, with its frozen sea and downtrodden people, that seemed ideally suited to their mission. "For what we are attempting," he said, "this is the perfect place. We should be thankful God has forsaken it."

"Will there be time to pray when we arrive?" asked Saleem.

"Yes, rest assured. There is always time to pray."

ELEVEN

Slaton slept fitfully in a modest rooming house two blocks from the river. He woke at eight, showered to shake away the mental mist, and took a buffet breakfast on the first floor. A breakfast, most critically, that included a deep cup of coffee. At the front desk he arranged to keep his room for another night, and assured the manager that it required no attention from housekeeping—Slaton did not expect to remain until tomorrow, but it gave him a safe house for the balance of the day.

He set out on foot under clear skies and a cool breeze. The city in the light of day was much as he remembered: classic yet unpretentious, like an art museum that displayed fine paintings, but whose curator preferred the honesty of scratched frames.

Slaton had put no more than three blocks behind him when he confirmed his first tail. He shot a glance back while standing at a crosswalk, and noticed a young, slightly built man wearing a black jacket and sunglasses. He was idling at the entrance of a closed restaurant, pretending to study a menu in a wall-mounted glass encasement. Pretending, Slaton knew, because he himself had passed the same menu box and noticed it was empty. His eye had been drawn to the same man a block earlier when he'd hurried around a group on the sidewalk, only to then slow when Slaton paused at a store window. That kind of movement had but one logical explanation.

Slaton kept going, and within two blocks he identified a second man: tall, thin, blue ski parka. The two were clearly running a tag team, one drifting out of sight while the other kept a visual. They were coordinating by text message, evident by flourishes of intermittent tapping on their mobiles. It could be an effective method, done well. But these two were agonizingly obvious. No professional team would perform surveillance in the way they were going about it. He saw no one else, but it was always healthy to assume a bigger detail than could be seen. He figured three was quite possible. Five a stretch.

The question of who they were he put aside for the moment. Or at least he tried. Anyone following him here, today, had to be linked to Christine and Davy's disappearance. In that moment, Slaton would have liked nothing better than to double back, eliminate one of the men, and beat the other mercilessly until he divulged what he knew. There was a slight chance such a plan would work. A far greater one that it would backfire and precipitate a disaster of the highest order. Anger as a strategy was rarely effective.

Slaton kept walking, keeping to his task amid the morning throngs. He'd left the rooming house with only a vague sketch of how to prepare for tonight's killing. Now, having hooked two trailers as easily as a charter boat trolling for mackerel, his thinking evolved. He combined the presence of the men behind him with what he'd seen in the park last night. Considered why they might be here and what they might know. The answers that came were not to his liking. Up until that moment, Slaton had been unsure how to pursue tonight's assassination. Now his hand had been forced.

He kept walking—not because he had a destination in mind, but more because he didn't. He needed time to think. Slaton mentally blueprinted a number of schemes, and while none seemed perfect, he realized that certain essential elements were universal.

At a major thoroughfare, with the Hofburg Palace coming into distant view, he stopped to reference his phone. He selected a map application and typed a search for what he needed. Three options appeared, and based on their websites, the most promising was a mere twenty-minute walk to the west.

Slaton set out in that direction.

Along the way he made two unexpected moves. He began by crossing against a light. Soon after that he performed an abrupt reversal, referencing his phone as if lost. It would keep his pursuers on their toes, but wasn't enough to lose them. Not unless they were completely incompetent. As he made his way west, his plan gained definition. By the time he reached his destination, Slaton had most of the details in place.

Buoyed to be making progress, he strode decisively under a green and brown awning and entered the second largest gun shop in Vienna.

There were two sales clerks in the store. Both were busy with customers.

Slaton studied the place as he waited, his eyes wandering over pegboard walls and heavy glass display cases. One of the associates was a twenty-something man who, upon getting stuck on a credit card transaction, asked for help from the other. The senior man was in his fifties, and his quick response and commanding manner left no doubt—he was either the owner of the shop or the manager on duty. Either would suffice.

This was the man Slaton needed to talk to.

Conveniently, the man in charge was the first to become available. He bid good day to a customer in cargo pants and a camo jacket who walked outside with three boxes of .223 Remington cartridges.

Slaton approached the counter and asked, "Do you speak English?" Regrettably, German was not among the half-dozen languages he spoke fluently.

"Of course, sir. What can I do for you?"

Slaton put his hands on a counter made of thick security glass. In the case beneath all manner of arms were on display: handguns, optics, magazines, knives, cleaning kits. "I'm in town on business," he said. "When I have an hour to kill I usually end up in a place like this."

"I am the same," said the Austrian. "Are you a collector, or a hunter perhaps?"

"A bit of both, I suppose."

The man half turned and directed Slaton's attention to one of the racks behind the counter. "Are you familiar with this model?"

Slaton recognized an FNH FNAR .308 with a MIL-SPEC fluted barrel, forward laser rail, and ambidextrous mag release button. He said, "Not really."

The Austrian was reaching for the rifle when Slaton said, "Actually, I've been searching for a piece that's a bit out of the ordinary."

The man looked at him blankly, neither eagerness nor caution in his expression. Slaton explained what he wanted, but only in a general sense, knowing it wasn't the kind of thing kept on sales racks. The specific make and model, he went on to say, was of little concern. "Would you have something like that?"

A long hesitation. "I should ask . . . why would you need such a weapon?"

Slaton gave a shrug that he hoped was relaxed. "I suppose the same reasons anyone would." He quickly shifted his gaze to the glass case. "Also, I am in the market for a good sight. You have the Schmidt & Bender T96?"

The man's expression brightened, finalizing Slaton's earlier deduction. *Owner.*

"Yes, a fine scope. Excellent for low light conditions. It also has a wide range of adjustment, making long-range shots easier." He leaned in conspiratorially. "It is the scope that turns us all into the marksmen we wish we were."

Slaton smiled agreeably. "At that price, one would hope. I have had my eye on it for some time."

The owner pulled the scope from the case and put it in Slaton's hands. He studied it in silence, nodding admiringly.

After a time the owner cocked his head slightly, and said, "As for the other . . . I might have something that would interest you."

TWELVE

The proprietor curled a finger to draw Slaton to the back of the store. They walked together, separated by the long display case, until the owner pushed through a curtain. Slaton followed him into a storeroom where dozens of rifles and shotguns were locked down on racks. There were a half-dozen gun safes, and boxes of ammunition were stacked neatly to one side. The smell of gun oil permeated the air.

The owner kept going, past the storeroom and turning down a hall. They ended in a small office. Slaton saw a desk littered with invoices and files. A computer to one side was a classic, a tower model whose plastic case had yellowed severely with age. Thick wires connected to an old cathode-ray monitor the size of a file box. On the wall were plaques of appreciation from gun manufacturers and framed certificates from weapons-training courses. An eight-by-ten photo showed the owner kneeling beside a trophy elk.

The Austrian reached behind a cabinet in one corner and pulled out a matte-black shape that was intimately familiar to Slaton. "M16," he said, impressed.

"Military surplus. I took it only recently as . . ."

"A trade?" Slaton ventured.

The owner grinned sheepishly. "Army reservists often manage to keep such trophies when they retire—I suppose they should be accounted for more accurately, but one rather understands. It could never be sold openly, of course, yet for someone like me who might consider an exchange? I don't ask where it comes from, and they are happy to receive fair credit."

"I'm sure they are."

Slaton took the long black stock in hand, testing its weight and balance. He noted the texture of the barrel and stock, and deemed it to be in reasonably good condition. Perfect for what he had in mind.

"It is a one-of-a-kind item," said the Austrian.

Slaton knew otherwise, but didn't belabor the point. "Tell me," he asked, "are there any restrictions on such a sale?"

"Austria has many restrictions on gun purchases," said a man who would know. "But here, I think, an exception can be made. Tell me, you are Swedish, perhaps?"

"Yes . . . my English always gives me away."

The owner looked pleased.

Slaton set his prospective purchase down. "As you say, it's a unique item. How much would you ask?"

"Three hundred seems reasonable."

Slaton's eyes shot up. It was a ruinous price. But it *was* exactly what he needed.

"However," the owner hedged, "if you were to buy the sight as well . . . I think two hundred would suffice."

"Done." Slaton looked around the room. "Do you have something I can carry it in?"

"Of course," the owner said, adding a knowing

smile. "One cannot simply go waltzing around Vienna with such a menacing armament in hand."

On another day, Slaton might have laughed. It was undoubtedly the owner's go-to line for customers not wanting to be seen hauling fully automatic weapons through the peaceable streets of Vienna.

"You won't try to mount the Schmidt & Bender on that, will you?"

"No. It would hardly be of any use."

The owner nodded, then eyed Slaton curiously. "What is it that you do for a living, my friend?"

"As little as possible. I'm retired."

The Austrian looked at Slaton questioningly, perhaps skeptical that even Sweden could have such a lenient early retirement policy. When no further explanation was offered, the owner took it as his cue.

He disappeared into the storeroom, and soon came back with a long, narrow cardboard box. The only markings on the outside were serial numbers and a scrawled inventory reference. Generic as it might be, the size and shape of the box belied its provenance as a shipping container for a rifle. Inside were foam seats that cradled the black stock and barrel perfectly. Back at the front counter, the owner made room inside for the scope. As he sealed it all with the original packing straps, Slaton found himself again perusing the glass case.

"I'll take that KM2000 as well," he said, pointing to a sheathed combat knife on the bottom shelf.

The owner retrieved the blade happily and wedged it into the box. "Our most popular knife."

Slaton was not surprised. He knew it was a solid piece, and standard issue for the German Army.

"Will there be anything else?" the owner said hopefully.

Slaton pried his eyes away from a Sig Sauer 9mm in the display case. Tempting as it might be, that was a bridge too far. "No, that will be all." He pulled a wad of cash from his pocket, and the owner raised an eyebrow. It went down as soon as Slaton began peeling off bills.

With the transaction complete, the two men exchanged best wishes for the day.

Slaton headed outside into a warming midmorning. He turned left on the sidewalk and picked up a course toward his rooming house. Within the first block he caught a glimpse of a blue ski parka across the street to his right.

He made no attempt to keep track of his pursuers. Slaton still had no idea who they were. Not yet. But he was increasingly sure he knew *why* they were here. Any way he constructed it, he could see but one endgame. He would put that to his advantage, and without any trace of mercy or remorse. From Slaton's point of view, a line had been crossed. His family threatened. His first goal was simple: locate Christine and Davy. His second would be to get them safe. Only when that was done would one final act ensue—a more personal mission to ensure it never happened again.

Fifteen minutes later, with the scalloped awning of his gasthaus in sight, Slaton glimpsed the blue parka once more. His convictions only deepened.

Back in his room, he set the box across the arms of the sitting chair. He crossed the room to the window and fingered back the heavy blind. He saw no sign of either man. This raised his level of caution a notch. But only one.

Slaton spent ten minutes on the smartphone he'd retrieved from his stash on *Sirius*. He input information on a website, waited five more minutes, then headed back out to the street. He walked three blocks north, one west, and disappeared into the office of a well-known car rental agency. With his reservation and paperwork already completed online, he gave a warm smile to the indifferent attendant behind the counter. Ninety seconds later he had a key in hand and was out the rear door to the parking garage.

"What happened?" the Uzbek asked urgently. He was completely out of breath.

Around the corner from the car rental agency, three men huddled in a tight triangle on the sidewalk. The Uzbek, a squat fireplug of a man, presided over the hastily called conference. With him were a young Tunisian in a black jacket and sunglasses, and a lanky Somali wearing a blue ski parka. They stood together on a cold slab of sidewalk, a thousand miles from any of their birthplaces. Three men bound by little more than a loose commitment to Islam. On this day they were doing Allah's work in a way none could ever have imagined.

The Tunisian, who'd spotted their man when he left the gasthaus the second time, explained that he'd turned into a car rental agency around the corner.

"How long he has been inside?" asked the Uzbek. They had taken to conversing in rough Arabic—the two Africans were steeped in different dialects, and it was not a native language at all for the Uzbek. Yet, just as they'd done in Syria and Iraq with other comrades-in-arms, they managed to get their ideas across. When all else failed, they occasionally fell back on German phrases acquired during their months in Vienna, or bits of English taken from the decadent Hollywood films they all watched—conveniently ignoring whatever irony that presented.

"He's been there for ten minutes. I walked past the window only moments ago, just before you arrived. I didn't see him at the counter."

"The cars are kept in a parking garage in back," said the Somali, leveling his lifeless eyes on the Tunisian. The three men had met only a few days earlier, and as unfamiliarity subsided, tension came more readily. This too they'd all seen during the war. "He is gone now, and we have no way to follow him. You should have messaged right away when you saw him hiring a car."

The two exchanged a seething look.

The Uzbek intervened. "It doesn't matter. We have learned enough. He has a weapon now, and a car for an escape. This is what we were told to expect." He addressed the Tunisian. "You are certain he left the weapon at the gasthaus?"

"Yes. He wasn't carrying anything when he left the hotel."

"Then he will return," said the Tunisian. "We can pick him up there."

"Why?" the Somali hissed. "We already know where he will be!"

Indecision swirled, and the two Africans looked at the Uzbek. Awkwardness aside, he was in charge. He'd recruited the others at the Islamic Center in Floridsdorf, taking recommendations from a local imam. *I need two men I can trust, preferably with experience in the war.* There was no need to specify a particular campaign or country—jihad recognized no such boundaries. The imam had been helpful.

Without keeping résumés, he considered it his duty to know who in his flock was capable of what. Most came to the mosque merely to worship, others because they were hungry or needed help finding legitimate work. Yet there was always that faction who came sporadically and prayed fervently, and who had never quite acclimated to life in Austria. Young men who bore scars and suffered limps, and whose deadened gazes reflected atrocities both seen and committed. Most had arrived amid the great waves of refugees, although a few were homegrown, non-indigenous seeds in the tidy garden that was Vienna. The imam made it his business to know every one.

"We can do nothing more here," the Uzbek decided. "It makes no difference where our man has gone or what he is doing. He'll be back—and tonight we will be ready, God willing!" He waited, got mumbled echoes in return. He issued a time and place for their rendezvous, and admonished, "Do not be late."

The two North Africans turned away, disappearing in different directions. The Uzbek waited until they were gone, then pulled out his phone. He thumbed out a quick message on a secure application before setting out himself into the heart of Vienna.

Before he'd gone two steps, his tiny burst transmission had been converted for end-to-end encryption. It uploaded through an antenna two hundred meters away, flowed to a nearby base station, and from there wove a digital path of more than two thousand miles. The process then ran in reverse until reaching its terminus: a blinking notification on a phone in a safe house just outside Vienna.

THIRTEEN

The rental car was a dark Renault, the kind of compact sedan that seemed to clog highways all across Europe. Slaton was certain he'd lost the team who'd been surveilling him. It was time to lay his groundwork for the evening, and he needed to do it alone.

He left town by way of the A5, riding the Nord Autobahn through the rolling hills of Austria's Weinviertel, or wine quarter, where highly regarded Pinot Blancs and Welschrieslings found their legs, and more menacingly where Hitler's Wehrmacht was greeted with cheers and flowers in the 1938 annexation known as *Anschluss*. Slaton watched the traffic carefully, making doubly sure he hadn't been reacquired. Only when he was finally convinced did he set to his true mission.

He exited the autobahn and took up a minor tributary eastward. The road cut through forest and low hills, and he diverted to explore a network of gravel sidings. The one he ended up choosing was, if his tortured translation of the signage was correct, a forest management road. He drove through thickening woods for another ten minutes, and picked out a half-dozen landmarks. Satisfied, he reversed to the main road and continued east, eventually picking up a secondary highway back toward Vienna.

Near Prottes he made his first stop, a hardware store where he purchased a pair of wire cutters, duct tape, and heavy-duty zip ties. He placed all of it in the trunk of the car. He'd intentionally chosen a remote corner of the parking lot, and with the trunk lid still open, he used the wire cutters to sever the glow-in-the-dark emergency trunk-release handle. He lifted the carpeted floorboard to reveal the spare tire and emergency tools. He dropped the severed T-handle into the well and removed the lug wrench from the tool bundle. Slaton closed the trunk, put the lug wrench under the front seat, then set back out toward the highway.

On the southbound motorway he passed through the hamlet of Hagerfeld, and beyond that encountered countless dormant fields, the earth beaten into brown rows under a clear winter sky. He picked up the A23 as he neared Vienna, jogged west at the river, and circled the city center in a tightening noose. The park that was fast becoming familiar came into view, its tightly landscaped commons lorded over by the massive Reichsbrücke Bridge. Beneath the wide span an ever-patient Danube carried eastward, black and silent in its ceaseless mission.

Midway across the bridge, Slaton steered onto an exit ramp and descended to the island. He found a small but mostly empty parking lot adjoining the winding main path. His selection of a parking spot was governed by two criteria—he wanted to be on the western side of the apron near a dense line of trees, and also as far away as possible from any overhead lights. Once he'd made his choice, Slaton mulled the idea of backing the car into the space.

It would offer better geometry, given the cover and lighting. Yet it would also leave the Renault as the only car so situated. Conformity, he decided, was the better choice.

With the car in place, he locked it and walked back to the bridge. His pace was casual, because that was how people walked in a public park. It was also completely at odds with his sensory awareness. For the first time Slaton crossed to the northern reaches of the main park. There he detoured along its lower shore, taking note of the stands of trees along the bank. One in particular he examined more closely—the one he'd seen two young boys disappear into last night. Finally, he began a swing toward the Donauturm itself. He paused at its base, as if studying the great tower admiringly.

Satisfied, Slaton headed back across the bridge and into the city. He made two final stops. The first was a small sundry shop where he purchased a prepaid smartphone, a package of gift wrap, and clear tape. Finally, at a sporting goods store, not far from the gasthaus, he purchased a cheap set of youth golf clubs and, in his assassin's equivalent of an impulse buy, a set of bocce balls in a drawstring canvas bag.

Ten minutes later he was back in his room. Slaton set his new purchases beside the box from the gun store. The phone he activated and set aside. The set of golf clubs included six short-shafted irons, and he wedged these into the long box. He removed the bocce balls from the drawstring bag and stuffed the bag into the pocket of his jacket. The remaining golf clubs and bocce balls went to the back of the closet.

He ran a mental checklist and was satisfied: everything was in place. Since leaving the rental car agency three hours ago he had seen no sign of the men who'd been following him. Now back at his starting point, he guessed they might be near. If his assumptions proved correct, it didn't matter—they would not approach his room.

And if my theory is wrong? he wondered.

Slaton decided to cover every contingency. He unlatched the locks on the second-floor window, and outside noted a wintering flowerbed to the left—a soft landing if it came to that. He drew the curtains tightly closed. Then, as quietly as possible, he pushed the dresser across the floor, blocking the room's only door. The door was rigged to swing inward, and the dresser *could* be pushed aside. But not without a tremendous amount of noise, and more to the point, a measurable amount of time. More than enough to react.

Precautions complete, he went to the bed and lay down.

Slaton closed his eyes, and let his thoughts drift to the places he knew they would. The South Pacific. The Mediterranean. Open sea. His shipmates.

Soon, he told himself, his deficit of sleep returning with a vengeance. *Very soon I'll have you safe.*

FOURTEEN

Park had deposited Boutros and his team in an old weatherboard cottage outside a village called Sinpo. The house was high on a hill and overlooked the sea, albeit set back sensibly into the first line of trees. There were similar dwellings on either side along the coast, a hundred yards north and south. Neighbors to be sure, but not elbow-to-elbow, and proof that waterfront property on the inhospitable shores of the Democratic People's Republic of Korea had not yet heeled to the influences of Western real estate developers.

The house had been built, according to Park, as a retreat for a founding member of the Central Committee, soon after the Armistice of 1954. Neither the years nor a series of obviously disinterested caretakers had been kind to the place—the wood-plank siding was loose in spots, and an ornate roofline had been put askew by too many seasons of ice and snow. But the fireplace worked, and the windows closed well enough to keep the warmth inside and the wind at bay.

"Weather maybe better in morning," said their host in rough English.

His name was Choe, a man of sixty-something

years, few words, and a wary countenance. Boutros thought he looked rather like a Korean Russell Crowe, add fifty pounds and some gray whiskers, subtract a few teeth and any trace of charisma. Like everyone Boutros had so far encountered in this land of shattered souls, Choe's eyes were dark and mistrustful, with a constancy that implied they had never been otherwise.

"For both of our sakes," said Boutros, "we will hope for it."

Choe only shrugged.

Boutros regarded the tan leather satchel on the table near the door—it was the one Park had been carrying all day. After arriving at the cottage and introducing everyone, Park had simply handed it to Boutros. He promised to be back the next morning, and gave firm orders to keep the team inside the house. *As if four Arabs would wander away into a North Korean snowstorm,* Boutros remembered thinking, but keeping to himself.

That had been three hours ago, and his men were now racked out on bunks in the back room. Everyone was exhausted after two days of nonstop travel. Boutros too felt the fatigue, yet he knew there was work to be done. He retrieved the satchel and went to the only table in sight, a beaten oak lowboy surrounded by four mismatched chairs. He picked the chair that looked sturdiest and sat down. Without invitation, Choe took the opposite seat.

Boutros had not yet looked inside the case, but Park had assured him it contained everything necessary to complete their mission—the kind of optimism all too often displayed by those on the handle of the spear.

He found multiple file folders inside, some thick

with paper, others holding only a few sheets. He removed the file on top, and as soon as he set it down, Boutros saw the first problem.

"I need more light," he said to Choe.

The Korean looked at him questioningly. The sun had set hours ago, and the only light now came from the fireplace and a lone candle on the opposite wall. For the first time Boutros realized there wasn't a light bulb in sight. Indeed, it dawned on him that he'd seen no evidence of electricity anywhere in the place: no refrigerator, no clock, no receptacles on the walls. Even at the height of the war in Syria they'd had generators for recharging phones, the occasional on-grid hour in the middle of the night. The rumors he'd heard were proving accurate: North Korea truly was in the Stone Age.

Choe grunted something in Korean, probably an expletive, and walked dutifully to a cabinet. He pulled out two more candles with holders, and used the one already burning to light them. He set both on the table and took his chair with an *Anything else?* stare.

"Thank you," Boutros said.

The Korean didn't respond, his glowering expression etched in stone—an effect magnified by the deep shadows and flickering light. Boutros remained impassive, although a new worry began to rise.

If this is the state of their homes, what will I find on the boat?

This was the essence of Boutros' inclusion in the operation—the reason why he, over any number of equally accomplished commanders, had been chosen to lead this mission. Kasim Boutros, as far as anyone knew, was the Islamic State's only officer with naval experience. He had long ago been commissioned in the Iraqi Navy, and spent a year commanding a British-built corvette, patrolling some of the most hostile waters on earth.

Ultimately, however, the war with America, in conjunction with long-running sectarian hostilities, had left Iraq's navy high and dry. Like a boat without a rudder, his career had gone adrift. He'd taken leave, gone home, and suffered through an interminable decade of infighting between militias. He watched family members fall to violence, saw the rise of an Iranian-backed government. When he finally committed himself to the Islamic State, it was less in devotion to Allah than as a prayer for stability. He'd fought well and hard for two years, rising through the ranks as a respected commander— Boutros might have been trained for the sea, but inspired leadership translated to any battlefield. Now his journey of service had come full circle: when the caliphate needed someone to assume command of a boat, tackle an unfamiliar ocean in the height of winter, it was only natural that Boutros got the call.

Choe got up and disappeared into the kitchen. In spite of his detached nature, he too was vital to the mission. According to Park, Choe was a fisherman from a nearby village who was familiar with the local waters and completely trustworthy. Trust Boutros never took for granted, but he would listen gladly to what the man could offer with regard to the boat and the sea. Even then, he knew this mission was going to take them far beyond the Sea of Japan—into waters where Choe himself had likely never ventured.

A conversation in rapid-fire Korean sprang from the kitchen. Choe was squabbling with the old woman. She'd been introduced as his wife, and Boutros had no reason to doubt it. A sinewy, hard-jawed peasant, she never seemed to stop moving, and had not left the kitchen since they'd arrived. The woman had so far delivered three meals, each worse than the previous. The first had been cabbage stew, followed by dried fish. After that had come a cold soup of some kind, the main ingredient being seaweed. Sami and Rafiq claimed to feel ill afterward, but they'd gone to bed without vomiting. Saleem had not been so lucky.

Boutros attacked the first file and found a collection of maps. He spread the largest over the table, anchoring the corners with candles and empty teacups. He saw marks on both their target and the intermediate rendezvous point. Both were surrounded by a seemingly endless expanse of blue water. It reminded him of ancient maritime charts, the kind whose edges were always adorned with serpents and giant squid. For a coastal pilot who'd spent his short career in protected waters, it was undeniably intimidating.

A shuffling noise caught his attention. He turned to see Rafiq.

"I couldn't sleep. My stomach is still not settled."

"Nor mine. We will not take any more of her meals. Politeness is not as important as mission readiness."

Rafiq leaned in and looked at the map. Boutros watched him closely, saw the realization strike home.

"This is where we are going?" Rafiq asked, uncertainty in his voice.

Boutros nodded. As a matter of security, only he had been briefed on their specific target. It was time to include the others. "Are you surprised?" he asked.

Rafiq grinned, still bleary-eyed. "Somewhat. It is certainly symbolic."

"Uniquely so."

"It seems very far away. Can we reach it from here?"

"As long as we all do our part . . . I don't see why not."

Rafiq looked at the stack of files. He began digging through, perusing a few pages from each. He separated one folder and opened it, revealing a pile of engineering diagrams.

His face took on a look of astonishment. "Look what they've done—it has been annotated in Arabic."

Boutros looked at the papers and saw flourishes of handwritten Arabic in the margins.

Rafiq kept going, flipping through pages of schematics and procedural lists. As he did so his enthusiasm waned. "Even so . . . this is going to require some study."

"You don't have to build it," Boutros said. "You only have to make it work . . . once."

Rafiq closed the file and dug into a second.

"What about Saleem?" Boutros asked. "Will he need guidance?"

Rafiq shrugged. "I doubt it. Of all the variables, Saleem worries me the least. He is an artist when it comes to explosives. As long as the basics are on board, he will find a way."

Choe's wife came into the room with a steaming bowl and set it on the table between them. Boutros saw a green liquid with tiny fish heads bobbing on the surface.

He exchanged a look with Rafiq. Without a word, the two Arabs retreated to the bunk room.

FIFTEEN

Slaton woke at six that evening as ill-rested as anyone headed for a stint on the graveyard shift. He made a cursory check out the window, saw a city deep into its long January dusk. When nothing worrisome caught his eye, he set straight to work.

The gift wrap he'd bought was dark blue, more refined than festive, and when he wrapped the box from the gun store it afforded the package an entirely new look—something cheerful and big-hearted. He pushed the furniture back where it was supposed to be, tucked the box under an arm, and locked the door as he left the room. From the gasthaus he hailed a taxi, preferring not to walk a mile through central Vienna with the package.

The driver dropped him along Wehlistrasse, one street removed from the river and behind the blessed frontage of St. Francis of Assisi Church. He skirted the soaring rust-tiled spires, the octagonal chapel, and ended on the southern bank of the Danube. Before him was the Reichsbrücke Bridge, and Slaton took the pedestrian walkway, arcing first above the churning river, then Danube Island and the calm estuary. On the far side he descended weather-hewn graystone stairs to the broad paths of the land-side park.

His eyes were alert as he crossed the gardens toward the tower. A dark night had taken hold, but the park was sprayed in patches of light from the city. Night always instilled its changes. Channels of light and pools of pitch darkness. In the distance yellow floodlights shone down on what appeared to be an athletic field. Given the rectangular configuration, he guessed it to be a soccer pitch, probably local clubs engaging in an amateur night-league match.

To the east, drifting in from the distant Vienna International Centre, he heard the sounds of a live concert. Bass reverbs, percussion, the high notes of a female singer. Concerts would be a natural fit for such a complex. He'd considered the park's own amphitheater, verifying that there were no shows tonight, but admonished himself for not having re-searched farther afield. Such an event could bring complications. Or conversely, opportunities.

Slaton refocused as his objective came near.

The Donauturm loomed before him, rising like a scepter into the impassive night. The uplit spire seemed to reach for the clouds, a solid ceiling that absorbed the city's lights with the warmth of a blan-ket. Slaton had in fact seen days when the tower did touch the clouds. Ever mindful of such compli-cations, he had already checked the weather. The forecast tonight was for modestly low cloud cover, a ceiling of two thousand feet above ground level. The tower was, and would remain, safely in the clear.

The treelines and hedges all around fell obscured, their lack of foliage less evident than in daylight.

There were few pedestrians in sight, the locals weary of winter and the tourists preoccupied by dinner hour. He heard traffic on the nearby streets, but only a few headlights were visible from the park's central walkways. Slaton arrived at the base of the Donauturm at precisely 7:51.

In twenty-four minutes, or perhaps a bit sooner, things would accelerate. One thousand yards south, across the slow-moving estuary, his target was to appear on a semicircle of concrete accented by Wetterstein limestone.

And when that moment came, Slaton would be ready.

He has gone inside.

The Uzbek sent the text from deep inside a stand of trees. He'd spotted their target as he materialized out of the park's darkness into the lights at the base of the Donauturm. He had arrived right on time and was carrying a long box—almost certainly the one they'd seen him haul out of the gun shop.

Everything was as expected.

The Uzbek's weapon was an arm's length away, a compact MAC-10 on the ground, resting against the base of a tree. His men were nearby, one to the right behind a garden hedge, the other in the shadow of a small service shed to the left. They had positioned themselves in a rough triangle, and soon their quarry would be centered amid three lines of fire. He watched their man disappear into the tower's ticket center.

This too was expected.

The Somali, who was better positioned to see inside, picked up, texting: He is at the desk. Laughing with girl at ticket counter.

The Uzbek waited patiently.

A minute passed.

Two.

He looked at his watch. 7:55. He tapped out: Is he taking the elevator or the stairs?

A delay, then: Neither yet. They are only talking.

The Uzbek looked at the tower. From so close it seemed astoundingly tall. Twenty minutes remained—still enough time for the man to position himself and shoot. All the same, the Uzbek had seen snipers operate in Syria. He knew them to be patient and methodical. And that required time.

Something is wrong, he thought for the first time.

Seconds later, a text came from the Tunisian: I think something is wrong.

"It's much colder in Sweden this week," Slaton said.

"It is always colder in Sweden," replied the smiling woman behind the ticket counter. She was a few years older than Slaton, not unattractive, and wore no wedding band. Her English was good, which was no doubt a prerequisite for her job—selling tickets to tourists at the Donauturm.

"We have an unfortunate reputation," he went on. "It's really not so cold, especially along the coast."

They talked about the seasons for another minute, a pleasant back-and-forth that ran straight through autumn. Flirting was too strong a word, but like any good operator, Slaton could be engaging when it served him. She was relating her experiences of last year's November blizzard when his eyes swept casually to the clock on the wall.

It was time.

"I'm sorry, but I should be on my way. As I said,

I'm heading to a party for my nephew. I somehow got turned around in the park, and thought you could steer me straight. I'm trying to get to Stuwerstrasse in Leopoldstadt."

She pointed out the correct path. "Take the Reichsbrücke Bridge. Once you are in the city, turn left at Venediger Park."

He smiled in thanks.

"Will you be in Vienna long?" she asked.

"I'm leaving tomorrow, I'm afraid."

"Pity."

"Yes, isn't it?" He edged toward the door, the gift-wrapped box secure under one arm. "The next time I'm in town, I will be sure to come back and visit your tower."

She said something as he neared the exit. Slaton never heard it. Every sense had been retuned to the night outside.

The Uzbek was getting anxious.

Moments earlier he'd texted again: Has he gone up?

The wait for a reply seemed interminable.

They'd been warned the man was an assassin, an expert improviser who would find a way to the top of the tower with his weapon. From there he would take one, or at most two shots at a target on the distant island. After that, the assassin had to make his escape.

Their assignment was simple. Once the killer had done his work, they were to ambush him on his way out of the tower. The Uzbek never doubted they could do it. Assassin or not, the man would not expect an encounter in the first seconds of his getaway. They had the element of surprise on their side, not to mention a three-to-one advantage. They also had superior firepower, three MAC-10s on full automatic. If that wasn't enough, the geometry was inescapable—their man would be trapped in the open amid three widely spaced lines of fire, while they would remain in cover. There could be but one result.

They only had to wait for their chance.

7:59.

He was contemplating another text when the Somali finally replied: He is moving again, near the elevator.

The text from the Somali had no sooner arrived than another came: At the front door now! Coming back outside!

The Uzbek shifted to his left, straining to see the entrance. Their target suddenly appeared. The box with the gun was still under his arm. The Uzbek checked his phone. 8:00. Something was wrong. Their man had never gone up into the tower. *He hadn't made his kill.*

They'd been given strict orders not to engage before that happened.

The Tunisian: What do we do?

The Somali: Shoot now?

Their target was walking past the base of the tower, backtracking the path by which he'd arrived. This had never been covered. They'd discussed the possibility that they might not hear the assassin's shot. And they had no way to confirm his kill. *But the man hadn't even gone up in the tower!*

The Uzbek knew he had to say something. He texted: Wait! Hold your fire!

He tried to think logically, and came up with one

possibility. What if the man hadn't been able to access the tower? Perhaps security was tighter than expected, or the elevator had gone out of service. In that case, what would he do?

Exactly what he's doing now. He's an expert improviser, and there is still time. He's looking for another location from which to shoot.

The Uzbek picked up his weapon, stuffed it beneath his loose jacket. He fired off another text: Follow him!

Slaton walked briskly.

A man on a mission.

He cut straight across the broad southern lawn using the city for a reference. He took up a course to the river and crested the small service bridge that passed over the A22, the autobahn that carved a swath through the lower park. The road was relatively quiet, the evening rush having subsided, and on the far side he descended into a nearly deserted greenbelt—the narrow strip that ran east-west between the motorway and the estuary.

And that overlooked Danube Island.

There was no one in sight on the walking paths ahead. Slaton forced himself not to check six. He veered toward the clusters of trees bordering the shore and found the one he wanted—the same outcropping where the two young boys had concealed themselves last night. It turned out to be ideal. There was a narrow gap in the foliage, an entrance hidden from nearly every angle by stout wintering hardwoods and evergreen underbrush. Once inside, he looked out across the water, toward the island. He easily picked out the semicircle of concrete and decorative limestone, and there, at 8:11—four minutes early—Slaton saw what he'd always known he would see.

The man from the photograph. The target he had been instructed to eliminate.

He put the box on the ground and began tearing away gift wrap like a kid on Christmas morning.

SIXTEEN

The thin man in the dark jacket stood waiting in the cold. His hands were thrust deep into his pockets—he had never adapted to Viennese winters. His flyaway hair was black and curly, approaching shoulder-length—as usual, a bit longer than it should have been. He pushed his wire-frame glasses up on his nose and searched the surrounding park. He saw no sign of the man he was to meet. Rocking left and right on his feet, he pulled out his phone and checked the time.

Two minutes to go.

Will he even come? he wondered.

He'd always known it was an open question. That he might be left standing on this semicircle, cold and alone, in the company of nothing more than hope. He wondered how long he should wait. Five minutes? Ten? An hour? He had no idea what the protocol was, but he decided he should allow something.

He startled when a stray dog trotted from behind a bench and ambled past. The mutt glanced up hopefully, but only once. Perhaps recognizing a fellow beggar. The man took off his glasses and rubbed the bridge of his nose. Clandestine meetings were not his forte. Certainly nothing he'd been trained to do. The fact that his first was taking place in a dark park on a cold night did nothing to make it easier. Yet he knew this was how it was done. He knew because he had watched it play out countless times, even if always from a safe distance. Video feeds from drones. Listening to secure comm links. He knew how such encounters were *supposed* to work.

He suddenly wondered if there might be CCTV cameras nearby. He hadn't thought about that. Would it matter to the man he'd come to meet?

He sighed and checked his phone again. The clock ticked ahead as he was watching.

8:15.

It was time.

The Uzbek almost lost the assassin on the service road overpass. Not wanting to get too close, he had waited until the man disappeared over the arched rise. After what seemed a reasonable delay, he made his own way across. On the far side he suffered a brief moment of panic when he didn't see his quarry. Then, thankfully, he caught a glimpse of a shadowed figure vanishing into a stand of trees.

There was no one else in sight, so it had to be their man.

He left the path and took cover behind an outcropping of brush. The others were close behind, and he considered how to manage things. He was most comfortable with hand signals, but night was always difficult. On top of that, he'd never worked with these two. Texting would be less prone to misunderstanding, he decided.

In a flurry of messages he directed the Somali and the Tunisian to separate. Soon his team was once again in the desired configuration—something near a triangle, centered on the outcropping of trees where their man was hiding.

He checked his watch. 8:16.

By 8:23 the Uzbek knew something was wrong.

It had been driven home that timing was critical. The assassin, apparently, hadn't gotten the word—he was supposed to have struck eight minutes ago. When their man repositioned from the tower to the stand of trees, there had still been time. Enough for a practiced killer to send one bullet. The Uzbek hadn't been told where the target would be, but he supposed it was across the water, somewhere on the narrow island.

No matter.

Something should have happened by now. Or did I miss it? Could the killer have used a silenced gun? Then a more problematic thought came to mind. *Could it have been someone else disappearing into the treeline? A homeless person or a kid doing drugs?*

The doubts began to fester. Multiply insistently.

He had to seize control of the situation—to get the night's work over with. He messaged the others, telling them to tighten the noose, then set out on a crouch toward the thick pocket of trees.

He worked the MAC-10 from beneath his jacket and tried to keep in the shadows. He came in low and quick, his eyes probing the stand of trees for anything out of the ordinary. As he got closer, he was rewarded. On the southern edge of the tree line, jutting into a spray of light, he saw an unmistakable protrusion—the barrel of a rifle.

His first thought, *Has the man already taken his shot?* was quickly replaced by, *I'm too exposed right now.*

He was twenty yards from a concealed killer. He couldn't see his cohorts, but he knew they were closing in on the opposite side. All too late, he realized he was committed—the element of surprise could be lost at any moment.

Adrenaline took hold.

He circled silently to his right. There was still no sign of the others, but he knew they had more ground to cover. They would arrive in thirty seconds, a minute at most. He heard the snap of a twig nearby, but couldn't say from which direction. *I'm exposed,* he thought again.

He couldn't wait any longer.

With his weapon poised, he shouldered into a gap in the brush and saw a natural corridor through the foliage. He felt a vibration, and realized his thumb was tapping the stock of his weapon. He forced it still. Carefully pushing aside a wet branch, he glimpsed a closet-sized space ahead. In the dim light he saw dormant grass tamped flat, broken branches on the ground. His index finger was poised on the trigger. The space was an ideal concealment, covered on every side but with a good view of the distant island. A perfect setup except for one glaring problem: the assassin wasn't here.

The Uzbek did, however, see his weapon.

He moved closer, his feet slogging through underbrush, his boots sucking into the mud. The rifle's shape was unmistakable, and on the ground next to it was the box the killer had been carrying. The gun was mounted on a series of poles—if he wasn't mistaken, two makeshift tripods constructed from a set of golf clubs. The arrangement put the weapon at shoulder height with the barrel extending beyond the brush—exactly what he'd seen from outside.

The Uzbek moved closer. He was generally familiar with weapons, but thought something about this one seemed different. He touched the stock, and felt a different texture from any gun he'd used before— an odd material, less conductive and more pliable. In the dim light he ran his hand forward along the firing assembly and handguard. It all felt the same until he reached the barrel, which was undeniably cold metal. He didn't know what to make of it. The Uzbek stood straight.

He was wondering where his cohorts were when he sensed something to his right. The slightest flicker of motion.

Before he could turn, his head was seized in what felt like a giant vise. His mouth opened, but no sound escaped. Had he been given another second, his muscles might have tensed, or a rush of adrenaline might have taken hold to give him a chance. He didn't have half that. With his chin pulled upward, a combat blade came to his throat. His last sensations on earth were twofold: the sound of a terrible gurgle, and a lightning-like bolt of pain surging into his brain stem.

The man with flyaway hair knew nothing about the killing taking place in a small stand of trees across the estuary. His earlier thought about waiting an hour was fading fast. He'd gone to great lengths to arrange this meeting, yet he knew a lot could have gone wrong. Not for the first time, his lack of field experience gnawed at him.

He looked in both directions, up and down the path. There was no one in sight. With a glance at his watch, he made his decision.

He would give it five more minutes. If his man didn't show by then, he would leave.

SEVENTEEN

It was the third adversary who was the most problematic.

He arrived only seconds after Slaton had broken the second man's neck. With the element of surprise gone, the third man had his MAC-10 nearly level before Slaton intervened with an upsweeping hand. He first controlled the stunted barrel, then wrenched the shooter's hand away from the trigger guard. With the gun pointed skyward and not under his control, the man gave up and began grappling.

He wasn't particularly large, but right away Slaton recognized a wrestler—the most common fighting art in the Middle East. His adversary spread his legs for leverage, tried to bar Slaton's left arm. Slaton blocked the move, but soon they were rolling in the dirt. Hopelessly entangled in near darkness, they fought more by feel than sight. Slaton's knife was sheathed on his lower leg, yet he couldn't reach it— every time he got a hand free, his opponent would reach for his gun or throw an elbow. Neither man seemed able to gain an advantage, and Slaton sensed a deadlock of sorts—like two prize fighters happy to get to the bell.

Then suddenly he was angry with himself. The

man he was up against was nothing more than a mercenary, a hired gun. Slaton's motivation was far more profound. He pounded his heels in the dirt furiously, incensed at the thought of a stalemate. He refocused his efforts, straining for all he was worth. Something gave in one of the man's arms and he screamed in pain. Slaton rolled on top of him, pried an elbow over his throat. He freed his other hand, and when he planted it on the ground for balance, Slaton felt something hard and round in the mud beneath. His fingers clawed and pried, and a softball-sized rock popped free from the earth. Shifting his weight, he created a clear line to the man's head. Two blows later it was over.

Slaton rolled away and lay next to the dead man. His lungs were heaving, his heart racing. Anger might not be much of a strategy . . . but it was a damned good motivator.

He sat up slowly, put his arms across his knees. Slaton realized he'd cut things too close. If the third man had arrived seconds sooner, he would have gotten off a shot. Had he been overconfident? Careless? Whatever the fault, he could not allow it again—on this mission, failure was not an option.

He stood gingerly, checked for damage. Aside from scrapes and bruises and other men's blood, everything seemed intact. It had been a close call, but his objective was met—all three men had met their end silently.

He moved to the shooting stand he'd built and looked out across the water. With considerable relief, Slaton saw his target still standing on the stone semicircle.

Having no idea how long that would be the case, he moved quickly.

The bodies went into a pile. It wasn't from any misguided sense of victory or to make a statement. The simple truth was that the best spot for concealing them, beneath a shadowed shelf of underbrush, was quite small. The police were going to have a hell of a time with their chalk outline.

The scene wasn't pretty. There was blood everywhere, its ferrous odor etched into the air. Slaton wiped the worst of it from his hands and clothing. Hopefully the night would cover the rest. He disassembled his makeshift shooting stand, dropping the golf clubs to the ground. The gun—which wasn't really a gun at all—he placed back into the box.

He'd known going in that it would be difficult to acquire a rifle on short notice, particularly in a country like Austria where gun laws, while not the most stringent, were unfailingly carried out to the letter. Given his tactical objective tonight, and the fact that things had to be done silently, he'd settled on a better way.

Unlike real guns, facsimile weapons were largely unregulated. They were designed for training, and used widely by police forces and military units. Thanks to their harmless nature, worn or dated specimens often ended up in private ownership, fated to become anything from private training tools to tap handles on kegs in basement bars. Slaton never doubted he could find something that would work, but he got a lucky break when the first gun shop he'd visited had not only a facsimile in stock, but a model that was perfect for his ruse. The M16 "Rubber Duck," with its black urethane body and metal barrel, was eminently convincing from a distance.

On a dark night one would have to virtually touch the stock to distinguish it from the real thing. As hoped, the fac had given him a perfect distraction, drawing his adversaries in like moths to a light.

He was glad there had been only three men. He'd gotten his final count after drawing them into the open: the small bridge over which he'd led his pursuers had served as a funnel, forcing them into the open one by one. From that point it had been little more than prioritization. A matter of divide and conquer.

He again checked across the water. His target was still there, and Slaton decided there was time for a hurried cleanup.

The bodies would be found sometime tomorrow morning—there was nothing to be done about that. A dog on its morning walk would catch the scent, or a vagrant might shoulder through the brush to urinate. The police would be called in, and by noon the little outcropping of trees would be surrounded by yellow tape and paper-booted detectives.

Fingerprints and DNA were not a concern. Slaton knew his profile was not on file anywhere, which put him in the clear as long as he wasn't taken into custody—something he had no intention of allowing. The one thing that had to be removed was the training gun. It was unique, and if the police took possession it wouldn't take long to discover where it had come from. In turn, the gun shop owner could give them his description, and video from the store couldn't be discounted—Slaton had done his best to avoid cameras, but it was possible he'd missed one.

He put the facsimile back inside the box. The knife remained sheathed to his leg. Slaton left the children's golf clubs on the ground, along with a half roll of duct tape and two crumpled balls of gift wrap. He imagined a baffled Viennese detective scratching his head. He picked up the rock that had saved him, then searched the ground and used the toe of his boot to loosen two more like it. These he fit around the fake M16 before working the packing straps back in place on the box.

He quickly searched the bodies and discovered a wallet on each man, complete with identity cards that might or might not be legitimate. After taking a picture of each with his phone, he left them in place. His earlier thought was reinforced: amateurs. Each man also had a phone. Two were cheap burners that had locked out, a password required to gain access. The last handset, from his first victim—and he suspected the leader—was a higher-end model that also had gone secure. This one, however, allowed either a passcode or a fingerprint—something to which Slaton conveniently had access. He placed the dead man's thumb on the home button, and after two tries the phone unlocked.

Slaton immediately went to the call log, then the contact list. He saw only two other numbers—certainly the burner phones on the ground next to him. He took a picture of the call log with his own phone, then moved on. He saw no voice mails, and the phone had not been set up for email or web browsing. It was a dead end. He briefly weighed taking the phone with him, but was concerned it might be tracked. He decided to leave it behind.

Slaton kept searching, and his hand came across a hard shape on the second man's ankle. He was surprised to uncover a compact Glock 26 with a full ten-round magazine. Without hesitation he pocketed the gun. The three MAC-10s he left where they were.

At that point his internal alarm activated.

He returned to the spot where the facsimile had been mounted and confirmed that his target hadn't moved. He began to turn back, then hesitated. Slaton took the Schmidt & Bender scope from his pocket and studied the man more closely. Again, there was a sense of vague familiarity. He would find out soon enough.

Slaton pocketed the optic, picked up the heavy box, and eased out into the night.

Slaton disposed of the box beneath the Reichs-brücke Bridge, taking particular care to avoid witnesses. It sank like three rocks. The water appeared reasonably deep, and he decided that if the detective assigned to tomorrow's triple homicide was particularly tenacious, the package might be recovered within a week. Otherwise he gave it a month. And if budgets or winter conditions precluded diving teams? In that case, the fac would likely be unearthed on the river's ten-year dredging cycle. None of it mattered to Slaton—one day, two at the most, and his work in Vienna would be done.

He hurried toward the island, still unsure how long his target would wait. So far his theory was holding. Someone was coercing him to kill the man on the island. The three Slaton had just dealt with, he was sure, had been assigned to eliminate him once that job was done. Within the borders of those facts, his assumptions so far appeared on target.

To begin, he himself would never have viewed the Donauturm as a good platform from which to shoot. The great spire was too public a place, and the extreme vertical confines gave but one way out. If those running the attraction were security-conscious at all, which Austrians generally were, any attempt to climb inside with a package sized for a rifle would raise blazing red flags. In the course of his reconnaissance, standing on the semicircle of concrete, Slaton had realized why the point had been chosen—because a non-operator might view the Donauturm as an obvious place from which to shoot. With that much figured out, Slaton knew he was being set up.

The simplest response: alter the battlefield to his own design.

He knew the men would be waiting for him outside the tower. In a more speculative assumption, he reasoned that since he hadn't completed his mission, they would follow him through the park. Every conjecture gave additive risk, but so far everything had held.

In a perfect world, he would have interrogated at least one of the three men, yet the complications of doing so were insurmountable. Slaton had one clear objective: to find out who'd taken his family. Of the four people who might tell him, three were now dead. They were likely no more than foot soldiers, and not particularly competent ones at that—men who probably didn't even know who'd hired them. Slaton's best chance for answers had always been the fourth man. The one standing in wait. He would know who was trying to kill them both.

Logical as it all seemed, Slaton sensed one disconnect: Why had the men he'd eliminated not simply been sent after the man on the island? Inept as they were, they probably could have managed it.

Why have I been brought here at all?

He saw no apparent answer.

As Slaton hurried toward Danube Island, he knew

his margin for error was slim. So far he'd been on target. The three men across the estuary had come to kill him.

He only hoped the last man could tell him why.

he pattern for error was slim. So far he'd been on target. The three men across the room had come to kill him.

He only hoped the last room would tell him why.

EIGHTEEN

Boutros woke well before dawn. The first thing he did was look out the window. He saw not a single light in the distant village, yet under a bright moon he could tell the swirling snow had dissipated.

He went to the main room and lit a pair of candles using the dying fireplace embers. He'd slept poorly, having been given nothing more than a blanket to spread on the cold stone floor. In a thought he would never have imagined, Boutros found himself longing for the straw bedroll he'd used throughout the war in Syria.

He and Rafiq had been up until midnight going over details of the mission. The files Park had given them were useful, yet complications had arisen. To begin, the nautical charts were labeled in Korean. Fortunately, Choe was a sailor, and he provided solid translations. More problematic were the engineering diagrams. Choe's grasp of technical terms was marginal at best. Their minder, Park, had promised to bring a technician in the morning. Boutros and Rafiq hoped he came through, and that whoever it was spoke a common language.

Boutros could see Choe through an open door—he was asleep on a chair in the second bedroom. He debated whether to wake the man. Even if the food had been awful, Choe and his wife had been mostly welcoming. As in most downtrodden corners of the world, the common people of Korea seemed exceedingly hospitable. All the same, he was impatient to move on.

Boutros decided on a middle ground—he targeted his boot on a tin chamber pot near the door and kicked out.

Choe startled awake.

"Sorry," Boutros said. "It is very dark."

The Korean rubbed his eyes, drew a hand over his gray-stubble chin. Just like Boutros, the fisherman's gaze went immediately to the window.

"The weather is better," Boutros said hopefully.

Choe got up, went closer to the window. He looked outside like a surgeon studying an x-ray. "We shall see."

The others stirred awake one by one, yawning and stretching and milling about the tiny cottage. Choe's wife came out with bowls of something that looked like mashed corn. On closer inspection, Boutros realized that was exactly what it was, only the husks and cobs had been churned in as well. Much like his musings on the sleeping arrangements, he felt a renewed fondness for the cuisine of war-ravaged Syria.

The front door opened and Choe walked in— he'd gone to the docks in the predawn. Right behind him was Park.

Boutros took this as a good sign. "Well?" he prompted.

Not surprisingly, it was Park who answered. "Choe says the weather is acceptable."

As a former naval officer, it was not lost on Boutros that their weather forecast was sourced not from any national meteorological office, but a long-toothed local skipper. It seemed strange to be doing Allah's work so far from the stolen lands, housed with representatives of the only people on earth whose hatred of America rivaled their own. Boutros did not delude himself that ISIS and North Korea were any kind of allies. It was more a matter of using one another to effect individual goals—whatever those might be.

He looked at Choe and asked, "Is boat the ready?"

"I have seen to everything," said the fisherman.

"Good. So we can go this morning?"

Choe deferred to Park who pulled out what appeared to be a smartphone. He began tapping on the screen. It was the first electronic device Boutros had seen since arriving in North Korea. He noticed his men watching as well, all three sitting behind bowls of soup that had not been touched.

It took nearly five minutes, the speed of Park's communications link clearly challenged. When the answer came, Park simply nodded to Choe.

The weathered skipper smiled. "We go fishing now."

The man Slaton was supposed to kill started moving at 8:29.

By 8:31 he was practically running.

Slaton hurried along the path, keeping a distant eye on his target. The man had left the meeting spot hesitantly, obviously not sure if it was the right thing to do. Then he began picking up speed.

Slaton lost sight of his quarry near the boarded-up boat rental office, and by the time he reached the wide paths of the northern shore the man was nowhere in sight. In a terrible moment, with his eyes scouring the tree-lined paths, he realized how easily his plan could fall to disaster. If he lost the man now, he might never see him again—and with him would go the best chance to find his family.

He was saved by a glimpse of a slight figure darting beneath a streetlamp. Slaton locked on like a radar. It was definitely his target—same slender build and light-footed gait, same dark winter jacket. He was moving fast across the island on a diagonal walkway, his silhouette framed by city lights. Having memorized the layout of the paths, Slaton knew the current geometry was unworkable. There was only one way to make up ground.

Turning from the path onto a grassy hill, he took an angle to cut the man off and broke into a dead run. It took less than two minutes to reach the walkway that traced the Danube's upper shoulder. This put Slaton ahead of his target. It also precluded any chance of stealth. His only option was to put himself on a pathway and stroll in the opposite direction. He saw his man right away, fifty paces ahead. Coming at him with fast steps and an edgy gaze.

A man who was worried. Even afraid.

Slaton wondered under what pretext he had been lured here, to the tranquil riverside arena of his execution. He'd obviously been expecting a meeting of some kind, no doubt arranged by the same party who'd tried to put Slaton on the delivering end of a bullet. A shared enemy, in a sense.

Or could it be something else?

It was time for answers.

With the geometry back under control, Slaton concentrated on timing. He checked the paths behind him, saw a handful of people in the distance on his right. No one was looking in this direction. He tried to govern his intercept with respect to three variables: minimizing the line-of-sight to any witnesses, selecting a spot on the sidewalk that wasn't illuminated, and keeping close to the tree-covered swales on his right—cover for reaching the rental car.

Slaton tilted his head down, a pose of contemplation. At thirty yards everything was going smoothly. At twenty he sensed the man watching him.

At ten it all went to hell.

NINETEEN

His target broke into a sprint across the grassy shoulder, making a beeline for the wooded glade.

Slaton ran to catch up, and soon had a new revelation—the man was damned fast. He flew into the woods like a startled deer, leaping over brush and darting between trees. Slaton was only a few strides behind but he felt like a lion chasing a gazelle. He got close once, only to stumble over a rotted log. He righted himself and kept going.

Losing this race was not an option.

Slaton pushed harder, straining for speed. He had to catch up before the man got back into the open—if that happened, someone might raise an alarm. The darkness of the glade was an enemy, almost no light penetrating. Leafless limbs slapped his face and stones gave way under foot. The only consolation was that his quarry faced the same obstacles. He registered little more than a dark shape crashing through the underbrush ahead. Then, suddenly, he seemed to close in, the scurrying figure only steps ahead. Slaton heard panting, saw brush snapping back barely an arm's length away.

The man *had* made at least one mistake—if he'd

run in the opposite direction he would have quickly reached the riverside. A very public place with bystanders and mobile phones. As it was, Slaton and his quarry were both out of sight. Even better—they were heading straight for the car.

If I could just catch the bastard!

He caught a glimpse of light: the edge of the glade looming ahead. Slaton had to catch the man before he reached it. He heard a grunt, a crash of vegetation, then saw him clearly—a tumbling heap in the wet underbrush. Slaton got a hand to him as he bounced up, but in the next instant he himself stumbled and lost his grip. Realizing he was going down, Slaton launched into a last-ditch dive. He swiped an arm in a desperate arc, like a defensive back trying to save a touchdown. His fingers clipped a leg, tripping the man a second time. Together they pitched headlong into a leafless sapling.

And then, finally, Slaton got a death grip on a handful of cotton fabric.

His hand became a vise. He leveraged his superior strength and weight, pinning the man to the ground.

There Slaton paused.

Both he and his captive were breathing in ragged gasps. The man started to say something, but before the first word came Slaton shoved his face into a pile of wet leaves. "*Not . . . a . . . word! Do I make myself clear?*"

Slaton said it in English, figuring that was his best chance of being understood. He felt the scalp in his hand nod. He continued in a low voice, words delivered with deliberate slowness. "We are going to get up now. If you do not cooperate completely, you will die. If you try to break away, same outcome. Do you understand?"

Another nod.

Slaton hauled the man to his feet and frog-marched him through the glade. He paused at the edge while they were still in cover. His rental was a mere fifty yards away, but they would have to cross open ground to reach it. He checked in every direction.

Night had taken a firm grip, the gloom punctuated by no more than a few pole-mounted globes of white above the parking area. The only pedestrians he saw were on the distant bridge. His captive was conveniently wearing a belt, and Slaton grabbed it near the rear waistband. It was an unbreakable grip, yet from a distance might appear collegial—a sober man guiding a friend who was three sheets to the wind. With a shove they set out in unison toward the car.

When they reached it, Slaton popped the trunk and turned the man around. For the first time the two stood face-to-face under a wash of light. Slaton was more certain than ever that he knew this man, but he still couldn't place it. With their faces only inches apart, it was the prisoner who seemed to have the revelation.

"I knew you would come!" he exclaimed. The words perplexed Slaton. Even more bewildering—they had come in Hebrew.

There was no time for questions. Not here, not now. Without responding, Slaton turned the man and put his hip against the bumper. He performed a rapid one-handed frisk—an acquired talent—and found no weapons, one phone, one wallet. He took the phone, then reasserted his grip on the man's belt.

Sensing what was coming, he protested. "No, wait! You don't have to—"

Slaton cut off the complaint with a knee to his prisoner's stomach. He doubled over, gasping for breath. The move actually filled two squares—he folded his captive into the trunk in that very position. Then, like a cowboy tying a calf at a rodeo, he bound the man's wrists and ankles in seconds using the heavy zip ties he'd purchased. A makeshift gag came next, duct tape and a rag, leaving space to breathe through the nose. Finally, he reached into his pocket and pulled out the drawstring canvas bag that had a few hours ago contained bocce balls. The last thing Slaton saw before putting the hood over his prisoner's head was a pair of frightened, wide-open eyes.

He thumped the trunk shut and made one last survey of the area. He saw no one watching. Slaton casually walked to the driver's door and got behind the wheel.

He steered onto the Reichsbrücke Bridge and blended into light traffic. It took all the self-control he could muster to drive at a sedate pace. He was desperate to talk to this man, uncover what he knew. Yet such dialogues had to be handled correctly. Had to be managed for optimum productivity. Which, unfortunately, required time. It was a level of patience Slaton wasn't sure he possessed.

He guided the Renault northbound on the route he'd mapped out that afternoon, keeping well under the speed limit and checking his mirrors regularly.

Not a single sound emanated from the trunk behind him.

TWENTY

Harbors across the world hold certain commonalities. They give shelter from high seas and heavy weather. They serve as hubs for crew and commerce. Within these constraints, however—as any skipper would tell you—ports across the globe are infinitely divergent. Monaco's harbor burgeons with megayachts, an unending competition between business titans and oligarchs and the odd royal family. Remote coves on the shores of Africa and Indochina are little more than white-sand beaches from which bronze-skinned boys push prams into the sea. The vast majority, of course, fall into a serviceable middle ground—places modified to the point of usefulness, but which retain a time-honed local character.

And that was exactly what Kasim Boutros saw in the light of an extended winter dawn.

The bay was shaped like a shell, a riprap breakwater added to enhance the calm. Three piers lay inside the mole, which on that hard winter morning was more than enough. Not counting a handful of launches, Boutros counted eight boats in the village fleet. Seven were of similar lineage—broad-beamed fishing trawlers that looked seaworthy, but only just. Their wooden hulls were scarred and pock-marked, their rigging conspicuously slack. Moored along the piers, weary and still, they had the aura of long-tenured employees resting in a break room.

The docks and surrounding sheds were a fitting backdrop—worn and beaten, gray from the elements, they looked in a state of functional disrepair. Wooden racks for sun-drying the catch lined every shore, empty until spring and tipped in snow. Even in midwinter the air was one with the sea, something between low tide and last month's catch—as if the essence of the wharf's mission had been infused into its planks and pilings.

Park was leading the way, a few steps in front of Boutros and Choe. At Park's side was a new man who'd been introduced only as "the technician." Boutros saw no need to inquire as to his specialty. The rest of his squad brought up the rear, trailing like a pack of disorderly schoolboys.

The boat that stood out from the crowd was at the end of the seaward pier, isolated and distinctive like a lone lost traveler.

"Name is *Albatross*," said Choe.

"I'll take your word for it," Boutros replied.

There was a name on her bow, and it might have been *Albatross*, but Boutros really couldn't say—scribed by hand, in black paint that had dripped badly, was a cluster of unfamiliar characters. Not Korean Hangul, he thought, but something farther south.

"Where is she from?" Boutros asked, the dock's worn planks complaining under his feet.

It was Park who answered over his shoulder. "Choe brought her here from Thailand."

"Why Thailand?" Boutros asked.

"Why not?" said the ever-sullen Park. "The important thing is that it is not a North Korean boat."

"I understand. It just wasn't what I was expecting."

"There is a bucket of paint and brush on board. Change the name to whatever you like, but only after you are at sea. And make sure it is not a Korean name."

Boutros wanted to say he couldn't create a Korean character if he tried, and that the undecipherable translation of *Albatross* was as good a name as any.

Halfway up the pier, a kneeling old man was applying putty to the hull of an overturned dinghy. Strangely, he never looked up as Boutros and the others passed. Boutros looked across the harbor and saw a woman with arthritic hands mending a net, two unsmiling boys hauling straw baskets from one shed to another. Like the man with the putty knife, every set of eyes remained averted. As if no one had noticed that a procession of Middle Easterners and North Korean intelligence officers were walking across the community pier. Boutros guessed aliens from outer nebulas would have gotten the same reaction.

Many years ago he'd witnessed Saddam Hussein's repression in Iraq, and more recently the Islamic State's occupation in quarters of Syria. Both had ruled through fear, but with a measure of targeted benevolence. What he saw here was something else. This was nothing short of subjugation, a populace not bent but broken, molded by generations of brutality and starvation.

As they made the turn to the final dock, Boutros addressed Choe. "Are there always so few boats here?"

"No. Others out working. In the winter most go south, to China Sea and Indian Ocean."

"In this village, one boat more or less will not be noticed," said Park, as if reading Boutros' thoughts.

Boutros looked skyward. Somewhere, he supposed, a few hundred miles up, there had to be satellites. Yet unlike Syria and Iraq, he doubted there were drones here—the North Koreans had an air force, after all, and they would relish the chance to shoot down anything that strayed into their airspace. He decided Park was right. The departure of one fishing boat from a quiet village might be recorded somewhere, but it would hardly draw notice.

When they reached the boat, Park said, "Keep your team here for a moment." Boutros didn't argue, and he watched the three Koreans cross a gangway onto the boat.

Rafiq came to his side. "I thought she would be bigger," he said.

"Be happy she's not. Smaller boats are easier to manage."

"But you will have our help."

"I know," Boutros said, thinking, *That's what worries me.*

The nautical challenge before him would be like nothing he'd experienced. To begin, he would be tackling open ocean without a single experienced hand. Boutros had schooled his men in some basics back in Turkey, during the days in the refugee camp while they awaited the final go-ahead. It had been little more than a safety briefing: how to not fall overboard, how to don a life jacket, the importance of keeping a clear deck. He hoped to teach them simple navigation, and was committed to assigning a watch detail—even if it was no more than keeping their eyes open for four hours at a stretch.

Anything beyond that, Boutros knew, was fantasy. The success of this voyage rested on his shoulders.

"She looks better than the rest," said Sami.

"A gift from God," seconded Saleem.

Notwithstanding the layman's nature of their opinions, Boutros had to agree. *Albatross* was sixty feet along the water line, he guessed, and her general condition was notably above that of the other boats in the harbor. Her rigging and fittings were not new, but less frayed than what he saw elsewhere. There were enough antennas to promise a decent electronics suite. If there was a shortcoming, it might be her fishing gear. She was rigged for purse seining, evidenced by the boom poised high over a brine-blanched working deck. The net was folded and stowed against the transom, yet it appeared dry and calcified, as if it hadn't been used in months. To the skipper of a naval patrol boat, which Boutros had once been, it seemed an obvious discrepancy in what otherwise looked like a reliable vessel.

"Let us hope the engine is as solid as the rest," he said to his men.

Park came out of the wheelhouse and crossed back to the dock. "Our technicians have gone over everything," he said. "You will have no problems. Long-range fuel tanks have been installed, so you can easily reach your destination." He pointed to an open stowage compartment along the port side. Roughly twenty jerry cans of fuel had been secured inside. "Those contain aviation fuel. They will be needed at your technical stop."

Boutros nodded to say he understood. He took in everything around him, and was satisfied with the logistics. The most important element, however, was beyond his expertise. "And the rest?" he asked.

"That," said Park, "is below deck."

Boutros exchanged a look with Rafiq, who nodded. "All right then, let's have a look."

TWENTY-ONE

Slaton repeated the course he'd taken earlier that day, driving northeast out of Vienna. The city's ring of hamlets began to fall away, and in the deepening night the Renault's headlights began cutting through heavy woodland. Gentle as the hills were, he was glad the weather was cooperating—even moderate snow might have forced him to a less isolated backdrop. Using the map on his phone he easily located the offshoot he'd scouted earlier—a well-maintained forest road.

The silence from the trunk was oddly insistent. Like a silent cry for help. Had he not been trained in the art of kidnapping—there was really no other word for it—Slaton might have wondered if his subject was suffocating or had gone unconscious. The cold truth was far more simple: the man in the trunk was scared to death. Bound, gagged, and confined in a pitch-black space, the lack of principal sensory inputs heighten others that were typically secondary. The air inside the trunk would become stale, infused with sweat and fear. He would feel the car bend through turns, and register the engine vibration with every acceleration and slowdown. He'd note the tires humming over asphalt and grinding over gravel. All of it would wreak havoc in his mind, spur questions about where they were going—and what would happen when they got there.

Slaton did nothing to minimize the effect. He even made a few unnecessary stops—silent pauses followed by rapid acceleration. At one point, on a section of wide-open road, he threw the wheel hard and began slaloming from shoulder to shoulder. If it was cruel, he felt no remorse—not with what was at stake.

The map on his phone became useless—forest roads were not displayed to begin with, and his mobile signal had gone intermittent. Slaton drove on methodically, times and distances to each turn noted, a handful of landmarks recorded. He found the intersection of two prominent fences, and soon after that spotted a unique section of guardrail—carefully selected points that stood out at night as well as they did in the day. He was still on course.

Inevitably, however, the clock in his head seemed to quicken.

I knew you would come.

His prisoner's words kept playing in his mind. It was as if the man had been expecting Slaton all along. Like he was greeting a guest at a cocktail party. Not an executioner.

Until Slaton had heard that one phrase, his assumptions had seemed on target. Three thugs had been brought in to eliminate him once he'd taken out the man in the trunk. That much was clear, and he'd dealt with it cleanly. Yet something about his target's reaction felt wrong.

I knew you would come.

For reasons he couldn't quantify, those words threatened everything. Made the clock run faster.

Whoever had abducted his family wasn't going to get a "mission accomplished" report from the killers. Had the controller of this twisted plot discovered how things in Vienna had played out? Perhaps. Either way, in the coming hours one fact would become clear. The three amateurs had met a bad end. The fate of the man in the trunk, however, along with his own, would remain an open question.

He decided he had a window in which to operate. A few hours at least. No more than a day. In that time, he had to get answers. He needed to find out who he was up against. Needed to make sure they understood the kind of war they'd be declaring if Christine and Davy were harmed.

Slaton had originally thought his prisoner would be useful in one of two ways—he would either divulge actionable information, or he himself would serve as negotiating capital. Now Slaton wasn't so sure.

He was expecting me . . .

He drove deeper into the forest, searching for his final landmark—a brown wooden sign at the head of a hiking trail. Just when he thought he might have gone too far—his troubled thoughts distorting the passage of minutes—the board with the painted hiker came into view.

After two quick turns, Slaton pulled onto a siding. He maneuvered carefully to cast the headlights on the base of a midsize oak tree. He turned the engine off, but left the headlights on with the high beams engaged. He got out, closed the door decisively, and walked with heavy footfalls to the trunk. He waited in silence for thirty seconds. Letting the imagination beneath the lid run amok. Trying to keep his own from doing the same.

The air was clean and cool, a departure from the city. The only sounds were those of the forest—a gentle breeze brushing the high canopy, a few insects buzzing. Still he heard nothing from inside.

He lifted the lid abruptly. The light snapped on and in the tight confines he saw his charge curled into a semi-fetal position. Slaton had not rented a full-size car for precisely that reason—to promote claustrophobia. A consideration, he was sure, few renters imagined.

The man was trying to say something, but the words were unintelligible through the gag.

"Quiet," Slaton ordered in English. He was sure the man understood, and it ignored his previous use of Hebrew. One more degree of control.

Slaton pulled him out roughly, then dragged his prisoner to the tree in front of the car. He backed the man up against the trunk, zip ties still binding his wrists and ankles. The stubs of a few old, broken-off branches jabbed him in the back like the spikes of some medieval torture device. Slaton used the wire cutters to briefly free his wrists, then wrapped them behind the tree and resecured them with new ties. He made sure it was uncomfortable, the shoulders trussed back severely. As a final indignity, Slaton used two more plastic ties to secure his belt to the tree. He doubted the man would wear one again for the rest of his life—however long that proved to be.

Finally, Slaton yanked away the hood.

Staring at the high beams, the man blinked and squinted. Slaton removed the gag, ripping the tape free like the world's worst wax job. One side of his captive's face was marked with red splotches, probably where it had been pressed to the floor of the trunk. His shoulder-length hair was mussed and tangled.

Slaton walked behind the tree, out of the man's line of sight. He waited for a full minute.

Completely silent.

Completely still.

When it came to interrogations, Slaton was well versed in standard practices. He recognized the importance of forethought and planning, and knew that an insulated working area was essential. Employing multiple interrogators was always the preferred method. Most critically of all—the best results required both time and patience.

He had none of that.

Yet he was not without tools at his disposal. Most important among them was sensory control. Light, temperature, time, sound, touch—all could be manipulated, turned to extremes in one moment, removed altogether in the next. If necessary, he could accelerate things with degrees of discomfort. Whether that advanced to something worse was up to his captive.

"Let me explain how this works," he said. "I need information, and I need it quickly. I will do whatever is necessary to get truthful answers. To begin, I'll tell you that I came to Vienna because of a message that came to my phone. That message instructed me to kill you, and threatened people I care very much about if I failed to do so. I chose not to carry through, primarily because I don't know who's behind this scheme. In essence, someone tried to coerce me into killing you. Are you following me so far?"

A nod.

"Good. You should also understand that I can re-visit my decision at any time."

Another nod.

"All right. So let's start with the obvious question. Who would want you dead?"

Slaton waited, watched every tremor in the man's expression. In his years with Mossad, he had rarely taken a direct role in interrogations. Yet he'd witnessed more sessions than he cared to remember—sometimes live, more often on video, terrorists and criminals confessing to acts so heinous and reprehensible that Mossad had committed to its ultimate response. They had called in Slaton.

Through the course of it all, he'd acquired a knack for reading men under duress. He had watched them conjure lies. Seen them break and tell the truth. What Slaton saw now was none of those things. The scrawny thirtysomething man he'd strung to a tree showed nothing but bafflement. On the question of who wanted him dead, he didn't have an answer. Utter confusion was steeped into his delicate features.

Slaton said nothing. After an interminable silence, he saw a response begin to build. Whatever came, he thought, was going to be something unexpected and raw. Perhaps even truthful.

"I can tell you exactly who brought you to Vienna," the man finally said. "It was me."

TWENTY-TWO

A relationship with a boat is like any other. The first meeting is always awkward, little mistakes made and movements tentative. As things progress, irritants are revealed and confidences gained. Only with time does trust develop.

This was how Boutros regarded *Albatross* as they cleared the breakwater into the rush of an oncoming sea. The boat shuddered ever so slightly as her big diesel dug in, feathers of black smoke lifting from her stack into the stone-gray morning. Choe was at the helm, Boutros beside him in the covered wheelhouse. Rafiq and the Korean technician had gone below for transitional briefings. Boutros had sent Sami and Saleem below to settle into their quarters, and he imagined them fighting like kids over who got the top bunk. Park had drifted alone to the aft deck, and was standing near the transom—bundled in a heavy parka and a knit cap, he looked like a tourist watching for whales.

"Waypoints go here," Choe said, showing Boutros how to input coordinate sets on the multifunction display. The navigation unit was a Garmin product, and Boutros saw *Made in America* on the bottom of the case. The irony was inescapable.

"Is the weather function operable?" he asked.

Choe tapped the menu to call up the radar display. A few distant rain showers painted along the forty-mile arc. Boutros knew it wasn't a state-of-the-art system—he noticed what looked like a coffee stain on the plastic frame—but all the essential modes seemed to work.

"What speed can I expect?" he asked. This had been one of the few requirements—to acquire a boat that was reasonably fast.

"Fourteen knots uses the least fuel," Choe said, pointing to the fuel flow gauges. "Twenty-one is highest for cruising."

"How much more will she do?" Boutros asked.

Choe shrugged, as if to say he didn't know. Boutros didn't buy it. "You brought her here all the way from Thailand. You must have let her run at some point."

The Korean tipped his head to one side. "There was one night, very late. I saw twenty-four knots, maybe twenty-five. But not for long—the engine made noises I did not like."

Boutros didn't respond, his apprehension returning. He had no mechanic on board, no engine manuals or spare parts. *Am I overstepping my abilities?* he wondered for what seemed the hundredth time.

From the aft deck Park shouted something in Korean, and soon he and Choe were engaged in a staccato back-and-forth.

Boutros edged out of the wheelhouse and stood along the starboard rail. He pulled up the collar of his jacket against a bitter breeze and looked out reflectively across the water. Cold lay over the sea like a great slab, and the cloud-mottled sun seemed chained to the horizon. Unlike his homeland, dawn here was a process of hours. In the distance he saw islands of seaweed choking the camo-green shoreline, and wind-driven whitecaps chevronned the surface as far as he could see.

He wondered how long the Koreans would stay aboard. At some point, he'd been told, another boat would come to collect them. Boutros was in no hurry. He wanted time for Choe to explain all of *Albatross'* quirks—every boat had them—and for Rafiq to learn the workings of what lay below deck. Once the Koreans were gone, they would be on their own. Their initial course would skirt the coast of Japan. Beyond that lay the real challenge. Not the bathtub that was the Persian Gulf, but the vast North Pacific.

Daunting as it was, Boutros knew things could have been worse. By all accounts, this winter had so far been one of the warmest on record, and the seas today were modest. The timing of their mission had always been more dependent on opportunity than the weather or seasons. They'd had to wait for the final component of their weapon. Soon it would be delivered, and from that point the race would be on, every delay increasing the chance of exposure.

Boutros looked out and saw a container ship in the distance, a churn of white at the bow. From his naval training he recalled someone giving him a rule of thumb about estimating the speed of a vessel based on its bow wake. The details escaped him, causing him to wonder how much his skills had atrophied. He'd been a decent ground commander, his ISIS units performing well in the heat of battle. He had laughed with his men in the good times and sent them to die in the others. He'd always been faithful in writing letters to the mothers of the martyrs.

This operation, however, was something he never could have imagined. Boutros was, to use the mariner's term, running in uncharted waters. He was here today, at the gates of the Pacific, because his naval experience was unique within the caliphate. And because an opportunity had arisen for an audacious strike against America—far beyond anything ever attempted.

He turned away from the rail and returned to the wheelhouse. He addressed Choe. "How long will you stay with us?"

Choe looked at the navigation display. "Twenty-four nautical miles—we will rendezvous with a patrol boat. Two hours, no more."

"Is that enough time to show me everything?"

"Everything? I have spent my life on the sea, and I still have much to learn. But I see you have experience. I will show you how I brought *Albatross* here from Bangkok."

Boutros looked at the Korean appraisingly. "Tell me . . . did you ever serve in your county's navy?"

Choe looked at him with surprise. For the first time in two days he smiled. "I am but a simple fisherman. Right now, my boat has no engine so I cannot use it."

"Then I hope they are paying you well."

The smile disappeared. "One new engine—that is all I ask for."

Boutros nodded, but didn't pursue the thread any further. He looked to the aft deck. "Do the nets and winches work?"

"Yes. On the voyage from Thailand I was with my usual crew. We set the nets once, only to be sure. But I warn you to not try it with your men—they are not fishermen. You might foul the propeller."

"You're right. Anyway, there is no need. Having the nets on deck is enough for appearances."

"Appearances?" Choe commented, seeming unsure of the word's meaning.

Boutros didn't expand. For the first time he wondered how the Korean must view this whole affair. He had to know who they were, at least in a general way, and by extension that they were plotting an attack. He might have glimpsed the equipment below, although he could hardly grasp its purpose. The question of why four Islamic militants were in the Democratic People's Republic of Korea, taking over a Thai fishing boat he'd been hired to procure—it had to be mindboggling to Choe. Much as it had been to Boutros himself three months ago. But here they both were. The product of unforeseen opportunity.

Boutros asked more questions about the boat, and Choe gave knowledgeable answers. Bilge pumps, fire equipment, engine operation, autopilot. He said *Albatross* felt top-heavy in high seas, but that angling into the wind helped considerably. Choe's briefing took the best part of thirty minutes, after which he relinquished the helm to Boutros. It seemed symbolic, like a change of command ceremony, minus the bosun's whistle and salute.

After getting his bearings, Boutros double-checked the course to the first waypoint. So far, he reflected, things were going well. The only hitch had been Adnan's detention in Frankfurt. Even so, like any successful commander, he assumed their run of good luck *would* come to an end.

The only question was when.

TWENTY-THREE

"I sent you that message," said the man tied to the tree.

Slaton tried to keep a dispassionate expression. Surely he failed. Of all the responses he'd imagined, this was not among them. "You sent me a message ordering your own execution?"

"No! I mean . . . yes, I sent you a text. But not what you're saying! Look . . . I know we've never actually met, but you must be him. You're David Slaton . . . the *kidon*."

Slaton didn't bother with a denial. "I know you from somewhere," he said. "And since you speak Hebrew, I'm guessing it's Mossad?"

"My name is Paul Mordechai. I served for a time as a special assistant to Israel's minister of energy. After that I worked for Mossad."

Long-forgotten details merged in Slaton's head. It went back years, and in a harsh irony, to the very mission in which he and Christine had met. "You were the technician. My last formal Mossad op."

"Yes. I served as an adviser to the senior leadership. It was my idea to requisition a deep-water drone to search for a ship on the bottom of the Atlantic—*Polaris Venture*."

"You never found her."

"No. But what I *did* find was more relevant—it helped uncover a conspiracy."

"I remember all too well," Slaton said.

Mordechai wriggled his right shoulder, and a grimace swept across his face. "Now that you know who I am, would you mind? My arm is going numb."

Slaton's expression never wavered. "Keep talking."

Mordechai heaved a long sigh. "Anton Bloch was the director of Mossad at the time. He liked my work, and recruited me into the Technology Department. Within eighteen months I headed up the section."

"The youngest ever to do so, I recall hearing."

Mordechai nodded.

Slaton remembered Bloch explaining that a brilliant young scientist had taken over the department, a man with a knack for converting promising technologies into operationally useful tools. He said, "I've seen your face."

"Have you been to Glilot Junction since you left?" Mordechai said, referring to the headquarters complex.

"Once or twice."

"Maybe you saw my photo somewhere or passed me in the hallway."

"Possibly. But you're not with Mossad anymore," Slaton said, no rising inflection to imply a question.

"I left three years ago."

Slaton's gaze narrowed. Better than most, he knew the cutthroat turnover rate inside intelligence agencies. He also knew the odor of scandal.

"Why did you leave?"

"I was forced out. I had been pushing hard for better funding on cyber initiatives. We were woefully lacking in defensive capability. The new director, Raymond Nurin, insisted it wasn't a priority. So I decided to prove my point. I hired a very sharp graduate student from the Weizmann Institute of Science to hack into two supposedly secure email accounts—those of Director Nurin and the prime minister."

"And did he succeed?"

"Spectacularly. He took over the accounts, leaving a single email informing them of the breach and adding that I had authorized it."

"And for that you were fired?"

"*Reallocated* was the word Nurin used. I admit it was all a bit theatrical. The prime minister was furious, and Nurin still had no interest in the vulnerabilities we'd revealed—he only wanted my head on a pike."

"Was there anything incriminating in the emails you hacked?"

"I never went through them all. We're talking tens of thousands, and that was never the point. All the same, it gave Nurin a reason to reassign me."

"Why only a transfer? If he was so angry, I'd think he would sack you outright."

"I can only tell you what he told me. He said I wasn't fit to be a senior manager, but that an opportunity had arisen—one for which I had all the necessary scientific credentials. He said a high-level position was coming open at a well-respected international organization."

"Which one?"

"The International Atomic Energy Agency."

"Which is how you ended up in Austria?"

"Yes. I work in the Department of Safeguards."

Slaton turned his gaze briefly across the dark forest. "Excuse my pessimism, but considering that you were posted here by Nurin . . . it sounds suspiciously close to an operational assignment."

"Not at all. I was actually transferred to the foreign ministry—my post is loosely considered a diplomatic assignment."

"Diplomatic?"

"The IAEA is an agency of the world—they pride themselves on having inspectors representing as many different countries as possible. When this position came open, there was not a single Israeli in its senior ranks. That gave Israel the inside track. I've been in the job eighteen months now."

"And you no longer report to Director Nurin?"

"No. Although in all honesty, I suspect he had that in mind when he steered me toward the job. Among other things, my division is responsible for monitoring the Iranian nuclear agreements. Nurin pulled me aside at a social gathering before I cleaned out my desk and suggested Mossad would very much like to have an insider during those visits."

"What did you tell him?"

"I said I was done with the Office."

"You turned your back on Mossad?"

"Some bridges are destined to be burned. But it wasn't merely spite. I've always believed in the IAEA. It's a good organization, an important one. Each day when I go to work, I'm surrounded by well-meaning scientists and technicians, people whose mission is to safeguard the world from nuclear annihilation."

"Sounds pretty idealistic."

Mordechai glared at Slaton, taking him by surprise. "Perhaps it is. But in a world where the design of bombs is available to anyone with an internet connection, the last line of defense is keeping rigorous safeguards on nuclear material."

Slaton saw conviction in the scientist's eyes, and also perhaps the vanity of a gifted mind. Someone convinced he was always the smartest man in the room . . . and who was usually right. "Okay, so you work for the IAEA. How does that translate into me getting blackmailed to kill you?"

If Mordechai was acting, he was good. He truly looked mystified. And more than a bit worried. "I don't know. I *did* try to get in touch with you. I sent a text message, but—"

"How did you get that phone number?"

Mordechai hesitated, and for the first time Slaton sensed evasion.

"Up until now, you've been making sense," he said. "Don't ruin it."

"It was one of the few hacked emails I did read—Nurin's account. I think it was dated last summer. Apparently, Mossad was trying to track you down, and they somehow acquired that mobile number."

Slaton's glare grew more intense. He had no knowledge of Mossad tracking him last summer. All the same, it was well within their dubious nature to try. Precisely the kind of thing Nurin *would* pursue. In recent years, Slaton had also been intermittently on the CIA's radar. He relented that there was only so much one could do when the world's preeminent spy agencies came looking for you.

"You don't have to worry," Mordechai said. "The uncovering of your number was kept at a very high level. For my part, I was stunned—the legend of your demise has long been taken as fact within Company halls."

"You realized that I'd gone off-grid."

"I suspected as much."

"Okay. But why did you try to contact me?"

A long pause. "I need help, and I don't know where else to turn. I'm persona non grata at Mossad, and I'm not sure who I can trust here in Vienna."

"Trust with what?"

"Perhaps we could discuss it under more civilized conditions?"

Slaton caught a flash of motion to one side. He saw the silhouette of an owl glide past and disappear into the treetops. He retrained his attention on his prisoner, his face steeped in calculation.

What Mordechai was telling him contained elements of truth. Indeed, Slaton had not yet sensed a lie. Hesitation perhaps, but not deception. His story was completely plausible for a desperate man in a tight spot, one who'd had a recent falling-out with Mossad. That alone, in Slaton's private ledger, was a checkmark in the plus column.

It was time for a decision, and it came down to believing what Mordechai was telling him . . . or not.

He reached down his leg and pulled the combat blade from its sheath.

TWENTY-FOUR

Slaton made Mordechai drive while he watched every move from the passenger seat. They passed a great windmill farm, rows of massive blades turning lazily in the starlight. Snow-bordered fields all around stood waiting for spring. After fifteen minutes civilization reemerged, a few cars and pitched-tile roofs at first, until a place called Mistelbach was introduced by a road sign.

Mordechai claimed to be hungry, and Slaton decided an hour of good cop might be in order—a decision perhaps colored by the fact that he himself hadn't eaten a decent meal since breakfast. He saw bright light spilling from a window in the center of town. It was a corner café, and from the street the place looked modestly busy—probably because there were few other options in Mistelbach at eleven o'clock on a weeknight.

They parked directly in front of the café, and were led to an outdoor patio. It was less busy than the main room, and not unpleasant with multiple space heaters cooking away. Slaton requested a corner table, both for its discretion and the proximity to one of the radiant furnaces. After a brief study of the menu, a busy waitress in a frilled blouse pinballed to their table. Mordechai ordered roast lamb, Slaton the chicken goulash special, and she was gone in a flurry of flowered embroidery.

"Tell me again," Slaton said. "The exact message you sent."

Mordechai was rubbing his wrists where the flex-cuffs had dug in. "Give me my phone back and I'll show you."

Slaton put the phone flat on the table, but anchored it with two fingers—trust was still an issue. It forced Mordechai to swipe and type in plain view. He navigated to his messages, tapped on one, then turned the screen to face Slaton.

> My name is Paul Mordechai. You know me as the technician who tried to locate the wreckage of Polaris Venture. I urgently need your help on a matter of national security. This Wednesday evening at 8:15. Meet me on the north shore of Danube Park in Vienna, the westernmost semicircle backed by three benches and three trees. Please come—this is of utmost importance. I can think of nowhere else to turn.

Slaton took his hand off the phone. He sat back and looked at Mordechai. "I never got that message."

His tablemate looked stymied. "But you must have . . . you came tonight."

"I got the time and place. But the message I received didn't say anything about a meeting. It said you would be there, and that I was to eliminate you. Once I'd done so, the sender promised I would get my family back."

Mordechai went ashen. He looked at his phone

blankly, the message glowing like an electronic omen. His eyes came up to meet Slaton's. "But you didn't go through with it."

"Killing you? Of course I didn't."

"Why not?"

"For the same reason you don't negotiate with terrorists—it doesn't work."

"Yet you killed three other men."

"I didn't see a lot of options."

"Who were they?"

"A good question. Thugs, presumably. On appearances they were Middle Eastern. Beyond that I have no idea. They could have been Palestinians or ISIS. Maybe home-grown Austrian jihadists. I think it's a mistake to assume that's relevant—their heritage may have had nothing to do with why they showed up tonight. I can only tell you they were at Danube Park to kill me. I would have preferred to talk to one of them, but circumstances didn't allow it. So my goal now is to find out who sent them— which circles back to my earlier question. Who would want you dead?"

Mordechai averted his gaze, scanning the room. He looked like a schoolboy about to spill a secret. As Slaton waited patiently, he made his own survey of the surroundings—one that he hoped was more subtle.

"I work for the deputy director general at IAEA," Mordechai said. "He heads up the Department of Safeguards. Our division is responsible for inspecting nuclear facilities and safeguarding material thought to be at risk. It's a big undertaking. Last year we visited over a thousand sites. Power plants, uranium mines, research and enrichment facilities. It's a lot to keep track of. But I also have a secondary job—when I'm not in the field, I'm responsible for auditing our inspections."

"Auditing?"

"I go over the records of site visits, check for discrepancies. We have a multi-layered system for tracking material."

"One would hope," Slaton said dryly.

"Roughly six months ago, I was going over the inventory numbers from a visit—it involved the extraction of fuel from a research reactor."

"Where?"

"Kazakhstan."

Slaton wasn't surprised. Even decades after the fall of communism, many of the Soviet-era republics remained awash in nuclear detritus. "What kind of material?" he asked.

"Our department is concerned almost exclusively with the two fissionable products that can be weaponized—plutonium and highly enriched uranium. This was HEU."

"Enriched to what level?"

Mordechai looked at him appreciatively. "You know your physics. The tranche in question was documented as ninety-two percent U-235."

"Anything over ninety percent is weapons grade."

"Effectively, yes."

"So what happened? Did this material go missing?"

"No—that would have been a full-blown crisis. To begin, you should know that we go to extreme lengths to track and store samples securely." Mordechai launched into an explanation of IAEA procedures for analyzing and recording radioactive material. Slaton let him talk, suspecting the relevance of his briefing would soon become apparent.

"Every batch of HEU is unique, and once logged,

its signature remains in our database forever. Regarding the shipment from Kazakhstan, I went over the entire acquisition process. The audit procedures were followed to the letter—everything checked. The material was transferred to a French facility to undergo downblending."

"Downblending?"

"Weapons-grade material can be made safe by diluting it with depleted uranium. Taken to the right concentration, it can actually be reused as fuel in commercial reactors. Most people don't know it, but for nearly two decades ten percent of the electricity in the United States came from downblended HEU sourced from Soviet-era nuclear warheads."

"But you're saying everything checked in the audit," Slaton said, steering Mordechai back from his excursion. "So where was the problem?"

"I had been giving thought to how our inventory methods might be made better. To test one of my ideas, I went a step beyond the usual audit procedure. I looked back at the original plan for that site visit to Kazakhstan. Going in we had expected to extract forty-one kilograms. The records showed that only thirty-six kilos were recovered—material that is now incontrovertibly secure on Austrian soil."

"It hardly seems damning—not recovering as much as had been promised in a planning document."

"I thought the same thing. But it caused me to keep looking. I studied protocols, signatures, interviewed a few of the team members—all of that was uneventful. It affirmed that the lower amount was received. But as a last resort I went to a highly unconventional source."

"Let me guess—a Kazakh source?"

Mordechai's expression changed. He was either impressed or alarmed that Slaton had made the same connection.

"Yes."

The waitress interrupted, sliding a plate in front of both of them. As soon as she was gone, Mordechai picked up his story. "You should understand that the relationship between the agency and the countries it monitors often borders on hostility. Yet among scientists there are sometimes relationships."

"Even between Kazakh and Israeli scientists."

"I studied for a time in France, and was friendly with a Kazakh who later became a senior researcher at CERN, the European Organization for Nuclear Research. He is now the director of nuclear security in Kazakhstan. After the fall of the Soviet Union, the country was left with huge inventories of nuclear material, but little funding to maintain and track it all. Other countries stepped in to keep inventories secure, and the IAEA did its best to remove high-level waste and surplus fuel stocks. Still the government struggles."

"So you reached out to this friend," Slaton surmised.

"Yes, in a strictly unofficial capacity. He supplied me with inventory numbers from internal records."

"And these confirmed a discrepancy?"

"Very precisely. Five kilos of HEU were unaccounted for after the IAEA transfer. The more I looked, the more I realized that only one person could know what really happened—the team leader for the site visit is the final authority for verifying quantities and signing off."

Slaton nodded, more pieces falling into place. He

felt his world shifting ever so slightly, something heavy and ominous blanketing his quest to find his family.

"There is more," Mordechai said. "Once I discovered the discrepancy, I quietly performed audits on other recoveries. I went back two years and found three other visits in which the numbers didn't add up—all extractions of HEU that were destined for downblending to commercial-grade reactor fuel. There was one kilogram from a research reactor in Ghana. Six each from molybdenum-99 production facilities in Belgium and South Africa."

Slaton composed a very cautious reply. "You're telling me that an inspector at the IAEA has been skimming highly enriched uranium?"

"I know it seems incredible, given the security measures in place—but I'm not talking about just any inspector."

"Who then?"

Mordechai hesitated, then said, "This is the reason I tried to reach you. The lead inspector on all four suspect acquisitions was the deputy director himself—the man who oversees the Department of Safeguards."

"What's his name?"

Mordechai told him.

TWENTY-FIVE

Tarek El-Masri tore the seal off a plastic bag. It contained a standard swipe kit: two pairs of latex gloves, a box of aluminum foil, ten cotton swabs, and ten small ziplock bags, each labeled with a distinct tracking code. He looked around the room, wondering where to begin.

El-Masri and his team were situated fifty-two meters underground, deep inside the PAAR II nuclear research complex outside Islamabad, Pakistan. The room was the size of a handball court and dominated by lab equipment. There were three others inside: two of his inspectors standing by with equipment, and the facility director, Dr. Khan. Khan was a pug-faced man with light-adapting glasses that had gone rose-colored in the laboratory's harsh glare— El-Masri thought the lenses resembled the bottoms of two tiny wine bottles. Khan stood squarely at the entrance, putting him, perhaps coincidentally, directly beneath the only clock in the room.

As head of the Department of Safeguards, El-Masri did not spend a great deal of time in the field. He was selective in the assignments he took, and even more so in choosing his support staff. That he ventured from his plush Vienna office at all was a departure from the practice of his predecessors. The inspectors who worked under him took it as a positive sign that the head of their division was not afraid to get his hands dirty—a word never used carelessly among nuclear scientists. What none of the rank-and-file could know was that this particular site visit had long been on El-Masri's radar.

It was two o'clock in the morning, and the bleary-eyed Dr. Khan had met them at the gate. The groundwork for the transfer was complete, having been laid in recent months, and the material had already been loaded for shipment. All that remained was a final inspection of the reprocessing lab. The unconscionable hour was quite by design—transporting highly radioactive material on public roads was hardly a task for rush hour, particularly in places like Pakistan where the observance of traffic laws was aspirational at best.

El-Masri spun a slow circle to check the cameras near the ceiling. There was one in each corner of the room, fish-eye lenses that left no angle uncovered. All were secured in hardened housings with tamper-proof seals, and from there the units were hard-wired to a computer. The computer, kept in a secure vault of its own, retained a digital record of everything. From there a satellite dish on the roof uplinked the feeds to monitors in Vienna. El-Masri wondered idly if anyone at headquarters was watching them at that moment. He decided it was unlikely. All the same, he knew his every move was being recorded for posterity.

He donned a pair of gloves, smoothed out the sheet of aluminum foil that would serve as his workspace, and selected a swab. He dragged the first swipe over the metal grill of an air conditioning intake, then for good measure ran it along the foot of the exterior door. The swab went into the first bag. He sealed the bag, labeled it, and photographed the bar code using an application on his smartphone. Nothing on the bag itself revealed the site, or even the country where the sample had been taken—a necessary measure of anonymity, as per procedure, for samples that might be tested anywhere in the IAEA's constellation of oversight laboratories.

His assistants joined in, and thirty minutes later they had what they needed—twenty-one samples that would be scanned for the most minute signature of telltale radioisotopes. Unused seals, labels, and components of the swab kits were retained in a designated trash bag. All of it would be inventoried back in Vienna—one more layer in the onionskin of security measures.

El-Masri deemed their inspection complete, and he and his assistants headed for the elevator. Dr. Khan fell in behind. They all rose to ground level, and at the main security station El-Masri was met by his second-in-command for the visit, a young Frenchman named Henri.

Henri said, "Here is the HEU sample taken from the first cask." He presented El-Masri a golden metallic vial, along with a clipboard with authentication forms and duplicate verification seals.

El-Masri regarded the vial, checking the tracking number against those on the clipboard. This was the primary objective of today's mission: the removal for downblending of twenty-nine kilos of 93 percent highly enriched uranium. The inspection of the reprocessing lab was a secondary errand—in effect, filling an administrative square in the quarterly Verification and Reviews quota. The nuclear inspector's equivalent of two birds with one stone.

Convinced the paperwork added up, El-Masri signed his name and meticulously printed his IAEA employee number in the correct box. He then handed over the vial, which was promptly—and within his view—slotted into a lockable carrying case. Six other vials were already so secured. That done, the carrying case was itself sealed, and both El-Masri and Henri scribbled their initials on the paper-thin security strip.

"Are we done below?" Henri asked.

"Yes," said El-Masri, "the Tier-3 inspection is complete."

"The aircrew reported in. The preflight of the airplane is complete—they are ready to receive the shipment."

"Good. Then we won't take up any more of Dr. Khan's time."

Everyone followed El-Masri outside. There, under the tall floods surrounding an asphalt parking apron, a minor convoy had formed. There were two heavy SUVs, and between them a great flatbed truck that seemed to suffer beneath three ponderous shipping casks, each the size of a Volkswagen. Certified to Type B standards, the containers had been tested to withstand a forty-foot drop onto a hard surface, a thirty-minute immersion in fire as hot as 1,500 degrees Fahrenheit, and even a broadside strike by a speeding locomotive. Notwithstanding these attributes, the casks had been securely chained down for the journey.

Henri placed another clipboard in El-Masri's hand, and as the final authority, he climbed onto the flatbed to certify the load. He moved between the casks, comparing inventory numbers, and verifying that one frangible security bolt had been affixed to the lid of each. The bolts had unique numbers of their own, along with an embedded RFID chip.

Satisfied everything matched, El-Masri again signed, one scribble on each of three sets of paperwork. He patted the last cask on the rump as one would an obliging trail horse, and stepped down to the parking apron. He took shotgun position in the lead SUV, and soon the formation began to move. They rolled toward the main gate, and once outside were surrounded by an armada of security: eight armored personnel carriers, three troop trucks, and a pair of light assault vehicles—one took the lead, while the other played caboose. The convoy set out at an unconscionably safe speed toward PAF Murid, a military airfield twenty miles south.

In the lead SUV, a mystified Henri sat in the back seat behind El-Masri. The Frenchman had been with the agency less than a year, and this was his first trip into the field. In preparation, and because he was accompanying the head of the department, he'd asked colleagues what to expect from El-Masri. The response had been virtually unanimous: El-Masri was outgoing and garrulous, and everything he said came at a fast-forward pace, as if his lips couldn't keep up with the rapid-fire thoughts in his mind.

As the convoy crawled through dark Pakistani countryside, Henri saw none of it. Indeed, he wondered if it had all been some kind of joke. El-Masri sat in the front seat looking precisely as he had since they'd left Vienna: adrift in utter silence. Henri had twice seen him surreptitiously pop pills into his mouth, and a stolen glance at the bottle told him they were for pain. At the moment El-Masri appeared to be staring forlornly at something in his hand. In the dim reflections of light from the instrument panel, Henri couldn't quite make it out.

After nearly a minute, curiosity got the better of him.

Henri pulled out his personal phone as if checking email, tilted it slightly so the screen's illumination cast between the front seats. It did the trick. El-Masri was holding a standard film badge—the personal dosimeter they all wore to measure cumulative radiation exposure. Having no idea what to make of it, Henri turned off his phone, pressed back into his seat, and got comfortable—they were in for a long day of travel.

Back at the PARR II facility, Dr. Khan watched the convoy patiently. It took ten minutes for the last taillights to disappear. As soon as they did, he sent a one-line text on his secure phone. Seconds later, behind a nearby equipment shed, a lone vehicle rumbled to life. In that moment, it was the only vehicle in the compound not owned and operated by the Pakistani army. A standard box delivery truck, it was neither new nor old, although the diesel engine churned with well-tuned smoothness.

The truck's headlights flicked on and it began to move. As it approached the main gate, Khan stood waiting beside the guard detail. He personally waved the driver through, and as the truck passed, Khan nodded to the three men inside. Their round faces and bowl-cut black hair attested that they were not locals. If the guards questioned why the director was waving a truck carrying three Asian men through the gate, and without any kind of inspection—a breach of every protocol ever hammered into their heads—they kept it to themselves.

The truck groaned as it bumped over a saw-toothed barrier—the kind meant to keep intruders out—and ran an ungainly slalom through four concrete barricades. Springs creaked with each carving turn and the transmission groaned. On the gentle incline to the access road, the truck spewed clouds of black smoke into the deepening night. At the main highway the driver turned left—opposite the course taken by the IAEA convoy—and took up a decidedly less cautious pace.

When that final set of taillights was out of sight, Khan pivoted to face the two guards behind him. Both stiffened slightly, and as he looked at them in turn, the senior man nodded.

Without a word, Khan walked away.

TWENTY-SIX

The patrol boat came right on time and was straight from central casting, a gunmetal gray dagger of armor with a high-mounted deck gun. Boutros watched the craft materialize out of the mist, its lone stack belching exhaust like a train clawing up a mountain. He supposed the North Koreans ran boats like this by the dozens, a beehive navy for a country that could never afford cutting-edge missile boats or heavy cruisers.

The high bow, stamped with the Roman numerals 623—which somehow seemed a concession to the West—sided up to *Albatross* with all the deftness of a bumper boat. Ropes laden with truck tires were lowered to serve as fenders, and lines were secured fore and aft. Even on the relatively calm seas, the two vessels thumped together asynchronously—incentive for a quick transfer.

A boarding ramp drawbridged down to connect the two boats. Without so much as a "good luck," Park was the first to cross, his pudgy frame curiously nimble as he bridged the gap. Far less certain was the next man across the gangway, Park's bespectacled technician who, given his two-handed death grip on the rail, had likely never been to sea in his life. Last to make the crossing was Choe.

For the first time, Boutros saw hesitancy in the skipper's movement. At the midpoint between the boats, he glanced back to the wheelhouse and made eye contact. Boutros saw something new in his gaze—not the confidence that had been there all along, but something deeper. An understanding between two sailors.

As soon as Choe was across, two crewmen from the patrol boat appeared from a passageway. Ominously, both were carrying machine pistols. Boutros watched as Choe and the technician were ushered below.

"What do you think will come of them?"

Boutros turned to see Rafiq. "Who can say," he replied. "Choe has served his purpose. The technician is more valuable." He found himself thinking about the fisherman's wife, with her foul fish soup and rotted teeth. "Whatever their fate . . . I doubt the world will notice."

Rafiq regarded him thoughtfully.

"Does my callousness surprise you?" Boutros asked.

Rafiq shook his head. "No . . . we cannot afford the luxury of compassion."

"Is that a quote from our caliph?"

"I can't remember where I heard it. Perhaps the imam in Cologne."

"One more man who has never seen the blade of combat," Boutros said reflectively.

The crew of 623 raised the gangway and pulled the lines connecting the boats. The vessels quickly drifted apart and the fenders were drawn in.

"I have seen battle," said Rafiq, "but not like you and the others. I would never sit in judgment of those who have bled."

"Sami, Saleem, and I . . . we *have* sacrificed. Yet your time in university may prove more valuable." Rafiq didn't reply, and Boutros sensed a hesitation as they watched the patrol boat begin its shoreward turn. "What is troubling you?" he prompted.

Rafiq heaved a sigh. "When I first arrived in Syria, my commander showed me a video taken here in North Korea. It showed 'Dear Leader's' uncle being executed with an anti-aircraft gun."

Boutros shrugged. "I have not seen it, but I can imagine such a thing. I would say the man was lucky."

"Lucky?"

"He met a quick end. I hope you and I are so blessed on our passage to paradise."

"Perhaps. But I remember my commander asking my opinion afterward—he wondered if we should try something similar. His idea was to put a few Christians in front of a twenty-three-millimeter ZSU, then upload the image online."

"What did you tell him?"

Rafiq was quiet for a time, as if trying to remember. "I told him I had no opinion on the matter. This seemed to disappoint him."

Boutros considered it. "It would have disappointed me as well."

"Why?"

"Because it wasn't truthful. There are only two possible opinions regarding such an act. Some would call it justifiable in a time of war. You thought it abhorrent, yet didn't have the conviction to say so."

Rafiq didn't reply.

Boutros suddenly felt the weight of his commander's duty. His own reason for being here was twenty years in the making. Sami and Saleem, he was sure, would never waver—personalities aside, they were core jihadists, molded in madrassas and radical mosques, forged in the fire of battle. Yet he'd always sensed a difference in Rafiq. He was driven by something else.

"I must ask you," he said, "what we are attempting ... will you have any hesitation in carrying through?" He captured Rafiq's eyes and held them, demanding a response.

"No," he replied assuredly. "I will make this device work. God willing, we will bring fire to America."

Boutros held his second-in-command's gaze for a time, long enough to be sure. Satisfied, he nodded. Rafiq went below.

He turned to watch the patrol boat wheel westward in a churn of whitewater and smoke. *Albatross* rocked gently in its wake. 623 disappeared in no time, hazing into a shoreward fog bank. Boutros considered turning the radar on to track the boat's progress, but there seemed little point to it. As the drone of her big diesel ebbed, the sea fell quiet— *Albatross*' own engine had been shut down for the rendezvous.

With strange suddenness, Boutros realized he was again in command of a ship. By any measure, the flagship of the Islamic State Navy. It was the kind of revelation that should have invited reflection, yet he was not so inclined.

Not with so much work ahead.

Not with so much sea in front of them.

He went to the helm and cranked the engine to life.

TWENTY-SEVEN

The roast lamb at table 18 was not savored as it might have been, the guest behind it distracted by the fact that he had, at various times that evening, been targeted for assassination, folded into the trunk of a car, and interrogated while bound to an oak tree. His tablemate, who had been directly, if not enthusiastically, responsible for it all, downed the chef's special like a stoker feeding coal to a furnace. Any appreciation for the tastes or textures of the meal was lost on Slaton—and so it would remain until his life was righted.

He chased the final gnocchi around his plate, and asked, "Have you shared your suspicions about El-Masri with anyone else, either at the IAEA or Mossad?"

"I didn't have enough evidence to make a formal accusation," said Mordechai. "What I found in the audit was circumstantial, so last week I decided to look for something more solid. Proof that would be incontrovertible."

"What kind of proof?"

A hesitation. "I suppose you could say I repeated my previous great mistake—I hacked into El-Masri's work computer."

Slaton's fork went gently to his empty plate.

Mordechai expanded, "The agency issues all senior personnel a hardened laptop, for official use only. These are of course very secure devices."

"But you found a way in."

"As it happens, I oversee information security for the Department of Safeguards. One of our technicians recently reported to me that he'd found a weakness in our internal encryption software. He explained the details of the fault, and assured me he'd seen no evidence of a breach. I told him to create a patch, and he assured me he could have it installed within two weeks. In the meantime . . ."

"You used this weakness to access El-Masri's computer."

"Yes . . . or at least I tried. Unfortunately, it wasn't as easy as I expected. He had apparently installed a secondary firewall of some kind."

"So you didn't get access?"

"No. In fact, I may have done more harm than good. I think he was alerted that someone was attempting to breach his system. And if he learned I was the guilty party—it would make everything that's happened in the last few days far more logical."

"Would it? Even if El-Masri figured out you were responsible, it seems a pretty big leap to the rest."

Mordechai thought about it, his face furrowing in the way it presumably did when he ran equations on radioactive decay. He pushed away his half-eaten meal. "Earlier this week, before I tried to send you that request for help . . . I detected irregularities on my own computer. A few messages I had sent disappeared. I didn't think much of it at the time, but now . . ." His voice trailed off.

"You think El-Masri turned the tables?"

"It's possible. If he saw someone trying to breach his system, he might have reversed the hack."

"Is that easy to do?" Slaton asked.

"No, it's not. I doubt El-Masri could have managed it. He's a knowledgeable physicist, but a bit old-school—computers aren't his game. Yet he might have enlisted help."

"And if he succeeded, he would have learned you were trying to contact me."

"Yes. I showed you the version of the message I tried to send. I was desperate for help."

"But I still see a gap. There wasn't anything in that text to suggest who I was. How could he have figured that out?"

"A good question."

Both men thought about it as the waitress scurried up and took their plates. She left with an order for two cups of coffee.

Slaton said, "Whoever replaced that message with the one I actually received—they knew a lot about me. Not only that I worked for Mossad, but also what my specialty was. And they knew I had a family that could be leveraged. That's not common knowledge."

"I would concur. Even at Mossad, there are only a handful of people who know you're still alive."

Slaton performed another survey of the room. "But you *did* mention *Polaris Venture* in your message. That could have been a trigger."

"In what way?"

"Consider the bigger picture. If El-Masri really is stealing weapons-grade material, he's not doing it alone. You just told me he would need help to take over your messaging account."

"True . . . but who could he be working with?"

"I don't know. It could be anybody from a state intelligence service to a terror group."

"El-Masri is Egyptian—would their Mukhabarat know your history?" Mordechai was referring to Egypt's iron-fisted intelligence service.

"It's possible. But Egypt is fractured these days. Aside from the government, you've got the Muslim Brotherhood and ISIS offshoots. El-Masri could just as easily be working with a Libyan militia or Iran. We can't assume anything." Slaton leaned back into his slatted wooden chair and pulled a hand across his chin. Mordechai watched him intently. As if expecting him to have all the answers.

"Is El-Masri in Vienna now?" Slaton asked. There was nothing ominous in his tone, but given the circumstances the question could not be construed benignly.

"No—he is actually on another site visit."

"Where?"

"Pakistan—the PARR-II reactor, outside Islamabad."

Slaton's eyes narrowed. "Let me guess . . . another HEU extraction? Material to be downblended?"

"Yes. Pakistan doesn't allow oversight of their nuclear weapons facilities, but PARR-II has long been under our watch—it's classified as a research reactor."

"When will he be back?"

"I don't know the exact schedule, but typically an extraction team will stay with the material all the way to the receiving laboratory. I can tell you they've been downrange for three days. I would guess he'd be back tomorrow, possibly the next day."

The coffee arrived. Mordechai immediately began

cutting his with cream and sugar. Slaton took no such half measures.

"Where do we go from here?" Mordechai asked.

"We?"

Mordechai waited, his spoon stirring patiently.

For the first time Slaton weighed the merits of a joint effort. He preferred working solo, but he'd made exceptions in the past. To include Mordechai meant trusting him, at least to a point. It would present twice the security headache. But also twice the research capacity.

"Well?" asked Mordechai. "Do we do this together?"

Slaton reached for his coffee and took a long draw.

TWENTY-EIGHT

Thirty minutes after taking command, Boutros had *Albatross* cutting smoothly through gentle seas. He summoned everyone to the wheelhouse, and with all three men present he went over the basics of how to run the boat. Their journey would take nearly a week, and while the boat had an autopilot, everyone would be expected to take a turn on watch. When he finished, he gave Sami the conn and ordered Saleem to assist him.

He motioned to Rafiq, and together they descended to the cramped lower deck. The crew quarters and galley were forward, but Rafiq led Boutros aft down a tunnel-like companionway. Dim yellow lights along the ceiling gave the aura of a passage to a dungeon. Dankness gripped the air along with a fetid odor, some belowdecks bouquet of bilge water, fuel oil, and caustic cleanser.

The engine room lay at the end of the passageway, fully astern, but Rafiq took an offshoot into a separate compartment. The amidships room spanned the beam of the ship, and was roughly fifteen feet from front to back. Overhead a large hatch connected to the main deck—Choe had never explained the room's purpose, but Boutros assumed it to be the hold where the nets were typically stored. At the moment, they would never have fit.

It was Boutros' first look at the hardware they'd been promised—the reason they were here—and his impression was a positive one. Brilliant work lights covered every corner of the compartment with lumens to spare. The floors, ceiling, and bulkheads shone with a spotlessness that was at odds with the rest of the boat. Machine equipment lined the walls, and a workbench was racked with every hand tool imaginable.

Centered amid it all was the focal point of the room.

Boutros closed in for a better look at the long metal cylinder. It was chained to a professional shop stand, which in turn had been bolted to the deck—a nuance that made Boutros' inner captain smile. He saw Cyrillic characters stamped on the side of the cylinder, leaving no doubt as to its source—it was a Russian item.

He looked at Rafiq, who'd had a chance to study the device in detail. "So . . . will it work?" he asked.

Rafiq canted his head to one side. "I don't see why not. The principle is quite simple, and Saleem assures me he can do his part easily."

"Explosives are easy?"

"He is very good at what he does."

Boutros took a step closer, then hesitated. "There is nuclear material inside, is there not?"

"Yes, highly enriched uranium. But only part of what we need."

"Is it safe?"

Rafiq looked at his commander incredulously. "Nothing about what we are doing is safe. But yes, you can go near. There is no immediate danger."

Boutros leaned in. He had been imagining it for months. Up close the weapon looked simple and innocuous, belying the revolution of warfare that it was. He ran a hand over the smooth metal tube. It was perfectly round, six inches in diameter and nearly seven feet long. Aside from having been truncated on one end, Boutros recognized it for what it was. "An artillery barrel," he said.

"Originally, yes. A one hundred and fifty-two millimeter field gun. This particular barrel was cast in Russia, as you can see. The end has been capped and modified."

"Modified in what way?"

Rafiq set his hand on the barrel's end, which was twice the diameter of the rest. "A graphite reflector has been installed. It serves to contain neutrons, which slows down the first-order expansion. Without such a tamper, the reaction tends to happen too quickly in the initial stages. This way, the same amount of material gives a much higher yield."

Boutros ran his eyes to the breech end, which was threaded like a great bolt. "And there?" he asked.

Rafiq gestured to a work stand along the port side. An inversely threaded end piece lay waiting. Like the opposing cap, it was larger than the diameter of the barrel. It also looked more complex than the rest. Boutros saw hardware inside, and wires snaked from three sealed ports—the paired ends had all been stripped of insulation, and their copper tips shone in the light like the fangs of so many snakes.

Boutros took in the rest of the room. "And the explosives?"

Rafiq put his toe to a heavy footlocker strapped to a bulkhead. "Inside."

Boutros nodded, then noticed an even heavier

container nearby. It looked like a floor safe, and the door was ajar to reveal that it was empty.

"What is that for?" he asked.

"Our final delivery will include a beryllium-polonium neutron initiator. It helps the explosion gain critical mass, lessening the chance of failure. But there is a degree of risk. Polonium has a very short half-life and is highly radioactive. Handling it will be the most dangerous task we face."

"Sami will see it through, God willing."

Rafiq nodded. "There is also this," he said, pulling a nylon backpack from behind a toolbox. Rafiq unzipped it and pulled out a compact machine pistol—Boutros recognized it as a PP-2000, a Russian 9mm weapon, buttstock removed. "There is also ammunition," Rafiq added as he restowed the weapon.

"It might come in useful," Boutros said. He took in the room as a whole. "Our Korean friends seem to have thought of everything."

"Perhaps more than we realize." Boutros looked at him inquisitively, and Rafiq gestured around the room. "The tools are from Hungary, the wire from Italy. A Russian gun barrel. There is even an American drill press. As far as I can tell, nothing on this boat can be sourced to North Korea."

"Including, I think, the four of us."

Rafiq blew out a humorless laugh. "I suppose you are right. But in the end, everyone gets what they want."

"Everyone," Boutros corrected, "except the Americans."

Five minutes later Boutros was back on deck, completing his survey of *Albatross* on more familiar ground. As the lone sailor on board, it was critical that he understand the operation of every winch and pump, know the placement of every line and cleat. He paused at the stubby bowsprit, which anchored a cable running to the wheelhouse. He didn't know what the cable was for, but noted it all the same.

With the growl of the boat's diesel steady behind him, Boutros looked out and saw not a single ship on the horizon. He filled his lungs with the brine-laced air. The sea settled his nerves, as it always had, and he had a distinct sense of life coming full circle. It had been nearly twenty years since he'd commanded a boat. In his days with the Iraqi navy he'd plowed the azure waters of the Persian Gulf, engaging in endless games of cat and mouse with American warships. He recalled at the time feeling like a rebel pilot in a *Star Wars* movie—guiding a tiny fighter against the evil Death Star.

He turned and studied in the foredeck. In the middle, secured to its cradle, was a sixteen-foot utility boat with a Honda outboard. The craft would be integral to their plan in the coming days, yet as he looked at it now, it seemed almost symbolic. Like some icon of final hope. Could he allow even a private thought that he might survive this mission? No, Boutros decided. Given the nature of their strike, his fate and that of his crew was sealed. He was at peace with his fate—even eager, in a way.

This was the opportunity he'd long been searching for.

He wondered if his ISIS commanders had known all along—the reason behind his fearlessness on the battlefield. Why he had always volunteered for assignments in the Kurdish and Iraqi sectors. Boutros was a religious man on the best of days, but his commitment to the cause had far less to do with God than vengeance.

His father, an officer in the Republican Guard, had perished in battle during the Gulf War. Less heroic, but profoundly more tragic, was the fate of his sister in the next campaign. The bomb had struck a hundred meters from their home that night, taking out a gun emplacement. Yet the force of the shock wave, milliseconds later, had taken down the entire north wall of their house. They dug Irina out to find her paralyzed below the waist. She lived another year, mostly in pain. Their mother tended to her day and night, dreaming of medications and therapy that might have been available outside war zones. When Irina succumbed to a simple infection, festering out of control, it had been nothing short of mercy. Boutros' mother died soon after, not from any kind of direct fire, but a victim of sheer despondency, the source of which was no less clear than the bomb that had collapsed the wall.

The Americans.

Always the Americans.

They'd marched halfway around the world, killing from arm's length with their deadly technology and Special Operations heroes. When the powder keg that was Syria ignited, the Americans sided with the Kurds and a new Iraqi army. For that reason alone, Boutros had thrown himself in with ISIS. Opportunities for retribution had so far proved scarce—the Americans put few boots on the ground, preferring to own the skies and employ others to do the dirty work. When the caliphate crumbled, like everyone knew it would, Boutros had followed the lead of the other survivors: he'd melted away. Lying in wait for the next battle.

And now, he was sure, he'd found it.

That Boutros considered this mission personal would have no bearing on its prosecution. If any tenet of warfare was too-oft forgotten, it was that no army, no matter how dominant in the field, was immune to the power of imagination. Bin-Laden had proved it on 9/11. So too, the lone wolves who regularly drove cars and trucks onto crowded European sidewalks. *Albatross*, in microcosm, was perhaps the ultimate response: one devastating weapon deep inside her hold, delivered by a handful of committed individuals.

Imagination indeed.

A stray gust of wind swept over the deck. Boutros looked aft, saw the Korean peninsula fading fast into a gauzy marine haze. He went to the helm and took over, sending Sami and Saleem below. He checked the engine gauges and the latest weather data. In his navy days he might have recorded the time, position, and heading in the ship's log. This voyage, he decided, was best left unchronicled.

Boutros would never come to realize how prophetic that choice was. As it turned out, not a single soul on earth noticed when, at 9:06 that morning, a Thailand-registered trawler named *Albatross* departed North Korean territorial waters. She set to sea skippered by a former officer of Saddam Hussein's navy, and with a crew consisting of a mechanical engineer, a bomb maker, and one chipper suicidal jihadist.

Her course was steady at 070 degrees. Speed twenty-two knots.

Also left unrecorded was any hint of her destination: a remote chain of islands over two thousand miles east.

TWENTY-NINE

The change imparted upon Austria by the gig economy was like it was anywhere—a case of technology outpacing the grasp of rules and regulations. Seemingly overnight, web-based companies mushroomed into existence. They skirted labor laws to employ workers without customary benefits, and formed virtual corporate structures to evade taxes. Workers went along with the game. School-teachers moonlighted as online tutors for a few extra dollars. Doctors wearing pajamas gave diagnoses over the phone. Carpenters rented out nail guns not being used that day. From warehouses to bicycles to boudoirs, the world was running in entirely new ways.

None of which was lost on the world's intelligence agencies.

For spies, the online marketplace was the greatest advance in defensive tradecraft since the invention of sunglasses. With little more than a valid credit card, one could summon a car, hire a nurse, or rent a forty-foot motorsailer. Hot food, toothpaste, and burner phones could be delivered to one's doorstep, eliminating risky forays to busy shopping areas.

It was shortly after midnight, on the third day since his family's disappearance, that Slaton leveraged one of the most practical applications of the new order: the ability to anonymously book a short-term safe house.

The software infrastructure was already in place. On his phone were applications for no fewer than ten online services, each with an active account and method of payment established: Uber, Lyft, Priceline, Amazon were all there, clicks away from delivering critical mission support. So it was, while sitting on the fast-emptying patio of Café Leandro, and with fewer keystrokes than it took to dial a mobile number, Slaton arranged lodgings on short notice through an online booking site.

Thirty minutes later he was thumbing a four-digit code into a lockbox on the door of a two-bedroom flat. Located in Leopoldstadt, Vienna's second district, the building was an unpretentious walk-up, three brick-and-mortar stories on a quiet residential row. It was also, not coincidentally, a twenty-minute walk to IAEA headquarters. He and Mordechai had agreed that such proximity, at least in the near term, was a practical necessity.

The first thing Slaton did on entering the apartment was use the prepaid phone he'd purchased to check the local news on three separate websites—two run by newspapers, the third by Vienna's main television channel. None made any mention of three bodies being discovered in Danube Park. Slaton gave the story an 80 percent probability of breaking by noon. More critically, he knew the leader of the team he'd eliminated had not yet reported back to his taskmaster. One way or another, whoever had commissioned the hit squad would soon realize their fate.

He considered turning on his primary mobile to

check for messages, but decided the risk of giving away their location was too high. He'd last done so as they left Mistelbach, calling up the compromised messaging account for the fourth time since arriving in Vienna. Slaton had found himself holding his breath as the connection ran. In the end, he saw only the same altered message thread, now forty hours old.

Vienna, Wednesday evening, 8:15. Do what you do best.

Disappointing as it had been, Slaton refused to dwell on it. If what Mordechai told him was true, El-Masri was complicit in a scheme to steal highly enriched uranium. That kind of operation needed the help of larger players. The kind of people who could effortlessly hack into phones and computers. Who could abduct women and children. And who dispatched teams of assassins. He couldn't simply wait for a message that might never come.

Slaton performed a walk-through of the apartment. There were two bedrooms, but only one had a window. He decided that would be his—the window provided a way out, and allowed him to watch for anyone with the opposite idea. His overnight bag bounced once on the bed, and he returned to the main room.

"How long will we stay here?" Mordechai asked as he looked over the small kitchen.

"That depends on a lot of things. Right now whoever wanted you dead has to be wondering what happened. As long as you stay out of sight, your fate is an open question. It buys us a little time."

"I have meetings scheduled at work tomorrow."

"We'll worry about that tomorrow. For now, you can't go anywhere near IAEA headquarters or your apartment. Don't call anyone, don't answer calls, don't send any texts."

"How could I? You still have my phone."

"In time."

Mordechai seemed unsure. "What if I leave? What if I get up while you're sleeping and go home?"

"Then I would be forced to fulfill my contract after all."

The little Israeli looked at him severely. Slaton couldn't read his expression, but it wasn't fear.

"Look," Slaton said, "staying out of sight is your safest move. Like it or not, you and I have parallel interests. You believe you've found a conspiracy that needs to be exposed. I want my family back safely. We need to figure out a way to make both things happen."

Mordechai thought about it, then nodded acquiescently.

"But know one thing," Slaton cautioned. "If those two objectives ever get crossed—have no doubt which is my primary."

Slaton kept Mordechai up until two o'clock that morning. What had begun as an interrogation evolved into a strategy session for the following day.

"El-Masri is working with someone," Slaton said. "We have to find out who it is."

"There might be hints in the files at the agency. I could research which inspectors were with him on the site visits where material went missing. If certain names recur, it could mean he has internal collaborators."

"A possibility. If I gave you access to a computer, could you do it from here?"

"Definitely not. The security protocols give me access from our internal network. But from the outside—I could never do it, not without raising alarms."

Slaton didn't argue the point. "Let's concentrate on how the message you sent me got altered. You think someone hacked your phone, supplanted the text you sent with the one I received."

"It is the only thing that makes sense. They knew the location in the park, and when I would be there. The only place I ever mentioned that was in the message. They altered it in a way that would eliminate me, then sent killers to deal with you in the aftermath."

Slaton weighed it. "Something about that still doesn't seem right. To begin, I would never have come based on your original message. You had no way of knowing it, but I wouldn't have left my family alone for the sake of a stranger, no matter how desperate you sounded. And whoever lured me to Vienna had an even bigger bridge to cross. They not only had to make sure I came—they had to give me a good enough reason to kill a stranger."

"Which is why they abducted your family."

"Apparently. But even if that's plausible, it's harder to understand how quickly and efficiently everything materialized. You sent your message on Monday. Within twenty-four hours my family was missing and I was on my way here."

Mordechai sank into the biggest chair in the living area, an over-upholstered recliner that seemed to swallow his slight frame. "Yes, I see what you mean. That wouldn't be easy."

"Not at all."

Slaton noticed Mordechai looking at him with more than a trace of suspicion. "What?" he asked.

"I can't help but wonder . . . what were your intentions when you left for Vienna?"

"You mean was I really going to kill you?"

Mordechai nodded.

"No. But as I told you earlier, it was nothing altruistic. The kind of people who concoct blackmail schemes like this . . . they're not the sort who keep bargains. I came to Vienna looking for answers. I got the first one when I realized I was being followed. From there, it was a matter of making things break my way."

"And have they?"

"I've made progress. But my wife and son still aren't safe."

Mordechai rose from the chair and began wandering the kitchen. He opened the refrigerator door, found it empty. "What comes next?" he asked.

"Are you any good with phones?"

"What do you mean?"

Slaton pulled out his phone and called up the photo he'd taken of the dead man's call log. "Each of the men I killed in the park had a phone. I was able to unlock one—I think it was the guy who was in charge." Slaton showed Mordechai the screen. "I'm pretty sure these were calls he made to his cohorts' burners. Can you do anything with that?"

"You didn't keep the phone?"

It hit Slaton hard—Mordechai was right. He should have kept the handset. At the time he'd been concerned about the phone being tracked. But he could have turned it off, removed the battery. He didn't like mistakes, and this was a clear one. Had he been task saturated? Worried about losing sight of Mordechai across the estuary? No, he decided. As much as he didn't want to admit it, the prospect of losing Christine and Davy was like nothing he'd ever faced. It was deep and personal. And it had put him off his game.

"This is all I've got," Slaton said, trying to hold back his irritation. "Can you *do* anything with it?"

Mordechai looked at the numbers like they were random draws to a lottery. "With Mossad's resources, I might have. I could have given you something geographic—what relays got used, some triangulation. I might even have been able to figure out where they were purchased, when they were activated."

"And without Mossad?"

The scientist shrugged. "I don't have the assets."

Slaton heaved a sigh. He felt fatigue weighing down. Not only his limbs, but his mind. The bed in the next room called. He had no idea if he would be able to sleep. But he knew it was important to try.

THIRTY

Albatross battered her way through solid swells, plowing obediently eastward under the high midday sun. From the protection of the wheelhouse, Boutros steered a course ten degrees north of his desired track. Conditions had degraded since leaving the protection of the coastline, and with a northerly wind rising, he thought it best to square the boat into the seas.

Explosions of spray flew over the gunnels, more from the windward port side, and water slapped the wheelhouse in rhythmic sheets. He eased the throttle back a second time, hoping things wouldn't get worse.

He heard footfalls and turned to see Rafiq.

"Do you need a break?" he asked.

"No," Boutros replied. "Another hour, then someone can take the watch."

"It will have to be me."

Boutros looked at him inquisitively.

"Sami and Saleem are both in their bunks—seasick."

"At least they were able to eat before it overtook them. We must all keep our strength." Their first meal on board *Albatross* had been rice with spicy chicken.

Sami had prepared it, and everyone agreed it was far better than yesterday's fish soup.

"The seas have risen, and it may get worse. The good news is that the body acclimates. Make sure they take water to avoid dehydration. A day, maybe two, and they'll be used to the seas."

Rafiq nodded compliantly.

"And you?" Boutros asked. "Are you feeling any . . . effects?"

In truth, Rafiq didn't look well. He appeared pallid, and was leaning against the console.

"I puked once and feel a little dizzy . . . but it is only the sea."

"Yes, I'm sure you are right."

Boutros was confident his men were suffering from no more than mal de mer. All the same, he knew what his deputy was thinking.

They had discussed it in the premission planning. Of the four men going to sea, three had never been on anything larger than a rowboat. Seasickness was to be expected. Yet they'd also had a discussion with the caliphate's chief and, in fact, only remaining physician. He had gone over the primary symptoms of radiation sickness—nausea, vomiting, headache, dizziness, weakness—all of which were shared with motion sickness. The material belowdecks—half of what would eventually be utilized—was well contained inside a steel tube. This, the doctor had explained, offered a reasonable amount of shielding, and so the risk of exposure was minimal. That would change during the next stage of the operation. Their first and only stop necessitated the direct handling of material. After that, more serious symptoms were certain: hair loss, stomach maladies, ocular bleeding. For at least one of his team—in all likelihood, Sami—this fate was inevitable.

Rafiq interrupted Boutros' inordinately dark thoughts. "Is this our route?" he asked, addressing the electronic chart near the helm.

"Yes."

"We will be very near Japan," Rafiq said, tapping his finger on the narrow passage between two large islands.

"The Tsugaru Straits, between the main island of Honshu and Hokkaido to the north."

"How wide is it?"

"Roughly twelve miles at the narrowest point."

"Does that not put us in Japanese territorial waters?"

"Typically, it would. Luckily for us, Japan has designated unique sovereignty limits to that area—only three miles from the coastline."

"Why?"

"To provide passage for the American navy. By declaring the channel as international water, America's nuclear-armed warships can pass through without violating Japan's constitutional ban on nuclear arms. They bow to the Americans. And it fits our needs perfectly."

Rafiq smiled thinly. "How appropriate."

"The route will save us a day over any other passage. Now . . . go check on the others."

As Rafiq disappeared into the cabin below, the boat lurched. Boutros made another correction on the wheel. He eyed the vessel monitoring system. The VMS unit, given away by its dome-shaped antennas, was the first thing he'd noticed from the pier. The hardware was becoming standard on fishing fleets across the globe. It had nothing to do with navigation or security, but was designed to give fishery authorities and environmental groups the ability to track individual vessels. The intent was to ensure that catches were lawful and protected waters honored. VMS units transmitted position, course, speed, and in some cases went so far as to issue catch reports.

At least when they were operational.

Choe had already taken care of *Albatross'* unit, having cut the wire to the antennas somewhere in the South China Sea. It was a crude but effective shutdown. Boutros had been told to expect a boat with Southeast Asian provenance, and he'd done his homework. According to Thailand's regulations, any boat greater than sixty gross tons was required to have a VMS transmitter. He also knew the requirement was relatively new, and that enforcement was a work in progress. One technical malfunction among thousands of boats would hardly be noticed. Doubly so given that the vessel's ownership had recently changed hands, getting duly obfuscated in the process—the North Koreans were better than most at cloaking transfers of money and title. In a month, perhaps two, a letter of noncompliance would arrive at an attorney's office in Panama. Or perhaps the regulators would get an emailed complaint from Greenpeace. Either would be far too late.

More problematic than an inoperative VMS, Boutros decided, was the chance of a random inspection inside someone's two-hundred-mile economic zone. That the ship's holds contained not a single fish, and that her nets would never once touch the water, was of limited consolation. She might be a boat with nothing to hide when it came to fishing, but if *Albatross* was ever boarded, Boutros would be faced with two great problems. Most obvious, of course, involved what *was* in the net storage compartment. The second was that any competent inspector would fast recognize a crew who knew nothing about the sea. There was little Boutros could do to mitigate either issue. If a boarding appeared imminent, he could do little but cover up the device and tell everyone to keep their mouths shut. If that didn't work—they had at least one weapon with which to make a stand.

It was all of course speculative. Chances were excellent that they would soon become lost in a vast ocean. Still, if Boutros had learned anything in his years at sea, it was that forethought could prove decisive in times of crisis.

And when that wasn't enough? Then he and his crew would gladly put themselves in the hands of Allah.

Events in Danube Park went much as Slaton predicted. The bodies were found before dawn—the consequence of an errantly thrown tennis ball, delivered by a pastry chef preparing for an early shift, and one easily distracted German spaniel.

One phone call later, and on the backside of a slow night, the police descended in legions. Before sunrise the crime scene had been cordoned off and guards posted all around. The light of a new morning was prodding the eastern sky when the lead detective arrived. He found himself presiding over a scene that included three bodies, a great deal of blood, a notable absence of murder weapons, one roll of duct tape, three MAC-10s, and a partial set of children's golf clubs.

Each of the three victims was carrying a phone, although it was fast determined that all were pre-paid items, had been activated within the last two days, and contained no relevant information save for the fact that they were tied to one another— hardly a shock for devices taken from three bodies piled like cordwood.

The identities of the men were easily determined— each was carrying an Austrian-issued identity card. Unfortunately, it was subsequently discovered that the addresses were fictitious in every case. This com-monality was not lost on the detective, nor the fact that all three men appeared to be of an age and— profiling or not—an ethnic origin that might sug-gest either terrorism or a hate crime. With this in mind, the inspector, a thoughtful man with a broad mustache and beer-drinker's build, ran the victims' names through departmental task forces that had been set up to combat both.

Over the course of the morning, photos would be taken and imprints cast of various marks on the wet earth. The bodies would eventually be moved, with all possible decorum, to the departmental morgue. Later that day, the detective would garner a few vague details about the victims when one of his sub-ordinates flashed photos, sourced from their iden-tity documents, around a certain local mosque.

As it turned out, the coming days would be full of investigative setbacks, many of them foreshadowed from the very outset. Indeed, if the inquiry could be encapsulated to a single image, it might have been the thickset detective himself. As he stood taking in the scene at first light, he was visibly perplexed.

Had he been there to see for himself, Slaton would have admitted but one point of defeat: instead of scratching his head, the poor man cupped his jaw in an ode to his bafflement.

THIRTY-ONE

Rain was tapping the window when Slaton woke. It wasn't a downpour, but more of a wandering shower, the meteorological equivalent of a stray dog. He looked at the bedside clock. Its big red digits glared back like a warning.

7:12 a.m.

He rolled toward the window. At the top he saw a black void, and below that was the valley between buildings where feeble streetlights battled the mist. Slaton pivoted his legs to the floor, picked up his phone from the nightstand. He hesitated, then turned it on. There was nothing new, only the cryptic message that had turned his life upside down.

He turned it off, switched to the prepaid phone he'd purchased, and launched a search of the local news. Slaton held his breath while the browser wheel spun. When the results flashed to the screen they were conclusive, and not unexpected. Two articles, very similar, could be collectively distilled to the headline of the first: "Triple Murder in Danube Park."

His work had been discovered, and somewhat sooner than anticipated. The reports added nothing to what he already knew. No identities of the victims were given, and there was nothing about suspects or evidence. Details would trickle out in time, he knew, the pace slowing as police realized the depth of their investigative ditch.

But time was not a luxury Slaton had.

A series of visions clouded his thoughts, arriving sequentially like a slide show. A verdant park. A playground. Davy leaping off a platform into a mulch bed, looking for all the world like a commando jumping out of an airplane. It seemed an arbitrary set of images, nothing to do with the facts before him.

And absolutely everything to do with them.

Slaton stood and went to the wash basin in the bathroom. He ignored the mirror, turned on the tap, and splashed water on his face, not bothering to wait for the warm side to kick in. Finally, he looked up and found himself whispering to the image before him.

"How long can I go on like this?"

It had been nearly four years since he'd left Mossad. Yet somehow, the more distant his past became, the more relentlessly it infringed on his new life. With concerted effort, he turned away from what he knew was a gloomy mental cul-de-sac. There was only room for the here-and-now.

With the hopefulness of a new morning, he rejoined the facts of last night. Surprisingly, a new clarity emerged. He used a towel to dry his face, then walked quickly to the second bedroom.

Mordechai was sound asleep in the double bed.

"Wake up!" Slaton said sharply.

Mordechai remained motionless. His feet were clear of the blanket, and Slaton smacked his soles with an open hand.

Mordechai startled awake.

There were two lamps in the room—one on the bedside stand, the other high on a Louis Quinze dresser. Slaton turned them both on. Regrettably, the energy-efficient LED bulbs didn't give the effect he was after. *How does anyone conduct a proper interrogation anymore?*

"What is it?" Mordechai mumbled. His eyes were slits and his head bobbed when he sat up. Rip van Winkle on Valium. Slaton wasn't surprised. The man was unaccustomed to stress, to playing in the life-and-death league. His hands fumbled over the night-stand for his glasses.

"I've changed my mind," Slaton said.

"About what?"

"You need to show up at the office today."

Mordechai put his glasses on, blinked twice. "But last night you said—"

"Circumstances have changed. The three bod-ies were discovered early this morning in the park. The police are investigating. Whoever abducted my family has seen the same news reports."

"Have the victims' identities been made public?"

"Not yet."

"Then . . . isn't it possible they'll think one of the bodies is mine? Or even yours?"

"There will be a period of uncertainty. On the other hand, we can't dismiss that whoever we're talking about might have connections inside the po-lice department. If so, they'll know their hit team failed. Either way, it's only a matter of time."

"Have you gotten any new messages from them?"

"No, and I'm not waiting. We need to go on the offensive. El-Masri is the key—we have to find out more about these suspect site visits. To do that, I need you in the headquarters building."

"But if I show up at work, it will be clear you didn't fulfill your part of the bargain. Won't that put your family at risk?"

"I'm guessing no more than they already are. But there is one thing we can do to minimize the threat. When you go in to work today, carry on like nothing has changed—just another day at the office."

"You don't think these people will suspect we've joined forces?"

"No. When I put myself in their shoes, I see a more likely scenario. They'll suspect I spotted their thugs, took them out, then let you run because I thought I'd been double-crossed. Right now, they're probably wishing they'd hired more competent killers."

Mordechai considered it. "That's not far from what actually happened."

"Not far at all. And it gives us back our biggest advantage—having you on the inside. I need to know when El-Masri is due back. After that, dig into his background. Personal, professional, everything."

Mordechai sat on the side of the bed. He leaned forward and ran his hands through his riotous hair. "And after work tonight? Do I return here?"

"No—go to your apartment. You and I can't be seen together. But we do need to stay in touch." Slaton instructed Mordechai to buy a fresh phone on the way to work, then provided the number of his own burner.

"All right," Mordechai said. "I will call you tonight."

"Good. But before you go . . . I need to know a few things about El-Masri."

"What could I tell you?"

"You probably know more than you realize."

"But I don't—"

"Is he married?"

"Yes."

"Is his wife here or in Egypt?"

"Here in Vienna. And also a son."

"What's his address?"

Mordechai looked at him severely.

Slaton kept an unwavering gaze.

"Twenty-three Eicherstrasse, Kapellerfeld."

"Does he have a dog?"

"I . . . I don't think so."

"A mistress?"

Discomfort. "No," Mordechai said. "At least, not that I know of."

"Does he exercise regularly?"

"Never that I've seen."

"What kind of car does he drive?"

"An Audi sedan."

"Color?"

"Silver."

And so it went for twenty minutes. At that point, Slaton and Mordechai parted.

The scientist was first to leave, taking the sidewalk east along Novaragasse on a course toward the river.

Slaton allowed a five-minute interval. From the building's entry alcove he searched the streets for anything out of character. He saw well-dressed bankers, briefcases penduluming at their sides. Students holding cell phones like modern-day divining rods. Elderly women in dresses walked to choir practice, while younger ones in yoga pants headed for the studio. All people for whom Vienna offered nothing more than an easy Thursday morning. And also nothing less.

His survey complete, Slaton turned west, a direct course to the nearest Metro station. He fell in with the masses, everyone around him absorbed in appointments and conversations and workaday routines. And for the first time in his life, Slaton wondered what it would be like to be among them.

THIRTY-TWO

Kapellerfeld turned out to be a pocket village ten miles north of the greater city. In America it would have been called a suburb, yet unlike the States, the township was not the product of a "visionary" developer who brought a flurry of clear-cutting, paving, and cookie-cutter construction. As with most European hamlets, it was a community in the truest sense, maturing over generations much like the vineyards of the surrounding hills. There was a school and a church and a highly regarded confectionery. A train to address wanderlust and a nursery to provide roots. If the great city to the south loomed, it did so at arm's length. An urban shadow not yet gone to eclipse. Kapellerfeld was small and tidy and clean. And a place where senior officers of the IAEA, apparently, could feel secure.

The rain had ended, and under the gloom of an overcast morning Slaton drove to within a mile of El-Masri's address before setting out on foot. Having studied the neighborhood using online satellite imagery, he went in with a mental portrait of the surrounding streets. He made his initial approach in a calibrated manner, a series of right-hand turns in an ever-tightening pattern.

His pace was resolute, his posture huddled. A man heading to the dentist to have a tooth pulled. Wearing khaki pants, a dark jacket, and a categorically bland expression, he was tedium personified. Only once, out of necessity, did he utilize the same street twice, and on that occasion he used the opposite sidewalk—in quiet residential neighborhoods, people noticed recurring strangers. The dismal weather was in his favor—he passed only a handful of people, shopping bags in hand or tending to gardens. He nodded cordially to a few, and none responded with anything more. For this Slaton was thankful—his German was no better now than when he'd arrived.

He spent twenty minutes on his approach work, logging one-way streets and bus stops, and taking particular notice of two narrow alleys—wide enough for foot traffic, but effective chokepoints for a pursuing car. He twice used his phone to inquire about a ride on Uber—not because he wanted a car at that moment, but rather to gauge response times. In doing so, he input a destination address that was centered in Vienna—drivers preferred to accept trips that ended in districts where follow-on work was likely. He was happy to see that, in spite of the early hour, a car could be summoned within minutes if necessary.

When he was finally comfortable with the field of play, Slaton made the turn onto Eicherstrasse. The homes along the street were a mix of themes, art deco here, contemporary there. He spotted number 23 from a distance. It was a half-hearted ode to Tyrol, a two-story affair with faux shutters and a brown shingle roof. Not the largest on the street, nor the smallest. Slaton had no idea what it was worth, but he speculated—because that was what one did when weighing suspected spies—that the home was not beyond the means of a department head for a major international agency. The main house was sided by a driveway, and in back he saw a BMW SUV parked near a detached garage. Mordechai had told him El-Masri drove an Audi, so this was likely Mrs. El-Masri's car. Here again, the ownership of two expensive German vehicles was notable, but hardly out of reach for a senior government official. And positively ordinary in the gilded burgh of Lower Austria.

As he neared number 23, Slaton studied the periphery. He saw a stone wall on the north side, and another along the rear property line. Either could easily be vaulted. A few cars were parked along curbs up and down the street, although he was sure the count would be higher tonight as city commuters returned home. A row of leafless trees stood sentry along the road, gray bark peeling from their trunks and naked branches shivering in the chill breeze.

Minutes earlier, canvassing the street behind, Slaton had gotten a look at the home's rear façade. There was a door, a sidewalk leading to the garage, and one frill-curtained window overlooking it all. He figured the window for the kitchen, but that could be verified later. To the positive, there were no signs of any soffit-mounted cameras or motion-activated exterior lights. It had initially struck Slaton as odd that there were no children's toys or play sets. Then he realized he hadn't asked the age of El-Masri's son. A mere oversight? Or was his perspective skewed in ways it never had been?

Either way, a question for Mordechai later.

As he passed directly in front of the house—the

only time he would do so in the light of day—Slaton took out his phone and pretended to thumb out a text. He looked up momentarily, as if awaiting a reply, and as he did the camera drifted casually to record a panorama image of the home and surrounding grounds. He glanced once at the house itself, noting that one room on the first floor was brightly lit, as was one on the second. The other two front windows remained dark.

The house slipped behind, and Slaton crossed the street to avoid a pair of elderly women, two doors down, who were chatting amiably across a white fence. At the first side street he turned right—he'd drawn the women's notice, but he was reasonably sure they weren't alarmed.

Altogether, it was a neighborhood like a hundred others around Vienna. A place with nominal security to counter a nominal threat. A place much like the one he and Christine had shared briefly in Virginia. How long had it been? Three years? The memory seemed so detached it felt like a dream.

He reached the Renault ten minutes later. Ten after that, Slaton was merging into the river of traffic heading south toward Vienna.

THIRTY-THREE

Tarek El-Masri watched the final cask as it was removed from the huge airplane. The jet was an Antonov AN-124, the largest cargo aircraft in the world, and had been chartered from the Russian heavy lift carrier Volga-Dnepr. There were Western freight carriers that might have been more reputable, and certainly more expensive, but the Russians knew their protocols when it came to shipping high-level radioactive material. Truth be told, there was also a more basic logistical reason for choosing the AN-124: it was the only airplane on earth with enough lift capacity and deck strength to haul three Type B shipping casks, each of which weighed as much as a main battle tank.

They had landed at Évreux-Fauville Air Base, two miles outside Évreux, France. The three heavy trucks receiving their loads faced a long journey, the AREVA reprocessing facility in La Hague being over a hundred miles distant. Fortunately for El-Masri, that would be an ordeal borne by others—French security teams were now responsible for the material. For his team, the worst was behind them: in particular, last night's nervous trek across the lawless Pakistani frontier.

"Our charter flight to Paris is running late."

El-Masri turned to see Henri with a smartphone in his hand.

"How late?" he asked.

"Two hours. We will miss our connection."

El-Masri sighed. He was extremely tired, his limbs feeling like they were filled with lead. He looked wistfully at the Antonov. Unfortunately, it had fulfilled its contract, and for the ride home they'd all been booked on a charter out of nearby Caen, then a connection at Paris Charles de Gaulle to Vienna.

"What are our options?" El-Masri asked.

"I have talked to Air France—they said we may be able to get home tonight."

Had it not come from Henri, El-Masri would have remarked on the incompetence of France's flagship air carrier. As it was, he lifted the clipboard in his hand and went back to signing. Authentication forms, RFID verifications, security seals, chain-of-possession documents. He was thankful the weight of the paperwork hadn't grounded the Antonov in Pakistan.

El-Masri was midway through the fifth page when the signature line seemed to blur. His hand began shaking right before his eyes, and he suddenly swooned. The world went black. The next thing he knew, he was sitting on the ground with Henri at his elbow.

"Monsieur . . . are you all right?"

El-Masri blinked a few times. The world seemed to reappear. "Yes . . . yes, I'm fine. Help me up."

Henri did, and once back on his feet an embarrassed El-Masri swatted the dust off the seat of his pants.

"We should go inside and sit down," said Henri,

pointing to the small aviation operations building. "I will get you something to drink."

"No, I'll be fine. We've had a difficult schedule for the last few days. I'm not as young as I used to be."

"All the same, you should at least take some water."

El-Masri nodded, more to divert Henri than because he thought it would do any good. The Frenchman turned toward the building, and El-Masri said, "We'll be done here in an hour. Call the airline and see what they can do to expedite things." Henri said he would, and El-Masri called out after him, "And once the plans are confirmed, send word to the main office. I think we have all earned a day off tomorrow."

Henri waved.

El-Masri picked up his clipboard, a pen hanging from the attached string. With his free hand he rubbed his forehead. He was glad this would be his last trip. *I don't think I could manage another,* he thought. In a rush of optimism—something he'd rarely felt lately—he decided the timing of this final site visit had worked out perfectly. Any later, and the entire plan would have come up short. It had all begun eighteen months ago, shortly after his diagnosis. Now God had granted him just enough time to see it through.

God.

It occurred to El-Masri that he hadn't prayed in days. He'd never been particularly devout, yet time was running short to make amends. Like heathens across the ages, he supposed, the relevance of piousness seemed more clear at the end.

He cast the thought away and focused on getting home. Tomorrow he could relax, take a long week-end. Perhaps drive to the mountains with his wife and son. Monday he would schedule an appointment with the director general and explain his situation. Announce that he was taking his final leave.

A few more months—that was his doctor's best guess. But of course, it was only that. He might linger for half a year or fail within a few weeks. Whatever happened, El-Masri was glad he'd made the most of his remaining time. Indeed, that was why he was here today: to finalize the legacy to his family. The last funds would soon be transferred and put in his wife's name—even if she knew nothing about it. The Bahamian account, the villa on the Red Sea coast. He had even arranged acceptance into a good Swiss university for his son. A future guaranteed.

He took the pen and began signing again, the lines on the forms seeming suddenly more sharp. He scrawled his name in flourishes, giving no heed whatsoever to the thick blocks of legalese printed above. In time, he knew every page would be scrutinized. An internal investigation to be sure, and probably less familiar faces from the outside. Police forces, intelligence agencies. But that would all take time. And time, for El-Masri, was in perilously short supply.

Henri approached from the administration building. He was walking quickly with a water bottle in hand. He twisted off the top before handing it over—as if El-Masri himself was incapable.

"I'm fine," El-Masri said more sharply than he should have. He took the water all the same.

"I have talked again with Air France. They assure me they can get us home tonight, but very late."

"Then very late it is."

Henri stared at him with concern. "I hope you

don't mind my saying it, monsieur, but you don't look well. Perhaps you should see a doctor."

"I have, and he assures me it is only fatigue. I've been working too hard. Now . . ." El-Masri handed the clipboard to his subordinate, ". . . go and finish the readings on the Antonov."

The Frenchman took the paperwork and set out toward the now empty transport.

El-Masri pulled his phone and composed a text message to his wife: Home very late tonight. Don't wait up.

He sent the message, and seconds later a phone vibrated on a granite counter in the warm kitchen of 23 Eicherstrasse, Kapellerfeld. It was picked up by his wife.

What El-Masri could not know was that his message, via a bit of cyber trickery, had also been directed to a second receiving number. The echo of El-Masri's text took a few beats longer to reach the second destination, for the simple reason that it was physically farther away. Much, much farther.

An alert chimed on a computer in the basement of a blasé building in Datong, China. Even for a country not known for adventures in contemporary architecture, the brooding rectangle of cinder blocks was remarkable in its unremarkability. It could have passed for a small business, a modest warehouse, or even a lesser government agency.

The building's true vocation had been a matter of some speculation to those who lived and worked nearby. Neighboring shop owners, the residents of nearby buildings, and a handful of Datong's city elders all had their opinions. The workers who populated the place were definitely not locals. They were a silent bunch who kept to themselves, and who shared a tiny hovel on the far side of town. The local police seemed complicit in the whole affair, and it was rumored they'd been instructed by higher authorities to give the building and its occupants a wide berth—the kind of "suggestion" from national that was never questioned. So no one complained, and whatever was happening inside the place kept happening. Even the resident colony of marmots burrowed beneath the building's foundation seemed oblivious to the goings-on.

The truth, known by few, was that the outpost in Datong, situated on the frontier of Inner Mongolia, was staffed not by Chinese nationals, but a team of twenty-six North Koreans. The cell was part of a unit called Bureau 121, a title as nondescript as the nameless chain of buildings through which it operated. "The Office," as it was internally known, fell under the firm but shadowed control of the Korean People's Army. Bureau 121 cells were spread widely across China, and a few farther afield—in countries where the leadership was either grossly incompetent or reliably corrupt.

For North Korea, the concept of foreign-basing intelligence work, risk-laden as it might seem, was ultimately a matter of necessity: the country was itself entirely unsuited to hacking operations, with a power grid and internet infrastructure lacking basic functionality.

Bureau 121 cells were composed of between twenty and fifty hackers, and its technicians were an exclusive lot, hand-picked from the elite University of Automation in Pyongyang. By North Korean standards, its recruits were well paid, and they enjoyed the rarest of perks—the benefit of living outside the workers' paradise of the People's Republic. Escaping no one's attention, however, was that the families of Bureau 121's technicians invariably remained behind on the peninsula. And while wives and children and parents enjoyed accordant privileges, their ability to travel abroad was strictly prohibited. The question of what might happen to them in the event of a defection was better left unasked.

The text message sent that day by El-Masri had been scribed in English, but it was effortlessly translated into Korean—all of Bureau 121's technicians were English-proficient. Indeed, it was a point of internal pride that no fewer than sixteen languages could be translated within the building. A senior man had been assigned to monitor El-Masri's devices, and when he received the text he was battling a terrible headache—the result of a fourteen-hour shift wearing a headset that fit like a shop clamp. His orders were to forward any results, through their best encrypted link, directly to headquarters, skipping any attempt to analyze the material. He followed them to the letter.

Which was how, thirty seconds after El-Masri sent the text to his wife, General Hai-joon Park began reading it in his office thousands of miles away. He went through the message twice, combined it with what he knew, and found himself consumed by one thought: *It was time to tidy up the burgeoning mess in Vienna.*

THIRTY-FOUR

On the way back to his rented room, Slaton made one critical stop: at a large electronics store he purchased a tablet computer.

Back in his room he stood up the computer on the kitchen counter. Next to it he placed a small stack of printer paper pilfered from the bedroom desk. He connected to the apartment's Wi-Fi—the password had been included in the rental confirmation, and he decided the network had no more chance of being compromised than any other available to him.

Once online, he downloaded a popular application that allowed prospective buyers to view real estate listings. With the app installed, he selected English as his preferred language, then typed in "Kapellerfeld," followed by "23 Eicherstrasse." Seconds later a map came into view: El-Masri's home was at the center with the surrounding property lines thickened like walls on a prison diagram. As expected, the home was listed as "Not for Sale." Undeterred, Slaton zoomed in, clicked, and was rewarded with a screen full of information.

According to Mordechai, El-Masri had been working at IAEA for roughly three years. Before that he had lived in Egypt. On the website Slaton confirmed that a buyer, almost certainly El-Masri, had bought the home thirty months earlier for 300,000 euros—roughly 350,000 U.S. dollars. A substantial sum, but again, not eye-catching, particularly since the Egyptian government might well have subsidized the purchase. All in all, interesting— but it wasn't what Slaton was after.

Because the sale was recent, and because real estate agents strove to generate interest in properties, the photographs from the old listing were still viewable. He saw a slideshow with twenty-four pictures: everything from outside shots with curb appeal to staged interior views of every room. In an exercise he'd performed before, generally in the role of assassin, Slaton poised a pencil over one of the blank sheets of paper.

He used a piece of cardboard packaging from the tablet computer as a straightedge and ticked off a makeshift scale in one corner of the page, settling on five-foot increments. He first referenced the streetside façade of the house, approximating the outer walls, and adding doors and windows with the greatest of care. He cross-referenced the panorama shot he'd taken earlier with his phone, and flicked between exterior shots on the website. In the end, he had a reliable blueprint of the home's periphery.

From that template, Slaton moved inside. He studied pictures of each room, relating different angles, and paid particular attention to the scenes through windows. These were invariably open during photo shoots to provide a bright and airy look. For his purposes, the windows provided geometric relations to points outside—and, in his previous life, lines of fire. Using furniture as references, he linked together passageways between rooms. Slaton moved back and forth between images, drawing lines for interior walls only when he was certain they were accurate.

After twenty minutes, he moved to the second floor. This was smaller, and a more simple setting: three bedrooms, a bathroom, and one large storage closet. He also noted a ceiling-mounted access door to an attic.

When he was done, Slaton sat back and for the first time regarded his work as a whole. The scale was not perfect, and the furnishings inside today would be El-Masri's—more rugs, he supposed, fewer soft-cushioned chairs and knock-off Old World paintings. Those details aside, Slaton was confident he had what he wanted, and an image he would spend the next thirty minutes memorizing—one reasonably accurate tactical diagram of the home he was going to invade.

Heeding Slaton's advice, Mordechai spent the morning going through his normal routines at work. He culled his email inbox, and attended two scheduled meetings. The first was a briefing on new security protocols that were coming down the bureaucratic pipeline, the other an interdepartmental lashing by the senior personnel director—the Department of Safeguards' sizeable Ukrainian contingent had "gone Cossack" at last month's Christmas party, laying ruin to a local bar and throwing an ice sculpture through a window. Mordechai had listened along with the other department heads, nodding and wishing he were anywhere else.

It was at one o'clock that afternoon, with most of the sixth-floor staff still lingering over extended lunches at nearby cafés, that Mordechai began his day's true work. He rode the elevator three floors down, and turned into an office marked TRAVEL DEPARTMENT. He told the receptionist who he was and what he wanted, and she directed him to a cubicle in a corner suite. There, an officious-looking older woman behind a desk glanced up. Mordechai was quite sure he'd never seen her before, even though he'd had his share of dealings with the department. Whether that was good or bad, he couldn't say.

"Can I help you?" she asked in Austrian-accented English. This was the lingua franca of the little United Nations that was IAEA.

"Yes, I'm Paul Mordechai, Department of Safeguards. I work under Deputy Director El-Masri." His identity card bobbed obviously from the lanyard around his neck, its blue border verifying that he was indeed a senior administrator. "The deputy director is out on a site visit, the PARR II inspection. They're due back soon, but I don't have a precise schedule. Can you tell me when they will arrive back in Vienna?"

A hesitation. The travel arrangements of inspection teams were closely guarded. A matter of security.

"The site visit is complete," Mordechai said, "so there is no longer any need for secrecy. Dr. El-Masri typically gives me the schedule, but it must have slipped his mind. I've got to arrange a meeting for the two of us with Director Ingalls, and I don't have his availability."

Dropping the name of the director himself seemed to do the trick—Dr. Ingalls, certainly, was beyond reproach. She began typing, and moments later Mordechai had what he wanted: the inspection team was expected to arrive tonight on a commercial flight from Paris, shortly before midnight.

Mordechai thanked the woman and returned to the sixth floor. There he diverted down a lengthy hallway. The north wing of the floor was not his customary working area, yet it wasn't completely foreign ground. Many of the faces he saw seemed familiar, and a few he knew on a first-name basis. The most important of them he spotted eating a sandwich at her desk—Ingrid, El-Masri's able assistant, and guardian to the gates of the deputy director's office.

Mordechai sidetracked behind a wall and pulled out his phone. He called his own assistant, an ambitious young Viennese named Rolf, and gave very specific instructions. When the call ended, Mordechai waited a few beats before setting out. He governed his speed to arrive at Ingrid's desk one minute later. As he neared, he noticed that the door to El-Masri's private suite was open, although none of the lights inside were on.

Ingrid was early forties, stout build and bosomy, with overmanaged blond hair. She noticed Mordechai approaching and smiled, perhaps more pleasantly than usual. She used a napkin to wipe a bit of mustard from one corner of her mouth.

"Good afternoon, Mr. Mordechai," she said.

"Hello, Ingrid. I'm sorry to disturb your lunch. The deputy director has some contracts on his desk that are due to be signed. I know he won't be back for a day or two, so I'll have to take care of it."

She looked at him questioningly. Ingrid was a classic nine-to-five soldier among the agency's army of civil servants. In the course of his work, Mordechai had regularly come to see El-Masri in his office. Never before had he gone inside alone. Ingrid opened her mouth as if to say something, and Mordechai seemed ready to forestall her words, when the phone interrupted them both.

She picked up the handset on her desk. Mordechai listened to half the conversation. *Contracts? . . . Why, yes, he's here right now . . . Let me write down the full list . . .*

Taking his cue, Mordechai gave a slight wave and walked straight into Tarek El-Masri's office. He nudged the door partially shut behind him and turned on a light.

THIRTY-FIVE

Mordechai didn't bother booting up the desktop computer on the arm of the L-shaped desk—he was quite sure El-Masri already suspected cyber intrusions, which meant he likely had strong passwords and security measures.

Not sure what he was even looking for, Mordechai began at the desk. He rifled through two drawers of paper files, stealing an occasional glance at the partially open door—Ingrid's desk was fortunately around the corner, and he heard her still talking to Rolf on the phone. He went through standard personnel files, site visit plans, technical specification manuals—many were twins of files he kept in his own desk. The third stacked drawer contained the usual array of office equipment, a handful of radiation badges, and a disassembled Geiger counter.

He moved on to the flat top drawer. Inside were the usual pens and pencils and Post-its, along with a handful of flash drives. Most of these had printed labels he recognized, deeming them as products of the agency's internal IT department. The only exception were three generic plastic sticks. One was white, another black, and the third was red with a sticker depicting the Egyptian flag. The three were labeled respectively in black Sharpie: CV, OFFI-CIAL PHOTOS, INSURANCE.

CV, he was sure, stood for *curriculum vitae*. In this age of career instability, no scientist was without one. The others seemed obvious enough, and equally useless.

He closed the drawer and moved on to the closet. There he spent three minutes rummaging through shelves, and finally two cardboard boxes on the floor. Still he found nothing. Desperation set in. Mordechai was feeling through the pockets of a suit coat hanging on a hook in the closet when he heard Ingrid say, "Yes, I will . . . And you have a good afternoon as well."

He watched the door, expecting her to come through at any moment and see his hands deep in the pockets of her boss's emergency dinner jacket. Then he heard the crumple of a sandwich wrapper, followed by something else being unwrapped.

He still had time.

Mordechai spun a slow circle, his eyes taking in the room. A picture of the Great Pyramid graced one wall, a diploma from Cairo University another. Next to the diploma was a small decorative mirror engraved with the IAEA logo. His eyes kept moving. A long bookshelf might have been promising had it not been stocked with thick technical treatises with mind-numbing titles. He was walking tentatively toward the shelf when a single word echoed uninvitedly in his mind.

Insurance.

He looked again at the desk. Mordechai returned, opened the top drawer, and pulled out the flash drive with the Egyptian flag. The one labeled IN-SURANCE. It seemed a long shot, yet something about the title seemed odd. *Who keeps their insurance information in a drawer at work?* He looked at the image on the stick.

Quite literally, a flag.

A flash of movement near the door.

Without even time to put the drive in his pocket, Mordechai pressed it between the knuckles of two fingers. He was nudging the drawer closed with his thigh when Ingrid appeared.

"Have a nice afternoon, Mr. Mordechai," said Ingrid as she watched the Israeli leave.

Having returned to her desk, she held her smile until he disappeared down the hall. When he did, she waited just a bit longer, then got up and went to the open office door. There she paused at the threshold. She scanned the room with her secretary's eye, and wondered what he'd taken.

When Mordechai first asked to go inside, it had struck her as odd, although not particularly suspicious. Her curiosity was piqued, however, when his own assistant called with an obviously pointless chore. That was when Ingrid began watching the mirror.

Dr. El-Masri had asked her to mount it on the wall last year after receiving it as a longevity award—because what else could you do with something like that? Ingrid had done so dutifully, but taken the liberty of placing it at a perfect angle between his desk and her own. She supposed it was rather nosy, but it made for an engaging diversion—shift in her chair slightly, and she had a perfect view of her boss. Today, however, it hadn't been Dr. El-Masri. In the reflection she'd seen Mordechai rifling through desk drawers, and later she'd heard him going through the closet. At the end, she saw him quite clearly snatch something from the top desk drawer.

Ingrid stared down the hall.

She knew she ought to report the incident to security. Then again, she had nothing against Mr. Mordechai. He was actually rather attractive, in a rumpled sort of way, and single, or so she'd been told. He had always treated her kindly, which was more than could be said for her boss. She supposed it was cultural, an Egyptian thing, but El-Masri treated her like dirt.

Ingrid went back to her desk and sat. She wondered if Dr. El-Masri might himself be in hot water. That wouldn't be so bad, she reasoned. It might even give way to a new deputy director, one from a place where women were treated with respect. A Swede, or perhaps an Italian. *Oh God, yes . . . an Italian.*

That thought swimming in her head, she went back to work on an interoffice memo: she would let Mordechai's indiscretion pass.

Ingrid Hoff would never know the consequences of that decision. Never understand how, if she had made the call to security, the course of world events in the coming days might have spun in an entirely different direction.

Mordechai was back in his office within minutes. He pulled the flash drive from his pocket, closed the door behind him, and inserted the stick into his personal laptop. He fully expected to find a security screen staring back at him, some rock-solid encryption algorithm that might take weeks to break.

What he saw was nothing of the kind.

After opening the main file, he saw a menu of the holdings of the drive. The first file was a text document. He opened it and read an astonishing three-page letter. It began with an overview of the entire uranium-skimming scheme. More critically, it explained *why* El-Masri had gotten involved. A revelation Mordechai could never have imagined—and one that made perfect sense.

After reading it, he navigated back to the file menu. He saw names that implied an array of useful information, and clicked on the most promising: HEU.INVENTORY.

He stared in disbelief as detailed reports blossomed to the screen. It seemed too good to be true, and he found himself scrolling through spreadsheet after spreadsheet. He half expected a puff of smoke from his laptop, a laughing cloaked cartoon to take over the screen while everything disappeared—it was simply too easy a victory. The file was as damning as it was comprehensive, a complete list of the suspect shipments El-Masri had been assembling for over a year. Everything in one document, completely unprotected. And then, all at once, Mordechai understood—the name scrawled on the plastic cover.

Insurance indeed.

He was looking, for all intents and purposes, at Tarek El-Masri's confession. The kind of mother lode a man in very deep waters leaves with a trusted lawyer. *To be opened in the event of my untimely demise.* Only in lieu of a lawyer, El-Masri had simply left the trove in his top desk drawer. Mordechai wondered if he'd been planning to give it to someone. Or perhaps he'd had second thoughts.

Or maybe the drive was exactly where he intended it to be.

He realized that if anything happened to El-Masri, his desk was the first place any investigator would look. Mordechai returned to the file menu. By the time he closed the fifth folder, he was convinced—everything necessary to prove the plot was now in his hands.

He checked the clock. Four in the afternoon. A bit earlier than his usual quitting time, but not unreasonable. He *had* to get in touch with Slaton. Mordechai shut down the computer, locked his office door, and headed outside.

The late-afternoon air was crisp and clear. Traffic was building on the nearby autobahn, yet as was his habit, Mordechai headed for the nearby U-Bahn. Arriving on the platform with five minutes to wait, he took one look around before sending his two most important messages of the day. He selected the first contact he wanted, pecked out two words, and launched them on a cyber route toward Europe. Keep moving. Where exactly those words would land he couldn't say.

He then fired off a two-part text to Slaton. The first segment alerted him that El-Masri would return home late that night. In the second verse Mordechai explained he'd uncovered a significant cache of information.

His train arrived within seconds of sending the final text. Mordechai pocketed his phone and boarded. The train shot out of the terminal toward the river and his flat in Landstrasse.

Mordechai had no expectation of a reply to either of his messages. In fact, none came, although for reasons more intricate than he could have imagined.

The two-part text sent to Slaton completed its course on the strength of two advantages: the handsets, by chance, were tied to the same carrier, and the message was routed locally. The text sent to Mallorca, on the other hand, did not reach its anticipated address—at least, not in its intended form. That missive was relayed to a secondary server where it passed through virus-infected switching software. Flagged, isolated, and shunted to an altogether different destination, the message made its electronic landing on a computer in the lower level of a cinder-block building on the frontier of Mongolia.

At a basement workstation, the same technician who had earlier received diverted messages from Tarek El-Masri, and who was unknowingly situated above a flourishing population of marmots, performed his customary translation. These results he forwarded, like the others, to some unknown recipient at headquarters.

Riding in the back of his staff car, the severe-visaged General Park smiled for the first time in a month when the intercept from Bureau 121 came through. It was a thread they had not before captured—and one he very much wanted. After a thoughtful moment, he dictated a reply that suited his own needs: Stay where you are. I'm coming for you.

The electronic diversion continued, first to Bureau 121, then running through the usual series of commercial routers and relays. Twelve minutes after Mordechai's original text had launched, the subverted message was pinging across eight time zones toward its intended destination.

———

As it turned out, the burner phone the message was meant to reach lay next to a canopied bed in a seaside retreat in Mallorca. A long-limbed woman, whose auburn hair was streaked by the sun and whose eyes were an emerald green, lay propped by pillows beside her son on the bed. He, in turn, sat transfixed by her reading of his favorite Dr. Seuss story. Christine was just turning the page to reveal Thing 1 and Thing 2 when the altered message arrived at its destined server.

It did not, however, make the final leap to the handset on the nightstand, and for the simplest of reasons: as had been the case for two days, the phone was turned off.

THIRTY-SIX

Passage through the Tsugaru Straits was uneventful. Boutros had planned their arrival carefully to traverse the narrows in the small hours of the morning. It seemed to work. He'd made a good nighttime survey of both islands, and they appeared quiet. A constant stream of ships had passed uneventfully, clusters of amber drifting off the port beam that invariably faded. Best of all, there had been no radio calls, no curious patrol boats silhouetted under the clear half-moon.

Now, with sunrise imminent, Honshu had disappeared, and Hokkaido was but a jeweled string of topaz on the aft quarterdeck. Ahead lay the Pacific, calm for the moment but thick with menace in the season of ice and darkness.

With the Straits behind them, Boutros turned off the VHF radio. There had been no option but to monitor radio traffic in the busy corridor. Now, with open sea ahead, security became the priority. He shifted his gaze to the other electronics. They weren't the best money could buy, but typical of what one would find on a vagabond purse seiner from a developing nation—Boutros knew because he had boarded more than his share of such boats while policing the Persian Gulf.

Equipment, of course, had advanced since those days. The VMS tracker he'd already disabled, yet he was aware that certain nav and comm units, when left on, initiated regular electronic handshakes. Boutros had no reason to suspect anyone would be searching for them in the coming days. All the same, there was nothing to be gained by giving their position away cheaply. From this point forward, aside from the occasional satellite message or weather forecast, everything would remain powered down.

He looked out ahead and was struck by the desolation. Everything around him seemed unfamiliar. There was something bleak and endless about this northern sea. Even the waves appeared to lift and break in a different manner. Visibility was good in the gathering dawn, and he was happy to see no sign of precipitation on the horizon.

Boutros heard a clatter from the companionway. He saw Rafiq topping the stairs, his cheeks gone dark with two days' growth of beard. They'd all shaved in order to travel, but after arriving in North Korea Boutros had told his men there was no longer any need to keep it up. Saleem was winning the contest.

Rafiq looked aft. "So it is done—we made it through."

"One more step behind us in our journey. Did you just wake up?"

"An hour ago. I've been in the workroom going over the assembly sequence. When the final pieces arrive, we must be ready."

Boutros nodded. "Good. And Sami and Saleem?"

"They are sleeping."

"No doubt dreaming of the things young men dream of."

Rafiq looked suddenly uncomfortable, and Boutros imagined he was thinking of a woman. He wasn't married—commanders had to know such things about their men—but certainly a young girl somewhere had stolen his heart. He considered asking, but then thought better of it.

"Would you like me to take over?" asked Rafiq.

"Yes. It's been a long night, but we are in the clear now." Boutros stepped away from the helm. Rafiq moved in and got his bearings.

Boutros referenced the electronic map. "The sea opens up here. It's time to steer a new course. Make the heading one hundred and eight degrees."

Rafiq turned the wheel, and the bow swung gently to the right. "How long will we remain on this course?" he asked.

"Until our next stop."

Rafiq looked at him with a raised brow.

"It's that easy," Boutros said. "For the next four days we will bide our time, prepare."

"And then?"

"And then things will happen very quickly."

Surveillance ops run by intelligence agencies were typically months in the making. Safe houses with prized overlooks were procured, staffed, and provisioned. The latest electronics were installed to capture every acoustic signature, the slightest electronic emanation. Targeted individuals were monitored by teams who rotated on a strict schedule, while distant analysts pored over the flow of information, combing data for vital details and returning updates to those doing the watching.

Slaton stood alone behind a garbage can in the shadows of Tarek El-Masri's garage. The luxuries of surveillance he'd enjoyed in the past were all but a distant memory. He had no electronics, no analysis of what he saw beyond his own. His only backup was the stolen Glock in his jacket pocket. With nothing more than that, he was determined to seize the last thread that might lead to his family.

The message from Mordechai had come late that afternoon: El-Masri was expected home shortly after midnight. Slaton arrived an hour early, and he saw few changes from his earlier reconnaissance. His position was less than ideal, but it seemed the best option in line with his objectives. The darkened recess lay between the detached garage and a small garden shed. The space was no more than two feet wide, and Slaton was forced to blade his body to make it work. There were spiderwebs and an old rake to push aside, and his feet were mired in mud. The garbage can at the top of the channel provided decent cover if he kneeled, although it was hardly necessary in nearly complete darkness. For all Slaton's advanced training in special tactics, he knew what any experienced operator knew: that in the real world, plans often digressed into something little removed from a common house burglary.

On this night, that was what the situation demanded.

The back of the house was roughly thirty feet away. From where he stood he could see the back door and every rear-facing window, and was close enough to hear two muffled voices engage in sporadic conversation—unfortunately in Arabic.

His position did have notable drawbacks.

Most obvious was the inverse of the hide's main advantage—he was *very* close to the house. That could backfire in any number of ways. There was a greater chance he might be seen or heard—and if that happened, there was no excuse for his presence that wasn't nefarious. He was operating on the assumption that the El-Masris didn't have a dog. He'd seen no evidence of it in the backyard—no chew toys strewn about, no freshly dug holes, no telltale brown piles. That put the odds in his favor, but Slaton never took it as a sure thing—not since he'd seen a deftly planned Mossad mission ruined by one thoroughly unnerved Pomeranian.

Another shortcoming was that he didn't have a view of the entire home. The north-facing wall and driveway were not visible from where he stood. A few steps toward the garbage can solved the problem, but it also highlighted him in the spray of a neighbor's floodlight.

Voices again from inside. A woman, motherly and directive. A muffled male response, grudging teen acquiescence. Tenors that were universal across languages.

This gave Slaton pause.

The true reason he'd arrived early had nothing to do with getting a better look at the house or a feel for the neighborhood. That was all established, having been set this afternoon by his earlier survey. What Slaton had wanted to mitigate was the one great complication. He was desperate to find his family, which meant pressing El-Masri for information—if the Egyptian didn't know where Christine and Davy were, he certainly knew who was responsible for their disappearance.

The problem: El-Masri had a family of his own. Slaton was determined not to involve them. Determined to defeat his enemies without becoming like them. The driveway, he'd decided, was his best hope.

He had checked the garage when he'd arrived, peering inside through a side window that was crusted with grime and the residue of a hard winter. In the scant light he saw the silhouette of the BMW that had been in the driveway earlier. There wasn't room for a second vehicle, which meant El-Masri would park outside—based on existing tire scrub marks, almost certainly on the driveway offshoot between the niche where he now stood and the back door. That small concrete pad, at the top of the L-shaped drive, became Slaton's area of tactical operation. The tiny battlefield where he would do what had to be done.

He envisioned intercepting El-Masri in the awkward moment when he climbed out of his car. The preferred option was to shove him back inside, occupy the back seat, and force him to drive to one of three quiet spots he'd already identified: the selection of which would be based on traffic and El-Masri's level of compliance. Slaton allowed five minutes for travel, ten more to get what he needed from the Egyptian by any means necessary. At that point Slaton's plan reached its end. He'd thought through a few contingencies, but without knowing what information El-Masri could provide, there was no point in taking it further.

An exterior light on the house suddenly snapped on, illuminating the rear driveway with the brilliance of a miniature sun. The back door opened and Slaton saw a young man appear. He was seventeen, plus or minus a year. Rail thin, he had a mop of black hair and was carrying a white plastic bag.

A trash bag.

Slaton took a knee behind the trash can. It was a bulky plastic item, four feet tall and two feet square, wheels and a handle on the backside. He heard light footsteps approach. Felt the can jostle once. Thankfully, the lid pivoted from the front on the hinges above Slaton's head—a detail he'd already noted that had just gone critical.

The big container rattled against his left shoulder. Something wet and granular slopped over the back, peppering his face and hair. By the smell, spent coffee grounds. The lid fell back into place. Slaton heard the boy mutter something in Arabic, an expletive he was sure—Mossad assassins had heard them all.

The footsteps receded. The door to the house opened again, then banged shut. The driveway light went out. Slaton listened closely, waiting for the distinctive *clunk* of a deadbolt tumbling into place. He never heard it, which wasn't surprising. Austria, after all, was a very safe country. Far more so than Egypt.

Slaton ventured a look. Everything was as it had been a minute earlier. The only difference—one more bag of kitchen waste in the garbage can. He drew in a deep breath, exhaled slowly, and checked the time.

12:21 a.m.

He watched.

He waited.

THIRTY-SEVEN

Slaton found himself thinking about the teenager. What if he came outside again?

From an operator's point of view, the boy was at an awkward age. If faced with an intruder, there was no telling how he would react. Would he bolt back inside the house? Or might he have a yellow belt in some martial art and try to be brave? There was a reason wars were fought by young men between the ages of seventeen and twenty-three. That was when they were fearless. Indestructible. The specific age at which that myth took hold varied, but this kid was definitely in the window.

I'll have to be careful, Slaton thought. *I should—*

His musings were interrupted by headlights sweeping across the side fence. He heard the purr of a big engine, tires squealing around a turn.

Right on schedule, a silver Audi coasted smoothly to a stop. Behind the wheel Slaton saw the profile of a dark-haired man wearing glasses. A face he had seen before on the IAEA leadership web page—researched that afternoon.

Tarek El-Masri. His best hope to find his family.

He edged closer to the entrance of the tiny passageway. Slaton was still in shadows, less than ten feet from the driver's-side door.

He planned his path carefully—around the right side of the garbage can, then left to reach the driver's door from the rear quarter. He would surprise El-Masri early, as his left leg swung out over the rocker panel. His cue would be the door opening. Slaton was in place, ready to move, yet the Egyptian seemed to hesitate.

Slaton was confident he hadn't been seen. Then he noticed a faint glow of light on El-Masri's face. He was checking his phone. A perfectly normal behavior. He made a mental note. *The phone would have to be secured.*

He kept waiting.

A few more seconds.

Then everything went to hell.

A second set of lights strobed across the side fence. Slaton saw a dark van rush up the driveway, the engine thundering as it careened wildly. It skidded to a stop in a perfect blocking position.

El-Masri's Audi was trapped.

Slaton watched two men scramble from the van's front doors. Three more burst from a sliding side door.

El-Masri saw it too. With surprising agility, he leapt from his car and bolted for the back door, shouting in Arabic as he went. He disappeared inside.

Slaton had his Glock in hand, but was frozen by the fast-moving situation.

The first two men rushed the back door in pursuit of El-Masri. Each was carrying what looked like a

Russian Vityaz-SN 9mm, distinctive with its pistol grip and thirty-round box magazine. None had suppressors. The three who'd bailed out the side door disappeared toward the front of the house. As far as Slaton could see, no one remained in the van—the kind of assumption one never relied upon.

He tried to make sense of it. Who were these men? The way they moved and handled their weapons told Slaton they were trained. The thickness in their torsos suggested body armor. He wondered if it could be some kind of police raid, a SWAT team here to apprehend El-Masri. Perhaps he and Mordechai weren't the only ones to have learned that a senior IAEA inspector was skimming uranium.

But that theory felt wrong. The van was beaten and worn—either freshly stolen or bought on the fly. A throwaway vehicle. That wasn't how special tactics teams operated. Then he considered the lack of any verbal warnings—nobody was shouting *"Police!"* or ordering El-Masri to surrender. Of the men near the back door, one wore night optics and a black knit beanie, so his face was largely obscured. Yet the other Slaton saw clearly in a spill of light. He was definitely Asian.

One of them spoke in a hushed voice. Chinese, Slaton thought. Possibly Korean. Neither case made sense. It all coursed through his head in a flash, and two truths crystallized. Tarek El-Masri, the key to finding his family, was inside the house.

And these men had come to kill him.

The two Asians paused at the back door. El-Masri had burst through moments ago, confirming that his son hadn't locked it. Yet El-Masri almost certainly had. Slaton watched an exchange of hand signals between the men, and one of them leveled his weapon while the other positioned to kick in the door.

To Slaton's eye, the door looked solid.

He moved quickly, silently, using the Audi for cover. He heard a distant crash—the front door giving way—and shouting from inside the house. The first kick on the back door failed, the man stumbling back. The second succeeded and the door slammed back on its hinges. In that moment, Slaton recognized his chance: both men had their undivided attention on the room they were clearing.

It is Hollywood fantasy that elite operators invariably shoot off-handed, or on a dead run from fifty yards. In reality, they never choose to engage while hanging upside down or in mid-leap between buildings. Not when more effective methods are available. Not when lives are on the line. What sets the best apart is far more mundane: they do the simple things well.

Very, very well.

Magazines are exchanged with incomprehensible speed. Recoil is little more than an ordinary rhythm. Clearing jammed weapons falls to second nature. From a hundred yards, with most weapons, a first-tier operator will rarely miss. Yet they prefer to be at ten, because that's where they've fired a million practice rounds. It is the ground they own.

Slaton engaged with precisely that mindset. He used the Audi as both cover and a stable platform. Situated seven yards behind his intended targets, and with the Glock in a comfortable two-handed grip, he addressed the figure in front who was advancing through the back door with his Vityaz sweeping left and right. Adjusting his aim-point to account for the body armor, he sent two rounds. The first struck his target in the neck, the second at the base of his skull. He dropped like a shotgunned pheasant.

His partner reacted quickly to Slaton's unsuppressed shots, spinning to locate some previously unknown threat.

Much to his detriment, he found it.

Slaton put him down instantly, two rounds grouped marginally beneath his night optic.

It was as simple as it was ruthless.

But then, there was no silver medal in a gunfight.

Slaton ran toward a door hanging on broken hinges, the Glock leading the way. He glanced at the two men as he passed, verifying there was no life in either. The sound of his shots would have registered with the front-door element. They might or might not realize they hadn't come from a Vityaz. Either way, they would know something wasn't going to plan.

As if to confirm the point, Slaton heard a muted burst of radio chatter. He looked more closely. Both men were wearing earpieces and tactical mics. Their lack of response would confirm something had gone wrong.

How many am I facing? That became the critical question. He had seen three men bail out of the van and move to the front door. Could there still be anyone in the van? Might there be a second vehicle, perhaps parked along the street? Slaton had seen and heard only the van, so the odds were good he was facing manageable numbers. But that was all he had—decent odds. If this were a Mossad mission, gambling for the good of Israel, Slaton might have pulled back to assess the tactical situation.

As it was—he had no choice. He *had* to interrogate El-Masri.

He retrieved a Vityaz from one of the dead men. It wasn't a high-end weapon, but reliable enough. The high rate of fire and big magazine gave it a brute-force edge over the Glock. Slaton checked the box mag, found it full. The fire selector above the trigger was set to "ОД", the semiautomatic setting—some ancient vestige of his training kicking in when he needed it.

He secured the Glock in his rear waistband and edged toward the main room. Stepping past the breached door, he entered the kitchen, clearing every space as he went. His senses were on high alert, processing every sound and sight and smell. He logged a heavy table that could be upended for cover. A large kitchen knife in the drying rack near the sink.

A sudden torrent of shouting broke the silence. It came from upstairs, cascading, Slaton knew, down the narrow stairwell in the main room—five steps ahead, then a ninety-degree turn to his left. Next came a crash, like a piece of furniture being over-turned. Something big and weighty, probably in the northern front bedroom. As he neared the main living area, Slaton was thankful to have the precise layout of the house in his head.

With that diagram in mind, he placed himself in his adversary's position for his next assessment: he allowed a fifty-fifty chance that one man had been stationed at the nearby front door. That put either two or three on the second floor. Everyone would have heard the shots downstairs. And they would know by now their rear element wasn't responding on the radio.

Slaton neared the threshold that connected to the main room. He peered carefully around the corner, the Vityaz ready, and saw the big street-facing window. The front door had caved and was flat on the living room carpet. The room itself was clear. No El-Masri. No wife or son. No hostiles. There was also no guard outside—at least, not in his field of view.

Another crash and a scream from upstairs. Then, sickeningly, the report of tightly spaced shots. Three groups of three echoing through the house. Slaton looked up the staircase, fearing the worst. He saw a shadow shift on the second-floor ceiling. Otherwise, nothing out of the ordinary.

Unless they were fools, they would have positioned one man there, covering the top landing. Slaton would have placed him to the right, where the wall gave solid cover. A position that commanded the top of the staircase.

He, however, owned the bottom.

It was a standoff of sorts. The men upstairs were trapped, facing a force of indeterminate size. Slaton was frozen below. He knew the numbers, but time wasn't on his side. Shots had been fired, and he needed El-Masri.

Needed him alive.

He looked pensively at the staircase. To go up was to die. He racked his brain for another way to reach the second floor. He considered the windows outside, the shape of the roof. He weighed how the physical situation had altered from the blueprint in his head. Slaton realized there might be one chance.

He kicked over a floor lamp, sending it tumbling into the main room. An attention-getter.

He quickly reversed into the kitchen. On the way to the door he noticed a stainless steel trash can. He grabbed it and set it on the slab outside the back door. He heaved the damaged door shut. It no longer seated properly in its frame, but he was able to wedge it into place. Which actually was ideal. He leaned the metal trash can against the outside of the door at a thirty-degree angle. If anyone pushed through, instant alarm.

Slaton ran flat out to the side of the house.

THIRTY-EIGHT

Slaton cleared the van first, found no one inside. He saw discarded clothing, a few water bottles, two ammo boxes—nothing that altered his perception of the situation. With a better angle, he looked out front and saw no suspicious vehicles in the street. His assumptions were holding. A team of five professionals had come to engage a family of three.

From El-Masri's point of view, hopeless numbers. As far as Slaton was concerned, however, the situation was improving: two down, three to go.

He saw a key with a fob dangling from the van's ignition. He removed it and put it in his pocket. A mistake on their part. But then, they hadn't been expecting any real opposition. They'd expected one stunned physicist, his wife, and a teenage son. He could hear the briefing now: *Get in, get out. One easy night.*

The Vityaz had a simple strap, and Slaton shifted the weapon behind his shoulder. He opened the passenger-side door of the van and laddered upward, stepping sequentially onto the running board, the dash, and finally the seat back. He hauled himself onto the roof of the van.

From there his plan evolved.

The driveway was close to the house, and he looked across at the nearest section of roof: four feet above the top of the van, the same horizontal gap. The roof was sharply pitched, but near the edge he saw a circular vent—a bathroom, he knew, lay directly below. The vent looked solid. A decent handhold.

What could go wrong?

From the far side of the van's roof, Slaton accelerated as best he could in two giant strides. He launched himself through the air at the rows of shingles, one hand reaching for the vent. He hit hard, his hips banging painfully on the edge, his legs dangling in midair. He reached the vent with his fingertips, but his first attempt to grasp it failed. With no purchase from below, he tried to stabilize himself, one elbow on the lip of the roof, the other hand clinging to the overhang. He tried to writhe higher and gained a few inches, enough to touch the vent. Taking a better grip on the roof's edge, he steadied himself momentarily before heaving upward. This time he got a handful of the vent—a solid cast-iron pipe. He worked himself upward, clambered over the edge, and got silently to his feet.

Slaton wasted no time, heading straight to the northern window. He ran in a crouch, trying for soft footfalls on the weathered shingles. His eyes never stopped moving—the small front yard, the street beyond, the van behind him. There had been no new sounds, and he feared he was too late—the tightly grouped shots weighed ominously.

Move faster!

He shouldered to the outer wall next to a four-pane window. The lace curtains were thankfully drawn open—as they'd been all day. Slaton readied the

Vityaz. He knew that the window fronted the master bedroom. There would be a doorway straight ahead, a bed to the left. He carefully leaned toward the nearest pane of glass.

What he saw caused his heart to sink.

There were three bodies on the floor. All lay still, and each was centered in a crimson pool. El-Masri and the boy he recognized immediately. The other was a middle-aged woman of Middle Eastern extraction.

Bastards!

Slaton felt an unfamiliar rage well up, something deep and irrepressible. El-Masri might have earned this, made himself a target. But not the others. The frustration he felt at losing El-Masri as a source of information was overwhelmed by the greater tragedy before him—and, if he were honest, the equivalency to his own situation. Whoever these men were, they had no hesitation in eliminating innocents.

Aside from the bodies, Slaton saw no one in the room. He imagined three men in the central hall, looking tentatively down the stairwell. Guns poised and listening. Debating who would go down on point. Or perhaps they were already on their way. Movement across the street caught his eye. A neighbor, an older woman framed in her front window. She was looking outside with a phone to her ear.

Time was becoming critical.

Slaton weighed his options. The easiest choice was egress. Move to the backside of the roof, get out the way he'd come in. Let three killers go free. Then logic began to intervene. These men had come to kill El-Masri, which meant they were almost certainly linked to the greater scheme. Linked to whoever had taken his family. It occurred to Slaton that this team might be a better source of information than El-Masri himself. One link closer in the chain. He made his decision without respect to justice or payback. At least that's what he told himself.

He eased lower along the roofline, and took a knee above the front door. He directed the barrel of the Vityaz menacingly downward. Below him was the brickwork leading to the front door. On any other day, the stonemason in him might have noted quarry-stone pavers in an edged herringbone pattern, an attractive bull-nose step fronting the threshold where the door had been.

As it was, Slaton waited with absolute stillness for one of two things.

The clatter of a metal trash can on the rear doorstep.

Or the appearance of three men directly below.

He didn't have to wait long.

THIRTY-NINE

The first thing Slaton saw was a sweeping gun barrel. The oscillations stopped abruptly, and he heard a flurry of hushed words, again in a decidedly Oriental dialect. The gun barrel lowered slightly and three men appeared. Cautious and alert.

Three heads swiveled left and right with the precision of a metronome.

Slaton's finger tensed. They paused as a group, and one backtracked toward the house. Slaton heard him trying to pull the ruined front door into place. He either succeeded or gave up, and soon Slaton was again looking down at three crowns of close-cropped black hair. All still scanning left and right. The lead man wore a night optic device. Apparently satisfied with what he saw, he quit scanning and rotated his glass up and away. They began walking toward the van.

As offensive scenarios went, the one before Slaton was among the most simple he'd ever seen. He was looking directly down at three unsuspecting targets. Two he would kill outright. The third had to be incapacitated. If there were more time, he might try to determine who was the commander. Unfortunately, in seconds all three would disappear around the side of the house.

He paired his rounds. The first two hit the leftmost man at the base of his neck. It certainly destroyed his spinal column, and he dropped as if crushed by some invisible force. The other two went rigid, a primal instinct—and exactly what Slaton expected. Before the first target had hit the ground, the right-hand man was suffering the same fate. Two bullets flew through the collar of his vest, no doubt tumbling as they decelerated, tearing bone and tissue, and rebounded off the inner faces of the hard plates. Armor having the opposite of its intended effect, the consequences surely fatal.

In an epiphany, the third man looked up. Yet before he could focus on the kneeling, shadowed figure on the roof, Slaton had sent two more rounds. In this case he aimed for the hips. One round hit, but the second missed as the man spun. He went flat on the ground, and Slaton put two more rounds high on his right arm—the man's strong side for shooting based on how he was holding his weapon.

Slaton paused to evaluate.

The first two killers were still. The third lay writhing in pain, his weapon beneath a contorted arm. Slaton put another round into his left shoulder. Nothing to do with malice. Everything to do with certainty.

The man groaned loudly, his movement slowing.

Without taking his eyes off his target, Slaton rotated his legs over the edge of the roof. He gripped the shingled edge with one hand and launched into space. His grip on the roof interrupted his fall—not completely, but enough that the remaining five-foot drop was manageable. He landed with bent knees on grass, rolling onto a hip for good measure. He sprang straight to his feet, and within seconds had a knee on the wounded man's chest.

There was little resistance. One foot kicked out, and the man's right arm rose slightly before dropping limp. His eyes were half-shut, blinking like a light bulb with a failing filament. Slaton checked his wounds. Blood was pooling fast on the pavers on one side—a major artery severed high in his right arm. Or perhaps fragments of the round had deflected off a bone or a Kevlar plate, taking a detour toward his heart.

Slaton felt no remorse. Not for a man who'd minutes ago taken part in killing three people, two of whom were noncombatants. Yet the man was fading fast—that hadn't been Slaton's intent. He'd always been good at the killing. But sometimes better than he wanted to be.

"Who do you work for?" he demanded, having no idea if the man spoke English.

A flutter of the lips, then his eyes drifted shut. He was breathing, but shallow ragged breaths.

"*Who?*" Slaton shouted.

No response. He didn't have long.

Slaton drew a sharp breath of his own, trying to hold steady against an onrushing sense of dread. In another situation he might have attributed his pause to the aftermath of battle, an ebb of adrenaline. Or even regret at the senseless loss of life. Yet the man dying beneath him seemed eerily symbolic. He wasn't watching one more soldier slip away—it was something far more precious.

He grabbed a fistful of the man's plate carrier, felt the armor beneath that had proved so ineffective. *"Where are my wife and son?"* he shouted ferociously. *"Where?"* He shook the man frantically, desperate for his eyes to open one last time. He only needed one minute. A few hard questions.

The eyes remained closed.

He put a finger to the man's carotid. No pulse at all.

"Dammit!"

Slaton's head sank low. He closed his eyes as disjointed thoughts caromed through his head. First El-Masri. Now this. Two failures on the same mission. Frustration went to anger. Anger to hopelessness. Slaton felt as if he were drowning, his body not responding. His thoughts faltered.

He tried to push it all away—there wasn't time.

Keep going! Find another way!

The sound of a distant engine brought him back.

He checked the street, saw it was clear. The lights of a car passed on a nearby side street and quickly disappeared.

Slaton weighed his situation. There were not yet any sirens approaching. He had only intended to incapacitate the third target. Get information, then leave him for the police. The minimum force necessary to get the job done. But no such outcome could ever be guaranteed. There were too many variables when bullets started to fly.

He released the vest. The limp body inside settled to the ground. Slaton began searching. Every pocket in the man's black cargo pants, every pouch on his vest. There was no ID, no phone. Only spare mags, a flashlight, a utility tool: the usual gear a professional would carry on such a mission. He glanced at the other two and knew it would be the same. Slaton was about to rise when something caught his eye. Clipped to the front of the man's vest was a small tube. The tip glistened in reflected light, like the eye of some tiny electronic viper.

A tactical camera.

By feel he traced the fiber-optic tube. It ended in a comm unit. Other wires led to a tactical mic and an earbud. Everything was still in place, and a faint red light shone on the transmitter. The unit was active. Slaton knew internal comm was standard in small units, thus the earbud and mic. Yet this device was fairly large, and the addition of a camera implied something else.

Something he might be able to use . . .

General Park could only stare at the video feed.

He sat in the SSD command center, deep inside the headquarters building in Pyongyang. The concept of what he was doing—watching one of his best tactical teams conduct a mission in Austria in real time—was an entirely new experience for Park. The Russians had given them the gear after years of asking, and this was the first mission to leverage the technology. Unfortunately, it was now a mission gone wrong.

The first images had been of success: Tarek El-Masri and his family, confirmed killed on the upper floor of their home. Park had nearly left the room at that point, but then the audio began picking up chatter about possible resistance. Now he was staring at a nightmare scenario.

On the eerie low-light feed before him were images of disaster. The lens of one of the two tactical cameras was being swept across the scene by some unseen hand. Three of his men lay bloody in front of El-Masri's house. The other two had not been heard from since the first moments of the mission. After completing the terrible panorama, the camera was redirected to a close-up of a very determined face.

Park sat staring at a man he'd never seen before, although he was quite sure he knew who it was—the legendary Mossad assassin. The man Mordechai had brought into the picture. David Slaton. He had sandy hair and a few days' growth of beard. The expression on his face was . . . resolute.

The killer lifted a microphone to his lips, put an earbud near one ear. He said, "Are we going to talk?"

The two technicians next to Park looked at him expectantly. One offered up a headset with a microphone. Park pushed it away without comment.

After what seemed an eternity—actually only ten seconds—the man in the video feed said, "No, I didn't think so. So you can just listen. I want my family's safe return. If it is not confirmed to me within forty-eight hours, through the messaging account you've already used to contact me, I will provide to multiple media outlets documentation of the theft of highly enriched uranium by Tarek El-Masri." The man looked up, away from the lens, and Park thought he could discern the alternating tones of a distant siren in the audio. The man re-addressed the camera. "Alternately, if my family is harmed . . . I will learn who you are. I will make it my life's mission to hunt you down, and I will not fail. Forty-eight hours."

The video failed suddenly and the audio feed went to a harsh white noise.

Park sat motionless for a time. He considered what he'd just seen, combining it with the intercepts he'd received only an hour ago—Bureau 121 making itself useful again. In addition to Mordechai's text to Mallorca, he'd sent another—presumably to Slaton—claiming to have uncovered damning information about El-Masri. The Bureau had seen that message, but there had been no chance to alter it.

Slaton.

He was becoming a tremendous complication. Based on what Park had just seen, his only interest was in finding his family. To that end, he'd gone after El-Masri—no doubt for information. *I should have predicted that,* Park thought. More pressingly, he wondered what Mordechai had uncovered. If there *was* hard evidence of their plot, it had to be controlled. He only needed a few more days . . .

"I must talk to Khang!" he barked.

There was a burst of typing by a tech at a nearby console. Thirty seconds later Park was given a standard phone handset.

The man named Khang had also been watching the video feed, and from only a few miles away. Park's muscular lieutenant, who'd served ably to this point, was situated in a rented farmhouse just outside Vienna. He had, in fact, planned tonight's operation—which made it that much more difficult to watch his men die.

Wrath was evident in his gravelly voice when he asked Park the obvious question.

"It can only be this assassin," Park answered. "The one Mordechai called in."

"The same man who eliminated the three Islamists in the park."

"That was a mistake on our part," Park said, a

surgeon unconcerned he'd lopped off the wrong leg. "We should never have used such fools."

"You had your reasons," Khang replied woodenly, reminding Park it had been his decision. The complications introduced by Mordechai had come on suddenly. Khang's team had not yet arrived in country, and Park insisted on hiring locals to quash the problem.

When Park didn't reply, Khang sensed he'd gone too far. He added, "If things had gone to plan in the park, it would have been simple for my team to clean up."

"But things *didn't* go to plan. Not in the park, and not tonight. This man is creating too many problems."

"Does it matter? Our primary mission in Vienna is complete. El-Masri has been eliminated—he was the threat."

"No longer," said Park. He explained Mordechai's claim of unearthing damaging information. And that Slaton also claimed to have it.

"One problem can be solved easily," said Khang. "But as to the other . . ."

Park let silence run. He himself had never been a field operative. He'd risen through the ranks of SSD not by cutting throats, but by cutthroat politicking. Even so, he knew men like Khang were sometimes necessary. And he knew there were times they should be listened to.

"Do you have any more information on Slaton?" asked the killer in Vienna.

"We've been working on it since he became involved. We believe him to be a former Mossad operative. Beyond that we've uncovered almost nothing.

Yet there is one possibility . . . he seems to believe we've taken his family."

"His family?"

"It's something I should have pursued sooner. We captured a communication stream between Mordechai and Slaton, and so we know how he was drawn into it—Mordechai arranged the disappearance of his wife and son. Yet we neglected to follow up. We waited too long to pick up their trail."

"Do you know where they are now?"

"Not precisely," said Park, "but the Bureau is getting close. They have been tracking a phone and a certain credit card in the Western Mediterranean. Can you finish things alone in Vienna?"

"Yes," Khang said confidently. He then added, "But I must ask . . . what about recovering my team?"

Park nearly blurted that he didn't give a damn about five men who'd failed. Then he remembered that soldiers could be an eccentric lot. They were oddly predisposed to retrieving their dead—some code-of-honor nonsense.

"Can they be identified as North Korean?"

"No. We entered the country separately, by way of Slovenia and Hungary. We have been staying in a farmhouse, very remote. Everything was arranged by an advance team who are all clear. The strike unit was sanitized for tonight's mission—mandatory for foreign operations. The police will find no identity documents, and of course there can be no biometric matches."

Park was always wary of overconfidence, but in this case Khang was right. It was one of the minor benefits of living in a totalitarian state—no one outside North Korea had access to national records. There was a chance the police could run DNA profiles, establish

Korean ancestry for the deceased team members, but that could just as easily point to their brothers in South Korea. The bodies outside El-Masri's home would prove completely untraceable—five men who might as well never have existed.

"No," Park decided. "We can't jeopardize the operation to repatriate the bodies."

Khang was silent, but didn't argue.

Park knew there would be a broader investigation of tonight's events, most relevantly into El-Masri's work and personal finances. He had already discounted the risk that presented. The Egyptian's misdeeds were always going to be uncovered sooner or later. Yet unless Mordechai or Slaton could give the authorities a head start, any investigation was going to plod along for weeks, or even months. By then it would be too late.

Park said, "I will instruct the Bureau to emphasize tracking down Slaton's family. Contact me once you've shut things down in Vienna. And use caution—Slaton is still nearby."

Khang's tone changed ever so subtly. "With all respect, sir . . . he has killed five of my men. The time is past for caution."

FORTY

Slaton got out of harm's way the same way he'd gone in. He scaled the rear wall of El-Masri's property and dropped into an adjoining backyard. It was a virtual junkyard of tires and old appliance shells. The windows of the attendant house had been dark all night, and he was quite sure it was unoccupied.

He ran flat-out for the first three minutes, distance more important than stealth. Only as he approached his car did he slow to a purposeful walk. The Renault was fast approaching its sell-by date for surveillance work. That was just as well—he would soon put Vienna behind him.

He found the car right where he'd left it, behind a small grocery store that had been closed for hours, but whose parking lot took overflow from a pub across the street. As he set out toward the main road, Slaton was overwhelmed by an avalanche of theories, new facts displacing old assumptions. His encounter two nights ago in the park had been with men of Middle Eastern extraction. Tonight, Asian involvement. A senior administrator at IAEA stood accused of thieving highly enriched uranium. Not coincidentally, El-Masri and his family had now been murdered.

Christine and Davy had never seemed so far away.

He steered the little car down an unknown street, his only destination being somewhere different. It seemed an apt metaphor for his life, and gave rise to an even more unthinkable idea.

What if I fail?

That was a question Slaton had never before asked. In his line of work, one that couldn't be allowed.

Certainly not here.

Not now.

He stepped down hard on the accelerator.

The Renault's feeble engine responded.

Why so many changes? Mordechai wondered as he stood by the chained-shut doors of an opera house.

For the last hour he had been getting a stream of text messages from Slaton. He'd instructed Mordechai to collect the information he had unearthed on El-Masri and bring it to a rendezvous.

The first meeting place given had been the southbound platform of the Schwedenplatz U-Bahn Station. Mordechai pocketed the flash drive and arrived within ten minutes. Seeing no sign of Slaton, he'd stood baffled on the platform, and forced himself to check the timetable now and again—as any normal person would. He thought it was a strange meeting place. There was hardly any traffic at this hour, and it seemed too public, too well monitored by cameras and police. He'd been staring forlornly at the entryway stairs when the next message buzzed on his phone.

And so began a breathless series of excursions. He had been sent, in turn, to a nearby park, the courtyard of a church, and finally this—the ticket kiosk of a closed opera house. Then, finally, as he stood winded beside locked doors through which the arias of Wagner had flowed only hours ago, Mordechai realized what was happening: it had to be a counter-surveillance routine of some kind.

He'd never had that kind of training, but he knew this was how it worked. He imagined Slaton watching him from a distant balcony or a darkened alley. Checking for tails, prepared to intervene. The thought was as reassuring as it was discomforting. The latter took hold when another text vibrated to his phone: Complications. Head home. Expect contact later this morning.

His nerves a wreck, Mordechai drew in a deep, long breath, like a swimmer about to dive the length of a pool. He set out back toward his flat, quick-stepping across vacant streets. No passing car escaped his eye. He gave a wide berth to a group of clubbing teenagers ambling by in an amorphous mass of giggling and playful shoving. It occurred to him that Slaton had said nothing about El-Masri. Mordechai had expected that he would force an encounter tonight, as soon as the Egyptian arrived home. Had Slaton decided to wait until tomorrow? Did he want to see what was on the flash drive first?

Questions tumbled in his head all the way to his flat.

FORTY-ONE

Mordechai entered his apartment and flicked on the light. He closed the door, threw the bolt, and leaned heavily into the wooden slab. He'd always thought it an extremely solid door, but never had he appreciated it more than in that moment. After catching his breath, he checked his phone—as he had five times on the way home.

No new messages.

It was nearly three in the morning. He pushed away from the door and looked wistfully toward his bedroom. He knew he could never sleep. It had been a desperately long day, and his stomach reminded him that he'd completely overlooked dinner. Over the course of the evening, he'd become increasingly consumed by the files he'd taken from El-Masri's desk. What he found in them was stunning, so much so that tonight, for the first time, Mordechai realized his original plan was shockingly shortsighted. The information was simply too important, the risk too great, to keep chasing his private agenda with Mossad.

He went to the refrigerator, opened it. Nothing piqued his interest. In the pantry he found a can of tuna and the tail of a loaf of bread. It would have to do. Minutes later he was sitting at the high-top counter, a wet tuna sandwich on a paper plate in front of him, wondering how Slaton would want to handle the trove of information. Suddenly the most dire of scenarios burst into his head. What if something had happened to Slaton? Successful as he'd been during his years with Mossad, everyone had their limits. He was destined to be a legend, but there was a price to having one's name inscribed on a wall.

Mordechai felt trapped between worlds. He had risen as a technician, strictly rear echelon. Yet he'd always felt he could relate to the operators, understand their needs. Only now did he see how much he'd been missing. In the field it wasn't about analyzing the latest satellite images or comm intercepts. It was about sleeping and eating when lives were at stake. About surviving to the next day.

At least I'm learning from the best, Mordechai thought.

It occurred to him that the memory stick was still in his pocket. He was reaching for the tiny flag-emblazoned drive when he noticed that the room seemed unusually cool. He also sensed more street noise than usual. *Or am I only imagining it?* He tapped his fingers on the counter as if playing a chord on a piano, and murmured to himself, "No . . . I'll never be cut out for this."

He walked across the room to the main window and looked outside. He saw what he always saw, albeit less of everything at three in the morning. Only a few lights glowed in the building across the street. Three floors down a lone taxi cruised past, and on the sidewalks a few people scurried through the chill night air.

For the first time Mordechai noticed the window. It was slightly ajar—less than an inch, but definitely cracked. He couldn't recall leaving it open, although he sometimes did in the winter—the flat's radiator had a mind of its own. He reached for the latches and saw the problem. The swiveling metal clasps weren't unfastened, they were simply . . . gone. Both above and below, he saw paired holes in the window frame where the latches had been. A shot of adrenaline surged as something else caught his eye—outside, a dark vertical line undulating gently in the breeze.

Mordechai heard a noise behind him. He turned and saw a man in the middle of the room. A powerfully built Asian in a tight black sweatshirt. Without thinking, Mordechai bolted on an angle toward the locked front door.

He never made it.

Slaton left Kapellerfeld with one immediate objective—to escape the scene of a crime. The chaos was miles behind him now, but he felt little relief. He was driving back toward Vienna, but what did it offer? A safe house that might no longer live up to its name?

He passed streets he'd never heard of, put city blocks behind him. At three in the morning Vienna was at its diastole. The sidewalks were largely empty. Street sweepers scrubbed the curbs because this was their chance. A few bartenders and nurses trudged wearily home.

Home.

In that moment, Slaton knew no such place. He felt impossibly adrift. Vienna, Danube Park, Kapellerfeld. At every juncture, one step forward, two steps back. He saw a stray dog trotting on the side-walk, nosing into the occasional trash can. A mutt with pointed ears and a tail like a question mark. Davy had been asking for a dog for his birthday. It was no easy thing, keeping a dog at sea, but it could be done. He and Christine had so far punted. But they knew the inevitability of the situation. Or so they'd thought.

Slaton slammed on the brakes. A red light at a cross street seemed to appear out of nowhere. He pulled in a deep breath, straightened his arms and pressed his palms against the wheel. There wasn't another car in sight. No pedestrians on the side-walk. He waited in compulsory stillness.

He recalled once hearing a pilot talk about be-ing "behind the power curve." That, he'd explained, was a place you didn't want to be. The reference came from the tendency of jet engines to accelerate slowly from idle thrust. To have power when you needed it, a pilot had to think ahead, predict what was coming. For the aviator who got behind, the interval from idle thrust to something productive could seem interminable. *And the more you need it, the longer it takes.*

That's where Slaton found himself—behind the curve. It was time to think ahead. Time to push away the frustrations of the last hour. He began with what he knew. Three Middle Eastern men in the park. An Asian hit squad. An Egyptian who'd stolen nuclear material. Mordechai.

Mordechai.

He looked down at his phone. Slaton had been elated to get the text verifying when El-Masri would arrive. At the time that had been his priority, so he'd given little thought to the rest of the message.

Now he looked at it again: Have extensive new information on El-Masri. Will provide when we meet again.

In that moment it had seemed secondary. Something they could address in the morning, after the night's dust settled. Slaton had expected to be able to interrogate El-Masri. Then he recalled Mordechai's promise this afternoon: *I will call you tonight.*

Only he never had.

Slaton felt a new unease. He'd been disoriented, turned in circles by the fog of battle. Or more precisely, by the prospect of losing the two people he loved more than any in the world. Now everything came together.

And when it did . . . he realized he'd made a massive mistake.

FORTY-TWO

Slaton's first inclination was to call Mordechai. The encounter at El-Masri's made him reconsider.

He parked a block away from Mordechai's flat in Landstrasse—he'd gotten the address earlier, but had not yet seen the place. It turned out to be a narrow residential building, five architecturally bland floors shouldered between a pair of similar structures, the one to the north being one floor smaller. From the vacant far sidewalk Slaton studied the building.

In diagraming El-Masri's home, he'd had both the time and resources for precision. This was different, an off-the-cuff evaluation. And while the results might be more speculative, they were no less vital.

The ability to survey structures in the field is an essential skill for a sniper. By virtue of his training, and more critically having spent countless hours behind optics, Slaton was something of an expert. Bombed-out hospitals, gleaming skyscrapers, lean-to hovels—all buildings could be viewed with certain expectations.

Freestanding homes were always the most difficult to gauge—private architects took maddening liberties in the name of artistic license, and owners had a penchant for off-the-books modifications.

Apartment buildings, on the other hand, were far easier to deconstruct. To begin, nearly all were repetitive, each floor hosting a certain number of flats. The floors also tended to mirror one another. Top-floor penthouses were the exception, particularly in buildings put up during the last forty years—the period in which developers realized that the increased cost of non-conformity was outweighed by premiums from ego-driven buyers.

Slaton diverted casually into the shadow of an entryway. The portico was on a diagonal from Mordechai's building and led to the locked entrance of a rising stairwell. A placard next to the door introduced a wealth management firm. If the door was unlocked before 8:00 a.m. Slaton would be stunned.

With an unobstructed view of the building, his first chore was to identify the correct unit—Mordechai lived in 304. The third floor seemed obvious, although caution had to be exercised—a handful of countries assumed the non-standard convention of having a "ground" floor to begin, and naming the second story the first floor. Thankfully, the organizational paradise that was Austria fell under no such delusions.

The building was relatively small, and Slaton saw only three units facing the street on each floor, distinguishable by paired windows—one large, presumably the main living area, and another for a bedroom. Having glimpsed the backside of Mordechai's building on arrival, he knew the arrangement there was similar. Simple enough—six flats on each floor, making 304 almost certainly a center unit. The only question: Was it in front or back?

Fortunately, this too was a matter of convention.

From the main entrance on any given floor, odd numbers were customarily assigned the left side of a hall, evens on the right. The main entrance in this case would be the elevator, and this too Slaton could distinguish. On the roof he saw two cinder-block structures. The one on the left was larger with a single access door and heavy electrical conduit—the equipment room for an elevator. The rectangular block to the right was smaller, a standard emergency stairwell providing roof access.

Altogether, it was no more than a series of deductions. Yet for Slaton it held value. He gave it an 80 percent chance that Paul Mordechai lived in the middle, third-floor, front-facing unit. A unit which, at that moment, had bright lights burning in both windows. At three o'clock in the morning.

Thin curtains had been drawn over both windows. A minor caution sign. Then Slaton's eye was caught by something more damning. It took a moment to even realize what it was—but once he recognized it, his suspicions were sealed beyond any doubt. From the roof of Mordechai's building, a thin black line snaked down to the main window of 304. If Slaton wasn't mistaken, an item of compound design with very high tensile strength.

A tactical rappelling rope.

Time seemed to accelerate, the implications clear.

For an operator, the ability to climb or descend along the side of a building is core curriculum. Freshman-year. A seventy-foot drop to the sidewalk aside, the primary risk in the set-up Slaton was looking at involved being seen by a bystander. Yet at this hour, on a quiet street, and with a bit of watchfulness—the risk would be minimal. Acceptable even, given the reward of easy access. Anyone well trained could make the drop in twenty seconds.

It didn't escape Slaton's notice that the line had been left in place, presumably as an egress option if things went sideways.

Which was precisely where he was going to send them.

Because leaving the line in place was a mistake.

Mordechai had never known such pain in his life.

His thoughts were disjointed, fading in and out of coherent function. Both his hands had been smashed, the bones crushed. It felt like his nose had been driven through his skull. He knew he'd passed out multiple times. Then it would all come back. The man pounding his face, shaking him back to consciousness long enough to ask a question or two. When no answers came—could he even speak if he tried?—the man invariably tilted the chair back and poured cold water up his shattered nose.

He tasted blood, smelled urine. A sensory nightmare of his own making.

He could see no more than shadows and shapes—one eye had knotted shut, and the other seemed blurred by something viscous and red. His tormentor, who was terribly strong, had bound him to a chair with some kind of rope. Mordechai knew he was North Korean. Not because the man had Asian features, but because Mordechai had been reading the files on El-Masri's flash drive.

The flash drive . . . he thought. *What if he finds—*

That hazy thought seemed to be struck from his head quite literally—something hard clouted his skull, just above the right ear. Mordechai saw bolts of white light. His head slumped, but he somehow clung to his senses. The questions kept coming, clumsy English that seemed oddly distant.

"Where is Slaton?"

Mordechai felt bile rise in his throat. He choked it down.

"Why are you working with him?"

Working . . . ? Who . . . ? Sensing a blow coming, his hands instinctively clenched. An agonizing mistake with so many crushed bones.

"Is Israel involved?"

Questions. So many questions . . .

Mordechai began fading again. Soon the spinning world disappeared.

And for the first time since it all began, he embraced the darkness.

FORTY-THREE

Slaton accessed the roof easily from an unlocked stairwell in the neighboring building. He found the black tactical rope anchored to the housing of a ventilation fan—directly over the window of what had to be Mordechai's flat. As expected, it was a good-quality line, composite weave nylon core with a polyester cover. He was glad for that given what he was about to attempt.

In climbing circles it was known as the Dülfersitz method. Absent any harness or hardware, the technique was used to lower oneself with nothing more than a single rope. The method was generally considered an emergency procedure, a last-ditch maneuver used by climbers or hikers to reach a safe place.

Slaton doubted very much that was where he was heading.

He routed the line carefully: between the legs, over the lower hip, across the chest, and over the upper shoulder. From there the line fed down to his guiding bottom hand. It was an awkward procedure, and he wished he had a pair of gloves. To the positive, he'd trained extensively in the technique, and, with a mere thirty-foot drop to negotiate, Slaton was sure he could make it work. The far greater problem: What would be waiting when he reached the window?

He stepped over the edge.

Hanging from the rope, with his boots firm against the building, Slaton was reminded of the last time he'd been similarly situated. Less than a month ago he'd raised himself up *Sirius'* mast in a bosun's chair to repair a loose spreader. On that day his only opposition had been a few gusts of wind, the North Atlantic Gyre having its way with the boat's rigging.

What a difference a few weeks make, he thought as he lowered himself in snatches down the sheer stone face.

The key to the method was maximizing contact points with the rope, effectively dispersing weight and minimizing friction. Slaton had mastered the technique wearing a full combat ruck, so that was in his favor. Tonight he was carrying nothing more than one Glock tucked securely under his belt. On the more sobering side—this wasn't training.

Passing the fourth floor, he got a good look at the window below. It was clearly cracked open, and as he closed in, with his feet nearly touching the upper frame of the window, he saw why—there were two sets of holes in the wooden frame where the latches had been removed. Whoever had gone in knew the basics. Exterior windows with no ground-floor access tended to be less secure—because less secure was cheaper, and builders cut corners to save money.

As he'd already done twice, Slaton checked the street for pedestrians. Then he scanned the windows of the opposing building for stunned faces. He saw neither. In truth, it wouldn't be a showstopper if he *were* to be seen. He expected to spend no more than two minutes in Mordechai's flat. Any more than that would mean something had gone wrong.

The rope was secured so as to be centered over the window. He searched for handholds on either side of the frame, and decided the best options were the window hinges themselves—a pair of six-inch-long mounts, upper and lower, jutting from the weathered brickwork.

When his boots touched the top of the window frame, he looped the rope twice around his lower wrist to anchor his vertical position. He bent his knees and pushed off to one side. Not unlike Davy working a swing, he shifted his momentum rhythmically, each cycle gaining separation to one side. With careful timing, he dropped far enough on the last oscillation to get a toe on the window bracket. Slaton twisted to steady himself there. He almost lost his balance, but corrected and dropped lower until he had a hand on the top window hinge. At that point, he was stabilized next to the window where he couldn't be seen from inside. He checked the line over his head. It now angled slightly toward the anchor point on the roof.

His first close look at the curtains was encouraging. They were still drawn, but made from a particularly sheer fabric. It was time to retrieve the Glock. This was no small feat—both his hands were busy on the rope. He contorted until his stronger right hand was free, then gripped the gun carefully—to drop it now would not only leave him unarmed, but the clatter on the sidewalk would announce his arrival like a doorbell. In that moment, had anyone been looking up from the street—and no one was—they would have seen something akin to Spider-Man with a rope and a 9mm.

Slaton got another break with the curtain—aside from its sheerness, it had been drawn closed tightly at the center, leaving a gap at the outer edge through which he could see much of the apartment. At that moment there was no one in sight. The layout looked typical: a main room, beyond that a compact kitchen, and a door to one side that was certainly the bedroom. Everything was brightly lit, the furnishings unremarkable.

What *was* remarkable was the condition of the place. It had been turned over in a reckless search—the kind people undertook when they wanted something badly and didn't care who knew. The contents of bookcases had been swept to the floor. Chair cushions lay askew, their fabric sliced open and foam shredded. Every cupboard door in the kitchen was open, and what had been on the shelves was now on the floor. Slaton saw a handgun on the island counter, a piece he couldn't identify from where he was, but some kind of mid-caliber semiautomatic. Next to that was a half-eaten sandwich.

He wondered about the gun. Might it be Mordechai's, perhaps turned up in the search? Or a careless intruder's? And how many intruders were there?

Slaton was still studying things when, through the partially open window, he heard a wet smack, skin-on-skin, followed by a moan. Moments later he saw a thickset Asian man emerge from the bedroom. He was a few inches shorter than Slaton, with an extremely muscular build—the physique of a competition body builder, all bulk and rigidity. His skin was like a husk, and there was an odd angle to the part in his hair. No, not a part, Slaton realized. An elongated scar across the crown of his scalp. As if someone had tried to split his head with a hatchet. *Scarhead.* More ominously, in an all too literal sense, the man had blood on his hands. He set a ball-peen hammer on the kitchen counter.

Slaton fought an urge to go in right then. As disturbing as the scene was, he had to pick his moment. Was the man working alone? Given his method of entry, it seemed likely. But an accomplice or two couldn't be ruled out. Either way, Slaton was looking at a sadistic man. The kind for whom throwing people under a bus wasn't metaphorical.

He twisted away from the window, keeping an eye on the gap in the curtain. The big man began searching the refrigerator, tossing a jug of milk and an egg carton on the floor. Slaton didn't know what he was looking for—not exactly—but he guessed it had to do with the message Mordechai sent. *Have extensive new information on El-Masri. Will provide when we meet again.* The fact that this man was Asian was damning in itself: he had to be tied to the bunch who'd murdered El-Masri and his family.

That didn't bode well for Mordechai, who was no doubt in the bedroom. Slaton was glad to have heard the moan—otherwise he wouldn't have given odds on Mordechai being alive.

There it is again, he thought. *Odds.*

Slaton was reasserting his grip on the window hinge when he got his worst break of the night. A police siren blared out of nowhere. He saw blue lights reflecting off a building on a cross-street. By their movement, he deemed the patrol car to be heading away, responding to some distant urban crisis. A regular occurrence in any big city. Unfortunately, the timing couldn't have been worse. The siren would naturally draw Scarhead's attention as well.

Through the gap in the curtain, Slaton watched

him turn away from the refrigerator and head toward the window.

Dangling tenuously against the outer wall, Slaton pushed as far away from the window as he could. Scarhead wouldn't be able to see him without getting very close to the window, and even then he would have to look to his right at an acute angle. He would easily discern that the police car wasn't a threat. Yet there was a far greater problem: he might realize that his rope, which had been dangling squarely outside the center of the window, was no longer in sight.

FORTY-FOUR

The best fight, Slaton knew, was the one you didn't have.

But sometimes that wasn't an option.

He edged closer to the window frame—if Scarhead noticed the missing line, Slaton *had* to know. He watched him stop two paces short of the window, saw him register the fading blue lights two streets away. That was followed by a half turn, and then . . . a distinct pause.

Slaton tensed his grip on the line.

Had Scarhead noticed the missing rope? Had he heard the muted sound of boots scuffing for purchase on the building's gray-brick frontage?

Whatever it was, Slaton saw him turn slowly back to the window. The look on his face, seen through the gap, was something frozen—a mental process caught in that awful abyss between alarm and indecision. Like a soldier realizing he'd just wandered into the middle of a minefield.

The next four seconds seemed like an eternity.

Slaton's initial impulse was to lean away from the window. That proved to be a mistake. The move only increased the strain on his hands, and left him helpless to direct the Glock with any accuracy. It also put him farther outside the center of gravity beneath the rope's high pivot point. Worse yet, by trying to back away from the window, he'd inadvertently committed himself to a return oscillation—one that would surely be seen. He made an instantaneous decision. Instead of trying to fight the physical forces, Slaton went all in.

He bent his knees and pushed hard off the wall, springing away from the stone face and arcing out in front of the window. He again tried to guide the Glock, but Newton's Third Law got the better of him—with the rope entwined tightly around him, his gun hand was pulled low and away. He couldn't train the barrel on his target.

He flew through the air like a bad circus act, all flailing limbs and opposing forces. To the man in the window, Slaton knew he would initially appear as no more than a shadow in the darkness. In a bad sign, the man was already reacting, setting a wide stance and raising his hands in a classically defensive posture.

Slaton had pushed himself eight feet away from the wall, but now he was heading back—accelerating like a human wrecking ball. In the moment before impact he prepared as best he could, feet together and knees bent. In the last instant he tucked his chin tight and turned his arms inward, protecting vital arteries from a smooth sheet of glass that was about to go to jagged shards.

The old window didn't so much shatter as explode. In a crystalline shower Slaton flew into the apartment. He'd closed his eyes on impact, but on his last look he'd seen a vector taking him straight at Scarhead. Sightless, he tried to time a two-legged kick at the man's head. He actually made contact, but not the decisive strike he'd wanted. Slaton crashed to the carpeted floor and immediately faced a new problem—he was hopelessly entangled in the climbing rope. He spotted the big man—he hadn't gone down, but he was off balance, righting himself near a bookcase.

Slaton tried to lift the Glock, but was again stymied by the rope. Scarhead recognized his advantage—he grabbed the line. With one great pull he sent Slaton into a half flip that spun him onto his stomach. Without time to look, Slaton tried to predict the man's next move. He rolled to one side, and in the next instant Scarface landed where he'd been. Yet it wasn't a complete failure—he locked onto a fistful of Slaton's shirt.

Slaton knew what was coming. Anybody so muscled would favor a close-in fight. He would want to incapacitate his opponent, a chokehold or breaking bones. Slaton himself was no stranger to close-in fights. He had the strength of a mason, hands that in recent years had become accustomed to cutting stone and hauling mortar.

He needed every bit of it.

Slaton landed a quick elbow to the man's nose. Scarface responded with a fist like a cinder block that glanced off Slaton's head. Scarhead rolled on top of him and seized the rappelling line—it had ended up at the base of Slaton's neck.

Recognizing what was coming, Slaton thrust his left hand under the line in the instant it went taut. The Asian tried to twist the rope into a nylon garrote. It worked to a point, but Slaton's hand kept the worst of the pressure off his windpipe. Scarhead's face went crimson as he strained to finish the job, veins bulging in his neck. Slaton's left hand was getting crushed and his shoulders were pinned to the floor. He wondered how long he could last. Would his hand go numb, become ineffective? Or would the Asian get impatient and try something new?

Slaton knew he had to change the dynamic.

Fortunately, he had more than raw strength—he had some of the best training in the world. While his left hand was striving to keep an airway, his right, which had ended up twisted behind his back, began working. Through all the chaos, the Glock was still in his grip—the Asian probably didn't even know he had a weapon. Trapped beneath the small of his back, the gun's grip was squarely in his hand, but canted with the trigger out of reach.

Slaton spread his legs wide for stability.

Scarhead responded accordingly, like a wrestler expecting a reversal from his opponent.

Slaton had to build space behind his back, the slightest gap in which he could maneuver. His left hand was going numb, nerves pressed to bone, circulation nearly stopped. His right hand was relentless, determined to not lose control of the Glock. Searching for the trigger guard. Finally, after one great shift of his hips, he felt it.

Proficiency with any weapon is a perishable skill, and owing to his newfound seafaring lifestyle, Slaton hadn't visited a firing range in months. Fortunately, the thoroughness of nearly two decades saved him. He'd learned to shoot from countless stances in training. A lesser but notable number in operational settings. Left-handed, right-handed, every imaginable grip from every conceivable position. Including, thankfully, "point-shooting" blind from his hip.

The main complication involved targeting—you had to aim not by sight, but by feel. With the gun against his hip, Slaton altered his grip to extend his trigger finger along the lower frame for a reference while curling his middle finger on the trigger. The Glock became an extension of his hand. The second problem was estimating where his target was vulnerable.

With his left hand quivering beneath the wrenched nylon rope, Slaton pulled the trigger. The Glock answered, sending a round low and toward the only available part of his target—his lower leg.

The first thing he saw was surprise in the face above him. That was followed by a grimace. The second shot produced what he wanted—desperation. Now it was Scarhead who needed to change the situation.

Slaton fired a third time, still aiming for the man's legs. Hoping like hell he didn't shoot himself in the foot.

When Scarhead released his grip on the climbing rope, Slaton knew he'd scored at least one hit. The relief on his crushed left hand was instantaneous. The Asian rolled clear and attacked Slaton's right side, seeking the gun. Slaton predicted the move, and rolled in the same direction—the same essential move practiced by every street cop in the world. *Protect your weapon above all else.*

With his grappling getting him nowhere, Scarhead suddenly changed tactics. He leapt to his feet. Slaton expected him to go for the gun on the counter. Instead he stumbled toward the door.

The ropes had loosened from all the twisting. Slaton could move again.

He freed himself from the line and leapt to his

feet as the big man disappeared. Slaton ran to the door, the Glock ready, and paused at the threshold to clear the space outside. He looked down the short hallway just in time to see Scarhead disappearing into the stairwell. There was no chance for a shot.

He ran a decision matrix.

Pursue?

The Asian had been limping badly, and a heavy trail of blood on the hallway runner would make him easy to track. Slaton looked down and saw blood on his own arm, felt a searing pain in his right thigh. Two gashes, almost certainly from broken glass. He checked each to make sure there was no arterial involvement. The lacerations were deep, particularly the one on his leg, but didn't appear life-threatening. He shook out his crushed left hand, flexing it twice into a fist. Everything seemed to work. Circulation was returning.

With one last look down the hall, Slaton turned back inside, shut the door, and threw the bolt.

He ran to the bedroom.

FORTY-FIVE

He found Mordechai on the floor. He was bound to
a chair and had been beaten savagely, his face a crimson horror. A belly wound was bleeding profusely,
and one of his hands covered it instinctively. His
skin had gone pale and his eyes were closed. Wispy
breaths carried through lips that were trembling
uncontrollably. Slaton glanced at the room around
him. It looked like a Laundromat had exploded.

The first thing he did was pull out his phone and
call 112, the emergency number in Europe. He gave
the address and said an ambulance was needed immediately. He hung up before answering the operator's questions. Hurrying to the kitchen, he pulled
a clean dishrag from the counter and a steak knife
from a drawer. He used the knife to sever the ropes
binding Mordechai to the chair—short segments of
the same line he'd rappelled down minutes earlier.

He lifted Mordechai's hand and pressed the rag to
the worst of his wounds. It was like putting a Band-
Aid on a colander.

"It's okay," Slaton said. "You're going to be all
right."

Mordechai's eyes cracked open, the barest of slits.

"I wanted . . ." he croaked wetly, "I only wanted to go back."

"Go back where?"

"Mossad. I wanted back in and . . . and this was my ticket. When I saw what El-Masri was doing, I wanted to run an op."

Slaton stared at him, trying to understand. He looked again at the belly wound, then noticed a bloody knife nearby on the floor. He'd undergone extensive training in combat field medicine, both care under fire and evacuation prep. Enough to know there was nothing more he could do. Not without pressure bandages or clotting agents or plasma. Mordechai's only chance was a rocket-like response by emergency services.

"Hang in there. Help is on the way."

Mordechai's head slumped to one side, then suddenly righted. "There's something you should know," he said, coughing weakly. Blood dribbled from one corner of his mouth. If nothing else, Slaton wished he had a dose of morphine or fentanyl.

"Your family," Mordechai said, "they're okay. Park doesn't have them."

"Who's Park?"

"The stick . . . look at the stick. I tricked your wife into thinking I was you . . . the phone you shared. I told her to buy a new one and go into hiding. She's out there, still moving. They're okay . . ." His voice faded and his eyes fluttered closed.

Slaton tried to make sense of it. His family in hiding? "You took over our private comm? You gave her instructions in my place?"

Mordechai's eyes opened again—this time in pain, agony seizing his every fiber.

"How do I get in touch with her?" Slaton implored.

"The stick," Mordechai repeated.

Slaton again heard sirens—a recurring theme tonight. This time, hopefully, because he'd summoned them himself. "Where?" he asked. "Where is the stick?"

Mordechai opened his mouth as if to say something but no sound came forth. His right hand came near his lips. Then, suddenly, his eyes glazed over like a machine that had lost power. Slaton checked his carotid. There was no pulse.

He closed his eyes briefly, said a silent prayer. As he'd done too many times before.

The sirens were nearing. Slaton stood and scanned the room. *A stick?* The man was an engineer—he had to be talking about a flash drive. But where?

He rushed to the kitchen where he'd seen a laptop. There was no data stick in any of the ports. One siren arriving, a squeal of tires. Blue lights rolled over the façade of the building opposite like a spastic lighthouse beam. Slaton rifled through drawers that were already open, pushed aside magazines on the counter. He didn't see a flash drive anywhere.

Scarface had been looking too. Might he have already found it? Slaton saw a jacket on a hook by the door. He rushed to it and searched every pocket. Nothing. He paused, recalling Mordechai opening his mouth.

Had he been trying to say something?

No . . . his hand had nearly touched his lips.

Slaton looked at the kitchen counter, saw a half-eaten tuna sandwich. He rushed over and lifted the remains of the sandwich. Beneath it was a small flash drive decorated with an Egyptian flag. One word was scrawled on the side: INSURANCE.

Shouted commands echoed in through the shattered window. Slaton pocketed the drive, took one last look through the bedroom door. Poor Mordechai. He had wanted to get back in Mossad. To be involved in operations. Wanted it so bad he'd put Slaton and his family at risk.

. . . this was my ticket. When I saw what El-Masri was doing, I wanted to run an op.

And so he had.

Slaton turned and ran through the front door. He headed for the stairwell, retracing the bloody trail across a carpet drawn in floral tones—pink and jade and lavender. Past the fire door he saw the glistening trail continue down the steps.

Slaton turned the other way. He climbed quickly, and on reaching the roof he backtracked the way he'd come, across to the neighboring building and down its tight stairwell. He reached ground level in less than a minute, exited through the back door, and rushed into the night.

FORTY-SIX

"How do they survive so far from land?" asked Sami, who was standing at the helm.

Boutros pulled his eyes away from the chart. He looked up and saw a lone bird circling overhead, a tern perhaps, some Pacific species he was not familiar with. The creature seemed unfazed by the gusting wind, its unmoving wings holding it effortlessly in a clear sky. Boutros cocked his head indifferently, then readdressed the map. "They come because the fish are here," he said distractedly.

"But there is no land for hundreds of miles. Don't they need a branch on which to rest? A place to build a nest?"

Boutros again forced his eyes up. This time he looked at Sami. He was staring at the bird with the wonder of youth, that naked curiosity through which one builds opinions on the mysteries of life. Given their circumstances, it seemed entirely pointless.

Unable to come up with a sage rejoinder, he said, "I am going below to see Rafiq."

Boutros stepped into the gloom of the lower deck and found Rafiq where he'd been most of the voyage, in the makeshift workroom. As Boutros came in, Rafiq was hanging a long-sleeve shirt on a peg near the bench—he typically wore only an undershirt when he worked.

Rafiq picked up a device of some sort from the bench—it was the size of a lunch box and had a probe connected by a cord.

"What is that?" Boutros asked, announcing his presence.

Rafiq's eyes flicked up in mild surprise. On such a small boat, he was learning, there was no such thing as privacy. "A Geiger counter—it measures radiation."

Boutros went closer. On the box he saw a gauge with a needle. Rafiq ran the probe across various points in the workshop. When it finally came near the heavy steel container the needle jumped suddenly.

Boutros stiffened ever so slightly. He had witnessed more danger in the last few years than most men saw in a lifetime. Yet the hazards of Iraq and Syria were tangible in their manifestations. Lead, shrapnel, fire. Even Assad's chlorine bombs one could see coming—the deadly yellow-green mist falling ominously from the sky. Here Boutros sensed a different kind of threat, one that could not be seen or heard or smelled. One that killed silently, slowly, and with profound certainness. Something about it seemed innately evil. But then, he supposed that was part of its effectiveness—not one fleeting burst of carnage, but a weapon to instill fear that would last a lifetime.

"How much material is inside?" he asked, pointing to the barrel's end, which already contained a perfectly machined cylinder of highly enriched uranium.

"Less than half of what we need for a viable bomb," replied Rafiq.

"But the rest we will have soon."

"So General Park tells us."

Boutros stepped back. "It doesn't seem enough for such a great explosion."

Rafiq set the Geiger counter on a bench. "When it comes to nuclear bombs, 'enough' is a relative term. This target cylinder contains sixteen kilos of HEU—perhaps enough to fill a few beer cans. The next batch will contain slightly more."

"A six-pack?"

Rafiq grinned. Even for Islamic fundamentalists, it was a reference they could all imagine. He went on, "Surrounding our target cylinder is the neutron initiator. To achieve critical mass, there must be a flood of neutrons in a very short period of time. The initiator, which is made of polonium and beryllium, releases additional neutrons when the two masses collide. And as I mentioned earlier, there is a graphite tamper to further contain the neutrons."

"It sounds complicated," Boutros remarked.

"Actually, once everything is in place, the operation is quite simple. The remaining uranium will consist of six rings—donuts if you will—that must be installed at the breech end of the barrel. Once I have done that, the rest will be up to Saleem." He put all ten fingertips together and burst them outward. "Boom!"

"What kind of explosives will he be using?" Boutros asked. This was more familiar ground for an ISIS commander.

"Czech Semtex—a batch acquired from a group in Libya. Saleem has worked a great deal with Semtex, and he was given instructions on how to shape the charge for maximum effectiveness. The explosion will drive the rings up the tube and into the core, initiating the chain reaction."

"What could go wrong?" Boutros inquired. As a commander, it was a question he always asked.

Rafiq thought about it. "I am an engineer, not a physicist. But from my readings, I gather the most common problem is for things to happen too slowly. If the explosion is not forceful enough, the two masses collide with insufficient speed, starting the reaction prematurely. Everything is blown apart before it reaches a supercritical state."

"So the tube explodes before an atomic blast is achieved?"

"Something like that. This device is the product of years of research by the North Koreans. Ultimately, they gave up on uranium gun-type devices—it's the most reliable method, but could never be mounted on top of a ballistic missile. For that one needs a smaller implosion warhead, which requires plutonium. According to the technician who briefed me, the Koreans built this device early in their program, and for years they've wondered what to do with it."

"Now they have decided," said Boutros. "They have given it to us."

Rafiq nodded. "A turnkey operation."

"Will that not be suspicious?"

"What do you mean?"

"In the aftermath . . . will it not be said that ISIS could never have built this alone?"

"It would not be impossible. With enough time, enough money, anyone can fashion such a bomb. The difficulty is in acquiring weapons-grade uranium."

"Yet after this bomb explodes, I am told traces

of the material can be identified. How can we take credit if that points to the North Koreans?"

Rafiq cast his eyes down at his wrench. "That is the part I have yet to understand. The Koreans assured us they would be able to deny any involvement. They must be supremely confident about that—otherwise, they would be inviting a nuclear response by the United States. I suspect the final shipment of material will somehow absolve them of responsibility."

Boutros remembered these Korean promises from the planning meetings—ISIS would get sole credit for the strike. He had never understood the details, yet Rafiq seemed convinced. And on technical matters, Boutros trusted his judgment. "Very well," he said.

Rafiq lifted the lid of a toolbox and extracted a wrench. Boutros decided to leave him to his work.

As he was walking away, he again noticed the shirt on the peg—in the breast pocket was a letter. The envelope was creased and wrinkled, as if it had been opened many times. He could just make out an old postmark. The unit commander in him wanted to take a closer look. The sea captain thought otherwise. What little privacy could be had was to be respected.

He walked down the companionway to the galley. There he found a half pot of coffee on the burner. It looked like something drained from the engine sump. Still, Boutros decided he needed a lift. He plucked a Styrofoam cup from a stack.

As he filled it he looked around the room. In one corner were neatly rolled prayer rugs, and next to the sink a wash basin and clean towels—necessary for the ablution. This was where Sami and Saleem prayed.

Boutros sometimes envied such men.

There were two essential camps in the caliphate. Most obvious were the ardent jihadists, men like Sami and Saleem who ran at death with their willful conviction. Yet others were less fervent, men and women who were deeply religious, but whose motivation to fight was sourced elsewhere. He and Rafiq fell in that category.

He took his first sip, found it lukewarm and bitter. Boutros added some powdered creamer, began stirring with a plastic spoon. He found himself thinking about Rafiq. He was the most highly educated of them all. Unfortunately, education counted for little these days in Syria. Even with the government taking charge, the country was better fitted to gangsters and black marketeers than scientists. He knew Rafiq had no wife or children. He also knew that he'd seen little direct fighting in the war—yet by all accounts, he'd made himself useful behind the lines. The caliphate, no doubt, needed such men. Needed them to keep power grids running and sewers from overflowing. To keep mobile towers connected so that the word of jihad could be spread across the world.

He found himself staring at the two rugs. He had seen Rafiq pray once or twice, but not like the others. Not like the martyrs who seemed to treat piety as a kind of competition. He felt an unease, although couldn't put his finger on the source. Rafiq? Sami and Saleem? Or was it something to do with himself?

The coffee was unsalvageable. Boutros dumped it in the sink and set a new batch brewing. He would have Sami bring him a cup at the helm later. Boutros zipped up his jacket and started up the stairs.

FORTY-SEVEN

Slaton drove fast and west out of Vienna, the Renault darting through Salzburg and skirting the Bavarian Alps. The sun was barely a glow in his mirror when he crossed uneventfully into Germany. There he rounded Berchtesgaden, where Hitler's Nazi Party had established its alternate Chancellery, and where the infamous Eagle's Nest lorded high on a summit. Soon townships gave way to forest, and Slaton found himself on a minor road in thickening woods, skirting the Bavarian National Park.

He steered the car around hairpin turns and through the occasional tunnel. His thoughts seemed to correspond—alternately veering and darkening. Most dominant was Mordechai's dying confession: that he had drawn Slaton into his personal plot to return to Mossad's good graces.

I wanted to run an op.

Mordechai had managed to establish a communication link with Christine, assuming Slaton's identity in their last-ditch connection. He ignored any regrets about letting it happen to concentrate on more pressing questions. Where were they now? Still in hiding? Or had this far-reaching Asian contingent become involved?

With each passing mile his desperation mounted, like a wave driving into ever-shallowing water. He knew the police in Vienna would eventually make progress. There was always a chance his face had been caught by a camera he hadn't noticed. Or perhaps a neighbor had seen him leaving one of the murder scenes. This alone was something of a personal best—or worst, depending on point of view. To be involved in two deadly incidents within a matter of hours. In both cases he'd tried to intervene. Tried to keep killers from doing their job. In both cases he'd been too late.

The wave climbed higher. Cresting in a way he couldn't control.

Slaton needed to find out what was on the flash drive. But first he had other priorities. To begin, he needed freedom to operate. It was time to ditch the Renault. Munich, he decided, was the best place for a tactical reset. One more hour west. He would abandon the car outside town, take a train the rest of the way. Blend in with the early commuters. In Munich he could find everything he needed. A computer, web access, all manner of transportation. It was time to burn the identity he'd been using and assume that of his last passport. This was a Canadian item. Thomas La Pierre of Edmonton, Alberta. Importer of fine European stone. *Keep with what you know. Operate from bases of fact.*

With a rough plan in place, Slaton decided there was time for some desperately needed rest. Two hours, no more. It was not a random number. His sleep cycle had once been clinically determined by Mossad. Every individual has unique rest patterns, and the agency wanted its assassins, who could spend countless hours in wait of a target, to know both the limits of their endurance, and the length of time needed for one restorative cycle of deep sleep. Slaton's personal recharge: one hundred and fifteen minutes. He'd initially been skeptical of the idea, but having applied it over the years he found it unerringly accurate.

He began scouting sidings and service roads, and eventually chose what seemed an inviting path. Little more than two gravel ruts separated by a line of dead weeds, the road was a challenge for the Renault. What would be potholes in the summer had gone to pockets of ice, and shallow rivers of snow lined either side of the raised roadbed. The trail curved through trees and ended at a small tarmac parking apron. All around were the remnants of some bygone construction project—a few rusted pipes, scrapped sections of guardrail.

Slaton K-turned to leave the car facing back toward the main road. He left the keys in the ignition and climbed into the back seat. He rolled up his jacket for a pillow, put the Glock in the seat back pocket, situated for his preferred right-hand grip.

He closed his eyes with deliberate slowness, intending to mentally sketch his next five moves. He was fast asleep by number two.

One hundred and fifteen minutes.

The palace was officially referred to as Residence Number 55, a name whose provenance—rather like the bunkers of the People's Strategic Rocket Forces—was of dubious numerical merit. Situated eight miles northeast of central Pyongyang, the residence borders the fringes of the Ryongsong district. Through the vision of the people's architect, the palace lies centered in a pleasantly wooded glade, ostensibly because its occupant was a lover of nature, although among the select few who worked inside, and who knew its ostentatious scale and luxurious accouterments, the quiet theory floated that the surrounding forests had more to do with the concealment of riches than bonding with fauna.

Among the trappings was a swimming pool with a water slide on which Dear Leader himself enjoyed the occasional splash during summer. The adjacent running track, on the other hand, had never been graced by his presence, nor the nearby athletic field. A shooting range saw limited use, which was just as well for the traitorous exemplars who took the place of paper targets. The locals outside the high fence referred to the palace as the People's Luxury Mansion, a peculiarly contrarian label that was as accurate in fact as it was at odds with any classic view of communist ideology. Even so, with the shooting range in the back of everyone's mind, few complaints were lodged.

General Park made his way down a long corridor in the massive main residence, his aggravation evident as he passed between paintings that might have been credited to Old World masters, and beneath crystalline chandeliers the size of cars. He was irritated he'd been forced to go through three security stations to get this far. Park no longer carried a weapon. He had done so many years ago, as a rising young officer eager to impress, yet he'd advanced to a point in his career where others could be relied upon for that sort of thing. He was now the senior officer others tried to impress.

The final anteroom was a gilded cavern of silk and tapestry. Here, he knew, the final indignity awaited.

He was frisked by two separate officers—one straight after the other, and each man being watched by a supervisor. Park had been through the drill many times, yet he always marveled at the implied mistrustfulness. Here he was, a former army general and now head of SSD, North Korean state security, and even *he* was made to go through the motions. It smacked of paranoia, of the deep-seated mistrust Chairman Kwon assigned to even those duty-bound to protect him.

Park looked about the great foyer. He saw six members of the chairman's personal security detail. He knew there were between eight and ten others nearby, guarding other entrances and waiting in reserve. Those in front of him looked serious and competent, each acutely alert—no doubt more than usual due to his arrival. Park had screened every one of these men, plucked them from elite military units. As head of SSD, he knew the security measures of the palace better than anyone on earth. Most disquieting among them: at each shift change, firearms were handed out randomly to the oncoming detail. Only one in three contained live rounds, the others being loaded with blank cartridges. In Park's opinion, it was one of Kwon's most unsound initiatives. Fearing a rogue agent inside his protective circle, he'd decided the scheme bettered his odds. Decided it introduced a calculus of failure into any lone-wolf plot. The security men had all been briefed on the situation—which of course was entirely the point. There was grumbling, Park knew, but only one man had ever formally complained. Kwon got wind of it, and the man had never been heard from again.

He was finally cleared. The two unsmiling men at the door stepped aside.

Park wondered if it was that stoicism, the unswerving masking of what was beneath, that had driven the Chairman's scheme in the issuance of bullets. As twin doors opened in unison, he stepped through and thought, *Then again, maybe the man has a point.*

FORTY-EIGHT

Park was greeted by a stunning woman in a white servant's coat and knee-length skirt. She smiled like the hostess of an upscale restaurant, bowed once, and ushered him forward. He mounted a long red runner whose hue, he'd always thought, conveyed all the humbleness and dignity of a Macau casino.

The room was less an office than a stage. Each picture, each piece of furniture, had been chosen for a certain image and posed accordingly. The familiar, and surprisingly modest, mahogany desk was a case in point. Park supposed it was a deliberate nod to the working class, yet he thought it wholly inadequate for a man who served not only as Supreme Leader of North Korea, but also Chairman of the Workers' Party, Chairman of the Politburo, Chairman of the Central Military Commission, Marshall of the Republic, and Supreme Commander of the Korean People's Army.

A busy man indeed.

Kwon Il-sun was a rather short, rotund man, with pale skin that magnified his youth. He was dressed in an impeccably pressed dark tunic and pants. He wore no jewelry or accessories, which had always struck Park as odd—he knew Kwon regularly sent emissaries on shopping trips to Beijing and Hong Kong where they would spend millions of dollars on jewelry and watches. Where it all ended up Park had no idea—but then, such were the mysteries of the Kwon dynasty.

As Park approached, the chairman was busy writing at his desk. When he finally looked up, Park felt his first moment of true unease.

Kwon rose and greeted Park joyously. A hands-on-the-shoulders embrace, a gleeful smile. Kwon led him by the hand to the wide sitting area. The chairs there were the deepest in the room, with traditional upholstery depicting bamboo and birds. They took opposing seats, and Kwon sat looking at him expectantly. A child waiting for the start of his favorite show.

Today, apparently, it was the happy dictator.

Park was relieved—one never knew what to expect. The Supreme Leader's public persona was cast unerringly: in every published picture and video, he was the man now in front of Park. The one who found delight in everything from school choirs to ICBM launches. In those imageries, he was invariably sided by clapping, ever-smiling minions who walked the fine line between sharing their leader's bliss and standing in awe of his leadership. Park, being one of the few true insiders, had seen the other side. Seen the stare that would turn coal into diamonds. Seen the executioner who showed mercy to neither friend or foe. Or for that matter, family.

The attractive woman disappeared, and in her place came another who might have been a clone, perhaps a slight variation in the length of her hair. She too was clad in a white coat and skirt, and her effortless advance with a tray of tea and scones would have passed muster in Buckingham Palace. She set the tray between them and, without being asked, poured two cups of tea. The clone disappeared in a whorl of white silk and a whiff of jasmine.

Kwon plucked up a scone and bit into it carelessly, crumbs dribbling across his faultlessly fitted tunic. He said, "General Gae tells me you have sent a team to Vienna."

Gae was the head of military intelligence—Park had long come to think of him as more a nuisance than a rival. The man was a plodder who'd risen by family ties more than merit—his mother was a cousin to the dynasty. Still, Gae had resources, and more troublingly, he was outside Park's chain of authority. Which was why Kwon had brought it up— stirring a bit of healthy infighting.

"Military intelligence is useful close to home," Park said. "They'll tell you what is happening at American air bases in the South, or with our friends in China. But yes, I sent a few men to Vienna. It is only a minor operation. There have been reports that some of our expatriate workers in Eastern Europe are skimming their wages before transferring them home. I thought a private word might convince them this would not be in their best interests . . . nor that of their families."

Kwon gave a shrug, then used a fingernail to pluck something from an eyetooth. "What about the show we planned for the Americans? Have we been keeping open the doors of the right caves?"

He was referring to an ongoing campaign: manipulating which elements of their nuclear program should be put on display to enemy reconnaissance. North Korea's nuclear means had long been a guessing game for the West. Park was one of the few who knew the truth: on that day, they had to their credit thirty-one viable nuclear weapons. The count put them light-years beyond South Korea, who wasn't even in the game. Yet not yet in a league with Pakistan, and nowhere near the Chinese. The drive to catch up was ceaseless, draining resources that could better be used elsewhere. As for the Americans, they had their intelligence estimates, but a bit of showmanship to magnify what truly existed was undeniably economical, notwithstanding that it became a self-fulfilling prophecy. Much like rainbows, the splendor of nuclear weapons was a vision with no apparent end.

"We are managing things as best we can," said Park. "The Americans' satellites are predictable, but their spy planes less so. We believe they have a new hypersonic aircraft that can span our country in a matter of minutes." Kwon's carefree demeanor seemed to sink, and Park sensed an error. "But we don't think it can deliver any kind of weapon," he added quickly, and without regard to facts—a recent study by the army's technology division had suggested quite the opposite.

It was no use—Kwon's mood had flipped. "We have been in an appeasement mode for too long," he complained. "The Americans talk freely of reunification, yet they say nothing about lifting sanctions. As my father often said, 'It is time to make life difficult for another American president.'"

"I agree."

"What do you propose?"

Park tried to appear thoughtful, not believing his good fortune. He touched two fingers pensively to his lips. "I think we must show strength," he said.

"A threat with our nuclear weapons?"

"Yes, but . . . something indirect. Perhaps a new capability, one the Americans haven't yet had to worry about."

"Such as?"

Park told him, and Kwon seemed to consider it. For the second time in less than a minute, his mood reversed. "Yes!" said the chairman, his eyes brightening. "That will stir them up!"

"True . . . but again, we must be cautious. The threat can only be vague. Perhaps something about how miscalculations or mistakes might threaten either side."

Kwon nodded. "Will you draft the communiqué?"

Park smiled.

They discussed the idea for another twenty minutes, Kwon asking questions that Park mostly answered honestly. At that point the Supreme Leader of North Korea declared business to be at an end. He invited Park to join him for a meal, which of course was no invitation at all.

A table for two had been set in an adjoining room. Park was glad for the change of venue—the office had seemed unusually stifling. Over a buffet that could have sated a dozen hungry men, Kwon guided a wildly divergent discourse. Park conjectured as best he could as to the direction of NATO, the state of the Chinese economy, and confessed a hopeless lack of expertise on American basketball. They dug into platters of sushi, caviar, and fresh fruit from the tropics, notwithstanding the fact that large swaths of rural North Korea were enduring yet another winter of hunger.

A Bordeaux was uncorked and gurgled from its

bottle with traditional promise. Park took a glass because he had to, and nursed it with care. More than any place on earth, he had to keep his wits about him here. Kwon seemed not to notice, and by the time lunch ended he seemed slightly giddy.

At the end Park left the same way he'd arrived. In the anteroom he collected his coat, checked his watch, and heaved a great sigh. Two hours—not a record, but an extended session. *How many more will I have to endure?* he wondered.

He noticed that three of the security men were right where he'd left them, fixed like living statues. The others had been relieved by new men, these every bit as stone-faced. Without comment, the head of SSD turned and walked away.

As he made his way down the first hall, Park prioritized his tasks. The communiqué would come first. It had to be worded very precisely. Something about the dangers that vast nuclear arsenals presented. It would be colored indelibly in Dear Leader's signature phrases. No hint whatsoever of SSD in the background. Simple enough.

Park then addressed the thornier issue. Vienna had become a problem. Slaton had become a problem. If El-Masri's information made its way to authorities, the entire mission could be compromised. Khang might be able to stave off the trouble, particularly if Slaton's family could be leveraged. His jaw tightened.

Success was near, almost within reach. But things were moving more quickly than expected. Park saw but one recourse.

He wasn't sure if advancing the schedule was even possible. But he knew he had to try. He pulled out his phone, trusting its security measures like never before, and from the halls of the chairman's beloved palace, he placed a call that lasted twenty-eight seconds.

FORTY-NINE

General Park's fleeting call was received, and his orders carried out, on a very small island in the South China Sea.

Eight years earlier there had been no island at all—only a coral reef which, on mean low tide, had enough exposure to create the odd tide pool. The Chinese government was instrumental in correcting this defect. Over the course of eighteen months, it undertook the dredging of millions of cubic meters of sand from nearby shallows. Enough sand that an island was eventually formed. Soon after that came a runway, a few buildings, a small hangar, and— most important of all—a fifty-meter-tall flagpole upon which a red flag with five stars was flown in all its splendor. As land grabs went, the campaign was as audacious as it was clumsy. The newly created Glorious Dawn Cay was among China's first attempts to commandeer a foothold in the South China Sea.

It was also the least successful.

To begin, the location had not been adequately surveyed—the department responsible for "repatriation operations," China's Ministry of Natural Resources, had not been made aware that a sister agency, the Ministry of Foreign Affairs, was at the endgame of secret negotiations with Vietnam about who was claiming what. A third department, the oft-ignored Ministry of Ecology and Environment, also had an opinion on the matter, having declared in an internal government report that the shallows in question were the least economically viable zone of ten being evaluated—a report, not surprisingly, that had never been shared with the Vietnamese.

The final blow, however, was quite literal.

Her name was Super-typhoon Indira, and she ripped through the South China Sea one late October night, three years earlier, with a vengeance that seemed almost personal. By morning light, little was left standing on Glorious Dawn Cay. The runway was covered in sand, the lone pier damaged, and most of the buildings had simply disappeared. One small reinforced hangar stood in defiance, if a bit crookedly and minus its entry door, and a savaged fishing boat, which would curiously never be claimed, had washed ashore on the lone taxiway. The flagpole was never seen again.

It was here that China aligned its administrative ducks. Deep in a carefully worded foreign ministry statement it mentioned the island under a new name—Friendship Cay—and included a map that showed the outpost in international waters. In effect, not claiming the island, but also not ceding it to anyone else. The dredges moved on to reefs with greater promise, and without so much as sweeping the runway, the atoll was vacated. What remained fell into complete disrepair. Yet if the name Glorious Dawn Cay was forgotten, the island itself was not.

Which was how, when the leadership of North Korea made an inquiry with its most intimate neighbor about finding a remote island airfield from which a few flights might operate undisturbed, the Chinese government had just the place.

The first small boatload of North Koreans had arrived sixteen months earlier. In the equatorial heat, and working with nothing more than shovels and brooms, the crew removed enough sand to distinguish the eastern half of the seven-thousand-foot runway from the surrounding beach.

Weeks later a few generators were brought in, along with food, water, and a great bladder capable of holding three thousand gallons of fuel. The hangar was tidied up—although no effort was made to replace the door—and a tiny squad of men took up guard. While the improvements were largely unremarkable, the soldiers' arrival might have provided the first clue that something unconventional was in the works: the guards, notwithstanding their ragged appearance and casual manner, had been handpicked from the best Special Forces units in the Korean People's Army.

Three months after the activity began, the first flight arrived. The aircraft was a Y-5A, a Chinese variant of the Russian AN-2 Colt. The type had been in use since 1947, a testament to its ruggedness and reliability. A single-engine biplane, the Colt was small and ungainly compared to its more modern turbine-driven brethren. Yet what it lacked in sleekness it more than made up for with unique flight characteristics. Chief among them, owing to its dual wing configuration and high lift devices, was that the airplane had no stall speed listed in its operating manual. Approach speeds of thirty miles an hour were easily achievable, meaning that with a decent headwind, the Colt needed no more landing surface than a good-sized residential driveway.

The particular aircraft that made the deliveries to Friendship Cay was a study in contrast. On appearances it looked a shambles. Oil dribbled back from the engine cowling like legs in a glass of high-alcohol wine, and the few readable exterior markings were as generic as a brown paper wrapper. The paint job was frightful, chipped and pitted, particularly on the leading edges, giving the impression the aircraft had perhaps flown through a sandblaster—very near the truth, in fact, an effect that had taken a team of technicians hours to craft. A closer inspection would reveal something else altogether: the aircraft was maintained to the very highest standards, and the crew, like the attendant guards, had been handpicked, the best of the best of the North Korean air force.

The Colt arrived on that first day from the north, and perhaps a bit east, a weary traveler appearing like an apparition from the distant nothingness of the northern sea. In subsequent visits there were minor variations in the arrival track. More constant were the orchestrations that took place after the Colt landed.

On five separate occasions the transport taxied into the doorless hangar. The moment the engine shut down, a small forklift wheeled up to the modified cargo door and removed one small but heavy cargo container. The containers, each the size of a microwave oven, were deposited at the very back of the hangar and covered with a tarp. The aircraft was then partially refueled from the storage bladder—enough to reach Hainan Island with a minimal reserve—and the Colt departed again without respite.

The longest the drill ever took was eighteen minutes. The record was twelve. Including taxi time, the interval spent on the ground never exceeded twenty-two minutes. Had anyone ever bothered to audit the aircraft's flight plan—and no one did—they would be hard-pressed to prove that the Colt's scheduled journey to Hainan had been interrupted by a brief excursion to Friendship Cay. And so the pattern had run for over a year.

Today, however, things were different.

Park's message set off a flurry of activity. To begin, the Colt was already in place, sitting empty in the hangar. She had recently been fitted with auxiliary fuel tanks, and both were topped off. The original five containers were no longer present. A team of technicians had recently arrived by boat—a beaten coastal cargo vessel that anchored in the lagoon—and transferred the containers to the vessel. After three days, like a second-rate magic trick, they returned with one slightly larger and heavier shipping cask.

On Park's order, it was this container that was put aboard the Colt and carefully strapped down. In terms of volume, the auxiliary tanks and shipping container fit easily into the boxy cargo bay. Their combined weight was another matter, nearing—in truth, perhaps exceeding—the aircraft's 4,700-pound load limitation. The pilots noted this discrepancy with due concern, and took care in precisely where the cargo was situated—a center of gravity had to be maintained that would not upset the airplane's flight characteristics. It was the kind of procedural cloud that might ground a flight on any other day.

Here, however, given their mission and projected route, the pilots felt little duty toward regulatory compliance. Indeed, they'd long ago lost count of how many laws they were about to break.

After one last check of the weather via a satellite phone, the pilots cranked the engine. The trade wind was predictable as ever, favoring a northerly take-off. The laden Colt taxied to the end of the runway, pirouetted into the wind, and used half the available concrete during its takeoff roll—easily the most it had needed since beginning its sojourns to Friendship Cay. The little airplane lumbered upward, made a slight eastward turn, and set out steady and true into a forgiving midday sky.

FIFTY

Slaton woke shortly before ten that morning, strobes of morning light straining through the wintering evergreen canopy. The fog of sleep cleared quickly from his head, accelerated by the aches of the previous night. He checked the laceration on his leg, saw no further bleeding. His left hand ached with certain movements, but seemed functional. He started the car, turned on the heater, and set out toward the main road.

The township of Rosenheim appeared in his windscreen less than an hour later. He discarded the Renault in a parking area outside a busy IKEA store. A bus took him farther into town, depositing him, quite literally, in the spired shadows of the churches of St. Nikolaus and Holy Spirit.

Slaton stood for a time on the sidewalk, contemplating his next move and trying to tamp down his rising impatience. The streets were modestly busy, normal people going about their normal lives. He ignored the strains from his neglected stomach, instead settling his eyes on the church. It was a dominating bit of architecture, two white stone towers topped by mismatched onion spires.

The front doors of the cathedral stood invitingly open.

He found himself drawn inside. He stepped through the entrance and regarded the great inner hall. His gaze lifted naturally to the tall columns and an arched ceiling with intricate gold inlays. Transcendent as it all was, in the end he found his attention falling to the stonework at the base of it all—he'd performed repair work on many such foundations across Europe and the Mediterranean.

Slaton had never been particularly religious. As a boy he'd been put through the motions. Visits to temple, a barely remembered bar mitzvah. In more recent years he'd found little time for faith. To Davy, he and Christine talked about God as they might a much-loved but little-seen grandparent. Someone good and giving, but ever at a distance. He supposed he believed obliquely in God, if such a thing was possible. If not belief, then at least hope. So many years spent as an assassin seemed another obstacle to faith, and the last two days had dug that hole deeper. No manner of repentance or atonement could undo what he had done. Yet here he was, standing in a church, doing what the casually faithful had done as long as there had been religion: calling on God when you needed Him.

The pews were mostly empty, and he edged toward the nearest and took a seat. Slaton closed his eyes and made his peace as best he could. Then, perhaps predictably, he asked for the thing he needed most. He didn't bother consigning to the usual, and rarely kept, bargain: *Make this happen, and I'll commit to a life of goodness and devotion.* No, he decided. God had heard that one before. He simply asked for help. It was the best he could do in that moment.

He lifted himself from the wooden pew and began walking toward the arched entryway. He saw a donation box and reached into his pocket. He'd no sooner placed a twenty-euro note in the box when a figure appeared at the grand threshold.

Above a simple dress he saw a warm smile.

"I'm sorry," Slaton said in English, stepping back to let the woman pass.

"Thank you," she responded with a thick Bavarian accent, then added engagingly, "I am Sister Magda. I hope you have found what you need today."

"My name is David," he found himself saying. "And I hope so too. Your church is beautiful."

Again the smile. "We try to do it justice, but time takes its toll."

Slaton looked over his shoulder. "The window casings along the east wall . . . were they repaired after the war?"

She looked at him curiously, then said, "I only know because I am the unofficial historian, but yes, that wing was damaged in the air raids."

Slaton led her to one of the windows. He pointed to a joint of cracking plaster beneath a mosaic of stained glass. "Whoever mounted the replacement frames used a mortar mix that was too wet. It wouldn't be hard to fix." He went on for two minutes about the specifics of the repair.

"You are a mason," she remarked at the end.

"In the best of times."

"And in the others?"

Slaton smiled for the first time in days. "I try to get by."

"That is all any of us can do, my son."

"I don't want to overstep," he said hesitantly, "but I'm having some trouble at the moment. I've been unable to reach my wife and son. For the last few days I've been traveling and . . . would you have a computer I could use for a few minutes?"

She answered with an expression that was benevolence itself.

Slaton was minutes later installed in a tiny church office. The computer was smaller than the one he'd seen in the gun shop, yet every bit as aged, and its low-resolution screen made every image appear like an old photograph. But it worked perfectly well, credit due perhaps to the oversight of Christ on the cross, nailed to the wall above, hovering over every keystroke. As the bells in the nearby tower struck noon, Slaton drew a deep breath and plugged in the flash drive he'd found beneath a half-eaten tuna sandwich.

The first surprise was that the drive's contents were completely unprotected.

Could it possibly be so easy? he wondered.

Slaton clicked to view the files. The old machine made him wait for what seemed an eternity.

He couldn't recall ever feeling so helpless. His wife and son were out there somewhere. If Christine truly was on the run, as Mordechai had suggested, she would be looking for him as ardently as he was looking for her. It seemed a paradox of the modern world. Communications tracking, facial recognition, cameras on every corner. By striving so valiantly to stay *off* the grid, the era of connectivity had isolated them from one another. In essence, his single-link plan for staying in touch had been beaten by the most devastating shortcoming—Mordechai had inserted himself between them. And when he did, Slaton had lost control.

But now? he wondered. *Have others become involved?* Given what he'd seen in Vienna, it couldn't be ruled out.

As the tiny wheel spun, Slaton whispered the question he'd been asking for days. On *Sirius*. In a park in Vienna. In a church pew only minutes earlier. A question, he feared, that might never be answered.

"Where are you, Christine?"

FIFTY-ONE

His wife was, at that moment, knee-deep in the kiddie pool at a resort in the Balearic Islands. Davy was belly-down in front of her, studying the bottom of the pool through a cheap mask. His head popped up for a breath, then immersed again.

The resort was high-end, forty-two acres of understated comfort and tranquil recreation. There were waiters as thick as shorebirds, a concierge in every wing. The room had cost a pretty penny, but she'd made the selection thoughtfully. Not because she yearned to be pampered, but because when an assassin's wife went to ground she would be expected to choose something more off-track and rustic. That was what Christine told herself, and it might have been true. Hiding in luxurious plain sight.

"No fish in here!" Davy complained after popping up again. The mask was fixed crookedly on his face and half full of water, his white-blond hair matted to the top. She reached down and helped him straighten things out. She'd earlier taken him to the beach where a rocky outcropping had been teeming with fish.

"We'll go to the beach again later," she said, fearing it was a promise she might not keep.

"I'm hungry," he said. His toddler's metabolism had quickly adjusted to the resort's all-inclusive dining schedule.

"We'll eat again soon."

Davy's face went back in the water. She kept only half an eye on him. He could swim as well as he could walk, a consequence of having spent most of his nearly three years on a boat cruising the world's oceans. The balance of her attention went to the lounges and bar areas around them. She saw no one paying them too much attention, no faces that looked familiar. She was struck by the humor of that—there probably wasn't a familiar face within a hundred miles.

She sighed, reached into her pool bag, and pulled out her recently purchased burner phone. It was turned off now, as it had been for three days. She spun the blank screen in her hand, suspicious as ever. Her conundrum hadn't changed—and how would it ever? If she turned the phone on, she suspected there would be a message. But who would it be from?

Christine set the phone on her lounge chair. *I never would have guessed it's harder to come out of hiding than go into it.*

She'd never hesitated when she received David's first message. Sitting in *Sirius'* cabin in Gibraltar, a box of cereal between her and Davy, his instructions had arrived like a lightning strike on the emergency phone they carried whenever they were apart: Get clear now!

It wasn't their prearranged warning code, but the message couldn't have been more clear. She'd quickly set sail, taking *Sirius* into the bay. There she waited for David, only to have their standing plan altered by a second message: Barcelona ASAP. Ditch phone and buy new burner. Also included was a new contact number.

Her thoughts whipsawing, Christine had collected their prepacked emergency bag, retrieved the backup passports for her and Davy, and pocketed a wad of cash. Within minutes, the two of them had abandoned *Sirius* and were in the dinghy headed for shore. The phone went to the bottom of Gibraltar Bay. Soon after that, she had her arm around her son in the back seat of an Uber heading toward the train station. Destination: Barcelona. In her pocket was a fresh phone, its number already sent to the new contact she'd been given.

Then, for a time, there had been nothing. Not until later that day when, wandering the heart of Catalonia with a two-year-old in tow, the third message had changed everything. Something about the wording seemed wrong, a verbal construction David wouldn't use. That caused her to reconsider the other messages. Like a wave crashing down, she realized in a terrible moment that the instructions hadn't come from David at all. Some unknown intermediary had inserted themselves into the chain. At first she didn't know what to make of it. Had something happened to David? Why would anyone try to manipulate her in such a way? In the end, she decided there was no good in any of it. Whatever strings were being pulled, she had to sever them. She turned the phone off.

From the shadows of the train station, she'd taken a cab to Puerto de Barcelona. After a quick study of the ferry schedule, she and Davy hustled onto the next available departure—Mallorca, Spain. A mid-Mediterranean playground. Precisely the kind of place people went to leave behind their problems.

So here they were, three days later. Searching for a way back. She guessed any call she made to David's phone might be tracked. Yesterday, in a blaze of inspiration, she'd borrowed a phone from a concierge to call the marina where *Sirius* was docked—or at least had been before Christine had left her on the Bay of Gibraltar. Without saying who she was, she'd convinced a young woman at the desk to deliver a message. Christine soon got a callback from their next-door neighbor—the Scotsman in slip 96.

He explained that David had been searching for her.

He came back to the slip that morning and seemed surprised Sirius *was gone. He borrowed my launch, then came back with your boat an hour later. Said it was all a big misunderstanding.*

Christine asked if her husband had said where he was going, and the Scotsman seemed perplexed. *He told me the three of you were heading to Spain for some sightseeing . . .*

After thanking the man for watching over their boat, she'd ended the call quickly, wanting to avoid any more lies. Only then did she take the time to deconstruct what he'd told her: *sightseeing, Spain, a big misunderstanding.* Could there be some message hidden in those words? No, she decided. They were but the standard fabrications of a practiced spy. And another dead end.

She wondered how long it would go on.

Davy kept up his splashing. Christine kept scanning.

She saw a face she recognized, a middle-aged man seated at the tiki bar—sunglasses, watchful gaze, drinking what looked like water. She'd already pegged him as hotel security. It was the kind of thing she would never have noticed a few years back. She knew they should have stayed in their room. David would have insisted on it. She'd paid for two nights, at which point her plan was to move to a different resort on the island.

Christine was glad for David's foresight—he'd included a credit card with her ID. Unfortunately, she had no idea what its limit was or if the bill would magically be paid. It was a system of household finances few couples could imagine. She supposed the next hotel, if it came to that, ought to be something more economical. It struck her that at some point in recent years money had lost its meaning. She and David kept a handful of accounts across the world, but accessed them rarely. They weren't rich by any means, but along with a bit of income here and there from David's masonry jobs, and her dabbling as a physician, they could cruise more or less indefinitely.

"Playground?" Davy said. He'd popped up again and was pointing to a plastic pirate ship where a half-dozen kids were swarming. For a boy who spent most of his life at sea with his parents, it was a rare chance for socialization.

"Yeah, let's go," she said.

She got her son out of the pool, dried him off with a plush resort towel. "But first we'll need some more sunscreen." Christine pulled out a tube of high-SPF lotion, squeezed a blob into her hand, and began working it over her son's shoulders. When she was done, she finger-combed his hair back. "You need a haircut, mister."

"You told Daddy he needed one."

"Yeah, I did," she replied, remembering saying as much last week as they'd all sat eating pizza at a shoreside restaurant.

As she was putting away the sunscreen, Davy snatched up the phone on the cushioned lounger. "Let's call Daddy!" he said.

"Sorry, kiddo—can't right now. But we'll see him soon."

She wrapped him in the towel, and a rib tickle got a grunt of laughter. So distracted, it was in the next moment that Christine made her only real mistake of the week.

She took the phone back from her son, not realizing that he'd done what children often did—he'd pressed the button. She dropped the handset into the side pocket of her beach bag having no idea it had been turned on. Nor did she see the days-old message that flashed to the screen and remained for two minutes before the sleep settings removed it.

STAY WHERE YOU ARE. I'M COMING FOR YOU.

FIFTY-TWO

As the contents of the memory stick flashed to the screen beneath Jesus, Slaton recalled the words of a renowned Mossad hacker who'd once given him a primer on cyber tactics. The first rule when combing through electronic data: the more innocuous the subject line of a file, the more important the information tended to be. *Show me a message about a cancelled paper clip order,* Mossad's chief of cyber operations had said, *and I'll show you the secrets of Iran's nuclear program.*

It was time to put that theory to the test. Slaton saw a dozen options and opened the first, a three-page text document. Two lines in, he knew what he was looking at:

> *To whom it may concern,*
> *What follows is my confession . . .*

Having spent years as a Mossad operative, Slaton had seen such letters before. They were the kind of thing deeply compromised individuals placed quietly in the hands of trusted lawyers or safe-deposit boxes. This was the timeless *"If anything should happen to me"* letter.

Slaton knew that as a method of forestalling retribution from coconspirators, such letters were of limited effectiveness. In El-Masri's case, clearly, the strategy hadn't worked. All the same, they often proved a gold mine for law enforcement and intelligence agencies, exposing all manner of nefarious activities to be, depending on the mission statement, either prosecuted or exploited.

Slaton wasn't sure how he would use the material.

But what he saw was astonishing.

In three pages El-Masri laid out the details of the scheme, an eighteen-month-long conspiracy in which highly enriched uranium had been skimmed during five IAEA site visits. He gave detailed records of the amount of material diverted, including how it had been isolated and concealed for shipping.

Slaton was no expert in the transport of radioactive material, yet he saw right away the hallmarks of an effective covert operation. An overly complex regulatory system, a ponderous bureaucracy, countless government agencies involved. There were inspectors from a dozen countries, language barriers, outdated oversight methods. He'd seen many such schemes before. He'd *designed* his share. The most successful mirrored this one, conceived and executed by high-level insiders. With a bit of planning and the right support, virtually any organization could be corrupted by the person who oversaw its day-to-day operations.

The greatest remaining mystery—that of El-Masri's motive for his crimes—was answered on the final page. The Egyptian had been diagnosed with leukemia two years earlier. He'd undergone chemo and experimental treatments that kept the disease at bay for a time. Then a battery of tests brought the worst possible news: the cancer was winning. In the face of insistent queries by El-Masri, his oncologist admitted that yes, the variant of cancer involved could well be the result of long-term, low-dose radiation exposure. *I know you've taken precautions over the years,* the doctor had written in an email that was copied into the letter, *yet this type of cancer does have a higher level of occurrence among those working in your field.* Those words had clearly had an effect on the physicist—the dreadful irony that his life's work was destined to destroy him in the end.

Slaton considered the timing of the diagnosis, relating it to Mordechai's estimate of when the thieving of HEU had begun—it was roughly the same eighteen-month period. If nothing more, the letter explained the scheme's genesis.

As it turned out, El-Masri was not a man to rely on broad strokes. After the overview, Slaton found himself combing through IAEA spreadsheets and internal communications that documented every aspect of the thefts, as well as copies of El-Masri's personal bank and investment statements. Completing the picture were threatening emails from at least three attorneys implying that in recent years the deputy director had fallen deeply into debt from speculative investments and, perhaps reading between the lines, a bit of gambling. For the last sixteen months, however, his accounts had been shored by large cash influxes from banks in China and Singapore. He'd paid off substantial debts, and even set aside a nest egg in a nameless offshore account—a limited liability corporation admittedly structured for the benefit of his family. This, El-Masri pleaded at the end, would hopefully remain unchallenged in exchange for his post-mortem candor.

Slaton was about to open the final file when muted steps sounded in the hallway outside. The room was constraining: there was one door, no windows, and little room in which to maneuver. Sister Magda had told him the space doubled as a bomb shelter during the war, and he saw no reason to doubt it. The rough-hewn walls were probably half a meter thick, and the ceiling was reinforced by arches on all four sides.

The footsteps receded, followed by a conversation in the distance. Befitting a house of worship, voices steeped in warmth and compassion.

Slaton went back to the screen.

The most useful find in El-Masri's files came at the end. Slaton read the final document breathlessly, for this was the one that gave him direction. The one that could put him on the offensive. El-Masri named his primary conspirator, a man named Park. He was North Korean, and apparently a high-ranking officer in the SSD. For Slaton this was a home run. It meshed perfectly with what he'd seen last night: men who could easily have been Korean. The involvement of a rogue nation seemed almost predestined.

Energized, he went back to the beginning and read the entire package a second time. For nearly an hour he pored over documents, committing details to memory. Park Hai-joon he gave particular attention. El-Masri admitted to having no direct evidence of his meetings with Park. Every contact had been in person, arranged clandestinely, and El-Masri was always searched for wires or recording devices. It meant there were no emails or recorded conversations to tie North Korea to the pilfering of highly enriched uranium. Only the despondent confession of a dying man.

This had a ring of truth to Slaton—if Park truly was a high-ranking SSD officer, that was precisely how he would operate. Details regarding shipments would have been arranged in quiet meetings, no traces left behind. Slaton, however, didn't need that kind of evidence. The greater picture was clear enough: Tarek El-Masri had been terminally ill, financially stressed, and determined to leave something to his family.

He had also been desperately fearful of being double-crossed.

Which, as it turned out, had been all but a premonition.

ASSASSING REVENGE 325

knock simultaneously. Only the a spot since occasion
to dangerous that

This and a ring of fresh mechanical gray cases
when high-ranking SSD officer that was punched
how he would reaching. Despite a pinding side
queues, would an assume this pond bets (seeming
no raises fall behind, at nice fewer, us during wood
that kind of conspicer. The present price was seen
chough, the willy Alcoy had been permitted at it.
thousally agreed and a complied to Kent wood
thing to its gully

FIFTY-THREE

After completing his second run-through of the files, Slaton leaned back in the worn office chair. He rubbed his hands over his face and studied the high arches. As so often happened, the initial elation of getting a breakthrough gave way to new channels of doubt.

He was struck by two inconsistencies in El-Masri's version of events.

To begin, he wondered why North Korea would have any interest in acquiring highly enriched uranium. That country's nuclear capability had long been established, so where was the gain? On a lesser scale, he pondered the wisdom of extracting small caches of material from multiple shipments. In at least two cases—the removal of material from a research lab in Ghana, and another in Kazakhstan—it appeared that stealing a greater amount of material would have been possible. The risk of so many small thefts seemed unnecessarily risk-laden.

There had to be answers to both questions.

All the same, Slaton remained convinced. Too many verifiable facts aligned with El-Masri's confessional. Mordechai's initial research of the thefts. The Asians encountered last night. The targeting of both El-Masri and Mordechai. It all fell into place like tumblers in a lock.

For Slaton, there was but one overriding question: *How will this help me find Christine and Davy?*

The sound of voices in righteous harmony drifted up the hallway. Choir practice in the main vestibule. He racked his brain, wondering how to proceed. Did the North Koreans know who he was? Did they know how he'd gotten involved? He had to assume they did. What about Christine and Davy? Did Park know where they were at that moment?

Slaton felt a rush of despair. He could hold his own against a gang of amateurs in a public park. Even a small assault team.

But I can't take on an entire country.

He closed his eyes for a moment, shutting out the screen in front of him. The sacred sounds streamed up the hall.

All at once, Slaton realized what he had to do.

He removed the flash drive, did a quick cleanup of the computer. He composed a brief than-you note to Sister Magda, and promised that he would try to return someday to repair the window.

Slaton walked into a hallway washed in the harmonies of "Ave Maria." Near the end of the corridor he encountered a gilded mirror. He glanced at himself once, and thought, *I need a haircut.* A memory was triggered. Pizza on a red-and-white checkerboard table. The sea in the distance. And much more.

So much more.

Outside the church he encountered a dry wind and bright sun. Slaton's plan going forward was fast crystallizing. He knew where to begin. With a final look over his shoulder, he saw high clouds breezing past the twin onion-domed spires.

And he was thankful.

The flash drive in his pocket had indeed been a godsend.

Three blocks away from the church, Slaton turned into a small store that sold a bit of everything. He purchased a throwaway phone for cash and had it activated by the time he reached the first crosswalk.

The number he dialed, as far as he knew, was unique—a contact created exclusively for his use. He let it ring twice, then killed the call. He walked another two blocks, then paused in a square with a distant view of the river. The return call came as he was buying a gelato—not because he had a sweet tooth, but because he liked the area, in a tactical sense, and needed a reason to loiter. Ever so subtly, Slaton's mindset was shifting. After so many days of reacting, he felt the brace of something better.

"Hello," he said, after taking his change from the vendor and turning away.

"How are you?" asked a female voice, not insincerely.

"I've got a problem. So do you. I assume this is being recorded?"

"Of course."

"I have information, something I think you'd consider critical. It involves a man named Park Haijoon, North Korean—I've been told he's a high-ranking SSD officer."

A pause, then, "All right. I'd like to hear what you—"

"Not like this. I'm in Germany. I need to meet with someone you trust as soon as possible."

"Let me call you right back."

Slaton ended the connection a second time. The phone vibrated after seventy-six seconds.

"Frankfurt," the woman said. "Eight o'clock, Alte Oper."

Slaton checked the time, hesitated. He could easily get to Frankfurt in half that. Nine hours seemed an eternity. But what choice did he have?

"All right . . . I'll be there."

FIFTY-FOUR

The wind had risen, and so correspondingly had the seas. Eight-foot swells on the beam put a cyclic sway in the boat's progress. Boutros had lowered the speed, but at least two of his men—Saleem and Rafiq—were feeling the effects. Neither had come above for hours, and he doubted they were fit for a turn at the helm. Truth be told, Boutros himself could not deny a minor unease in the pit of his stomach.

Sami appeared from the companionway, looking carefree as ever. By some quirk of biology, he had somehow acclimated more quickly than anyone.

"I saw a high water level in the bilge earlier," said Boutros. "I'm not sure if the pumps are keeping up."

Sami looked at him blankly. "Bilge?"

Boutros sighed. "Never mind, I'll take care of it. I'd like you to relieve me soon. I need to show you how to run the boat in heavy seas—you'll have to steer manually."

"Of course. Is there time for me to go below and pray?"

"Yes, go ahead."

"What is the direction of the qiblah?" Sami asked.

Boutros checked the compass and pointed in the direction of Mecca.

Sami nodded and went below.

Boutros' eyes swept a horizon falling slowly to darkness. Early yesterday he'd seen a distant iceberg—a hazard he'd certainly never worried about in the Persian Gulf. Yet today the air was noticeably warmer, and he could see a distant thunderstorm to the south. He'd known running a boat across the Pacific was going to be a challenge. *Albatross* was slow and cumbersome, the ocean endless, and his crew was more interested in prayer than sea states. Yet so far the weather had cooperated, and it was forecast to remain relatively calm. There had been no mechanical troubles, nor any word that their mission had been uncovered. So far, a quiet passage through civilized waters.

But how long can it last?

Twenty minutes later Sami took over the helm. Boutros went below to find an unsteady Rafiq in the workroom. He was bent over the workbench with a screwdriver in hand.

"How are you feeling?" Boutros asked.

"Well enough to work," Rafiq replied. "I am checking the integrity of the firing squibs."

"Squibs?"

"Small detonators that will initiate the explosion."

Boutros nodded thoughtfully. "Is that not Saleem's job?"

"He is in his bunk, feeling the seas. He was able to finish modeling the shape for the explosive charge.

There is little left to do until we receive the final shipment. When will we reach the island?"

"If the weather gets no worse, two days," Boutros said. He saw unease in Rafiq's gaze. "Something is bothering you."

The boat lurched, and Rafiq closed his eyes for an instant before saying, "I didn't sleep well last night. It was the seas mostly, yet . . . I found myself thinking about our partners in this mission."

"Partners? You mean the North Koreans?"

A nod. "Do you trust them?"

"I see no reason not to. They have so far kept to our agreement."

"Something about it bothers me," Rafiq said. "Our reasons for being here are clear. We have been desperate to hit back since being driven from our caliphate. This is a bold strike that will truly hurt the Americans. But the North Koreans—what do they gain?"

Boutros pursed his lips thoughtfully. "I admit, I have wondered the same thing. The North Koreans have been at war with America longer than you or I have been alive, yet in recent years there has been talk of reconciliation. Change like that does not come without dissent, factions inside the government who think differently. Individuals who have an interest in keeping things as they are."

"Park?"

"He runs their intelligence service. That gives him a great deal of latitude. And Chairman Kwon—who can say what is in such a man's mind. Korea is a fractious place, and those divisions have granted us a golden opportunity. You and I can only trust that our benefactors will be on this island, waiting with what we need. The question of why it has all come to pass—I leave that for God."

Rafiq nodded. "Yes, I suppose you are right."

The boat lurched again, even more severely, and both men reached for hand holds to steady themselves.

Rafiq still looked uncertain.

"Is that your only concern?" Boutros asked. "The North Koreans?"

"I *am* curious. This island we will visit—is it far from our target?"

"I expect another three days at sea after our stop."

"Three days more. A lot could happen in that time. I wonder . . . can you put these places on the electronic map near the helm?"

"Of course. I'll show you later how to change the settings to look ahead."

A call came from above, Sami shouting something down the stairwell. "My presence is required," Boutros said.

Rafiq watched his commander go, then finished testing the final squib. That done, he found himself staring at the great bundle of wires before him. He thought the creation pointless, but Saleem had spent hours on it last night—stripping insulation, braiding pairs, twisting connections.

The wires, twenty-one in all, had come from a half-dozen spools: among them were three different gauges and six distinct colors. With something near glee, Saleem had woven what looked like a harness around the explosives chamber. He'd plugged leads into functionless fittings, connected others to dead batteries. Two wind-up analog alarm clocks had multiple connections. Saleem had brought everything from Syria. He referred to it as his "bird's nest," an innovation he'd developed as a cheap but effective countermeasure against tampering.

Over the course of the war in Syria, dozens of Saleem's IEDs had been uncovered by enemy forces. Most were simply predetonated, which invariably caused some kind of damage. Yet he swore that not a single one of the infidel explosives experts had ever been brave enough to try to disarm one of his bombs. By the end of the conflict, he proudly claimed the method as something of a calling card. When Saleem first saw what the Koreans had provided for this job—a simple single-action trigger, requiring but one cut to disarm—he was doubly happy he'd come prepared. He committed to building one final nest—the most complex ever for the caliphate's most magnificent weapon. Given Saleem's enthusiasm, Boutros had approved the idea. Rafiq, a mechanical engineer who'd spent years learning to create clean and efficient designs, thought it an inglorious application of skill.

A chanting cadence drifted through *Albatross'* diesel-infused lower decks: Saleem was praying yet again. Rafiq stepped back from the bench and walked to the tiny porthole across the workshop. He looked outside pensively, his eyes almost level with the riotous sea. The thought that had been brewing in his head for weeks grew more insistent. Since that morning in Suruç when the letter had finally caught up with him.

A correspondence he'd given up on more than a year ago.

As he stared at the sea, Rafiq knew he had but

one course. He would do his job in the coming days. He would make this weapon work. But he would also allow himself to look beyond that.

It might be for nothing, he allowed. *But today I am going to look at that map.*

Christine chased her son through the lobby breeze-way, towels wrapped around them both. Davy giggled as their wet flip-flops made squeaking noises on the tile. Christine saw a familiar face behind the front desk—the young woman smiled understandingly.

Davy led her in a merry pursuit, past the little-used business center, and then a faux library where wall-to-wall bookcases were stocked with weighty classic volumes. Without a dust jacket in sight, it seemed less a literary hub than the contrivance of some interior decorator.

With a skittering right turn at the first hallway, Davy raced toward their room. He bumbled to a stop in front of their door, both hands on the handle. "*SpongeBob*?" he said expectantly. He'd been reveling in the extensive channel selection on the room's TV—another indulgence lost when cruising the Seven Seas.

"First we read two books," she said, suspecting he would fall asleep after an active morning. Thankfully Davy hadn't outgrown his naps.

She swiped the key card, but didn't see the usual green light or hear a *click*. She was about to try again when the door cracked open slightly. Davy pushed through and ran into the room. Christine followed him for two steps.

She stopped cold when she saw three Asian men.

One was very muscular. He stood a bit crookedly and had bruises on his face.

The other two were perfectly straight. They had guns.

Davy came back to her without saying a word. She took half a step to put him behind her hip.

Protecting.

The door behind them closed.

FIFTY-FIVE

Slaton despised the waiting.

Always the waiting.

He had caught a standard train to Munich, followed by a high-speed to Frankfurt. He arrived four hours before his scheduled meeting. With time to kill, he went over El-Masri's files a third time in an internet café. After that he got two hours' sleep in a cheap rooming house. The previous night had left its mark on his clothing, and he decided replacing everything would be more efficient than scrubbing under faucets. At a second-hand store he purchased a tan shirt, dark green cargo pants, a light jacket, and was lucky to find a comfortable pair of hiking boots. He also selected one pair of heavy-knit socks. Thick socks were standard for any mission—add rocks or a can of beer, and you had an instant weapon.

He arrived at the scheduled rendezvous thirty minutes early.

The Alte Oper, or Old Opera House, stands proud in its Renaissance reincarnation. The original house was destroyed during World War II, bombed to the point of being anointed Germany's "most beautiful ruin." The replacement, however, was true to its parent, a three-story rectangular affair adorned with all the frescos and mosaics expected of a grand house, and a roof overseen by a full-scale rendition of Pegasus in bronze. Surrounded by gardens and a wide plaza, twin circular fountains stood sentry at the main entrance. And it was here, between dueling cascades of uplit water, that Slaton approached his contact.

Her eight o' clock profile, even in silhouette, he recognized instantly.

The woman he'd talked to on the phone.

"You made good time," he said, approaching her from behind.

"I was already in the neighborhood," Anna Sorensen replied, turning to his voice as if she'd known he was there.

Slaton's eyes swept the sidewalks before settling on her. "No you weren't."

"What makes you say that?"

"Your clothes are wrinkled, you're bleary-eyed. And nine hours? That's exactly what it would take to drive from Langley to Andrews, hop on an agency jet, and fly to Frankfurt."

She stared at him with something he couldn't place.

Slaton hadn't been surprised it was Sorensen who answered his call today. She had, after all, been the one who'd given him the number in the first place—his private emergency line to the CIA. He'd worked with the agency twice in recent years, Sorensen involved on both occasions. In those dealings, he'd always felt she was on his side, some measure of personal trust established. A baseline comfort level.

Tonight Slaton sensed nothing but tension.

"Okay," she admitted, "I was in D.C."

"Wouldn't it have been easier to send me to Berlin, have me walk into the embassy for a secure call? Why drop everything and come here yourself?"

"Because I can. I've been promoted—I'm assistant deputy director, SAD."

"Directorate of Operations, Special Activities Division? Congratulations—you're now officially in the black. Did I have something to do with that?"

"Those missions where you worked with me . . . with us . . . were very successful."

"Good. That means you and your agency owe me something."

She screwed her face into something unpleasant. Which wasn't easy. Sorensen was mid-thirties and extremely attractive. Fit and blond, she would have looked right at home in a commercial for a Peloton exercise bike.

"Tell me where you heard that name," she said, her eyes drifting to the uplit winged horse above the portico of the opera house.

"What name?"

"The one you mentioned in your call—Park Haijoon."

"The fact that you're asking suggests it's true—he really is SSD."

Sorensen didn't reply.

"High-ranking?" he said to the silence.

Still nothing.

"Okay, very high-ranking."

"He's the head," she said.

It was Slaton's turn to go quiet. He'd been rehearsing this juncture of the conversation for nine hours, and the decision matrix he'd built was now at its primary branch. He reached into his pocket and extracted the flash drive. He showed it to her, but then made it disappear in his hand with the theatrical flourish of a magician. "Like I promised in my message . . . there's a *lot* of good intel here. But I need guarantees first."

"Such as?"

He paused an extra beat. "It's pretty straightforward. Christine and Davy have gone missing."

For the first time he saw a softening in her gaze. Sorensen had spent three days safeguarding Christine and Davy on their previous convergence. She knew them both well.

"*Missing?*"

"It's only been a few days," he said, his voice hollowing out. "But honestly, Anna . . . it feels like a lifetime."

They shared an empty bench in the least raucous corner of the Opernplatz, the broad terrace adjoining the opera house. Slaton explained everything that had happened since Gibraltar. When he covered two killing sprees in Vienna, keeping oblique on details, he noticed Sorensen's gaze go distant. He imagined her recalling a briefing, sometime in the last twenty-four hours. Perhaps a junior analyst from the Central Europe desk going over the latest news from the Continent. Or maybe a curious wave of police reports from the Vienna station.

At the end he gave her a moment to digest it all.

"Highly enriched uranium has been stolen? By a senior man at IAEA?"

"He was senior before he was gunned down."

"And you're saying your family was dragged into this by a former Mossad department head who was working at IAEA?"

"That about sums it up. You need to understand—I never wanted to get involved in any of this. Unfortunately, my reputation has a way of following me."

"If what you say is true . . . then we have a problem."

"*A problem?* We're talking about bomb-grade nuclear material, half what you'd need to build a crude weapon! There's no telling where it's gone, Anna!"

She nodded slowly, as if the thoughts running through her head somehow dampened her movement. Slaton sensed something in the background, a secondary concern he wasn't seeing. That thought was interrupted by a new disruption. The phone that was supposed to be his link to his wife—the one he'd begun to ignore—was vibrating in his pocket.

In one motion he pulled it out and checked the screen. The stunned look on his face must have been evident.

"What is it?" Sorensen asked.

The phone was a reliable mid-range item, and as such, had a screen with decent resolution. Slaton saw a photograph that had been sent via text. He tapped until the image filled the screen and felt his blood run cold.

It was a picture of Christine and Davy. They were in the cabin of a small aircraft, some kind of business jet. His son was sitting next to his wife and grinning, full of innocent good humor as he was entertained by someone behind the camera. Christine was staring straight ahead. The look on her face was one of dread.

FIFTY-SIX

If there was one thing that set Slaton apart as an assassin, it was his innate ability to detach emotion from operational priorities. He felt fear and empathy like any sane person, yet when necessary had the ability to wall them off, shrouded behind the bastions of mission objectives. Sitting in front of the Alte Oper on a frigid January night, that ability all but left him.

His phone's screen was now facing Sorensen. "They're on a private jet," she surmised from the photo's background.

Slaton nodded.

"Do you have any idea where they departed from? Or where they're going?"

"No."

"Did anything come with that? Any text or an attachment?"

"Not yet."

"I need to send it to Langley. I'll tell our people to go over it—they're the best. We might be able to identify the aircraft, or at least the type."

Slaton was doubtful. He guessed the picture had been sanitized—edited before transmission so as to not give anything away. He set the phone on the bench, followed by the flash drive. Sorensen picked up the phone, tapped in a number, and sent the image. It would end up, he was sure, somewhere in the state of Virginia, but only after running some tornadic electronic routing that would prevent it from being tracked to its destination.

He watched her in silence. It was directly before him now: proof that his family had been taken. Never had he felt so close to surrender. Felt such soul-crushing guilt.

"I don't know what I'd do, Anna . . . if I lost them. If they're harmed because of me, because of what I used to be . . ."

"David, you can't blame—"

"Do you know what I did this morning?" he cut in, his voice distant.

She looked at him patiently.

"I went into a church and prayed. I can't remember the last time I did that."

"There's nothing wrong with it. But if God doesn't want to get involved . . . the CIA is the next best thing."

On any other day he would have smiled.

She handed back the phone. As Slaton took it she held his wrist for a moment. It had the desired effect—it got his attention.

"I know Christine," she said. "I know Davy. I will do everything in my power to help you get them back."

Slaton saw her level gaze. Her resoluteness.

"I'm glad you came," he said. "I mean . . . I'm glad it was *you*. It's rare for me to admit it, Anna, but I need help on this one. I can't do it alone. And I don't mean just the resources. I'm too close—not objective enough. I need someone I trust to help me see what I'm missing."

"Well . . . what the hell. I just came across a damned ocean, so I might as well keep going."

Whatever edge Slaton had been nearing, he felt himself pull back. The disorientation, the anger. It gave way to something better.

"I'd like you to promise me one thing," he said.

She raised an inquisitive blond eyebrow.

"I have a lot at stake here. I want the lead, from beginning to end."

"You know I can't guarantee that, David . . . not all the way. But for the time being, you've got a big head start. So what's our next step?"

"Park. I think he's the one who's taken Christine and Davy."

"But you can't be sure of that."

Slaton considered it. "Not completely, no. But I am sure their disappearance is related to this uranium theft. It's exactly the kind of thing that causes people to take hostages. That makes them send out kill teams."

After a thoughtful pause, Sorensen said, "This friend of yours from Mossad, Mordechai . . . his message to your phone got hijacked and replaced."

Slaton picked up the handset from the table. "I think so."

"And Christine had a phone exactly like it."

"Yeah."

"So we can assume she was manipulated in the same way."

"Most likely."

"That takes some know-how," she suggested.

"Park again? North Korea?"

"It fits. Of course, there are other rogue states, and even a few criminal enterprises with techies who could play that game. But the signature is solid—it's how the North Koreans run their cyber."

The flash drive was still on the bench. Slaton pushed it toward her. "This will be more useful to you than me. You've got the resources to dig." She took the drive and inspected it. Slaton held up his compromised phone. "Over the last few days, I've been turning this on regularly to check for messages. I'm guessing it could be used to track me?"

"Probably. Keep checking, but at random intervals. If they're sending you proof-of-life pictures, they'll be in touch again. They want something."

"I'm guessing they want me. With El-Masri and Mordechai out of the picture, I'm the only one who knows enough to threaten their scheme." Slaton paused for a time, carrying that thought forward. "The big guy who killed Mordechai . . . I think he was searching for the flash drive. I think they knew it existed. Maybe El-Masri told them about it."

"They also tortured Mordechai."

Slaton nodded. "But now they don't know where it is. There's a chance I've got it, but . . ." He let his voice trail off, inviting her along.

"But they can't come out and ask, because *you* might not know about it."

"Exactly."

Slaton turned his burner off. He felt like a man overboard at sea on a dark night watching the only life ring get pulled back on board.

He said, "The first file on the drive is El-Masri's confession. What would happen if you copied that, then sent it to my phone from an untraceable IP address here in Frankfurt?"

"They'll see it—and it would prove you have information that could compromise their operation."

"Exactly," Slaton said.

"Which forces their hand—they'll have to get in touch again."

He looked at her encouragingly.

"We might be able to trace any incoming call or message."

"It's worth a try."

"Not bad," Sorensen said. "But if this *is* North Korea, or any competent state actor . . . it probably won't get us much. There will be cutouts, electronic cul-de-sacs to keep us from tracing any contact."

"Probably. But it'll at least rattle some cages. Make it so they're the ones reacting."

Sorensen's thoughts seemed to drift for a moment, then she said, "You're right about Christine and Davy—their being taken is connected to this HEU theft. Yet there could be more to it."

"Like what?"

"I don't know . . . something."

He looked out across the plaza, the sharpness in his gaze back. "How long will your people need to go over that photo of Christine and Davy?"

"We should have an initial take within an hour."

"All right. In the meantime, you can send me that page from El-Masri's cover letter."

"And then?"

"Then we get ready to move."

"How?"

"What kind of airplane did you fly in on?"

"No, David. You can't be—"

"Serious?" His gray eyes held her like a gunsight. "This isn't only about my family. If North Korea has been stealing weapons-grade uranium, that's a serious national security threat to the United States. You want my help in getting to the bottom of it? Give me the support I need."

Sorensen sighed. "Citation Ten. I'll have it ready."

"Full tanks, fresh crew."

"By all means."

He looked at her imploringly. "I'm glad to have your help, Anna. But please tell your people to work fast. Give me a vector . . . show me where to start."

"And then?" she asked.

Slaton didn't respond.

FIFTY-SEVEN

General Park had left standing instructions to be informed immediately of any traffic on Slaton's mobile phone. Because his orders were always followed to the letter, he was awakened by a cautious knock on his door minutes before six o'clock that morning.

Park stirred.

For the first night in weeks, he had slept in the comfort of his private retreat on the slopes of the Taebaek Mountains, the north-south topographic spine of the Korean Peninsula. Conceived in the image of a Swiss chalet, the architecture was all exposed beams and weatherboarding and sharply peaked gables—a gingerbread vision, if ten thousand square feet of living space could be imagined as such. More critically, the retreat was situated 110 miles from Residence Number 55 outside Pyongyang—where Chairman Kwon had been for weeks, and where he would remain for the foreseeable future. As head of SSD, it was Park's duty to know such things.

Another soft knock.

Gathering his wits, Park half rolled and encountered something soft. The contact was followed by a gentle moan. The girl was still next to him, an ivory-skinned waif with short black hair. She wasn't as pretty as most, but she'd made up for it with surprising enthusiasm. If she had a name he'd forgotten it, so he simply nudged her bare rump with his knee.

The girl woke with a start, looked blearily at Park and vised her face into a smile. He responded with nothing more than a shooing wave, and didn't even bother to leer as she shuffled naked to the adjoining room.

After the girl was gone, he donned his robe, and said, "Come."

Jong appeared.

Even at this hour he was his decorous self. Park thought of him as something of an English-style valet, and he dressed the part in a rigidly pressed vest and trousers. He held a silver tray with both hands. On it was the usual pot of tea and soft-boiled egg, and between them a secure tablet device. The morning service of an intelligence chief.

"An urgent message, sir."

"Who is it from?"

"I was told Bureau 121. Also . . ." a hesitation from a man not prone to it, "your wife called last night."

"You explained how busy I have been?"

"Of course," said Jong.

Park rubbed his face with both hands. He had not seen his wife in weeks. In truth, he would be happy to never see her again. She knew about the girls but didn't much care. She'd most likely called to ask for another junket to Beijing. It was the only place she was permitted to shop for her essentials: Gucci, Hermes, Prada. The *real* ones, not the knock-offs the Chinese so openly hawked. Her trips came more or less monthly, and Park rarely denied them—the price of marrying Chairman Kwon's older sister. This was the bond that had installed him as head of SSD, one rung from the top of the ladder. And the bond that, so far, had kept them both alive.

"Tell her I will arrange a trip, but it will have to wait another week."

Jong bowed to say he would. Park sent him away with an order for a second pot of tea. It was going to be that kind of day.

He woke the tablet and pulled up the message in question. It contained an intercepted image that had been sent to Slaton's mobile phone. Park manipulated the screen to get a better look, and saw a photo of a document. He read it through once, his pace slowing with each word. If the signature and content could be believed—and he strongly thought it could—he was looking at the confessional of Tarek El-Masri. Wanting to be sure he had it right, Park read through once more, then went over the translation provided by the bureau. There could be no doubt. From his grave, El-Masri was laying bare the plot Park had so painstakingly orchestrated.

He stared at the teapot for a time, then very deliberately poured a stout cup. He walked to a window, drew the high curtains aside, and took in the sweeping view. The nearby hills were firmly in winter's grip, a dusting of new snow bright in the morning sun. He did not doubt the authenticity of the letter—he'd suspected there might be something like it. Given how things had gone off-rail in Vienna, he also wasn't surprised it had turned up in someone else's hands. He *was* mildly curious as to how it had been intercepted. Might Slaton have been juggling documents himself, sending them from one device to another?

Had a third party become involved? Or . . . had someone *wanted* him to see it over breakfast this morning?

He retrieved his phone and placed a call to the supervising officer at Bureau 121. "The images you sent to me—where did they originate?" he asked.

"We are trying to determine that, sir," replied a vaguely familiar voice. "It arrived only twenty minutes ago. We intervened and the transmission was interrupted."

"So this never reached Slaton's phone?"

"That is correct. Should we leave it that way or allow it to pass through?"

Park pondered his options. If Slaton had sent the image to himself via another device, he would become suspicious when it never arrived. On the other hand, there was a possibility that others were now involved.

"What are the chances of discovering where it originated?" he asked.

A hesitation. "That may prove difficult. From what we have determined so far, the routing is very complex, at least three consecutive address shifts upstream from the primary node which—"

"*What are the chances?*" Park interrupted in his general's tone.

"Poor," the technician admitted.

Park frowned. In truth, he'd been expecting such a leak. Even hoping for it, in a way. What vexed him was the timing—*he* needed to control the flow of information. For all its complexity, his plan was nearly realized. The only problem was Slaton. A complication, like Mordechai's interference, that Park never could have foreseen.

"All right," he said, "hold the message back. If

anything else is sent to this number, contact me immediately."

The supervisor, sounding relieved, said that he would and cut the connection immediately. Park regretted not having seized the last word—an ill-veiled threat to instill some motivation. He would make no such mistake in his next calls.

He retrieved paper and pen from the bedside stand, and composed a message in straightforward English. He read it through twice to make sure the meaning could not be misconstrued. Park called his personal aide at headquarters, dictated the message word for word, and with a final tirade that reflected his acidic mood, he ordered it sent to *Albatross*.

The next connection took time to run, utilizing a specially encrypted radio link. Khang finally answered, his voice backed by white noise.

"When will you land?" Park asked.

There was a pause while Khang researched the answer. It took nearly a minute. "We arrive in Urumqi in two hours and ten minutes," he finally said.

"Tell the pilots to waste no time. I am advancing our timetable."

"Advancing . . . but I thought—"

"We planned for this contingency! If you had handled things better in Vienna, there would be no need!"

Khang didn't reply.

"Is your injury serious?" Park prodded, pressing his advantage. Of course, he already knew the answer. He'd spoken to the embassy doctor in Vienna. Two gunshot wounds to Khang's leg had left him limping—a handicap, but no permanent damage.

"It is nothing," Khang said.

"Good. The woman and boy . . . you have followed my instructions?"

"They are completely unharmed."

"Very well. Now here is what I want you to do . . ."

When the call ended three minutes later, Park stood pensively in front of the window. He noted an antenna on the top of a distant hill. Other than that, there was not a marker of civilization anywhere in sight. The remoteness of his retreat was quite purposeful. It had nothing to do with the native birds whose droppings decorated the pitched roof, nor the odd bear who occasionally came to turn over the garbage bins. In the coming days, seclusion would be essential.

He found himself thinking about Khang. Park had recruited him five years ago, plucking him from an elite Special Forces team. In all that time, through scores of difficult assignments, he'd never seen anyone get the better of the man. Khang tried to brush off his failed encounter with Slaton, as any good soldier would. And since the debacle in Vienna, he'd mostly recovered. He'd abducted the woman and her son quickly and efficiently. Going forward, Park reckoned Khang would work hard to restore faith in his competence. It was good to have that kind of loyalty. Good to have such leverage over a man.

His thoughts advanced to the most important communication he would deliver—not today, but soon. He had already written the script, practiced it time and again. Eighteen precisely crafted words, and the most important of his life. At least, to that point.

He tried to rehearse it once more, but his thoughts foundered.

Not for the first time, he felt niggling doubts about the wisdom of abducting the family of an assassin—a man, he'd been told, who had a matchless reputation in the shadowed circles of Western intelligence agencies. Park, of course, had heavy security. And he almost never ventured abroad, preferring to keep to the confines of the most hermetic police state on earth.

Even so—

Recalibrating his thoughts, Park inhaled once, then recited his message clearly and precisely in a near whisper.

Soon, he thought afterward. *Very soon.*

FIFTY-EIGHT

While imagery analysts at Langley set to their labors, Sorensen and Slaton diverted to a nearby café. She ordered tea and a croissant, he a caffé americano. They discussed El-Masri's file, lost caches of highly enriched uranium, and what it all could mean for his family.

From the quiet corner table, Sorensen called for an update after precisely one hour. She tilted the phone away from her ear, allowing Slaton to lean in and listen—speaker mode was a bridge too far in such a public setting. They were briefed by a young woman with an upper Midwest accent—somewhere, Slaton guessed, very near the Canadian border.

"Our first goal was to identify the type of jet," she said. "It's not as easy as you might think. Business jet interiors are anything but standardized. They come out of the factory in dozens of different configurations. You've got your seating plan, entertainment amenities, galleys, and wet bars. It's a great pricing gimmick for manufacturers. Your standard Learjet—it's got more variations than a Starbucks latte. Gulfstream goes so far as to—"

"Okay," Sorensen cut in, "I get the picture. What did you find?"

If the woman was put off, it didn't enter her tone. "We're ninety percent sure it's a Challenger 300, built by Bombardier."

"Okay, good. What else?"

"Well, nothing with that degree of confidence—but we're still chasing some leads. We got distracted by one possibility right off the bat, but it turned out to be a dead end."

"What was that?"

"Do you still have access to the picture?"

Sorensen curled three fingers at Slaton in a beckoning gesture. He turned on his mobile and found the photo. "Got it," Sorensen said.

"Okay, in the background you can see the cockpit door. We blew it up as best we could given the resolution, and ran some filters and DEAs—detail enhancement algorithms. You see, every aircraft that carries passengers has to display its registration certificate—it's usually mounted in a clear plastic sleeve, either on the cockpit door or somewhere nearby. It's a regulatory thing ICAO insists on, like a restaurant having to show its liquor license."

Sorensen watched Slaton pinch the screen to make the photo bigger. "I can see the door," she said. "And on the wall next to it is a plastic sleeve. But . . . I can't tell what's inside."

"That's what we were trying to determine," the analyst said. "Turns out, the plastic holder is empty."

"They removed it before they took the picture," Sorensen surmised.

"That'd be my guess," said the voice from Langley. "We're still working a few other angles. Another hour and we'll have the aircraft type nailed down. If we're right about it being a Challenger, that's not good. It's one of the most common airframes out there. Over seven hundred flying around the world."

Slaton was still looking at the picture. His eyes, however, had moved away from the area around the cockpit door. He was looking at his wife. On first glance he'd been distracted by the worry etched into her face, her defeated posture. That in itself seemed wrong, despite the situation. Christine was a doctor accustomed to making life-and-death decisions, a sailor who'd tackled oceans. If she had one overriding trait, it was steadiness under pressure. She could never be the basket case she appeared to be in the picture.

Which meant she was telling him something.

Slaton scanned every part of the photo, and finally he saw it—her hands. They were just in view at the bottom of the shot, resting on a tiny hardwood table. Only they weren't in a natural position. Both sets of fingers were oddly set. He combined that with her puzzlingly vanquished expression.

All at once he understood.

On her left hand, the middle and index fingers were extended, the rest curled. Her right hand was set roughly in what looked like a Hawaiian shaka, or "hang loose" sign, the thumb and pinkie extended. Both arrangements were inexact, the fingers not rigidly straight. Subtle by design. Yet Slaton knew precisely what she was telling him.

"*H* and *Y*," he blurted.

Sorensen interrupted whatever the analyst was saying. "What?"

"The letters *H* and *Y*!" He pointed to Christine's hands. "We played around with sign language last month on the boat—Davy seemed to like it, like we had a secret code or something. The first thing you learn is the alphabet."

Sorensen looked at the photo. "And that's *H* and *Y*?"

"Or *Y* and *H*."

"What could that mean?"

The analyst, who'd obviously heard and followed along, said, "It could have to do with the country they're headed to—like an airport code or the name of a city."

"Maybe it's the initials of whoever abducted them," Sorensen ventured.

Slaton couldn't take his eyes off the picture. "I don't think so," he said. "Aircraft are like boats in certain ways . . . and Christine knows boats. I think it's part of the airplane's registration number."

Sorensen looked at him, and said, "The tail number?"

"It would make sense." Slaton edged closer to the phone. "There might be seven hundred Challengers flying around the world, but how many would have *H* and *Y* as the first, or maybe last letters of the tail number?"

"Statistically speaking . . . I'm sure you could count them on one hand," said the disembodied voice. "It's worth a try."

Sorensen looked again at the photo. "If it's not that, she's telling us something else. But you're right, David. Christine is definitely sending a message."

Boutros struggled mightily—even though he knew it was hopeless.

Both feet were in the dirt, sinking under the pressure. His hands were over his head, holding up the great wall that was tipping so perilously toward him. He called for help, yet knew there was none to be had.

He was alone now.

And that would never change.

His hands began slipping under the great weight, tons of stone gathering momentum. On the other side of the wall the storm blew incessantly, wind and rain and flashes of lightning. The sea in all its fury. He felt his arms weakening, felt failure upon him again . . . until something gripped his shoulder. That was followed by a distant voice.

All at once, the storm seemed to dissipate.

He opened his eyes, blinking away the sleep. When he finally focused, he saw Rafiq.

"What . . . what is it?" he asked.

"Come quickly," said Rafiq. "There is a message."

FIFTY-NINE

The entire crew was gathered in the wheelhouse. Saleem looked better than he had in days. Rafiq too was improved. The arrival of news relating to their mission had brought them together with high expectations. Unfortunately, as was so often the case in war, the news was not good.

The message had arrived via their encrypted satellite device, and was displayed on its backlit screen. They had been instructed to check twice each day for messages, at midnight and noon Zulu time. Until now there had been not a single contact. The message that finally came, at midnight Zulu, eleven hours removed from the time zone in which they were sailing, was a great disappointment.

"We are to switch to our secondary target," said Saleem. It sounded very near an accusation.

"Yes," Boutros replied distractedly.

"But why?" asked Sami.

Boutros read the message again. It was painfully brief.

> SHIPMENT TO ARRIVE ONE DAY EARLY
> INCREASE SPEED IF ABLE
> CHANGE TO SECONDARY TARGET

And that was all. No reasoning, no logic. No options given. Boutros felt the others looking at him. Waiting for their commander's interpretation.

"There has to be a reason," he said. "It is possible our plan has been uncovered. Or perhaps the American navy is planning an exercise that would keep us from reaching the primary."

He looked at his men, saw nothing but disappointment. Boutros felt it as well. Their primary target had been Pearl Harbor. The plan had been to detonate the weapon in the harbor entrance at dawn. It would have been an undeniably symbolic attack—the opening of America's last great war repeated, quite literally, in a flash. Also, proof that the world's greatest military power was not invulnerable. Allah's vengeance could be imparted anywhere on earth.

"It won't be the same," said Saleem. "Once the weapon is complete, no one can stop us from striking wherever we wish!"

"No," Rafiq argued, "we are running blind. We have no idea what we might face if we continue to Hawaii. What if the Americans are looking for us already? We've been told the timetable has been advanced—there must be a reason."

"You may trust these North Koreans," said Saleem, "but I do not!"

Rafiq glared at Saleem, and was about to respond when Sami argued, "Without them we would not have this chance to put glory to God! The Koreans are as committed to success as we are."

"Are they?" countered Rafiq.

Everyone looked at him, and a hard silence fell. The question that had long perplexed them weighed like a black hole.

Boutros put it into words. "If the North Koreans want so badly to attack America with a nuclear weapon . . . why do they need us?"

"I have wondered the same thing," Sami admitted. "They have given us nuclear material, a boat, and the hardware to make it all work. Why?"

His final word seemed to infuse itself in the air. *Why?*

The wheel turned silently left and right, the ghost that was the autopilot holding course in tireless obedience. The seas had been gentle since sunrise, and the air was warming. Only the sound of light waves slapping the bow broke the stillness.

"I think I might know," Rafiq said.

They all looked at him.

"This second delivery of highly enriched uranium, the back of our so-called gun weapon—it will be different."

"Different how?" Boutros asked.

"The technician who told me how to assemble the weapon mentioned something. His English was poor, but he said that 'material from others' had been prepared. It would be perfectly machined and ready to load. Yet something about the way he spoke of it seemed strange. I asked him where this second batch had come from. He seemed surprised by the question, and told me it had been acquired from five other countries. He mentioned Pakistan and Ghana . . . also Belgium, I think."

"Other countries?" Boutros repeated. "But why?"

"I am not a physicist, so it is only speculation . . . but I think it has to do with attribution."

"Attribution?" Sami repeated.

"The established nuclear powers, in particular France, Russia, and the Americans, keep an extensive library of the world's nuclear stockpiles. Every batch of weapons-grade uranium and plutonium created leaves traces in the atmosphere, in the soil and water around production facilities. And each has a unique signature. When a nuclear device detonates, identifiable traces are left behind."

Boutros nodded, seeing the connection. "So when our weapon goes off, and the Americans try to determine who is responsible . . ."

"There can be no answer," Rafiq finished. "North Korea will be a suspect, but no more so than Ghana or Pakistan. It gives a measure of deniability."

"How did they get this other uranium?" asked Sami.

"I have no idea. It seems likely they've stolen it, yet that could be hard to prove. And the North Koreans could say they too were a victim of theft."

"By using us to deliver this device," Sami added, "their excuse is complete. The caliphate will be eager to claim responsibility."

Rafiq nodded. "The Koreans get to use their weapon with impunity, exposing America's weakness."

Saleem said, "What does it matter? We will have what we want, glory be to the Prophet!" He quickly added, "Don't you see? If this is true, we owe nothing to the Koreans. They are only exploiting us for their own purposes. I say we attack Pearl Harbor, no matter what orders they give!"

"No!" argued Rafiq. "We don't know everything—there has to be a reason for the change!"

The two exchanged a hard look.

All eyes ended up on Boutros. He considered everything in the new light, then shook his head decisively. "No. The North Koreans want success as much as we do. They would not divert us without reason. It will take another three days at sea to reach Hawaii. Based on this message, I don't think we have that much time. And in the end, what does it matter? We can still bring a great victory."

"The secondary target will be only half a victory," Saleem argued.

"More than that," said Boutros. "The symbolism of the secondary target is nearly as great as Pearl Harbor. It will also be virtually undefended." Saleem began to say something, but Boutros cut him off. "That is my decision! We are going to strike the secondary!" He leveled his gaze squarely on Saleem, who scowled but nodded his assent.

"It's settled then," Boutros said. "I will take the helm. We can push the boat hard, gain a few more hours."

"When will that put us at the rendezvous?" Rafiq asked.

Boutros went to the chart table and ran a rough estimate. "If all goes well . . . we will take the delivery late tomorrow. At that point, we will have everything we need."

SIXTY

The "delivery" Boutros was referring to was, at that moment, touching down on the half-mile-long runway at Rongelap Airport in the Marshall Islands. The Colt bounced once before settling, the aircraft still ponderous despite her low fuel state. The captain taxied toward the terminal, which turned out to be a coral-block shack the size of a two-car garage.

No one came to meet the aircraft, which wasn't unexpected. The captain shut down the engine, got out and stretched, and began searching the tarmac. Near one edge he saw a pair of worn wooden blocks connected by a piece of rope. He retrieved them and chocked the airplane's left wheel front and back, although it hardly seemed necessary—the island was as flat as a duck pond. He instructed his copilot to prepare for refueling, then set out toward a tiny cluster of buildings a few hundred yards away— what was probably referred to locally as "town."

The captain had done his homework.

Situated among the western atolls of the Marshall Islands, the landing strip at Rongelap received only a handful of flights each week. Virtually all brought in supplies for the island's twenty-two residents. The bulk of this was food staples, since, for the last seventy years, nothing grown on the island itself could be safely consumed. For three generations, life on Rongelap had been governed by a unique series of events—and so it would remain for another thousand years.

The most egregious of these incidents had been code-named Castle Bravo.

Transpiring in March 1954, Castle Bravo was the largest nuclear test ever undertaken by the United States. Problematically, it was never intended to be. In truth, Castle Bravo was perhaps the greatest scientific miscalculation in history. Planned for a yield of 6.5 megatons, the bomb's experimental lithium deuteride boost proved disconcertingly effective, driving the yield to an unexpected 15 megatons—two and a half times the predicted energy.

In the blast's immediate aftermath, concerned physicists worked their slide rules feverishly, desperate to estimate the scope of their error. The resulting cloud of radiation, they quickly realized, would fast blanket islands for hundreds of miles to the east. Unplanned evacuations were hastily ordered, and military personnel were instructed to remain inside bunkers. Ships downwind were diverted away from the fallout. It was all quite reactionary, and of limited effectiveness: traces from the mushroom cloud climbed into the stratosphere and would in time circle the earth. The resulting international outrage led to stern limits on subsequent testing.

It was therefore with no small degree of irony that when General Park planned his delivery of a cache of weapons-grade uranium, he viewed the remote atolls of the Marshall Islands as a fitting waypoint. Rongelap maintained an operational airport, had fuel available—albeit at a ruinous price—and was ideally situated as a final stepping-off point to the rendezvous with *Albatross*.

Yet there was one complication. And that, Park had decided, had a simple solution.

All he needed was a second aircraft.

On appearances, the second Colt was a twin to the one that had yesterday left Friendship Cay. Its two pilots had even been drawn from the same North Korean air force squadron. Seventy miles south of Rongelap, outside radar coverage and not in voice contact with any air traffic control network, the second Colt was established in a low-altitude holding pattern above balmy crystalline waters.

The crew at her controls were an obedient pair—as North Korean pilots tended to be—and knew nothing of the greater mission behind their assignment. Their orders had been to take off from Marshall Islands International Airport—in Majuro, where they had been waiting for days—under a carefully crafted flight plan. They would proceed in the general direction of the tiny runway at Rongelap, giving wide berth to the closely monitored airspace around the American missile test site on Kwajalein. Once outside radar coverage, they would go into a holding pattern, induce a two-hour delay, then return to Majuro. It was as simple a mission as either pilot had ever flown, albeit with one peculiarity—they had been told to file their flight plan using a slightly altered aircraft registration number.

Everything went to plan.

The Colt from Friendship Cay, with its heavy load, progressed through its technical stop at Rongelap. The captain had no trouble locating the "airport administrator," a small and ever-smiling man with a walnut complexion, lounging inside his sun-beaten, thatch-roofed home. The man happily stamped the flight's paperwork as if it had come from Majuro, and because that departure point granted the flight "domestic" status, no consideration was given for customs or immigration inspections.

The laden Colt took on a full load of fuel, including topping off her auxiliary tanks. If the airport caretaker ever questioned why the aircraft was taking on five times the amount of fuel required to reach Majuro—and at a price per gallon double what would be paid there—his concern was lost when the skipper paid in cash, rounding up to the nearest hundred dollars. As a token of goodwill, and perhaps even more distractingly, the captain gave the caretaker a half-dozen pirated DVDs of the latest Hollywood movies. The native, who was clearly something of a city father, refused to let such kindness go unanswered. He went into the tiny airport office and returned with strips of dried copra, proudly proclaiming them to have been grown on the island.

Best wishes were exchanged, and soon the Colt was airborne on the next leg of its journey, a northeasterly vector over the open Pacific. Right on schedule, her sister ship, orbiting fifty miles to the southeast, took up a heading back to Majuro where hours later her arrival would be duly recorded.

Twenty miles outside Rongelap, the more heavily laden aircraft labored to climb over open ocean. The two pilots, whose sustenance for the last two days had been derived from vending machines across the South Pacific, exchanged a cautious look. The captain produced the strips of copra and handed them to his copilot. Without comment, the copilot cracked his window open and dropped them through one by one. In the Colt's wake, ten strips of nominally radioactive coconut meat fluttered down to the vast sea below.

Soon after leveling at their cruise altitude, the captain directed his first officer's attention to the west. In the distant equatorial haze, on the horizon, another atoll was clearly visible.

"Bikini," the captain said.

The chain of islands seemed still in the heavy air, as if remaining in some kind of topographical coma after the traumas of long ago. Both men reflected on the symbolism of it all. This was the theater of America's nuclear genesis. And in the sky above: the delivery of what would soon be its greatest defeat passed completely unnoticed.

SIXTY-ONE

"Hotel Yankee Eight Six Bravo," Sorensen said.

Slaton had been stirred from a deep sleep by a knock on his door. He answered it to find Sorensen standing in the hallway. As soon as he stepped back, she bypassed him without invitation. He leaned out to check up and down the hall, then closed the door behind her.

Realizing that Slaton's "vector" from Langley would take time, they'd driven to the U.S. Army air base at Wiesbaden. That was where Sorensen's Citation X was parked. The jet was ready to go, and the new crew, who'd been briefed to expect a fluid mission, were standing by on short notice. Once all that was settled, Sorensen had procured rooms for them both in the visiting officers quarters.

She turned to face him, waving a printed page. "I think we found the airplane in the picture."

"Hotel Yankee," he repeated. "Just like Christine said."

"Yes."

"How sure are you?"

"About as sure as things get in our business. To begin, it's one of only two Challengers whose registration begins with those two letters."

"And the other one?"

"Crashed landing in a snowstorm in Telluride last year."

"How encouraging." Slaton rubbed his face as if to massage away the fatigue. He checked the clock by the bed. It was five thirty in the morning. He'd gotten his two hours' sleep, plus a bit more. He was sure Sorensen was working on less.

"Then there's the matter of ownership," she said. "The aircraft is registered to a shell company in Panama, which is controlled by another in the Cook Islands."

"What could be more transparent."

"It was actually an easy trail to follow. This is an operation we've been watching for almost two years, and definitely tied to North Korea—that's what piqued our interest to begin with. More specifically, we think it was set up and run by SSD."

"Park?" Slaton queried.

"Like I said, slam dunk."

"Okay . . . I agree, that's solid. So where is this jet now?"

"That's the not-so-great news," she said.

He hazily remembered Sorensen saying something through the door after her first knock. Something about *good news and bad news*. "Let me guess—you can't find it."

"Actually, we know exactly where it is." She checked her watch. "Right now it's on final approach to the airport in Urumqi."

"Urumqi? As in Northwest China?"

"I doubt there's another one."

"Why would they be going there?"

"Urumqi's a decent-sized city, but it's a stepchild as far as China's ruling elite are concerned. The place is surrounded by desert, and cold as Siberia this time of year."

Slaton read between the lines. "Meaning there's nothing of intelligence value. And consequently, no reason for the CIA to keep a presence there."

"Basically."

"So that's the bad news? That you can't get eyes on this jet?"

"No. The bad news is a little more hypothetical. As it turns out, we actually track a lot of small jets through Urumqi—the airport has one particularly endearing quality."

"What's that?"

"Geography—it's halfway between Europe and most major cities in the Far East. For all its short-comings, Urumqi is the perfect transit hub."

"You're saying this jet was in Europe?"

"Yes. Once we had the tail number, it was simple to find its departure point—Mallorca."

Slaton nodded. An island in the Med, not far from Gibraltar. It was just the kind of place Christine might choose for a hideaway. "So you think the jet will continue elsewhere?" he asked.

"Almost certainly. We have aviation specialists on staff. They ran the numbers, and it turns out a Mallorca to Urumqi flight is right at the limits of the jet's range."

"So it's a refueling stop."

"I think that's a safe bet. It'll be on the ground soon, then probably airborne again within the hour."

"Can we find out where it's going next?"

Sorensen paused a long beat, forewarning her answer. "That's not so easy," she admitted. "We're good at tracking jets that go international out of China—those flight plans have to be filed with external networks. Unfortunately, the same doesn't apply to domestic flights—we could probably manage it, but to hack that server would be pretty provocative. Basically, it's a line we haven't crossed."

"Because you don't want it crossed in return," he said critically. "A gentleman's agreement."

"David, if it was up to me—"

"You're in the damned Directorate of Operations, Anna! You run special ops! If it's not up to you, then who?"

"Look, I know what this means to you."

"No, you have no idea! You've never had a child who might . . ." His words trailed off.

Sorensen's attention went to the only window in the room. It was perfectly square, four equal panes edged in frost. Outside was the backside of an institutional building, some kind of personnel center. Slaton kept his eyes on her. He knew Sorensen was on his side. She'd spent time with his family, and she and Christine had gotten along well. There was no need to make it personal. Yet he sensed she was holding something back.

"What else, Anna?" he asked.

She turned back to face him. "It's only speculation right now, but based on this stop in Urumqi, the distance and course remaining, not to mention the aircraft's ownership . . . our analysts strongly suspect your family is being taken to North Korea."

It was all Christine could do to take her eyes off Davy—but she knew she would have to at any moment.

He was sound asleep in a reclining chair, curled into a soft crescent with a blanket. She'd not yet

seen any signs of stress—no meltdowns, no clinging to her, no trouble sleeping. She took some of the
credit. In perhaps the most difficult night of her life,
she'd forced herself to characterize their abduction
as some great adventure. All smiles and excitement
and pointing fingers at new sights. It helped that
their captors had so far been civil—one of the un-
derlings had even tried to play chase with him in the
tiny cabin.

Civil. So far . . .

The clouds outside the triple-pane window were
thick—she could barely see the tip of the wing.
Then, all at once, the aircraft broke through a final
layer and a city appeared. Less than a minute later
they were on the ground.

Christine took in everything through the tiny oval
portal, desperate to learn where they were. She saw
an airport like any other, if a bit dated and worn.
There were a few other airplanes, and most didn't
seem Western. Not Boeing or Airbus, but Russian or
Chinese manufacturers. She hoped to see a terminal
with a *Welcome to Wherever* sign. Or perhaps some
distant landmark she recognized.

In time, the answer to her question came, albeit in
a general way.

A big China Southern Airlines jet.

Another operated by Air Nepal.

She saw Mandarin characters painted on a distant building.

So they were in China. Somewhere.

It was hardly a surprise. The men who'd marched
them out of their resort room in Mallorca—there
were four, and all were on board, along with two
pilots—Christine had figured for either Chinese or
Korean. She hadn't gone to the trouble of asking—

for Davy's sake, she'd sworn internally to do nothing to antagonize them. *And even if I knew where they were from, how would that help?* she thought.

Out of nowhere a large hand appeared from behind and slammed the window shade shut.

Christine startled, but held steady. She knew it was the thick-muscled leader. The man with a notable hitch in his gait.

"I was only wondering where we are," she said, not turning to face him.

No reply.

She was quite sure that he was in charge. She'd recognized the deference shown by the others from the first moments in Mallorca: during the smooth exit from the room, the rushed journey to the airport with everyone sardined into the back of a generic work van. She'd seen him make a call on a smartphone in the first minutes of the flight. Hours later, it was the big man with the scar on his head who'd posed her with Davy for a photograph—a thoughtful composition in which they'd been squeezed together in a chair and positioned with a certain background.

That had been her first break. Christine had no idea what these men wanted, but it almost certainly involved David. That being the case, when they lined her up for a picture, she assumed he would see it. Weighing how to put that to use, the sign language they'd been studying seemed a natural fit.

In Mallorca her captors had bustled her and Davy from the van to the airplane on a quiet corner of the airfield. Remote as it might have been, however, it was still a public place, which gave no option of putting a hood over her head—or, thank God, Davy's. So as she'd walked across the tarmac, Christine had gotten a good look at the scene. There were a few people in the distance, but all too far away to signal for help.

Then she'd seen the aircraft. Near the back, on the shroud of the portside engine and slightly beneath the T-tail, she saw the black and white registration number.

HY86B.

Hours later, when the camera came out, it seemed her best chance. With only two hands to work with, she'd signed the first two letters of the tail number. As a further attention-getter, she'd put on a look of terror.

Which wasn't hard to do.

Could it possibly work? she wondered, staring at the shuttered window. *Will David see my message?*

She sensed the big man behind her, sitting in complete silence. Her discomfort grew, and finally she turned to face him.

"Have you heard from my husband?" she ventured. It seemed a harmless enough opener.

He grunted, then said, "You are doctor?"

Christine nodded cautiously. "Yes, I'm a doctor."

"I have need."

He limped to the back of the cabin. She watched him more cautiously than ever, not sure what he had in mind. Perhaps not wanting to know. He returned moments later with the airplane's first-aid kit. He handed it to her, then took off his boot and sock. He raised the cuff of his trousers to expose his right leg. It was bandaged heavily, and blood had saturated what looked like an original dressing.

"Again," he said.

"You want it rebandaged?"

A nod.

She switched positions with him, putting him in the swivel chair and elevating his injured leg into an opposing seat. She opened the kit and saw only the basics. Gloves, gauze, tape, a tube of antibiotic ointment. It would have to do.

She retrieved a spare blanket from a nearby bin, worked it under his leg. She then accordioned his pant leg up. Christine unwrapped the original bandage, which seemed professionally done, and saw multiple wounds. The damage looked fresh—ragged tissue on the back side of the calf, and more on the outer heel.

"What happened?" she asked.

He didn't answer, but it hardly mattered. Christine had done enough turns in the ER to know she was looking at a gunshot wound. Or more likely, two. At least one entry high on the gastrocnemius, and a pair of exits near the ankle. Most of what she saw was soft tissue damage, probably including the fascia and tendons around the ankle.

"Did you have it X-rayed?" she asked.

"Is good. Only needs bandage."

She went to work in silence, happy her son was asleep. She donned the gloves and cleaned the wounds as best she could, noting a few sutures on the heel that seemed to be holding. As she set to her task, she had a curious flashback to her med-school rotation in psychiatry. She recalled discussing with her preceptor Stockholm syndrome, the irrational bonding of captor and captive during hostage situations.

Christine felt nothing of the sort.

As she tended to the wound, it struck her that her patient was watching her with inordinate intensity.

He also seemed to be smiling. It was as if a secondary storyline was playing out in his head. As if he was relishing some obscure victory.

Never, not in her wildest dreams, could she have known what he was thinking.

SIXTY-TWO

Slaton didn't let Sorensen out of his sight. Without her, and the vast resources of the CIA, he could imagine but one option: catch a commercial flight east, find a way to breach the North Korean border, and search an entire country single-handed.

A definite challenge.

But if that's what it came down to, he would do it.

Two hours after the meeting in his room, they were sitting side by side on a bench in the army dining hall. All around them enlisted personnel were having breakfast, loading up on calories for a day in the field. At least half of the males had either shot a glance or stared openly at the stunning thirtysome-thing blonde sitting next to Slaton. None could have imagined that, in the greater hierarchy of Washington, she was roughly four pay grades above the general in charge of their post.

Slaton was scooping wet powdered eggs from a partitioned plastic tray when Sorensen's secure phone rang. She took the call, listened for two minutes, then began asking questions. The tables around them were packed with too many loud and caffeinated sergeants to hear what was being said.

Less indistinct, however, was the way Sorensen's

face hardened during the call. If Slaton wasn't mistaken, he saw the beginnings of worry lines around her eyes. Subconsciously, he went on edge himself. By the time the call ended, a full ten minutes after it began, Slaton's fork was on his plate and he was leaning forward.

Ready to go.

"What was that all about?" he asked impatiently.

"There's nothing new about the jet carrying your wife," she said, clearly sensing his edge. "But we did discover something else. This company that owns the Challenger, the one controlled by SSD. It turns out they have two other aircraft on their books. Not business jets, but small transports, Chinese Y-5As."

Slaton tried to visualize the type—aircraft recognition had long ago been drilled into him by Mossad. A basic skill for a spy. "The original version was Russian," he said. "NATO calls it the Colt."

"That's the one. We put together a lookback analysis on these particular aircraft. We've got a new algorithm that can channel air traffic control records, ownership history, along with raw surveillance imagery of certain airports. Park's airplanes have been busy in the last two years—very busy. A lot of their flying was international, and we were able to track quite a few of the movements. Once that was done, we crosshatched some new data."

"Such as?"

"The files you gave us from El-Masri."

She gave Slaton a few seconds to put it all together. "Pakistan?" he queried. "Ghana and Kazakhstan?"

"Bingo. Of the five caches of HEU allegedly stolen by Park's group, we can place these aircraft at a nearby airport, and in the right timeframe, on three occasions. A fourth is probable, and we're working on Belgium."

"Okay . . . so you think you know how Park moved this material. But where was it taken?"

"There's not as much hard evidence, but I think we figured it out. In each case, after the theft, the aircraft flew in the general direction of Southwest Asia. From there the trail gets more sketchy, but we think we tracked one to a very small island in the South China Sea."

"Which island?"

Sorensen looked at him quizzically, then smiled. "I forgot—you and Christine were sailing there not long ago. It's called Friendship Cay today, but the name used to be something different."

"Glorious Dawn?" he said.

"I think that was it—you really do know the area."

"I know it was one of China's first attempts at dredging islands—and one of the few they gave up on."

"They were there long enough to install a small runway and a few buildings."

Slaton thought about it. "What better place to hide a couple dozen kilos of highly enriched uranium. Are you looking into this?"

"The Navy is diverting a littoral ship to take a peek. But I don't think they'll find much."

"Why not?"

"Because these airplanes both left the island—one last week, and the other early yesterday."

"How could you possibly know that?"

"I explained that we don't hack Chinese domestic air traffic control. I didn't say anything about Vietnam or the Philippines."

He looked at her incredulously. "Have I told you that I'm glad you're on my side?"

"No, but I'll take it under advisement."

"Do you know where these airplanes are now?"

"Almost. At least one of them turned up right under our noses. It's been found abandoned—Marshall Islands International Airport, in Majuro."

"When?"

Sorensen looked at her watch. "Less than two hours ago. The airplane is empty, but we have a team en route to go over it. The crew seems to have disappeared."

"You figured all this out since last night?"

"This is reaching critical mass back at Langley. Half the staff in my section are working various angles. The second Colt is the one we need to find. We're coordinating with the Navy and Air Force, going over radar logs, even reallocating a few satellites. Oh . . . and Director Coltrane wants to talk to me directly. I've got a call scheduled in ten minutes."

"Good. Have a nice chat, and tell him I said hello—right after you get that aircrew out to my jet."

"I figured as much. The crew will want to know where they're going."

"Right now, east."

"In the general direction of the Marshall Islands?"

"It's a start. Last I heard, my family is heading to North Korea, so it at least puts me within a few time zones. In the time it will take me to get there, I'm guessing you'll have something more specific."

He waited for Sorensen to argue against his logic. What she said was, "Sounds like a plan, but I can make it even better."

"How?"

"I'm going with you."

Slaton stiffened only slightly, then said, "Yeah, well . . . I guess it is your jet."

By six o'clock that evening, Hawaii-Aleutian Time, three sets of travelers were converging on a single point in the Pacific. They closed in at wildly divergent speeds.

The slowest was the trawler *Albatross*, making a steady twenty-four knots on dead-calm seas, her engine humming at redline. The four men on board were busy: managing the boat, preparing for their mission, and making regular entreaties to Allah for guidance.

Far to the southwest, a single-engine Y-5A churned methodically northward at sixteen thousand feet. Her weary pilots never gave a thought to divine intervention, concentrating instead on a Bendix weather radar to avoid lines of tropical thunderstorms. They did their best to conserve fuel and find smooth air as convective turbulence shook the little airplane mercilessly. After one particularly heavy jolt, the captain and first officer exchanged a look of concern. They both turned to see the heavy container in the cargo bay—which they knew held nuclear material—swaying ponderously beneath its tie-downs.

Five miles west, a Citation X sped inbound at nine-tenths the speed of sound. It carried two passengers, one of whom tried to sleep, while the other interacted nonstop with an intelligence agency halfway around the world. Both had marginal success.

SIXTY-THREE

Thousands of miles from any continent, and centered precisely in the world's most expansive body of water, a small ring of coral rises from an indigo sea. Little more than an uninhabited necklace of rock, it is shaped in the general outline of a nesting bird—an apt analogy for an atoll that serves as home to hundreds of thousands of seagoing terns, boobies, and frigates.

Nestled on the right shoulder of the international date line, the tiny island chain serves as an eternal counterpoint to Greenwich, England. Noon translates to midnight, day compares to night, and the urban London horizon is countered by endless expanses of sun and featureless sea. One of the most isolated places on earth, the atoll is called Mokupāpapa by native Hawaiians, Kure by the Americans, and far less agreeable names by the handful of sailors and airmen unfortunate enough to have been castaway on her shores.

At high tide the circle of cays remains but a few feet above sea level, as if taunting the warming globe to make its move. The largest strip of land, if it can be called that, was referred to as Green Island.

Less than half a mile long, and a quarter mile wide at its greatest reach, it is the site of the only enduring human mark—a tiny World War II–era runway left to ruin. Since those tumultuous years, the island had fallen to what it had always been: a tiny shelf of constancy surrounded by an ever-changing sea. Hard-scrabble plants sprout foliage year-round, rain comes like clockwork, and the sky keeps an unvarying shade of blue. Any notion of seasons is roundly ignored. The tropical wind blows incessantly, and on those few days when the sun goes missing, the balmy water takes over to avert a chill.

Against the white noise of the modern world, Kure Atoll was more ignored than forgotten. Its shoals are well marked and recorded, yet because the atoll lies in protected waters, fishermen keep well out to sea. Indeed, the only true pocket of human interest comes not from tourists or navies or even the odd scuba diving charter, but from one tight-knit group of individuals who come for the same reasons others do not: Kure, for all its glorious isolation, is celebrated by the world's ornithologists.

A few times each year, always during nesting season, they motor ashore in small groups. They set up tents and propane stoves, and for a week, sometimes two, they patrol the desolate beaches to count nesting pairs of various species with the lust of sailors on shore leave. When their mission is done, they break down camp, pick up their trash responsibly, and head home to enter data.

This narrow window each year, when humans can be found on Kure, is in fact quite predictable. What would come as a surprise to even the most committed ornithologist was that this research schedule had been painstakingly documented in a very recent, and narrowly viewed, report produced by North Korea's SSD.

The conclusion: through the long dregs of January, and at the height of the northern winter, there would be not a single mating pair of terns on the island's white coral shores.

The sun was touching *Albatross'* transom as everyone gathered near the bone-dry nets. Boutros had decided to convene his meeting on deck—the boat's autopilot was having no problem with the calm seas, and as the tropics took hold everyone was increasingly eager to escape the stifling air of the wheelhouse.

If he was thankful for anything, it was that the weather had cooperated during their crossing. They'd had one rough day early on, a few rain showers since, but the Pacific had, by and large, cooperated magnificently. Having done his research, Boutros knew it could have been otherwise. Winter on the North Pacific was a wildly unpredictable affair. These were the months when surfers in Hawaii watched the rise and fall of obscure weather buoys thousands of miles away, waiting for swells that would build for days to become twenty-five-foot monsters thundering down on the North Shore of Oahu. So far, *Albatross* had been blessed. The short-term forecast was for more of the same.

One more day, he thought. *God willing, that is all we need.*

"The charges are prepared," Saleem said proudly. "I will not connect the wiring until we are near our target. I have also checked the initiators and both batteries—there is a primary and a backup."

Boutros nodded, then looked expectantly at Rafiq.

"The device is ready," he said. "I had some difficulty setting the cap into place, but it was easily solved with a bit of filing and lubrication—the threading was still rough from the machining process. We need only the projectile rings to make our weapon complete."

All eyes went to Sami.

"I am ready," he said, his voice unwavering.

Boutros nodded respectfully.

Sami's involvement had so far been minimal. There was always room for a fighter if they were challenged by a patrol boat, and one could never have enough deckhands. As it turned out, Sami proved to be a quick learner and had become useful around the boat.

Yet his primary reason for being here would play out in the next twenty-four hours. Rafiq had explained everything to the young Libyan during the early planning stages, making sure Sami knew what he was getting into. He told him there was nothing particularly hazardous about handling highly enriched uranium. That would come in the form of a dense metal, heavy slugs machined to fit the weapon. Yet what made HEU good for nuclear bombs—its fissionable properties—had little bearing on its rate of radioactive decay. Due to an extremely long half-life, HEU was a low emitter of radiation. There were alpha particles, and a bit of gamma activity thrown in, but for the most part it was harmless. Best practices involved wearing gloves during handling, and taking every precaution not to inhale dust particles.

Yet there was a greater problem. The North Korean weapon they'd been given included a neutron initiator, and this was composed of polonium and beryllium. Because polonium is highly radioactive, with a very short half-life, the only option had been to include it separately in the final shipment. In any laboratory or weapons production facility, installing polonium would be done robotically. In the cabin of a fishing trawler in the middle of the Pacific—the only option was to do it by hand. If not fatal in the near term, it was an almost assured death sentence. Boutros would never forget Sami's response after that briefing—he had never hesitated.

"When will we arrive?" Saleem asked.

"Very soon," Boutros replied. "I think shortly after nightfall."

"Is that not a problem?"

Boutros frowned. "I had wanted to make our approach to the island in daylight. Unfortunately, the currents have been against us all day. Yet we will find a way, God willing."

"There are no new changes?" asked Saleem. "We are still being told to attack the secondary target?"

"Nothing has changed," Boutros said flatly.

Saleem nodded. The subject would not be brought up again.

Boutros looked forward, through the windscreen over the helm. His posture suddenly stiffened.

Sami was the first to notice. "What is it?" he asked.

Boutros took a moment to look at each man in turn. He then raised a bony finger, pointed to the horizon, and said in an oddly subdued voice, "We have arrived."

SIXTY-FOUR

For an assistant deputy director of the CIA, SAD no less, the idea of transiting Russian airspace in the course of an operation was a complete nonstarter. Resultingly, Slaton and Sorensen were denied a great circle route that would have gotten them to their destination hours sooner.

The question of what that destination was became solved somewhere over Bhutan. Sorensen returned from the cockpit after using the jet's communications suite for the sixth time—Slaton had seen the system, and recognized state-of-the-art technology when he saw it. Along the same lines, no expense had been spared on the jet's interior. There were chrome fittings, plush carpet, and six supple leather seats, all of which adjusted into sleepers. Courtesy of the American taxpayers.

"Midway Island," she announced.

Slaton paused a beat. "That's where our missing Colt is headed?" he asked. Visions of the great World War II naval battle filled his head.

"Probably not—but that's where you and I are going. Military radar logged hits tracking north out of the Marshalls—a low and slow target navigating through thunderstorms. Very few airplanes operate in that airspace, especially at low altitude, so it's almost certainly the one we're looking for. We projected the general course and took into consideration the airplane's range. There's no way they can make it to the main Hawaiian Islands, so they're heading to one of the islands west of there."

"You're sure?"

"The only other option is ditching in mid-ocean. But that still leaves a lot of ground to cover. The Leeward Hawaiian Islands extend for almost a thousand miles."

"And Midway is our best option?"

"It's the farthest-west airfield in the archipelago where we can land and get fuel."

"Okay. That makes sense." He glanced out the window, saw the Himalayas passing in the distance. "Can we get there from here?" he asked. They had already refueled once in New Delhi, and Slaton figured Midway had to be thousands of miles ahead.

"The pilots say we're good. This jet's got some long legs—one of the reasons I like it."

"Good. The sooner we find this Colt and put a stop to whatever the Koreans are up to, the sooner we can get around to finding my family."

Sorensen didn't reply.

"Anna . . ." he said cautiously. "Is there something else?"

"There is. The jet Christine and Davy were on, the one that passed through Urumqi . . . we think we know where it landed."

The sedan climbed smoothly uphill, its headlights slicing through darkness. For a time Christine saw only forest, thick and evergreen, with rough-hewn terrain in the gaps. There was a sensation of climbing, affirmed by a straining engine. Then, all at once, the foliage disappeared.

The night was clear, the moon bright, and in its glow she could see the compound clearly. It was relatively small, built into the side of a forested hill. On first impression it looked more like a fortress than a home, the bastion-like foundation lifting as if by some tectonic process from the valley of rock below. The upper levels of the house were completely at odds, almost Alpine in appearance.

The approach road was narrow and new, constant switchbacks hairpinning higher. The headlights illuminated the kind of jade forest that might be found in a hundred different places in the world. She wished she were in any of the others right now.

Christine was in the back seat, the big man in front, passenger side. He was silent as ever. There had been a few hand gestures during the flight, and he'd issued orders to his men in a language she didn't understand. To Christine the man had spoken few words since she'd dressed his wound so many hours ago. Four to be precise. Perfectly clear and distinct, expressed after they'd landed.

It had been a short ride from the airport, which seemed a mercy in itself. After thirty hours of travel and half a world of time zones, Christine was severely disoriented. She wished it was only the fatigue, but she felt herself falling into a bleakness she'd never before experienced. Had she been alone, it might have overtaken her, reduced her vigilance to something catatonic.

Only one thing kept her going.

Davy was awake at the moment. Bleary-eyed from the circadian upset, he was nestled to her right hip.

He actually seemed to be enjoying the sights. For a boy who'd spent most of his life cruising featureless ocean and exploring palm-tipped islands, the surrounding hills must have seemed like mountains.

"Are there bears outside?" he asked.

"No, honey. I don't think so."

"When will we be there?"

"Soon, I promise."

"Will Daddy be there?"

Christine pulled in a great breath. "No . . . but we'll see him soon."

The big man turned and gave her a stern look—the only one he possessed, apparently. Christine considered asking how his leg was holding up, but her compassion was forestalled by a thought she'd had many years ago with regard to another abductor—the one she'd eventually married: *Where was gangrene when you needed it?*

In the end she said nothing.

Neither did he, which left his input since landing at the four words he'd uttered back at the airport.

The four most unsettling words Christine had ever heard.

"Welcome to North Korea."

SIXTY-FIVE

Boutros looked out the window into blackness, his hands steady on the wheel. He turned his eye to the adjacent navigation display and pressed a button to zoom in. He didn't like what he saw.

Any approach to unfamiliar shallows demanded unremitting caution. Doubly so at night. Boutros was confident of *Albatross'* position—he'd made a number of crosschecks when they passed through the Tsugaru Straits, and the nav data was tight. In the era of GPS, that was rarely a problem. Less certain was the electronic chart he was working from. The software was a Chinese product, and the database two years out of date. Hardly a confidence builder.

Worse yet, he'd been warned that Pacific atolls were notoriously misrepresented on charts. Channels leading into ports were generally well marked, but the barrier reefs around uninhabited islands were rarely penetrated. Most Pacific atolls developed as nearly circular reefs, with only a few ill-defined gaps through which a ship might pass into the central lagoon. These barrier reefs tended to shift over time. Coral heads grew and currents shifted. Storms created new passages and closed off old ones. Owing to the capricious nature of such channels, few cartographers committed to plotting them on official charts.

In daylight, Boutros knew, the job would have been much easier. With gin-clear water and a blazing tropical sun, one could easily pick out trouble spots. Boutros was an expert by virtue of his days running the Persian Gulf. Coral outcroppings would stand out dark and ominous against the white-sand bottom of channels. And during daylight the flows of current through deeper gaps could be recognized on the surface. Now, two hours after sunset, he had no such guidance.

He looked ahead and saw Saleem, a dim shadow near the bow. Boutros had ordered every unnecessary light turned off for their approach. He doubted there was anyone on the island, but it was free insurance. It also kept everyone's night vision at its peak. He'd posted Rafiq and Sami to stand watch at the port and starboard rails. In effect, it gave Saleem and Rafiq maximum separation. The two had been increasingly at odds during the voyage, and Boutros realized he'd begun issuing assignments to keep them apart. A not unfamiliar situation for a commander, but a distraction all the same.

He nudged the throttle forward and referenced the chart. The boat crept forward twenty meters. *Run aground here,* he thought, *and our mission will be over.*

"Any luck?" Boutros shouted through the forward window—he'd lifted it open in order to communicate with Saleem.

"Still deep!" Saleem called back.

Boutros could see him coiling a line.

Albatross was fitted with a basic depth finder, but

no forward-looking sonar or other device to identify shallow water ahead. That being the case, Boutros reverted to the backup that had been used by captains for a thousand years. Saleem stood at the bow pulpit with a sounding line—essentially, a length of light rope with a lead weight tied to the end. Every ten yards or so, as the boat edged forward, he threw the line ahead to measure the depth. At the line's twenty-foot mark a rag was attached to serve as a warning—if it got that shallow, Boutros needed to know immediately.

Boutros had expected he would make mistakes during the voyage, but an hour ago he'd realized the most glaring. When Choe briefed him on *Albatross'* handling traits, Boutros had neglected to ask the most basic of all questions: How much water did she draw?

He was left to guess, and decided it had to be somewhere between eight and twelve feet. A twenty-foot alarm, he was sure, gave them room for error. But it also forced them to seek a deep channel—something that might not even exist.

In dim moonlight the outline of Kure Atoll was clear—a low panorama presented in shades of darkness. He could make out small islands, sandbars, and a few exposed coral beds. A whitewater arc of soft breakers completed the encirclement of the calm inner lagoon. Their objective lay to starboard—Green Island comprised the east side of the ring, a matte-black shadow protecting the atoll's right flank. The lagoon itself would be reasonably safe, protected waters deep enough to find any number of decent anchorages.

They only had to reach it.

"Breakers to the right!" Sami called out.

Boutros threw his head out the starboard window and saw the danger. It was thirty meters distant, and matched what was on the chart—a shallow reef next to the best natural channel on the southern edge of the atoll.

"That's all right," he called out. "We must keep it to the right. We are getting close."

"Fifteen feet!" Saleem shouted from the bow.

Boutros threw the engine into reverse, putting them dead in the water. He looked forward and saw Saleem displaying the flag on the sounding line, his hand pointing five feet farther down.

Boutros cursed under his breath. "We will go very slowly from here. Keep checking!"

Saleem coiled up the line and took the weight in his hand. He heaved it into the dark sea ahead.

"Show me!" said Slaton from his seat near the window.

Sorensen addressed the laptop she'd brought on the flight. She called up a map of North Korea that was definitely not a Google product. To begin, it was sectioned by tinted arcs from northwest to southeast. The swathes overlapped and each was labeled with a small data tag. Slaton recognized them as satellite coverage tracks. Instead of cities and national parks being identified, he saw the names of every military base and nuclear installation, along with official residences of the regime.

Definitely an internal app, he thought.

Sorensen zoomed in on a point in the southeast corner of the country—no more than thirty miles from the DMZ, and roughly ten inland from the Sea of Japan.

"There's a military airfield north of Mount Kumgang. We've been watching every airport as best we can, and this one got the hit."

She manipulated a secondary file, and one quadrant of the screen filled with an overhead image that could only have been taken from space. The resolution was excellent, and Slaton saw the airplane.

"Are you sure that's the right jet?" he asked.

"One hundred percent."

Slaton almost challenged her, but decided to concede the point. Nobody in the intelligence community, certainly not assistant deputy directors, gave that level of assurance without reason.

"We have two more images," she said, "both after the jet parked."

Slaton saw them in sequence. A shot of three people walking across the tarmac with a solid security contingent around them. He couldn't see faces, but the big picture was damning enough. One head and set of shoulders was very large, and in the middle were two others: one medium, the other very small. In the second image they all appeared to be getting into a dark sedan. Slaton tried to hold steady. The other image of his family he'd seen that day was far more staged. Here, captured clandestinely from above, he almost felt as if he could reach out and touch them.

"Where were they taken?" he asked.

"Our degree of confidence on that is a bit lower. A number of the North Korean elites keep retreats nearby—it's sort of like their Jackson Hole. We know which residence is Park's and the lights are on."

She called up another overhead image. Slaton saw a sturdy house built into the side of a large hill. Like

Sorensen said, the lights were on. The photo had enough resolution to distinguish a few dark shapes that Slaton instantly recognized. Two on the roof, two near the driveway entrance. One on a side lawn that appeared to be the only level ground. Security.

Sorensen's analysts had nailed it. This was where Christine and Davy were at that very minute. And likely where they would remain until . . . *what?*

Slaton was taken by an odd sensation. A familiar voice echoing in. A voice he always trusted. Something wasn't right. He thought back over the last day. During their refueling stop in New Delhi, he'd turned on his old phone and checked for messages. There had been no new attempts to contact him. Yet Sorensen hadn't seen him check the phone. Hadn't even asked if he had. That didn't compute.

More facts tumbled in, and soon it was like watching a demolished building collapse in slow motion. The way Sorensen had dropped everything and flown from Langley to Germany. The ease with which she'd given him access to the jet. The intel he was looking at right now. It seemed too good. Too timely. Too "one hundred percent."

"What's wrong, David?" she asked.

He reached slowly for the top of her computer and folded the screen closed. Slaton stared squarely at the head of the CIA's black operations division, his gray eyes a void. When he finally spoke, his voice was detached, as if coming from a different place. A place he'd been before, and to which he never wanted to return.

"You're not telling me something, Anna. I want to know what it is. And I want to know right now . . ."

SIXTY-SIX

Albatross reached the lagoon on her second attempt. The first channel turned out to be a cul-de-sac, forcing them back into open water. A second passage on the chart, slightly west, proved far superior. By Saleem's rough soundings, they never had less than eighteen feet of water beneath the keel. Wanting to use the same channel for their departure, Boutros marked it carefully with the GPS before idling into the lagoon.

He aimed for an anchorage a hundred yards from Green Island, the southern tip where the derelict runway began only steps from the high tide line. Boutros inched the boat forward, checking the depth finder constantly. The chart suggested the lagoon was mostly safe, yet there would always be a few stray coral heads. He'd picked up a weather report shortly before sundown, and it included a tide table for the area. Right now the tide was near a low, so by traveling the last quarter mile at minimum speed, there was little risk. If they ran aground on the soft sand bottom, they could simply wait a few hours for the tide to lift them.

The moon had nearly set, and by no more than starlight he guided the boat at a crawl to his chosen anchorage. They reached it uneventfully, and

Boutros decided to set two anchors—one fore and one aft. He didn't want the boat to swing once it was in place. Saleem had just secured the big bow hook when Rafiq came from below.

"A message has arrived. Our shipment will arrive shortly after daybreak."

Boutros smiled broadly. "The schedule is holding."

Rafiq looked toward the island. "Have you seen anyone?"

"No. Sami and Saleem have been watching closely. We were told these bird scientists only come a week or two each year."

"For their sake, let it be so."

"Did you acknowledge the message?" Boutros asked.

"Of course. I said we are in position."

"There is still one chore—we must lower the runabout into the water. Then we can rest and wait for first light."

Rafiq regarded the launch. It was a solid fiberglass shell, fifteen feet long, with a small outboard motor. "I hope it is seaworthy," he said.

"I've looked the boat over—it will serve our purposes."

Rafiq almost said something. Instead, he turned and went below.

"I'm cold, Mommy," Davy said as they walked toward the main house.

"I know, honey," Christine said in her most reassuring tone. "We're going inside now."

There was little wind, but the night air was bitter, the temperature in the teens if not single digits. Davy had never before experienced bitter cold, and when Christine picked him up and put him on her hip, he buried his face in her shoulder.

On arriving at the compound they'd first been directed to a small detached building, a drafty cabin with multiple rooms that had the look of servants' quarters. There they'd waited, until an officious older woman arrived with warmer clothes. The two of them were still dressed for Mallorca—T-shirts, shorts, running shoes—and so the oversized cotton hoodies and sweatpants were appreciated. Better yet in Christine's view: it seemed a continuance of the reasonable treatment they'd so far received.

The big man collected them, and now they were crossing the gravel parking apron to the main house. Christine took in what she could. Up close the place seemed architecturally disjointed, a fortress built into a hill with the trappings of an Alpine lodge. A rough stone staircase rose from the parking area to a peak-roofed portico fronted by gloomy wrought-iron fixtures. The foundation of the residence was cut in gray stone, the sides of which were highlighted by feeble exterior lights. Somewhere in the distance she heard the drone of a big diesel, no doubt a generator. Only then did it strike Christine that she hadn't seen a single light during the drive from the airport. She knew little about North Korea, but what she'd seen so far could be distilled to one word: medieval.

Her downcast reflections ended the moment she and Davy stepped into the main house. The temperature rose fifty degrees, warm air rushing through the doors. The next thing that struck her was the light. It was pleasant and inviting, and somehow encompassed every corner of the place. She saw a vast main room, everything in it contrary to the home's cold exterior: soft furnishings, plush carpet, foot-to-ceiling draperies cast in royal colors. There was artwork as well: sculptures on tables that could only be termed modernist, and paintings on nearly every wall, landscapes mostly, all of them bursting in the colors of summer.

She put Davy down, and at her side they held hands—he hadn't been more than two steps away in the last thirty-six hours. The big man, who she'd heard addressed as Khang by a guard at the airport, drifted behind her.

Nothing was said, and as Christine stood taking in the room, a man appeared from the side hall. His features were quintessentially Korean. The black hair had a slight dusting of gray, and he was dressed in dark trousers and a tunic—the style eminently communist, yet the material and tailoring something more. *I really am in North Korea,* she told herself.

His round face held no expression whatsoever, and the man seemed to study her for a time. He finally came closer and extended a hand. "I am General Park Hai-joon."

Having never been taken hostage in the Far East, Christine wasn't sure about the etiquette. She reluctantly shook the man's hand, and didn't bother to introduce herself.

Park addressed Khang in Korean.

She sensed a hesitation, then Khang departed silently into the same hall through which Park had arrived. Her host watched him leave, and only when the big man was gone did his eyes swing back to Christine.

He said, "I'm sure you are mystified by what has

happened to you and your son." Park's English was good, if a bit measured.

"I *know* what's happened. What I'd like to know is why—" Christine cut off the rest of her reply. She was determined to keep her internal promise: for as long as possible, she would say or do nothing confrontational. Not in front of Davy. Her ruse that they were on some happy little escapade, even in the eyes of a preschool child, had to be fast losing its legitimacy. Yet as long as these people were civil, she was determined to respond in kind.

She said, "I just don't understand the reasons behind it."

Park walked to one side of the room and motioned for them to follow. He stopped on a small carpeted area, at one side of which was an expensive-looking toy box. He said, "I have two grandchildren. Your son may use these." He opened the lid to reveal a pile of brightly colored toys. Christine recognized many of the Western standards: a stack of colored rings, giant Lego bricks, two Barbies, a bag of army men.

Davy didn't hesitate. He wriggled on her hand, and as soon as she released him he lunged for the box and began digging. Christine watched guardedly, not sure what to make of it all.

"You look surprised," said Park. "Perhaps you expected children in North Korea to play with lumps of coal."

She didn't respond. At his invitation, she took a seat on a nearby chair—it put her three steps away from her son. She shot a cautious glance at the corridor where Khang had disappeared.

Park drew a small end table close to Christine,

and then sat on it with his hands on his knees. When he spoke, it came in a curiously hushed voice. More than a whisper, but barely. "Your being here tonight was never planned. Honestly, your husband's involvement in our operation was never planned. It has created many complications."

"Yeah, my husband has always been good at that . . . complications."

"I am aware of his reputation."

"So why don't we start at the beginning," Christine said. "What the hell is all this about?"

"That," Park replied, "is a very long story. And one, I assure you, whose end has not been written . . ."

SIXTY-SEVEN

"Park contacted us six months ago," Sorensen said.

Slaton bolted upright in his chair. "Park Hai-joon . . . the head of North Korean state security? He made *contact* with the CIA?"

Sorensen nodded, then gave him a moment to digest it.

"Are you running him as an agent?" Slaton asked.

"Actually, a bit more than that."

"How could it be more than—" He stopped mid-sentence. "Why don't you start from the beginning."

"Okay. But understand, what I'm going to tell you is classified at the highest level."

"Higher than what I gave you on that flash drive?"

"Point taken." Sorensen's gaze drifted to the tiny oval window, the night sky outside an obsidian void. "Last summer Park reached out to us. He went through an intermediary—I can't say who, but it's not important. One of our people met Park for a few hours in Singapore. As I'm sure you know, Kwon rules with an iron hand, but his true authority is derived through the military. Park explained that the mood among North Korea's senior officers is unsettled. Kwon has made purges at the upper levels of the command structure twice in the last three years."

"That's hardly new."

"No, house cleanings are a regular occurrence. That's how strongmen like Kwon keep their generals and ministers in line. The previous head of SSD was executed two years ago. According to Park, a video was circulated internally of the man being used for target practice."

"That's not very original," Slaton said.

"It wasn't a firing squad. They used a 170mm self-propelled howitzer."

Slaton looked away momentarily, then gathered his thoughts. "Okay, that's original—and pretty off your freakin' rocker. So what—you're saying this made an impression on Park? He figures that in two years, maybe three, he'll be the one standing on the bull's-eye with a sabot round coming at him?"

"In part. But he isn't the only one. Park began as an officer in the Korean People's Army. That means he's close with a number of generals high in the command structure. They've all witnessed the same stunts, seen the brutality of Kwon's rule."

Slaton was beginning to see it. "So we're looking at a coup? Park told you the military is going to take over?"

"It's not so straightforward. Park said he confided in a handful of friends, and that he found some support. But there's never a shortage of vipers in a pit that deep. If word was spread too widely, sooner or later someone would play the loyalist and inform Kwon that a plot was being hatched. In the end, Park and his small circle decided that Kwon might be toppled, but not without a crisis. They needed to find a way to humiliate him, both internationally and internally. A reckless act the world couldn't ignore."

"Which is where stolen weapons-grade uranium comes in?"

"He didn't tell us that much, but apparently so. Park has gone through the motions of planning an attack, and without Kwon's knowledge. As head of SSD, he's the only one who could. He gave us almost no details as to how it would be carried out. He only told us it would be delivered by sea, and involve some kind of weapon of mass destruction. That could mean nuclear, chemical, or biological—he wouldn't specify."

"So when I called and brought up his name . . . that's why you came straight to Frankfurt."

She nodded. "We've been busting our butts trying to figure out this threat. As you can imagine, we don't trust Park completely. The information you uncovered about the uranium stolen from IAEA—that has to be tied in. Park has promised to give us enough notice to snuff out this attack. On his cue, we're supposed to intervene. He said the team chosen to deliver it could be easily overpowered. The device itself won't be hard to deactivate—a simple switch with a clock, and we'll have ample time. At that point we go public, show enough detail to convince everyone of the seriousness of the threat. We'll have dodged a bullet, and the Kwon regime looks incompetent."

"And the CIA gets a brilliant counter-terrorism victory."

"No, David . . . this is not about us. It's about Park fueling enough embarrassment to doom Dear Leader's internal support. Anyway, what would you have us do? Park is going forward with his scheme.

Knowing as little as we do, we have no choice but to play along."

Slaton shook his head slowly.

"What?" she asked.

"It doesn't make sense. For this to work, the attack has to be credible. With HEU, we're not talking about a dirty bomb—this is going to be a full-blown fission weapon. How could Kwon ever consider a strike like that? He knows that if North Korea hits the United States with a nuke, you'd retaliate a thousand times over."

Sorensen got up and began pacing the tiny cabin. "I know," she said. "That's the one thing that didn't compute in my mind either. But when he met with our operative, Park was very specific on the point. He said he conceived this attack very carefully. He guaranteed that as long as the intervention was successful, the plot could be tied to North Korea. Not only that, he said it would be obvious that if it had succeeded, they might have gotten away with it."

Slaton considered it. "I guess a nuclear blast has a way of destroying evidence. This has to be where the material pilfered from the IAEA comes in."

"No doubt."

"Tell me . . . by CIA estimates, does North Korea have any highly enriched uranium of their own?"

"Yes. The weapons they've tested and built to date are all plutonium designs. Yet we know they've long had a small stash of HEU—it's a by-product of their early efforts to get the bomb."

"So let's allow that they'd know how to make one using uranium. And if an HEU bomb were to be set off, and at least some of the material is identified as having been sourced from places like Pakistan and Ghana, the North Koreans could claim innocence.

It would eventually be discovered that the material was stolen by El-Masri through IAEA—a murdered Egyptian in the chain to complicate things further. Effectively, North Korea contributes their bomb-making know-how, maybe a bit of their own material, but separate themselves from the strike in every other way. Equipment, delivery, targeting."

"They might even use surrogates to deliver it."

"Surrogates?" said Slaton. "Like mercenaries or something? Who in their right mind would take that kind of assignment?"

"I know, it's a stretch. But Park mentioned it in his meeting—he said the strike team wouldn't be North Korean."

"Have you talked to him since then?"

"We have a line of communication set up, and I can tell you it's being monitored very closely. He's used it once, two weeks ago, to tell us the attack would occur soon."

"How soon?"

Sorensen hesitated over what had to be incredibly sensitive information. She relented. "Sometime in the next week, a target in the Pacific region."

"That's it? The Pacific? It leaves a lot of ground to cover." He tried to wrap his mind around it, then leveled a hard stare at Sorensen. "Do you understand how dangerous a game this is?"

"Yes, I do. As does the director of the CIA, the full national security council, and the president. They've all been briefed in."

"I think I'm beginning to see what Park gets out of this."

Sorensen didn't reply.

"Will he be any better than Kwon Il-sun?" Slaton asked.

"Could he be any worse?"

He looked at her severely.

"Our national leadership has decided the potential of a new, relatively friendly regime in North Korea is worth the risk of letting this play out. The only alternative is to go public with the entire affair, in which case Kwon would clean house."

"That would spell the end for Park," Slaton said.

"No doubt."

He shook his head. "What a mess."

Sorensen sighed and sat in one of the plush chairs. "I agree. But burning Park to the regime doesn't do anything to lessen the risk. I promise you we haven't been sitting around idly. None of us would be doing our jobs if we didn't pursue this with everything we have. We've been watching the DPRK closer than ever. We haven't seen anything relating to the strike. Not until you called yesterday. Now you've given us leads—*good* leads."

Slaton ratcheted down. He knew she had a point, at least from her "agency" point of view. Seated in the swivel chair across the narrow aisle, he thought Sorensen looked tired, spent. He too was feeling the fatigue. Too little rest, too many time zones. He would try again for sleep before they landed. Preparation. No different than topping off a magazine or freshening the batteries in a tactical flashlight.

But what were the chances?

His family's position seemed more impossible than ever. Not only were Christine and Davy being held deep inside the most repressive police state on earth, but now the country's leadership was facing an attempted coup. They were actually *inside* the home of the main conspirator. A man who was plotting a faux nuclear strike against the United States.

The number of potential disasters seemed incalculable.

Sorensen clearly read his distraction. "David . . . I'll do everything in my power to help them. But now that you know what's at stake, you understand what my priorities have to be. I'd like to have your help."

He paused reflectively, then nodded. "Yeah, I get it. And I'll help you as best I can. But just to be clear, I don't care about your priorities. I don't give a damn about regime change in North Korea or your agency or your spy games. All I want is to get my wife and son back safely."

"And I just showed you exactly where they are."

He nodded slowly, then leaned forward to close the distance between them. Not a threat, but a demand for clear understanding. "If I help you out of this mess," he said, "will *you* do what's necessary to get my family back? *Whatever* it takes?"

Because Sorensen was a spy, the shift in her expression was negligible. But there *was* something. Something he trusted.

"Yes," she said. "You have my word."

SIXTY-EIGHT

In the basement of the hillside residence, Khang stood gingerly. His leg hurt like hell. He drummed his fingers incessantly on the table where an array of secure comm units were mounted. The room was General Park's personal communications center, with direct lines to various agencies in Pyongyang, including SSD headquarters. Yet for all the available links, the handset he was holding was unique.

Khang had been here a number of times before—always with the general's permission—to talk to headquarters about missions or to make security arrangements. The receiver in his hand, however, was unfamiliar. Indeed, he had never even seen it used. It was supposedly a secure device, hardwired to a Chinese-made system that dated back to the eighties. He knew it routed signals underground—not through the air where the Americans and South Koreans could intercept them—and that it employed some manner of encryption.

The phone offered but one lighted button, and when Khang had selected it and lifted the handset five minutes earlier, it had taken three tries to get a good connection. In the end, however, it worked.

Now, as expected, he was waiting for the person he needed to reach.

Khang had become increasingly troubled in recent days. He didn't like what had happened in Vienna. Five good men lost. He was furious at having been shot in the leg by an assassin—a man he should have gotten the better of. He didn't like being ordered to Mallorca to snatch a pair of Westerners. That seemed incredibly reckless.

But what bothered him more than anything was what was going on upstairs at that moment—a continuation of the general's peculiar behavior. After dispatching Khang to Mallorca, Park had followed up with strict orders: be respectful to this woman and boy, handle them carefully. Now the general himself was treating them as if they were long-lost family. It seemed inconceivable to Khang—especially given whose family they *really* were.

A shot of pain fired through his ankle.

He also wondered why the schedule was being moved up. By necessity, he'd been involved in the strike since the early stages—he wasn't privy to every detail, but enough to do his job. He'd arranged security on a tiny island in the South China Sea. Requisitioned two small transports and the pilots to fly them. Eliminated two scientists in Vienna. The ultimate goal—an attack that now appeared imminent—Khang knew to be very closely held. He himself had not been told the target, but he'd overheard enough in the general's meetings, seen enough details in messages, to discern the ultimate aim: to vaporize Pearl Harbor.

Khang always assumed the attack had approval from on high. Yet now, with the general's behavior so increasingly erratic, doubts had begun worming into his head.

Thankfully, there was one way to find out.

The phone remained silent, nothing but a low hiss to prove the connection hadn't been broken. Khang looked warily at the empty staircase.

He shifted his stance, putting weight on his good leg. It had been all he could do to not show weakness when he'd walked the woman and boy inside.

The assassin's wife and child, he thought. *If it were up to me—*

The operator interrupted. "Your call is going through," she said.

A familiar voice came on the line. Chong Su-lok was an old and trusted friend. The two of them had been forged in the same fires: bunkmates in army boot camp, and later the same class during Special Forces training. Side by side, they had risen in concert, bonded in ways only soldiers could understand. They had eventually reached parallel positions at the apex of the state security service. Chong, in essence, was Khang's counterpart in the chairman's office.

As such, he was but one step removed from Kwon Il-sun himself.

Boutros rounded up Sami and Rafiq, and they went ashore in the launch. Saleem remained on board to mind *Albatross.* Once again, assignments that were quite intentional.

The residual voyage to Green Island was laughably short for a crew who'd halved the Pacific in recent days. In the early dawn they saw thick colonies of birds nesting on the northern half of the island. As they neared shore, with a steady trade sweeping in, they began to smell them as well, the stench of guano carrying on the wind.

Everyone clambered ashore, Sami and Rafiq uncertain on sea legs. After securing the launch, they set out in search of the runway, the sun bathing the horizon with its warm copper glow. Rafiq suddenly stumbled over something, and the procession came to a jagged halt. All three men looked down in unison, thunderstruck.

"This can never work!" said Sami, his tone disconsolate.

They found themselves standing on the runway, yet it was barely visible. Whatever material it had been constructed from seventy-five years earlier—concrete or smoothed coral or some amalgam of the two—seemed to have reverted to its natural state. Weeds and small shrubs grew to hip-height along the entire length of the strip, which they could now see was no more than a few thousand feet. The surface was pitted and crumbling, more a gravel path than anything meant to support an aircraft.

"How could an airplane land here?" Sami asked.

Boutros considered it. He knew a little about unprepared landing sites, having served in Saddam's navy during the war. But this *did* seem extreme. "Perhaps it is possible," he said. "The Koreans would not have planned a landing here without taking a look at the place."

The others regarded him uncertainly.

After a prolonged silence, Boutros announced, "We should do something useful."

"Like what?" Sami asked.

"We will perform a survey."

———

The inspection took twenty minutes.

The three men spread out and walked the length of the derelict landing strip. Boutros told the others to look for obvious trouble spots, and they found surprisingly few. Near the lagoon-side edge, Sami discovered a pothole the size of a car tire. Boutros pulled away an old fishing net that had ended up near the runway's centerline. Rafiq was the busiest of the three—walking along the seaward edge, he found endless bits of plastic flotsam that had washed onto the runway's eastern shoulder. He threw the biggest pieces back into the sea.

On reaching the far end of the strip the meeting reconvened.

"It looked bad at first glance," Boutros said, "but the grass and weeds are misleading. I see few real problems."

The other two appeared skeptical.

"We should go back to the boat," said Boutros. "I will send a message about the condition of the field. While I do that, the two of you must move the fuel ashore." The twenty-two jerry cans brought to refuel the airplane had yet to be transferred.

There were nods of agreement. As they walked back to the launch, all three men found their eyes drawn to the sky.

Back on *Albatross*, Boutros fired up the satellite unit. It was only to be used for urgent contingencies, but he decided this qualified. He typed out: RUNWAY IN POOR CONDITION. LANDING MAY NOT BE POSSIBLE. ADVISE.

A MESSAGE SENT confirmation echoed back.

Boutros waited. He watched Sami and Rafiq struggle with the big jerry cans of aviation fuel. Once they had ten in the launch, they went ashore and unloaded, then came back for the rest.

Boutros kept watching the sat-comm screen hopefully. They had received only a handful of messages on the device, and this was the first time they'd tried to initiate contact.

The sun rose higher and the heat began to build. The screen remained blank.

SIXTY-NINE

The airplane arrived shortly after nine o'clock that morning. Sami, who had the youngest and sharpest eyes, was the first to see it. It began as no more than a speck, a fleck of hope in the bluest of skies. The distant drone of the engine was next, a low-frequency vibration violating the dense tropical air.

Boutros hurried to the launch with his landing party, once again leaving Saleem to mind *Albatross*. With the last of the jerry cans ashore, the boat was feather-light as its bow slid onto the now-familiar spit of sand—the closest thing to a beach on Green Island. All three men clambered over the gunnel. No response had ever come to the warning Boutros sent about the condition of the runway. Now the point was moot. Given the airplane's expected fuel state, if the pilots didn't land on the runway they would be taking their chances in the lagoon.

The airplane gained definition as it came closer. Boutros discerned two stacked wings and a single engine. The design seemed familiar, although as a navy man he couldn't remember the type. Something Russian perhaps that had flown in Saddam's air force. It looked stout and utilitarian, with thick main tires that might give it a chance on the rough surface.

The airplane flew straight toward the southern edge of the runway, although it didn't appear to be slowing. Moments before Boutros thought it was going to crash, the pilot leveled out and buzzed the length of the strip.

"He's checking the surface," Rafiq surmised.

"Yes," Boutros agreed.

They all watched the biplane execute an ungainly, climbing turn to the left. After a wide oval pattern, the pilot again maneuvered toward the end of the runway. This time the airplane's speed was noticeably slower. Indeed, so slow that Boutros began to worry.

"It's barely moving," he said.

"It will fall out of the sky," seconded Sami.

"No, there is a strong headwind," Rafiq argued. "It will be fine."

By the time the airplane crossed the coral-sand beach it seemed to be practically hovering. They could clearly see the pilot through the side window—a Korean wearing some kind of headset and a baseball cap. He was concentrating intently.

The wings bobbled left and right, and the pilot's hands gyrated on the controls. The airplane touched down, bounced once, and came to rest in no more than two hundred feet.

The engine's deep rumble went to a lower pitch, and the propeller began chewing up the highest vegetation like an overblown weed eater. After one great mechanical cough, the propeller fell still. Save for a chorus of squawking from the distant seabirds, the island was once again silent.

The sleek Citation X landed at Henderson Field on the height of midmorning, settling smoothly onto 7,800 feet of high-grade groomed concrete.

Located on Sand Island, in the Midway Atoll, the airfield's lineage can be traced back to the Second World War. It is the island chain that lent its name to the pivotal naval battle of the war, when the tide in the Pacific turned—this only months after the surprise attack on Pearl Harbor.

The symbolism was not lost on Slaton.

Yet when he looked out the tiny side window, what he saw didn't strike him as anything legendary, let alone a battleground. It was an island like a hundred others he'd visited in recent years. He saw trees sprouting the coconuts Davy relished throwing into the sea, and the crushed coral sand along the shore that invariably found its way into his pants.

Slaton forced his musings away.

The jet came to rest outside a tiny terminal, the engines winding down wearily. When the boarding door opened, light streamed inside like a switch had been thrown. Sorensen led the way out, and Slaton was right behind her. The heat hit like a thermal wave. Standing on sun-bleached concrete, Slaton squinted against the sun. For the first time he missed the Ray-Bans he'd left behind on *Sirius*. He didn't beat himself up over it—he'd departed Gibraltar expecting a Viennese winter and a gunsight. Not a mid-Pacific atoll and a nuclear bomb.

He and Sorensen walked side by side to an operations building that looked like a '50s convenience store.

She said, "According to the pilots there's a nice

comm suite inside. They say the airfield is kept up pretty well so airliners flying across the Pacific can list it as a diversion airport—apparently that allows them to fly a more direct route between the continents and save fuel."

"But there's no regular commercial air service?"

"No. The airfield was closed to the public years ago. It's only open to official business now, run by the Department of the Interior. We're smack in the middle of a huge marine conservation area, and the Fish and Wildlife Service keeps a contingent here."

Slaton looked out and saw a small marina in the distance. There were three center-console offshore boats, all displaying the Fish and Wildlife Service emblem. A pair of small dinghies had been dragged ashore on a nearby beach, their motors tilted up. On the island's highest ground, a tiny neighborhood had sprouted, the architecture glaringly institutional. Every bit of real estate that wasn't developed seemed populated by nesting birds—a variety of species, all of them big and ponderous.

They went inside the operations building and found a staff of one, a young woman with the unmistakable genes of a Pacific Islander. After showing an ID, Sorensen was given clearance to use the phones behind the counter.

Slaton was left standing by a window-unit air conditioner that sputtered like a miniature typhoon, the occasional chunk of ice flying out like hail. He approached the young woman and introduced himself, in loose terms, as an associate of Sorensen's. She gave him a high-wattage smile, then responded with her name. Slaton could never have repeated it. He heard only countless vowels and a melodious cadence—a name like a song.

"Do normal cell phones work here?" he asked.

"You're kidding, right?" she replied, her voice expectedly lyrical.

"Yeah . . . I guess we take these things for granted."

"The satellite coverage is good. And I've got a ham radio in back. My husband is really into it. Operators all over the world try to reach him since we're so remote—sort of a contest, I guess."

Slaton's next thought was hopelessly predictable. *How can I use a ham radio to reach Christine?*

It was patently absurd, of course, and a reminder of the perils of an over-focused mind. It was also hardly necessary. He knew perfectly well where his wife and son were, and knew they were unreachable. As much as he hated it, in that moment there was nothing he could do for his family. He could only wait for a chance.

With Sorensen on the phone, he began to wander the place. He paused near a map of the world that filled an entire wall. The map was at least fifteen feet across, encompassing the earth in a modified Mercator projection. At the center of the flattened globe, predictably, was Midway Atoll. There was a red pin on the island, and hanging from that was a piece of string colored in alternating red and white segments—each segment, according to a note in the corner, represented five hundred miles.

He stretched out the string until it touched North Korea. Three red, three white. Three thousand miles, more or less. Nearly all of it water.

"Is that your next stop?" The singsong voice from behind.

Slaton let the string drop from Pyongyang. "Unlikely. I imagine there's not much demand for that route."

"North Korea? Hardly. I think the secretary of state stopped here once on his way to negotiations."

Slaton turned away from the map.

"Will you be staying overnight?" she asked.

"I don't know—I'm only along for the ride."

"Well if you do stay, let me know—I can show you a few things to do on the island. My cousin has some fishing gear and rents it out at a pretty reasonable price. One of the permanent-party ornithologists runs what's left of the old dive shop."

"Thanks," he said. "I'm sure the diving and fishing are great, but it's not really why we're here."

"So why are you here?"

"To get gas," Slaton said without missing a beat.

"Yeah, that's pretty much the story."

The woman took that as her cue to go outside and check on the refueling. Soon after, Sorensen returned from the operations counter. Before Slaton could get out a word, she said, "There's nothing new on your wife and son."

It caught Slaton off guard.

"I figured you were about to ask," she said, "so I thought we'd get that out of the way."

"Okay, fine. Anything about nuclear bombs?"

"We still don't know where the Colt ended up, but we've got to be in the right neighborhood—it's only a matter of scouring every active airfield within a thousand miles. They must have stopped somewhere, at least to refuel."

"Aren't most of the islands around here U.S. possessions?"

"Most of them."

"So if a Chinese transport lands on U.S. territory, carrying nuclear material . . . wouldn't that get noticed?"

"One would hope. Trust me when I say we're working on it. The good news is that we have time."

"How do you figure?"

"Highly enriched uranium is good for building a crude nuke. But even if you have all the moving parts, it takes time to assemble a device and move it into position for an attack."

"How long?"

"We know this material flew past the Marshall Islands yesterday. According to our analysts, we probably have a few days to figure out where it went. In the meantime—"

The jet's captain rushed inside. "Flash message for you, Miss Sorensen! It's highest priority!"

Sorensen hurried to the door, Slaton right behind her. In less than a minute a relayed message was displayed on her laptop. It had come from General Park, and was eighteen words in length:

ATTACK SET FOR SUNDAY 1400 LOCAL
   TIME
TARGET WILL BE MIDWAY ISLAND
DELIVERED BY FISHING BOAT NAMED
   ALBATROSS

Slaton looked at Sorensen. Neither spoke for a beat.

"We're standing on ground zero," she finally said.

Together they looked at the clock above the laptop's screen, which had converted to Samoa Standard Time, and subtracted a day after crossing the international date line. It was Saturday, 10:38 a.m.

"Your analysts were a little off," he said. "We've got just over twenty-four hours."

SEVENTY

Unloading the bomb material from the Colt was surprisingly straightforward. Boutros and Sami dragged the heavy cask toward the cargo door and, with the help of the pilots, heaved until it was resting on the hard coral surface.

They'd been warned the container would weigh nearly three hundred pounds, and Park, or someone under his watch, had had the foresight to include a furniture dolly in the Colt's cargo bay. Once the cask was on the ground, it was a simple matter to lever it onto the dolly. From there Rafiq and Sami wheeled it to the launch. When they were done, everyone paused to catch their breath. The only sound was the guttural chatter of nearby birds taking exception to the disturbance.

Rafiq pulled Boutros aside. "There is a problem," he said.

"What?"

"The initiator was to be shipped in a separate container."

Boutros had been so focused on their task, he hadn't noticed. "It's not on the airplane?"

Rafiq shook his head. "Perhaps something to do with the timetable being advanced."

Boutros felt a terrible pull in his gut. "What does it mean?" he asked.

"It's not that bad. As I told you before, the reaction builds with neutrons. The beryllium-polonium initiator serves to boost the weapon's yield. Even without it, everything should still work."

"But it will not be as powerful."

"Enough to obliterate our new target."

Boutros thought about it. "Yes, you are right—it doesn't matter now."

"And there is one advantage—Sami won't have to handle the polonium."

Boutros nodded, wondering how Sami would react. Would he be happy to not suffer in the final hours of his life? Or disappointed that he would not agonize in the name of Allah? The thought was interrupted when the airplane's captain, who was still wearing his baseball cap, came toward them. He said, "Petrol," and pointed to the jerry cans lined up next to the runway. As with Park, they were forced to revert to English for a common tongue.

Boutros gave the order, and Sami and Rafiq began hauling the cans to the airplane. "How long will you stay?" he asked the captain.

"Petrol," the man said. "Then we go."

Boutros saw the copilot standing by the airplane—he was unlatching a service door near the engine, a case of oil on the ground at his feet. Boutros didn't bother to ask what their next destination would be—he doubted this airplane could reach North Korea without stopping, no matter how much fuel they took on. Even so, he was sure they would find their way back—like a homing pigeon returning to its loft.

Once the fuel had been transferred, Boutros again

asked for the flight crew's help. It took all five men to lift the leaden cask into the launch. They set it on an arrangement of stout wooden planks in the center of the boat—the last thing Boutros needed was to capsize and sink their prize in twenty feet of water. That done, the five exchanged goodbyes, an awkward series of nods and waves between men who shared no language or heritage or religion— indeed, no bond whatsoever but that of a shared enemy. The three Middle Easterners pushed their overburdened launch into deeper water, and Sami fired up the little outboard.

Forty-five minutes after it had arrived, the Colt was thundering across the weed-laden runway like a bison across a grassy plain. After an unusually short takeoff run, it wobbled into the sky, reminding Boutros very much of the ungainly birds around the island. From *Albatross'* deck, he and his team watched the Colt rise.

"God's work is now before us," he said, wanting to refocus his men.

They were together on the working deck, and with the hatch to the main hold open, everyone looked down into a space designed for fishing nets. The heavy container had been lowered inside using the main davit and was sitting beside the weapon.

Boutros stole a glance at Sami and saw that he was smiling, giving an answer to his earlier question— he'd been told his martyrdom would not be as agonizing as expected.

"How long will the final portion of our journey take?" Rafiq asked.

"It is only fifty-seven miles," Boutros replied. "We

are right on schedule." He looked east and saw a handful of distant thunderheads—unusual for this time of day, but no more than isolated cells.

"Prepare to pull anchor. Everyone stays on deck until we clear the reef. Once we're under way, I'll stay at the helm while the three of you finalize the assembly."

Albatross easily cleared the outer reef, and was soon plowing through cobalt blue sea. With one left turn, Boutros settled the bow on an easterly course, toward a target whose name was synonymous with one of America's greatest victories. He imagined that name would soon hold very different meaning to the world's nearly two billion Muslims. Not that Boutros cared about any of them.

In that moment, only one name stuck in his head: that of his dear sister.

Irina.

A girl who suffered no longer.

Sorensen spent nearly an hour on the phone. She used the comm suite on the Citation, which was the most secure link, and when her series of calls finally ended she went out into blinding daylight.

She found Slaton under a palm tree fifty yards from the main building. He was scanning the harbor with a pair of binoculars borrowed from the operations building.

"What are you doing?" she asked.

"A little reconnaissance never hurt. If this boat really is coming here, I figure I can give a local area brief to whatever units are coming to the party. But honestly, if I was making the call—I'd order an air-

strike before that bomb gets anywhere near the island."

"That's one of the ideas circulating. As you can
imagine, the president and National Security Council are deep in session. The prevailing thought is to
try and intercept the boat at sea before the weapon
can be armed. That would provide good hard evidence to use as we see fit, along with some hardware
for our intel teams to study."

"And maybe a few releasable photos to help top-
ple Kwon Il-sun?"

"That's not a priority—we won't allow Midway
to be put at risk."

"What units are being called up?" he asked, putting the binoculars back on the harbor.

"Airborne radar is about to launch from Hickam
Air Force Base in Hawaii. That's fifteen hundred
miles from here, so it will take a few hours for them
to get on station. The carrier *John C. Stennis* is four
hundred miles north with its battle group—they
were on the way to a Southeast Asia deployment,
but they're being diverted. We don't have any Delta
or Seal Teams in Hawaii right now—the closest are
in Guam—so two companies of Marines from the
3/3 in Kaneohe are gearing up to board a C-17.
They should land here by nightfall. Inside eight
hours, this is going to be the most heavily watched
rock on earth."

"I guess that about covers it then," Slaton said,
still scanning.

Sorensen looked out across the harbor and saw
three boats moored in the lagoon. She felt a flutter
of worry. "It couldn't be any of those, could it?"

Slaton pulled down the binoculars. "Park said it

was a fishing boat—are you telling me you don't trust him? The head of North Korean intelligence?"

Sorensen frowned.

"Don't worry—those boats have been here for days. Two operate regular supply deliveries. The third is a motorsailer owned by a South African couple—they've been here five days waiting for a part to be flown in for their engine."

"You can tell all that just by looking?"

"No, I asked Lea-Lai . . . whatever her name is."

Sorensen looked at the sea beyond. "We could fire up the Citation and start looking ourselves."

"You could. But I've done that kind of search before—it's a really big ocean."

She heaved a sigh. "It seems like we ought to be doing something."

Slaton didn't respond. He put the binoculars back in place and began sweeping the horizon.

Park sat stoically near a roaring fireplace, light from the flames flickering over the great stone hearth.

The American child had been enthralled by the fire—he'd apparently never seen one "inside a house." He and his mother were now in the adjacent office, two guards at the door—civility was one thing, but guests they were not. Cots had been set up in the room, and Park knew they'd slept for a time, until the boy had awakened with a night terror and his mother had risen to comfort him. Now he heard them conversing in hushed voices. Park vaguely recognized the tones. An unsettled boy. A mother trying to mask her fear. He increasingly believed he'd done the right thing in bringing them here. However events played out, they would prove useful bargaining chips.

Park meandered to the wet bar and poured two fingers of bourbon into a clear tumbler. He envisioned one of two outcomes in the next twenty-four hours. The most likely was that he would fly to Pyongyang and assume control of the country. He was in close touch with his coconspirators, and all were on alert. Ready to facilitate a sudden and tectonic shift amid the senior military leadership. If there were any hitches, the takeover could be made certain using the backup plan—this involving one discreetly delivered 9mm round. The key to it all was generating—in every sense of the word—a firestorm over the Pacific.

Park had run the political calculations a hundred times in his head. The Americans wanted new leadership in North Korea, as did most of the world. Nonetheless, allowances had to be made for the other eventuality. Which was why he had sequestered himself to these remote hills. And why the two Americans in his study were such great comfort. They were his insurance should something go wrong.

He tipped back the glass and closed his eyes. Park heard the crackle of the fire. The distant hum of the generator outside. Gentle voices from the adjoining room.

"It's called a globe, honey."

"It's our world?"

"Yes."

"Where are we?"

A wobbly mechanical spin. "Right here."

"Have we been to this ocean?"

"Yes, we have, the Pacific. Here, here . . . and down here."

"Is that the place with the three palm trees?"

A mother's soft laugh. "I remember a lot of places with palm trees."

"You know, Mommy. Where I had two birthdays."

Park's eyes snapped open. A jolt of what felt like electricity surged through his spine. He jumped to his feet and rushed into the office. The woman pulled the child protectively into her arms. Park ignored them. He put a hand to the globe, looked at it disbelievingly.

He ran out of the room like it was on fire and descended to the basement. There he skidded to a stop at the communications desk. He tried to remember the codes and protocols. His hands moved quickly, clumsily—completely in line with his thoughts.

Finally, he made the connection.

This time there was no foresight or planning in the delivered message. He didn't bother to count how many words it contained, didn't so much as read through it once. If there was any backup at all, it was that in his agitated state he said the words aloud as he typed them. Park launched his missive into the digital ether as quickly as he could strike the send button.

SEVENTY-ONE

Notwithstanding the absence of the beryllium-polonium initiator, the assembly of the weapon went precisely as planned. Sami, wearing a pair of thick rubber gloves, removed six uranium rings, one at a time, and fit them into the receiver at the breech end of the barrel. Rafiq then positioned the assembly onto the attachment point, leaving the explosives portal exposed.

At that point, Saleem went to work, installing the shaped charge, and connecting the leads of the primary and backup initiators. With everything in place, Rafiq and Saleem together rotated the breech assembly into position and torqued down the containment bolts.

At that point, the weapon was ready to be armed. This would be Saleem's job—the chamber was surrounded by a spaghetti-like halo of wiring, and only he knew which were the critical two switches.

"It is almost time to pray," said Saleem.

Rafiq, who had not bothered to do so in days, said, "Perhaps later. I still have one last task."

"What is that?"

Rafiq pointed to the far end of the barrel. "With no neutron initiator, the access port must be sealed."

He retrieved a circular plate the size of a Frisbee. Made from inch-thick steel, ten heavy bolts encircled its perimeter. Rafiq worked the plate into position on the top of the target assembly, then began securing the bolts in a machinist's pattern—using minimal torque to begin, and alternating sides. With a final pull of the wrench, he backed away.

Boutros appeared from the corridor, having been relieved at the helm by Sami.

"It is done," said Saleem. "All that is left is to activate the arming switches."

Boutros stood looking at the tangle of wiring around the breech—Saleem's signature "bird's nest." Bright wires, batteries, two alarm clocks. With the target so near, it seemed a needless precaution. "Which are active?" he asked.

Saleem pointed to a pair of black plastic switches, each the size of a matchbox, buried deep within the harness. "These are the true switches. The time is set as scheduled. Depress one button on each, and the countdown will commence. One will send a detonation signal at 1400, the backup one minute later."

"When will we arrive?" Rafiq asked.

Boutros checked his watch. "We are right on schedule. The island should come into view soon."

"Let's go above then," said Rafiq. "I would like to look for the island."

Saleem deferred, leaving to pray in the adjacent compartment. As soon as he was gone, Rafiq looked pleadingly at Boutros. "Please," he said, "come with me. I would like a private word."

Boutros regarded him for a moment, then nodded.

Park departed the basement communications room as hurriedly as he'd arrived. In his wake the room fell silent. Only after a prudent interval did Khang emerge from the shadows of the closet.

He'd ducked inside minutes earlier, when Park had come trundling down the staircase. From inside, with his wide shoulders pressed against the wooden shelving, he had listened closely.

Khang's English was not good. But that very fact—that Park had moments ago mumbled in English as he'd typed and sent out a message—only hardened his suspicions. He'd only caught a few words. *Mistake . . . urgent . . . Saturday.* To whom Park had sent them, Khang could only speculate— and speculation was not among his assigned duties. He was a solider, no more and no less. And right now his soldier's instincts were on high alert. He sensed a battle brewing. A fight in the air.

He limped across the room to the phone he'd been using. Khang checked the wall-mounted clock. His comrade in Pyongyang had told him to call back in one hour. Eight minutes to go.

He hesitated mightily, his brawny hand wrapped around the handset. He finally gave in to impatience and made the connection. Khang recognized the risk he was taking. Yet if what he suspected was true—it had the potential to work out well for him.

He closed his eyes and imagined a phone ringing in a dimly lit room—one very much like the one in which he was now standing. A room deep in the bowels of Residence Number 55.

———

It had never been in Slaton's nature to waste time.

That being the case, while Sorensen was gathering updates from Langley, he persisted in exploring the island. He found himself drawn to a small cluster of buildings. The most prominent was a corrugated aluminum lean-to that housed a makeshift dive shop. It was clearly a contract operation, something called Omni Divers. The adjacent air-conditioned shack was labeled Omni Grocers, and in front of that was a five-hundred-gallon gas tank administered by Omni Propane. He supposed all had been more profitable in years gone by, when groups of tourists still came. Yet there was still a resident population of biologists and researchers and radar technicians, all of whom ate and grilled out and explored the reefs.

He found one man under the corrugated roof. He was tall and thin, with bleached blond hair, roughly Slaton's age. With an old captain's hat turned backward on his head, he looked like a U-boat commander in search of a periscope. Slaton remembered being told the dive shop was run by an ornithologist. That wasn't what he would have pegged this man for—but then, Slaton couldn't remember ever meeting one.

"G'day!" the man said, his Aussie accent unmistakable.

"Good morning," Slaton replied.

"New to the island? Haven't seen you round here before."

"Yeah. I came in on the Citation." Slaton imagined that with only a few arrivals each day, and a runway that could be seen from any point on the island, that was probably how locals referenced newcomers—the airplane they came in on.

"Staying long?"

"Not very, but possibly long enough to do a little exploring on the reefs."

The Aussie maneuvered around an air compressor and extended his hand. "Mark," he said, dropping the *R* as if it wasn't in the spelling.

"David," Slaton said, because going with the name and nationality on his passport—Thomas La Pierre of Canada—didn't jibe with arriving on a U.S. government aircraft. And also because here, on a rock in the middle of the Pacific Ocean, he saw no compelling need for tradecraft.

"Are you a certified diver?" Mark asked.

"I am, although I didn't bring my C-card." In truth, Slaton had been trained to dive by the Israeli Navy—and also to take part in underwater activities for which wallet-sized certification cards were hardly appropriate. "I was actually only thinking of a mask, snorkel, and fins."

"We can fit you right up."

"No need yet—I'm not sure if I'll have the time."

"No worries. If I'm not here, I'll be in the third hut on the right." He pointed up a narrow path that probably passed for a street.

"Good to know. So tell me—how many people live here on Midway?"

"Live?" Mark chuckled. "Most of us are a bit transient to call it that—but on any given day, I'd say there's thirty-five, maybe forty of us."

Slaton nodded, his eyes scanning the shop. He saw the usual array of gear, most of it used, and not lovingly. A handful of skimpy bikinis were tacked to the rafters like dollar bills over a bar. Then something else caught his eye. He nodded to a short metal pole and asked, "A lot of sharks around here?"

"Only thing that outnumbers the birds. But they're a harmless lot," Mark added with typical Aussie bravado.

"Do you have the rest to make that work?"

"I do. Have you ever used a—" His eyes shifted past Slaton. "Don't look now, mate, but your lovely friend is trying to get your attention."

Slaton turned to see Sorensen waving at him frantically from the Citation's boarding stairs. He whipped around and broke into a run.

As he hit his stride, Mark called out, "If you end up staying, I wouldn't mind meeting her . . ."

SEVENTY-TWO

The seas were still cooperating. Boutros looked out and saw thunderstorms building to the east and south, but they remained distant. From where he and Rafiq stood, on the point of the bow, he strained to see Midway Atoll. They were inside fifteen miles now, but he couldn't discern any land through the marine haze.

He turned to Rafiq, who was also searching—even more in earnest, it seemed, than Boutros himself. "All right," he said, "tell me what is on your mind."

Rafiq met his eyes, but said nothing. With a strong wind whipping through his hair and beard, he reached into his pocket. He pulled out a letter. The same one, Boutros was sure, he'd seen once before.

Rafiq handed it over.

Boutros kept his eyes on Rafiq for a moment, then straightened three folds and held the letter open. Wind whipped the corners of the paper as he read it. Because the letter was written in formal English, a few of the words escaped him. The greater meaning, however, did not.

He folded the letter carefully, almost delicately. "What are you telling me?"

"I want to accept."

Boutros' gaze never wavered. "You have been accepted into graduate school in Oslo, Norway. And you want to go there . . . from here?"

"I applied to a handful of PhD programs some years ago. I had always dreamed of going back to school, but I knew it would be difficult. There was a string of rejection letters, and I became very frustrated. Eventually, I told myself it was hopeless and committed to jihad. It all left my mind for a time. Then, recently, the Norwegian government began a special program, very small, in which they accept a few refugees each year into top-flight universities. This letter caught up to me at the camp in Suruç."

Boutros turned and looked across the sea in contemplation.

"By then I was committed to our mission," Rafiq went on. "I know how important it is to the caliphate. Even so, the thought of going back to school . . . it won't leave my mind."

Boutros let his eyes drift aft. "The launch?" he surmised.

Rafiq nodded.

Boutros tried to imagine it. "You could take it and head west, perhaps? Reach another island? Flag down a fishing boat?"

"Yes! I know there is a good chance I would only be captured. Or even more likely, lost at sea. The chance of success is very slight, one in a hundred . . . but at least there would be that one."

Boutros said nothing.

"I've done everything God has asked of me," Rafiq implored. "The weapon is ready. I am confident it will work, and our mission will be a success. Perhaps Sami could come with me and—"

"What are you talking about?"

They both turned to see Saleem approaching. Sami was at the helm, watching closely.

Boutros weighed a response, then held up the letter. He spoke loudly enough for everyone to hear. "Rafiq wishes to go to university."

"*What?*" Saleem replied.

"He feels his work here is complete. He wants to take the launch and attempt an escape. He says Sami can go with him."

"Coward!" Saleem hissed.

"I have done my part," Rafiq argued. "If I could survive, I might someday bring another attack, God willing."

"You will be martyred with the rest of us!" Saleem shouted. He reached into his pocket and pulled out a heavy wrench. He came at Rafiq ready to swing.

Boutros stepped between them and put a palm on Saleem's chest. It stopped him cold. "Enough!" he ordered.

Saleem stood defiant, still brandishing the wrench. "He is a traitor, I tell you!"

Boutros looked at the two men in turn. He held out an open hand to Saleem. "Give me that."

Saleem didn't move.

"*Now! As your commander, I order you to stand down!*"

After a lengthy pause, Saleem relented. His shoulders sagged and he handed over the wrench.

Boutros took it, then half turned. Everyone stared at Rafiq. With the boat carving smoothly onward, the foredeck acquired the aura of a tribunal.

Boutros finally said, "I understand your conflict.

You have done your part ably, and every man should have his chance." Rafiq's face brightened. Then with lightning-like speed, Boutros whipped the wrench in an arc, striking Rafiq squarely in the head. He collapsed in a heap and didn't move.

Silence fell, the only sounds being the drone of the big diesel and the sea cutting against the bow.

Boutros looked at Saleem. "May God have mercy on us all."

Seconds later, and without so much as a prayer, Boutros and Saleem together pitched the body into the sea.

"The international date line?" Slaton said incredulously. "He *forgot* about it?"

He and Sorensen were staring at a message from Park on her laptop. At that moment in North Korea, it was Sunday. Yet when Slaton and Sorensen had landed on Midway, they'd gone back one day by virtue of crossing the international date line eastbound. Where they now sat it was still Saturday. When Park realized his mistake, he'd sent an urgent message. The attack was going to take place *today*.

"This kind of thing has happened before," Sorensen said. "We almost lost four F-22s, our latest and greatest fighter, the first time they tried to deploy across the date line. Their software imploded—navigation, fuel system, radios. They only made it back to Hawaii by following their tankers. Hundreds of billions of dollars for a weapon system, and every engineer in the chain forgot about the correction."

She looked at the clock. "It gives us—"

"Thirty-eight minutes," Slaton said, having already done the math. "But I've been watching the harbor—there aren't any new arrivals. If this boat, *Albatross*, has been delayed, we might have more time."

"Let's hope."

"Can the Pentagon speed up their response?"

"They're doing what they can. The call-ups I mentioned earlier are still in the works. The airborne radar is two hours out, and *Stennis* is prepping to launch some Hornets—but even those are an hour away."

Slaton saw the binoculars he'd requisitioned earlier on a table. He grabbed them and hurried to the entry door. He ducked through, paused on the top step for elevation, and began scanning the horizon.

Sorensen was right behind him. "Do you see anything?"

The smooth arc of his motion began in the north, sweeping left across the horizon. Somewhere in the southwest quadrant, beyond the distant reef's whitewater, his movement caught like a gun turret hitting its stop. He paused for a few seconds, then lowered the glass.

"Where are the pilots?" he asked.

"Operations building."

He leapt down and sprinted for the door. By the time Sorensen caught up, Slaton was already inside issuing orders. ". . . no more than ten minutes!" he shouted.

The pilots, one of whom had a large coffee stain on his pristine white shirt, bolted out the door like they'd been shot from a cannon.

"What did you tell them?" she asked.

"I told them this island is about to get nuked. I

gave them ten minutes to collect every soul they can find, put them on the Citation, and get the hell out."

"You saw *Albatross*?"

"I saw a big fishing boat. I couldn't read the name from eight miles away, but I think we should assume the worst."

Before she could respond, Slaton was moving for the door.

"Where are you going now?" she demanded.

He paused, turned to face her. "Anna, at this moment there are roughly forty people on this island. If those pilots can round up half in the next ten minutes and evacuate them, they'll deserve a medal. But there's no way we can get everyone safe—not in that amount of time."

"So what can we do?"

"If I was you . . . I'd go get on that jet."

He spun away and disappeared through the door.

Sorensen rushed outside. She spotted Slaton sprinting for the tiny marina. Rotating in the other direction, she saw the sleek Citation. The woman with the singsong voice was running across the tarmac toward the stairs, a look of terror ruining her pleasant features.

Sorensen squeezed her eyes shut. *"Dammit!"*

SEVENTY-THREE

Every country has its corners of expertise when it comes to technology. North Korea's Bureau 121 is a model of larceny when it comes to the theft of communications and hard currency. Russia lays claim to some of the darkest corners of the web, the FSB backing shadowed hacking groups whose disinformation campaigns create chaos in the West. China's most lucrative front involves legions of hackers who mine secrets from defense contractors, and who thieve intellectual property for economic gain. Yet in one domain, there is not a nation on earth, or more concisely, above it, that has the capability of the United States. When it comes to space-based reconnaissance, America is dominant.

At the direction of the president, a veritable constellation of assets had been reoriented to manage the crisis. A satellite over the central Pacific, which employed infrared and laser sensors with remarkable resolution, recorded a lone athletic man sprinting toward the docks on Midway's Sand Island. From a similar orbital track, albeit greater altitude, the enhanced radar imaging sensors of a different bird were locked onto a suspicious fishing vessel: six miles west of Midway and closing in fast.

Far to the east, over the Korean Peninsula, a new geosynchronous unit fed real-time streaming images of a hillside retreat in the southeastern hills.

Impressive as it all was, the most impactful intelligence gathered that hour came not from the National Reconnaissance Office and its array of orbiting marvels, but from its even more shadowed sister organization—the National Security Agency.

Long the world leader in communications intercepts, the NSA, in close cooperation with the CIA, had been developing a revolutionary surveillance package to monitor Kwon Il-sun's primary residence outside Pyongyang. From NSA's point of view, the challenge all along in spying on the North Korean leadership was the regime's cave-dwelling level of technology. The lack of any meaningful digital infrastructure—the same reason Bureau 121 was forced to set up shop in marmot-infested buildings in Mongolia—meant that Dear Leader's primary residence had few computers to hack. Indeed, by one reliable source, there were but five computers in the entire main palace, and two of these ran nothing more than video games for Kwon's amusement. Altogether, it led NSA penetration teams to view North Korea rather like a General Motors salesman might view a country without roads: a place with limited opportunity. So it was, given that burrowing into code and co-opting signals was not an option, the agency's planners began to explore more direct eavesdropping.

Scientists in the research division were given free rein, and began linking advances on multiple technology fronts: drone miniaturization, stealth technology, power management, artificial intelligence, and signal networking. The NSA, in conjunction with

DARPA, the Defense Advanced Research Projects Agency, had long been developing a new class of tiny drones. For the mission in North Korea, existing designs were refined, and new technologies incorporated. The end result was something near a revolution.

Each tiny aircraft was no larger than a grain of rice. The drone's deployable wings unfolded after delivery, and once in position served a triad of functions: propulsion in flight, photovoltaic power source, and dual-use antenna. A second class of drone—a variant that was the size, and to a remarkable degree the appearance, of a certain species of praying mantis indigenous to the Korean Peninsula—was also developed, with power and transmission capabilities far more robust than those of its smaller counterpart.

Two days earlier, with the year-long project deemed mature and the situation on the peninsula becoming critical, the green light had been given. The initial insertion was accomplished using a stealthy "mother" drone—a doormat-sized arrowhead made of frangible composite material—that was delivered by an Air Force F-22, twenty-two miles outside North Korean airspace. The delivery was accomplished at extremely high speed and altitude. After release, the F-22 reversed its course while the drone was further boosted by a small rocket engine. Forty miles from the targeted residence in Pyongyang the motor fell away, leaving the drone to glide the remainder of its journey. With its energy dissipating, the drone navigated using GPS to a point three hundred feet above the palace. And there, the real party began.

With hand-wringing engineers monitoring the mission, the package burst open right on schedule releasing a swarm of 312 tiny drones. All but six were the smaller model, and on deployed wings they fluttered down en masse toward Residence Number 55. No sooner were they clear than a second charge detonated above, fragmenting the remnants of the mother ship into tiny shards—which by no coincidence looked very much like tree bark—across the palace's northern glade.

It was here that AI kicked in.

The mission was undertaken in the predawn hours of an unusually temperate night. Having been programmed with a diagram of the residence, including the location of three windows that were typically left open, the drones began their search. Of the 306 smaller variety, 295 successfully deployed and inserted themselves into the palace. From there they coordinated among one another to learn dead ends and identify successful passages.

Armed with intelligence gleaned from defectors, the drones infiltrated air-conditioning ducts, spun through hallways, and descended elevator shafts. In burst transmissions, they synchronized with one another to cover as many rooms as possible, and on reaching a valid destination, each used its dwindling initial power supply to alight to some high fixture in the respective room. Picture frames, fireplace mantels, and the canopy over Kwon Il-sun's bed were all covered. A few of the drones failed along the way, but this too had been anticipated by the engineers at DARPA—the tiny aircraft had been created in the image of the winged seed of a certain Chinese elm, hundreds of which populated the surrounding grounds. While not the correct season for such seeds to be fluttering to ground, in the coming days the housekeeping staff would sweep up dozens unknowingly.

The overall results were an unmitigated success. In the end, an array of over 240 microphones had been cast about the palace. They covered every room, closet, and bathroom. Even the wine cellar was monitored. In the name of power management, the units were voice-activated, meaning they only listened when conversations were ongoing. All results were relayed to the network of six faux praying mantises that had alit to trees around the palace, and from there everything was sent up to waiting satellites.

Which was how, in the early hours of that evening in the White House Situation Room, the nuclear crisis in the Pacific was overshadowed by a new intelligence report. After reading through the message privately, the national security adviser briefed everyone, including, at the head of the long table, the president himself.

"Within the last hour we've captured a number of revealing conversations from Chairman Kwon's residence. We are certain the coup has been uncovered. It is also clear that General Park has been identified as the leader. The palace is in lockdown, the military has been put on alert, and an overwhelming response is being assembled."

After a period of stunned silence, it was the chairman of the Joint Chiefs, a lantern-jawed Marine, who summed up the development most concisely. "Park is so screwed."

SEVENTY-FOUR

The nautical passage leading into the harbor of Midway Atoll was perfectly well marked. The approach was from the southeast, and keeping Sand Island to the left and Spit Island to the right, channel markers offer a virtual invitation to the smooth crystalline lagoon.

Keeping *Albatross* at idle speed, Boutros held tight to the green marker on his left, better to keep an eye on Sand Island. This was the lone populated island on the atoll. He saw thirty or forty structures of various sizes and purposes. No more than two hundred yards distant was the approach end of a runway that stretched the length of the island, the surface of which, not surprisingly, was in far better shape than the one on Kure. At the airfield's midpoint Boutros saw one airplane, some kind of business jet with two people boarding.

He checked the time on the navigation display. 13:38.

"I wonder if they will make it."

Boutros turned and saw Saleem watching the airplane. He had a nylon backpack over one shoulder.

"Who can say," Boutros replied. "Is the weapon fully armed?"

"Both the primary and backup. Everything is now in God's hands."

Boutros looked ahead at the harbor. The marina would pass to port, a tiny set of docks where three boats lay moored. All were less than thirty feet long with twin outboard engines, and by the emblems on the side they were clearly official. Had he not done his research, he might have feared they were run by customs agents or some kind of port authority. As it was, he knew the boats were part of a tiny police detachment that watched over the encompassing marine reserve—in effect, a handful of nautical game wardens.

"You have the gun?" Boutros asked.

Saleem unzipped the backpack to reveal the frame of their only self-defense weapon, a compact PP-2000 machine pistol.

"All right. Go aft and keep watch," Boutros ordered. "And keep a close eye on those boats. They are the only real threat."

Saleem re-shouldered the backpack. "If one of them comes our way, I will be ready."

Boutros wished they had more to defend with, but he'd already briefed Sami: if anyone attempted to board the boat, he was to do his best to support Saleem. Axes, hammers, flare guns. Whatever he could find.

Saleem went aft and took up a post by the nets. It occurred to Boutros that he was standing directly over the hatch under which a primed nuclear weapon was awaiting one surge of current. He decided Saleem was well aware—he probably wanted to be the first in line for glory.

He adjusted course slightly to port, keeping to the channel. His plan was to enter the main harbor, then reverse toward the island and get as close as possible to shore. He wondered if he should run *Albatross* aground in shallow water. The weapon, he'd been told, would leave a significant crater. He thought the best legacy would be to remove as much of the island as possible. Unfortunately, he wasn't sure how to go about it. Put the keel on the bottom? Or leave some water beneath?

It was like no nautical question he'd ever faced.

Boutros maneuvered carefully, slowly, and soon had *Albatross* fifty yards from the sandy shore. He paused there, stilling the boat in twenty feet of water.

Her bow was pointed at the island like a dagger.

Sami, standing forward, was the first to notice the threat—although, by any measure, it could hardly be characterized as such. In truth, had it not been for the baking sun, oppressive humidity, and diesel fumes backwashing from the boat's stack, he might have thought they'd made an early arrival in paradise.

It began with the sound of a small outboard motor, followed soon after by a tiny inflatable runabout rounding the breakwater of the marina. The craft was no more than eight feet long and carried but one occupant: at the stern, with her hand on the outboard's steering arm, a slim blond woman in a bikini. Sami turned to get everyone's attention, but right away saw it wasn't necessary. All three sets of eyes on *Albatross* were locked on the boat—or more precisely, its occupant.

The woman was steering for the middle of the harbor, where a lone motorsailer lay anchored serenely. That vector would take the runabout two hundred feet clear of *Albatross*' port side. The little boat was moving slowly, no more than five knots, its high bow plowing through crystalline water. As it came near, the woman waved in the general direction of *Albatross*. Only Sami returned the gesture.

The woman was very attractive. Very athletic. Her bikini seemed almost too small for her frame. The little boat was slightly past abeam when it suddenly came to rest. The engine went silent and the squat rubber hull settled on the water. The three men on *Albatross* watched closely. Saleem put his hand on the machine pistol inside the backpack.

The woman bent down and began fiddling with something at the base of the engine. For almost two minutes she pushed and pulled and rapped with her knuckles. Then, with one pull on the starter cord, the engine fired back to life. She set back out, still headed squarely for the motorsailer. The three men aboard *Albatross* kept watching, albeit with widely varied thoughts.

Saleem thought the woman's swimsuit offensive to his Muslim sensibilities.

Boutros, with his commander's mindset, viewed it as a cautionary event.

Sami was nothing short of enraptured.

Regardless of the effect, all three men were so diverted by the sight, each in his own way, that they never noticed one peculiarity—dragging behind the runabout was a twenty-foot-long line with a diving weight knotted to the end.

SEVENTY-FIVE

Slaton had never cared much for jewelry or fine accessories. All the same, at that moment, he was infinitely appreciative that Christine had splurged to give him a high-end Swiss diving watch as a Christmas present.

According to his Breitling Superocean, he had fifteen minutes.

He was by then directly beneath the boat named *Albatross*. On the ship's hull he saw a modest accumulation of barnacles and algae, and looking aft a school of fish was swirling around the rudder. The boat's engine was running, evident by a low rumble transmitting through the water, yet her propeller was stilled for the moment. He prayed it would stay that way.

Slaton was wearing a black wetsuit, long fins, and a mask. Strapped over his left shoulder was a small "Spare Air" oxygen tank with an integral mouthpiece. Designed as an emergency air source for divers, the miniature tank was rated to provide roughly fifty breaths. Since leaving the pier and getting dragged most of the way to *Albatross*, Slaton had counted thirty-two. It proved more than enough. He kept moving to the boat's starboard side—opposite where Sorensen was feigning a mechanical issue on the runabout. On breath number forty he surfaced.

He had two other items from the dive shop in his right hand. One was a modest length of rope, knotted every few feet, at the end of which was a weighted pouch from a diving rig. The other, hanging from his wrist by a looped cord, was one of the few weapons on earth he'd never employed.

Slaton made a cursory scan of the rails above. He was situated amidships, and above him was the wheelhouse. He'd been hoping the boat would anchor—the rope would have given him a way to reach the main deck ten feet overhead. Unfortunately, the crew hadn't bothered—with no significant current or wind, the boat lay dead in the water. Backed against the hull, Slaton saw no simple method of climbing aboard. He'd counted three men earlier, and while there might be more, he had no time for surveillance. The three had taken up stations: one forward, one aft, and one remaining in the wheelhouse. None displayed weapons obviously, but any might be armed—most conspicuously, the man aft was carrying a backpack for no apparent reason.

Slaton looked up, desperate for inspiration. He'd known this would be the weakest point of his plan— but then, he'd never hatched any tactical scheme in the space of two minutes that didn't have grave deficiencies. He saw a number of stanchions along the port side, and these supported twin lifelines along the length of the boat. He was sure he could heave the weighted rope over the lifeline, and with a few tries get it to return to create a secure loop. The problem: doing so would make enough noise to get everyone's attention.

It seemed a fatal flaw.

If an alarm was raised on deck, he would have no choice but to fight his way on board. That meant scaling ten feet up the side of a steel hull, one versus three, while supporting his own weight. He was already regretting his choice of weapon—there had been only two to choose from in the scuba shop. Most simple had been a spear gun, which in his present predicament might have proved more useful. Slaton had instead gone for lethality. Looped around his wrist was a device commonly referred to as a bang stick. Originally conceived by divers as protection against sharks, it was little more than a three-foot pole, at the end of which was a chamber, firing pin, and twelve-gauge shotgun shell. The bang stick solved the biggest problem of underwater ballistics—water was far more dense than air. But the bang stick was a contact weapon—you had to plant the business end directly on your target, giving an effective range of the combined length of your pole and arm. Great for incoming tiger sharks. Far less so looking up the side of a sixty-foot trawler.

Slaton checked his watch. Fourteen minutes remaining. There was simply no choice.

He rearranged his gear, making sure the coiled rope was free. He was about to attempt his first throw when the relative silence in the harbor was violated by the most glorious sound. The engines of a Citation X business jet winding up to takeoff thrust.

Boutros had been watching the jet intermittently since they'd arrived. He'd seen a handful of people climb aboard, and watched the jet taxi to the end of the runway—from where he stood, no more than a quarter mile away. Now, as its engines spun up to full power, the air seemed to reverberate. He saw birds scatter from the nearby island, and the jet began to move. Boutros nodded and thought to himself, *Now there are some lucky people.*

A different sound, more sharp, seemed to register through the din. He looked at Sami and Saleem—they were both watching the jet takeoff. Another muffled thunk nearly caused him to turn, but then his eyes averted to the woman in the runabout. Her tiny boat was circling behind the motorsailer, barely visible. The woman had donned a T-shirt. He mused that sunburn would soon be the least of her problems.

As it turned out, this was Boutros' final living thought—in the next instant, a sturdy metal cylinder imparted a crushing blow to his skull.

For two reasons, Slaton had viewed the man in the wheelhouse as his primary target. Based on position and demeanor, he was almost certainly the commander. He was also nearest the point where Slaton had come aboard.

Not wanting to expend his one-shot weapon, he'd gone with the Spare Air canister. Although small and light, it was made from high-grade steel. One vicious hammer blow had done the job. The leanly built man crumpled.

Before he'd even hit the deck, Slaton was rushing aft. The man with the backpack had a clear view of the wheelhouse. He'd seen what was happening and reacted predictably, digging into the backpack for what had to be a gun. If he had already had it in hand, it would have forced Slaton into cover.

Thankfully, the man with the backpack wasn't

a pro. A trained operator would never have tried to remove the weapon from the carrier—from such short range, he could easily have executed a blind shot straight through the nylon. As it was, he fumbled, and shouted, "Sami!"

Slaton closed the five-stride gap in less than two seconds.

Like a medieval warrior in dive gear, he held the bang stick like a lance and planted it squarely on the man's ribcage. The powerhead made contact and the twelve-gauge shell fired. The results were devastating. The man flew backward on the deck in a spray of blood and tissue.

Slaton never paused. He reached for the backpack and extracted his prize—a PP-2000 machine pistol. He took a two-handed grip, and as he spun to his right checked the fire-selector switch. It was already in auto.

His eyes swept the foredeck, ready to lay down fire—he had no idea if the last man was packing. Slaton didn't see him for a moment, and he instinctively began to move. Then a flash of blue fabric caught his eye along the starboard rail. He sent a short burst that splintered wood and fiberglass. There was a grunt, and the man stood straight behind the side window at the helm. Slaton unleashed an extended burst through the glass, and the man flipped over the rail and into the sea. He ran to the spot, saw him facedown in the water. Slaton double-checked the other two, confirming there was no life in either.

It was all over that fast. Fifteen seconds had he timed it.

He saw a stairwell leading below deck. Were there more men below? His instincts told him no, but there was only one way to be sure. And he was headed there anyway—like it or not.

He descended carefully, pausing on each step. The slowness was agonizing, but necessary. The first thing he saw on the lower deck was a large compartment: galley, prayer rugs, food wrappers. Slaton heard a comforting sound from above: Sorensen approaching in the runabout.

He cleared the room carefully, efficiently. Moving forward he encountered the crew's quarters—four beds with twisted sheets and pillows, four others untouched. Was there one more? He edged back to the companionway and moved aft, his weapon poised.

As he neared the last compartment, the first thing he saw around the corner was a workbench and tools. Then the array of bright work lights on the ceiling. Finally, as the center of the room came into view, he saw the rest. A long steel tube—if he wasn't mistaken, an artillery tube. It had been modified on both ends. Slaton hadn't had the time to envision what he was looking for, but the picture before him left no doubt. This was the weapon. And it was going to vaporize the island in—he checked his watch—twelve minutes.

Slaton moved closer, caution in every step. He searched for booby traps. Listened for any sound. He stared at the breech end of the weapon and saw a tangle of at least twenty wires. Batteries, clocks, small plastic cases. He recalled Sorensen relaying Park's promise . . . *The device itself won't be hard to deactivate—a simple switch with a clock, and we'll have ample time.*

Like hell, Slaton thought.

Someone had modified the general's plan.

He stared in disbelief. If he couldn't disarm the weapon, it was all over. It would detonate, taking him and Sorensen and Midway Atoll with it. And worst of all—any hope his family might still have.

Slaton felt a terrible twist in his gut.

There has to be a way ...

He turned and ran for the stairs.

SEVENTY-SIX

"Your phone," he shouted to Sorensen. "I need it!"

She had the dinghy lashed to his climbing rope and was struggling to get a good grip. "I'll be right up!"

"No time! Throw it to me!"

She hesitated, then reached into her pocket for the sat-phone she'd retrieved from the Citation—at that moment it was their only link to D.C. Sorensen lowered the phone, then pitched it up ten feet toward Slaton's waiting hand.

Except it only traveled eight.

Slaton snatched at the phone but couldn't reach, and he watched helplessly as it arced back down toward the lagoon. A wide-eyed Sorensen lunged and grabbed it the instant before it hit the water.

Slaton cocked his head. "A little more carefully . . . *please.*"

Sorensen took better aim, and on the second pass they connected.

Slaton rushed downstairs. He quickly took two pictures of the weapon and sent them to Langley. He then made voice contact. His call was answered by a voice he recognized—Thomas Coltrane, director of the CIA.

There was no time for catching up. "What do I do to disarm this thing?" Slaton demanded.

"Stand by. We're analyzing."

"*Stand by?* Do you realize—"

"We are aware of the time constraints," Coltrane broke in. "Keep sending images, the rest of the weapon." Slaton began snapping and sending pictures from every possible angle. As he did, he heard a gasp from behind.

Sorensen had made it up the rope.

"God Almighty," she said, edging closer and looking at her watch. "We have nine minutes," she said.

"And thirty seconds," he added, still feverishly sending images. "And let's hope their clock isn't running fast." After one last picture, he again put the sat-phone to his ear. "Well?"

"We're working on it," said Coltrane with the coolness of a man who had five thousand miles to spare.

"*Work faster!*"

"All right. Our techs say the wires are a nonstarter. If we had time we might figure it out, but it's almost certainly booby-trapped."

"I'm hoping you have another option," Slaton said.

"Do you see the circular panel on the right side?"

Slaton did. "A steel cover, the size of a dinner plate. Ten bolts."

"According to our people, that's our best chance." Coltrane told them what to do.

Slaton turned and found Sorensen staring at him.

"Okay," he said. "You find a bucket. I'll look for a wrench."

Sorensen found a ten-gallon plastic bucket on deck in the third compartment she checked. There was already a line attached, so she went to the port rail and dropped it into the lagoon. It took all her strength to haul what was probably eight gallons of water back up. By the time she got back below, Slaton had two bolts remaining. He was spinning the wrench like a man possessed.

When the final bolt hit the floor, he said, "Do I just pry the cover off?"

He'd put the phone to speaker while he worked, and a voice that wasn't Coltrane's said, "Yes . . . but try not to inhale excessively. If this section is what we think it is, it might contain highly radioactive material."

Slaton and Sorensen exchanged a pained look. He grabbed a flat-head screwdriver from the nearby workbench, pried off the heavy cover, and let it fall to the floor. Nothing happened. No explosion. No ominous glow inside.

Slaton tried not to breathe. It didn't work.

"Done," he announced.

"That's good," the same voice said. "Now the water."

Slaton took the bucket from Sorensen, stealing a glance at his watch. Six minutes. As carefully as he could, he poured the entire contents of the bucket through the aperture and into the barrel. At the very end there was backflow over the portal, implying the chamber had filled.

"Okay, now what?" Slaton asked, wondering if the steel plate had to be reinstalled.

Coltrane's voice returned. *"Now get the hell out of there!"*

Sorensen had the dinghy running full throttle when its rubber hull skidded onto the white sand beach. With less than a minute to go, she clambered out and turned toward the operations building. Slaton grabbed her by the wrist and wrenched her in the other direction. They took cover behind the great boulders that lined the breakwater, their backs hard against warm coral slabs, their feet in the sand.

The sun beat down, reflecting off the beach with overwhelming brilliance, dancing over aquamarine waters. They exchanged a glance.

"Do you think this will work?" she asked.

He looked across the island. In the distance he saw an unconcerned teenager walking with a fishing pole on his shoulder. "I have no idea."

"I'd like to say thanks—either way."

"Yeah. Either way. For what it's worth, I'm glad you didn't get on that airplane."

"If this *does* work out, I want you to know . . . I haven't forgotten my end of the bargain."

"Good," he said. "Because neither have I."

Slaton was about to say something else when the harbor was rocked by a massive explosion.

•

The scientific term for what occurred was predetonation, more commonly referred to as "a fizzle." The term is a deceptively bland one for the most inelegant of technical failures: what occurs when a nuclear weapon fails to achieve its intended chain reaction.

It would eventually be determined that the gun-type device on *Albatross'* lower deck attained less than one-tenth of one percent of its potential destructive power. The force of the primary conventional charge, instead of driving two uranium masses together to achieve criticality, was instead redirected by the seawater inside the tube. The end result was that the weapon, so carefully crafted by legions of North Korean engineers, and assembled by four ISIS jihadists, literally blew itself apart at the breech end.

Yet if the two uranium masses never collided, the explosion was not without consequences. Great chunks of forged metal burst outward in a hailstorm of shrapnel, most critically downward. The boat's steel hull was penetrated at a half-dozen stations below the waterline. *Albatross* shuddered violently with the initial blast, and soon after—as viewed by two cautious heads rising above the distant breakwater—geysers of overpressurized steam vented from the main stairwell like smoke from a dragon's lair. Soon after this, there was a gentle repositioning, the greater hull taking on a distinct list to starboard. The stricken boat came to rest on the sandy bottom, canted severely, a maelstrom of purging air and whitewater swirling about her wheelhouse.

In the end, it could be viewed that her death was not unlike those of hundreds of other ships since the dawn of the nuclear era. In places like Bikini and Eniwetok. *Albatross,* like those before her, assumed her final resting place torn, irradiated, and settled crookedly on the white-sand bottom of a distant Pacific atoll.

SEVENTY-SEVEN

It took two hours for the response to begin materializing. The first airplane to land at Henderson Field was a Kentucky Air National Guard C-130, which by chance had been passing fifty miles south of Midway when the weapon on *Albatross* detonated. The local residents who had not reached the Citation in time—fourteen, as it turned out—were rounded up for immediate evacuation to Honolulu.

The second arrival was a U.S. Navy C-2A Greyhound—a carrier-onboard-delivery aircraft, or COD—that had launched from *Stennis*. The COD taxied to the tiny terminal where a team of sixteen officers and enlisted personnel deplaned—these, in effect, were the first responders, carrying instruments for measuring levels of radioactive contamination. This was only the beginning. Across the Pacific, ships and airplanes and medical units found themselves being mobilized on a moment's notice. Their mission: to quantify, and if possible contain, the nuclear disaster on Midway Atoll.

Slaton and Sorensen were headed the other way.

Sorensen spent nearly half an hour on the phone. It didn't escape Slaton's notice that much of her conversation was out of earshot for him. He decided to let it go, and after what seemed like lengthy negotiations, she met him in the shade of a coconut palm near the operations building.

"We've got our ride out."

"The C-130?"

"No. We've been given permission to board the COD for the return flight to *Stennis*."

"And then?"

"Let's talk about that when we get there."

Slaton almost protested. Then he opted for patience—and to once again trust Anna Sorensen.

Two hours after averting disaster in a bucolic Pacific lagoon, Slaton found himself strapped into a utilitarian seat and slamming onto the flight deck of the *John C. Stennis*, flagship of the United States Navy's Carrier Strike Group Three.

The COD was immediately marshaled to a clear area, and Slaton found himself being issued ear protection. He put on the Mickey Mouse earmuffs, and was glad to have them moments later when he stepped into what had to be one of the loudest places on earth. An F-18 launching off the nearby catapult made his skull vibrate, and the visual image was a blur as men and women in color-coded vests scurried around deck. Slaton saw an officer in tan service dress beckoning him and Sorensen toward a door on the island beneath the bridge.

They all ducked inside, and only then did the man try to talk.

"Welcome aboard!" he said. He was smiling, and looked about eighteen years old—although as an officer he was probably ten beyond that. "I'm Lieutenant Ross."

Slaton and Sorensen pulled off their earmuffs and introduced themselves.

"The strike group commander, Rear Admiral Wilson, wants to see you."

They followed Ross up three flights of stairs, then through a series of hallways, ending in an empty conference room. They took seats on one side of an oval table. Ross waited with them, although Slaton noticed he'd planted himself in the farthest corner of the room. He wondered if Ross thought they might be contaminated. As it turned out, he was right, although not in the way he was thinking.

An admiral wearing service khaki appeared in the doorway. He was tall and lean, a living testament to regulation, and in his left hand was a manila file folder. The look on his face was nothing short of thunder.

Slaton had never technically been in the military, but he'd worked with a great number of soldiers, both operationally and during training courses, including sniper school—that being the case, he knew that when a flag officer entered the room, it couldn't hurt to stand. He did, and Sorensen followed his lead. This seemed to soften the admiral's visage, but only slightly. Wilson shook their hands stiffly, then took a seat across the table. Lieutenant Ross blended into the faux woodwork.

Wilson didn't speak right away, his eyes alternating between Slaton and Sorensen. They finally settled on her.

"Miss Sorensen . . . assistant deputy director, CIA." His tone was nothing short of an accusation.

"That's right."

"You certainly know how to pull strings, ma'am."

"Only with good reason."

A frown.

"Is that for me?" she asked, nodding to the folder he'd placed on the table.

The admiral pushed it across the hardwood surface.

Sorensen opened it and began reading. Because she held it at an angle, Slaton couldn't see what was inside. Wilson's eyes remained fixed on Sorensen.

Only when she finally closed the folder did the admiral divert his eyes to Slaton. "I don't know who you are, mister, but if you think—"

"Enough!" Sorensen said, getting up out of her chair. "You two, out," she said, looking alternately at Slaton and Lieutenant Ross.

Ross was out the door in a flash. Slaton stood, hesitated. He leveled a flat gaze at the admiral before exiting to the adjacent room. The door closed behind him. It was a heavy item, and Slaton couldn't hear what went on inside. He caught more intonations than words, and most of it seemed to be coming from Sorensen. After five minutes, the door opened.

Rear Admiral Wilson emerged. He walked up to Slaton with something new in his gaze. "I'm sorry," he said, extending his hand.

Slaton shook Wilson's hand a second time, and said, "It's okay . . . but for what?"

"Sometimes orders come down the pike and we're not told the reasons behind them. The one we received tonight, regarding you, was to say the least out of the ordinary. Miss Sorensen has explained what you did for our nation today. She also told me a little about your own troubles. I will do whatever I can to help."

"I appreciate that, Admiral." He looked theatrically

around the room. "Does that mean I now have command of a carrier air wing?"

Wilson half smiled. "Don't press your luck, mister. Commander Rhea will be waiting for you in the ready room." The admiral strode off and headed up a flight of stairs.

Slaton went back to the conference room. "Are you going to tell me what the hell that was all about?"

Sorensen pointed to a chair. "Have a seat, David."

SEVENTY-EIGHT

"We have new photos of the compound," Sorensen said.

She removed four overheads from the folder and slid them in front of him. Slaton pored over every detail and decided the place looked little different from the last images he'd seen. He noticed that guards were still posted, albeit in slightly different positions. "How sure can we be that Christine and Davy are there?"

"As sure as we can be without having eyes inside. I haven't seen it, but I'm told there's imagery that appears to have captured them walking across the driveway a few hours ago. We've been watching the place nonstop since then—no vehicles either in or out."

"Okay. So how do we get them out?"

"A mission is being put together at Camp Humphreys—it's an Army post in South Korea. SEAL Team Five was already forward deployed, and they're planning to go in using three low-observable helicopters, heavily modified UH-60s."

"Stealth Black Hawks—like the ones used in the bin Laden raid?"

"Even better—I'm told they've been upgraded.

That's good because the North Koreans have a decent air defense network."

Slaton stared at her for a beat. "When does this mission launch?"

"The timing is being determined."

He gave her a critical look.

"David, you need to understand something—launching a mission across the DMZ is essentially an act of war. We're watching the compound where your family has been taken with everything we have. The final decision on the mission rests with the president. He knows what you did for us, and he wants to bring them out safely."

"But it's not a done deal."

Sorensen hesitated.

Slaton suddenly saw the light. "You're waiting to see how Park's coup will play out."

She cocked her head noncommittally. "There is a measure of uncertainty."

He thought it through aloud. "You were supposed to capture *Albatross*, use her as your exhibit one. But now she's a radioactive wreck on the bottom of a lagoon."

"True."

"But you can still point the finger at Kwon Il-sun for this attack. You could argue it was even more reckless the way it turned out."

"It's not that," she said, heaving a sigh. "There's a complication."

His eyes narrowed. He'd heard that phrase countless times over the years—never had it been followed by good news.

She said, "Park's attempted coup has been uncovered. It happened right before *Albatross* went down. We have excellent intel from inside Kwon's residence—timely and very accurate. Pyongyang is in lockdown and a leadership purge is ongoing. A few of the generals who we think would have backed Park have been arrested."

"What about Park himself?"

"This house where he's taken up is remote—it's in the southwest corner of the country. Kwon knows where Park is, but he won't mount an assault until his own safety is assured. We need to figure out two things: how fast Kwon will move, and with how much force. Until we know that, we can't launch a high-risk exfiltration mission across the border. Otherwise we could end up with a SEAL team getting overrun by a battalion, outnumbered fifty to one."

A new revelation hit Slaton. He dipped his head and shook it somberly. "No . . . I should have seen this sooner."

"What?" she asked.

"You have a SEAL team prepositioned? The latest and greatest Black Hawks at Camp Humphreys? This isn't about my family. It's a contingency you've been planning since Park first contacted you. If the coup fails, you want to get him out as a defector. Grill him, give him a new life if he cooperates. There can't be any better source on the regime than the head of SSD."

Sorensen held his gaze. "Yes, we do want him. And yes, this op was a planned contingency. Are you surprised? Do you blame us?"

Slaton's voice went hollow. "No. I guess I hadn't really thought it all through."

"There's hope, David. We're watching very closely. It's not out of the question that Park's coup could still take hold. If not, we want very much to get him out—we just can't start World War III to do it."

He nodded, knowing everything Sorensen was saying was perfectly logical. He closed his eyes and rubbed his temples. He was weary of relying on that one word: *hope*.

He heard Sorensen say, "The move-up of the attack with *Albatross* took us by surprise. The SEAL team will be ready to launch in a few hours. A lot can happen in that amount of time, and we're putting every asset in place so we can react." When Slaton didn't respond, Sorensen repeated, "*Every* asset."

He opened his eyes, saw Sorensen staring at him with unusual directness. He hit the rewind button on her words. She kept staring at him, one corner of her mouth creased into a smile.

Slaton felt a stir. "Is that possible?" he asked.

"So I've been told."

He pushed up out of his chair. "Commander . . . ?"

"Rhea," she finished. "Black Aces ready room, two decks down, turn right."

Slaton lunged over the table and kissed Anna Sorensen full on the mouth. And then he was gone.

In his wake, a stunned Sorensen sat still for a moment, trying to recalibrate her thoughts. As she did so, she idly slid the contents of the file back into the manila folder. In an oversight she would only come to understand days later, she never took the time to inventory what was inside. Had she done so, she would have noticed that one of the photographs of Park's residence was missing.

SEVENTY-NINE

The Black Aces ready room was a busy place, a half-dozen officers engaged in various levels of business and socializing. The room was dominated by twenty airliner-type seats arranged in four rows. At the front two large screens displayed a compilation of maps, schedules, and notices.

"You must be my passenger," said a man in a flight suit as soon as Slaton walked in. He was roughly Slaton's height, a bit more lanky, with a broad mustache and Hollywood smile.

"Does it show?" Slaton asked.

The two shook hands. Slaton introduced himself simply as David, and Rhea went with his call sign. Sure enough, beneath the gold wings Slaton saw: Dan "Gonno" Rhea, CDR USN.

"Gonno," Slaton said, trying not to make it a question.

Rhea shrugged good-naturedly. "Yeah, well . . . Maverick was taken."

"Right."

The pilot got right down to business. "This little passage we're about to make—it's not like anything I've ever done before."

"For what it's worth, neither have I."

"The mission seems to be to get you to South Korea in the minimum amount of time."

"That's right."

"Well then," Rhea said, "here's how it's going to work."

He led Slaton to the big map at the front of the room. *Stennis* was represented in the center of the map, and that's where Rhea's index finger went. "We're going to launch in an F/A-18F—that's a two-seat Super Hornet."

"I'm familiar," Slaton said.

"I'd normally have a weapons system officer in back, but today I'm laying claim to being the world's only supersonic airline pilot."

"Exactly how fast is that?"

"That's what I've been trying to nail down since I was assigned this flight." He dragged his finger across the Pacific to their destination. "From where we stand, it's roughly two thousand six hundred nautical miles to South Korea. The Super Hornet tops out at a little over a thousand knots up high, but do that and you're burning fuel at a phenomenal rate. We've been given carte blanche on air refueling to make this happen—Air Force tankers have already been launched, and they'll show up wherever we need them. I should tell you, I've never seen that kind of clout in my life."

"You're welcome."

Rhea flashed his most gregarious smile. "This isn't like any flight planning problem I've ever solved before—going long-range, from Point A to Point B, in minimum time. I figured nine different profiles—speed and range with different numbers of bags."

"Bags?"

"Sorry—external fuel tanks. They let us go farther

in between refuelings. But they also slow us down. As far as I can figure, our best option is to load three externals, run until they're dry, then punch them off."

"Drop them?"

"It's a big ocean—and I got approval for that as well. After that we go as high and fast as we can, refueling twice. If everything goes as planned, Fast Eagle 2 should land at Camp Humphreys a little over four hours after we launch."

"That's our flight call sign?" Slaton asked.

Rhea nodded.

"Okay . . . then let's get moving."

Two enlisted men put Slaton in a flight suit, which was a notable upgrade—after his exertions of recent days, his clothes resembled an unmade bed, add a bit of grime and blood and sweat. Next he was fitted into flight gear: G suit, helmet, oxygen mask, boots, harness, and survival vest.

Rhea donned his own gear, and together they made their way to the hangar deck. The commander put Slaton in the back seat of a Super Hornet and went through a safety briefing—how to combat G-forces, emergency egress on the ground, and the procedures for an ejection. When Rhea began going over the basics of parachute maneuvering and landing, it became clear that Slaton was already well versed. This gave Rhea his first hint of his passenger's background. The second hint came as he was going over the survival vest.

"Where's my weapon?" Slaton asked, looking down at the empty sidearm holster on his vest.

"Easy, Killer. We carry Sig P228s, but only on flights into combat zones."

Not sure where he was headed in the coming hours—and never one to forego the acquisition of a perfectly good weapon—he said, "Let's fix that."

Ten minutes later Slaton was on deck, the clamor of air operations all around. He climbed a ladder to the back seat where a plane captain helped him strap in to the sleek F-18. The cockpit was tighter than he'd imagined, and before him an array of screens were powering up: flight data, navigation, weapons delivery. On that point—weapons—Rhea had been clear. With no combat mission, and shooting for maximum speed, they were completely unarmed. From Slaton's point of view, it seemed like having the most high-tech gun in the world and leaving the ammo behind. But then, he was just along for the ride.

Start and taxi were fast, and once the canopy came down the ambient noise level lowered considerably. Slaton watched an intricate orchestration of personnel and equipment as the Super Hornet taxied into position on the catapult. Steam swept across the deck in a surreal backdrop, and the sea all around was flecked with whitecaps from a steady breeze. More signals, more coordination. Then the engines began spooling up.

"You ready, Killer?" Rhea asked, having apparently settled on Slaton's call sign.

"Oh yeah."

It all happened in a blur. Slaton's head snapped back as the catapult kicked in. It felt like being shot from a gun, an acceleration like nothing he'd ever experienced. From zero to a hundred and fifty knots in two seconds.

There was a burble at the end as the deck fell away and the wings gripped the air. Then everything settled, a firm but steady push from behind as the Hornet accelerated on its own.

Rhea pitched the nose up, banked sharply to the left. Within seconds they were speeding west into the gathering dusk.

EIGHTY

Christine didn't know the details of what was happening. She only knew the situation was changing. She heard shouting in distant quarters of the house, orders being issued.

She and Davy had been moved to an office of sorts, a midsized room with comfortable furnishings. There was a heavy desk, and filled bookcases lined the walls. Two guards had been posted at the door, and she saw another outside the room's only other exit—a window overlooking a garden.

Davy was at that moment goose-stepping across the carpet. There was a television in the room, and Park had told her it was fair game. Unfortunately, there was only one channel to choose from, some state-run propaganda channel that at this hour was showing a military parade resplendent with tanks, missile carriers, and marching infantry. Davy had giggled at the high-step marching and was doing his best to imitate it.

More shouting from the main room, then a shuffle of motion. Christine was drifting toward Davy when Park and another man appeared in the entryway.

Davy came to her side, and Christine put an arm around him.

Park gave her an iron stare, then issued orders to a group of men in Korean. He turned away and disappeared.

There were now four men guarding the door.

Commander Rhea punched off the external tanks after seven hundred miles. Slaton watched the empty bomb-like shapes tumble toward the ocean until he lost sight. Rhea took the jet up to forty-two thousand feet and accelerated through Mach 1. The sun had already set, but they were now traveling at such a high speed and altitude that it began rising in the west—as unnatural a phenomenon as Slaton had ever witnessed.

Catching the sun, Rhea called it.

They hit the first tanker thirty minutes later—the supersonic speed had put serious miles behind them but also guzzled fuel at a prodigious rate. Slaton watched a veritable ballet as Rhea guided the Hornet behind an Air Force KC-10. He'd actually witnessed a similar aerial rendezvous two years earlier, although it involved different types of aircraft—and a very different perspective.

Rhea skillfully plugged the Hornet's receptacle into a drogue, and for the next few minutes he bantered good-naturedly with the KC-10's crew while fuel was being transferred. Tanks full, Rhea disconnected in a puff of vapor and once again climbed for speed.

They were making good time, yet Slaton hadn't wasted a minute. He studied the instruments and switches and levers. He figured out how to manipulate the main navigation display to overlay their course on a map. The Korean Peninsula was still over a thousand miles ahead. He memorized what was in every pouch on his survival vest, and decided he would like it a lot more if it held a few armor plates. His eyes went back to the nav display, and on a whim he reached into the leg pocket of his flight suit. He extracted the reconnaissance photo he'd stolen from Sorensen's file, and at the bottom saw what he wanted.

"Can you do something for me," he said on the intercom.

"Wanna fly upside down for a while?" Rhea asked.

"No ... I'm good on that. I've got a coordinate set—can you plug it into the nav data so it shows up on the map?"

"Sure, give me the lat-long."

Slaton did, and when Rhea was done he explained how to step the map forward until the fix was displayed. Slaton saw a green segmented circle over the hillside retreat, a waypoint Rhea had playfully named TRGT1. The map showed terrain, and conveniently scribed the inviolable borders of North Korea. A border which, if everything worked out, he hoped to cross in a Black Hawk in the coming hours.

He was studying the terrain near the residence when Rhea said, "You've got mail."

"What?"

"A message addressed to you via datalink. It reads, 'Convoy heading to residence in question from military base south of Pyongyang. ETA two hours. Mission scrubbed for now. Talk when you arrive. Sorry. Anna.'"

Slaton's world seemed to fall away. He pressed his helmet back into the headrest and squeezed his eyes shut. Never had he felt such helplessness. Such desperation. He was doing everything in his power to reach his family . . . but it wasn't enough. The mission being planned had always been a stretch. Yet now Slaton wasn't even going to get a chance.

He opened his eyes and stared at the electronic map. Saw the translucent green TRGT1. It represented the house on the hillside where his wife and son were being held. Now a North Korean army battalion was bearing down. He imagined the orders from the hermit king: crush any remnants of the failed coup. Park had no escape. There would be no SEAL team coming to his rescue. Slaton doubted the SSD chief would be taken alive. Doubted anyone in the misplaced Alpine lodge would survive.

Oddly, he suddenly began to think more clearly. Slaton found he wasn't racked by guilt or paralyzed by despair. Quite to the contrary, he felt strangely invigorated. Imbued with an astonishing sense of freedom. With this new information, an entirely new mindset took hold.

There were no longer any rules.

None whatsoever.

He glanced down at a lever near his left hip, his thoughts quickening.

"I take it this is bad news?" Rhea prompted.

"Remains to be seen," Slaton said. "But I do have a question for you."

"Shoot."

"On the ground you mentioned this lever in back—the ejection selector. What exactly does it do?"

"Don't mess with that," Rhea said quickly. "In the position it's in now, the one lableled NORM, if you were to accidentally eject, I would stay put."

"And the airplane still flies?"

"Not very well, but it does."

"Has that ever happened?"

"I've seen the video. A VIP in back grabbed the wrong handhold—the canopy blew, he ejected, and the pilot was left driving a convertible."

Slaton looked at the lever, then regarded the back of the helmet in front of him.

"I've got some news that might not sit well," he said.

His pilot didn't respond.

"That message you just read me was a coded assignment—we've got a new destination."

"*New destination?* Like where?"

Slaton referenced the map. "The place you input as Target One. I need you to drop me off there. Then you can make your way south."

"*Drop you . . .*" Rhea hesitated, then began laughing out loud. "Damn, Killer! You had me going for a minute. Take your ass *into* North Korea, let you eject, then fly away with the wind in my hair?" He kept laughing for a time, but his mirth gradually subsided under the weight of Slaton's silence. "You are *not* serious," he finally said.

Nothing from the back seat.

"Look, you have more chain-of-command mojo than anybody I've ever seen. But we would be facing SAMs, triple-A, fighter response—it'd be suicide."

Slaton let Rhea's one-sided debate run its course.

"There is *no way* the Navy would approve it— and without that, I'd get court-martialed six ways to Sunday."

"You won't," Slaton finally said.

"And why not?"

"Because you'll tell them you got hijacked."

Nervous laughter—this from a man who landed jets on pitching carrier decks in the middle of the night. "And who the hell would believe that?" Rhea asked.

"Everybody."

"Why?"

The shot that rang out sounded like a howitzer in the confines of the narrow cockpit. To Rhea's right, on the edge of his instrument panel, he saw a round hole dead center in his magnetic compass.

"You just shot my airplane!"

"I've got twelve rounds left."

Sitting in back, Slaton could all but hear the wheels turning inside the high-tech flight helmet in front of him. Realizing he was asking the man to risk his life, Slaton decided he owed Rhea more. He said, "Tell me something, Commander. Are you married?"

A pause. "I am."

"Kids?"

"Two daughters," Rhea said.

Slaton explained the true reason behind what he was asking—that his wife and son were being held in a compound at the given coordinates.

Gonno went silent for a very long time.

Slaton said, "If you want, I can shoot up your cockpit some more. Make it really convincing."

More silence. Then, "How old is your boy?"

"Two and a half," Slaton said. "He never lets you forget the half."

He knew he'd made his case when the navigation course line suddenly shifted northward. TRGT1, which had been offset to the right, was now directly in front of them. Its color changed from green to blue.

No longer a reference fix—it was now their destination.

"Thanks," Slaton said.

"You *will* owe me a beer for this."

"Maybe two."

EIGHTY-ONE

The last refueling went smoothly, and on Slaton's request there was no banter between Rhea and the tanker crew. He didn't want to broadcast his intentions to anyone—it would all become clear soon enough.

They flew high and fast for another thirty minutes. As they did, Fast Eagle 2 strayed farther and farther off their original course, north toward enemy lines. Slaton was sure that Sorensen, Coltrane, and the rest had by now realized something was going very wrong. To compound their worry, he'd directed Rhea to ignore all inbound communications. There had already been a half-dozen attempts to reach them, each more frantic than the last. Right now, Slaton guessed, there were some deeply furrowed brows in command centers all across D.C.

"Our best chance is to go in low and fast," Rhea said. "Coming in over water there's nowhere to hide. But since we're fast and alone, we might take them by surprise. Once we're in the hills, masking behind terrain is our best defense against missiles."

"Okay. How long until we reach our target?"

"After feet dry, it's about a forty-mile run. At the speed we'll be holding, maybe five minutes."

The term "feet dry," Slaton knew, meant crossing the beach.

Rhea added, "I'm seeing some radar activity, but no targeting yet."

"Keep flying, Commander. You're doing great."

"The coastline is painting now."

Slaton looked at the display and saw a ragged perpendicular radar return in front of them.

"Here goes," Rhea said.

They'd already begun a gentle descent, and from twenty thousand feet Rhea nosed over further. Slaton watched the airspeed build. The sun had set again when they'd slowed for their final refueling, and now blackness had taken hold. They were heading for the deck twenty miles from the coast, clean and fast at seven hundred knots. Slaton discerned a few lights along the coastline, which made it that much more real. That much more extreme. They were about to penetrate the border of the most repressive, unpredictable nation on earth.

He watched the radar altimeter as they got lower. Rhea leveled out thirty feet above the sea—almost low enough, he imagined, to leave a rooster tail. The airspeed was bleeding down now, high subsonic—Rhea had explained that avoiding sonic booms would be for the best.

"Seven minutes to target," he said, "feet dry in two."

Slaton closed his eyes. Running just below the speed of sound, skimming above the water, he induced his body to relax. It was an exercise he'd performed many times as a shooter. Tune out the chaos to place his body in a more restive state. Easier said than done—but it *was* possible. A shooter's trance.

He let himself think about Davy. The holidays

they'd shared only weeks earlier on *Sirius*. Baking sweet bread, stringing lights on the mast. He and Christine hovering over Davy's bed, watching him sleep with that peaceful innocence reserved for children.

For Slaton, this moment seemed a summation of his life. It all came down to the next hour. He would find them. Get them safe.

Nothing else mattered.

Nothing.

The variance in Fast Eagle 2's flight track had been noted immediately in halls across D.C. Concern grew markedly when all attempts to contact the Hornet were met with silence. With the jet on the verge of violating North Korean airspace, a conference call was set up that included CIA Director Coltrane, Anna Sorensen of the Special Activities Division, the chairman of the Joint Chiefs of Staff, and the president of the United States.

"Do we have any idea what the hell they're doing?" the president demanded, a staunch Christian who was not prone to strong language. "Is our jet launching some kind of attack?"

"This . . . Hornet is unarmed," the chairman of the Joint Chiefs said, having to check the f-bomb from his own response—he was, after all, a career Marine. "It's carrying no weapons that could be used in an attack."

Anna Sorensen, linked in from the comm room of the carrier *Stennis* half a world away, felt compelled to speak up. "Actually," she said, "I'm not so sure about that . . ."

She explained her suspicions, and after a brief

silence, the president said, "I don't see how that could work . . . but all the same, is the precaution we discussed relating to the Black Hawk mission available?"

It had come up in the planning stages, a back-pocket insurance policy managed by the NSA. The director of national intelligence said, "I'm told it's ready . . . all we need is your go-ahead, sir."

"Then do it," the president said.

Had Corporal Hwan Yoo not been nearing the end of his sixteen-hour shift, things might have turned out differently. The unpopular schedule was an initiative brought by their new commander: raising the number of staff required to be on duty with no attendant increase in manpower. Everyone knew new commanders had to do *something* to make their mark, yet on that evening the practical result was that after staring at a radar screen for fifteen and a half hours, Corporal Hwan's eyes were glazing over.

He was seated in the air defense complex at North Korea's Wonsan Air Base, a knot of six cold and clammy bunkers on the southeast corner of the airfield. If Hwan's attention was waning, it was not for lack of activity. Contrary to the intent of the commander's new model, he was at that moment monitoring Sector Four, which covered a large swath of the Sea of Japan, all by himself. The two other technicians assigned to his sector, both senior to him, had taken leave to the adjoining room. Twenty minutes ago, rumors began circulating that there was some kind of crisis in Pyongyang. All leave had been cancelled, and Wonsan was on lockdown. It was probably just another exercise, he thought, but his compatriots in the bunker were feverishly exchanging theories.

Hwan had a more pressing concern.

He'd been watching a target for the last ten minutes, coming in fast from open water. In truth, approaching so fast he thought it might be a technical glitch—their old Russian equipment was notoriously unreliable. Yet the blip kept coming. Hwan was on the verge of calling his supervisor back from the break room when his mistrust of the equipment was confirmed. His screen flickered once, then went completely blank. The lights in the bunker extinguished, and the emergency backups came on—or at least the ones that worked.

Hwan heard commotion from the break room, and his sergeant popped his head in the doorway. "Another power outage," he said.

Duh, Hwan thought, as he said, "Yes, Sergeant."

"Has there been any activity?"

Hwan paused wearily. If he said yes, the dodgy contact would have to be reported via landline to Command Central—assuming that phone still worked. Hwan would then face a mountain of paperwork, another hour at least before he could return to the barracks. Anyway, he decided, as fast as the target had been moving—it had to be an anomaly.

"No, Sergeant," he said, stifling a yawn. "Nothing at all."

EIGHTY-TWO

By the light of the half-moon, Slaton saw hills rushing past on either side. The infrared view out front dominated one of his displays, the oncoming forest converted to shades of light and dark. He kept checking the time-to-target clock in one corner.

"Ninety seconds," Rhea said, confirming what Slaton saw. "We're gonna pop-up now, slow to the speed we briefed."

"Do what you have to, Commander."

"Double-check that lever."

Slaton looked down. "NORM position confirmed."

"Okay." A pause. "Thirty seconds."

Slaton was pressed into his seat as the G-forces increased. The ground seemed to fall away. On the screen a distant man-made structure stood out, all hard angles and heat clear against the cool forested hillside—three miles on the range scale.

Three miles, he thought. *So close.*

"Last chance to change your mind," Rhea said.

Slaton didn't reply. His focus was elsewhere. On the map display. On the clock. Going over how he would handle the parachute. How he would find his way to the residence. Striving for any advantage in a situation drowning in obstacles.

Rhea whispered something from the front.

"What?" Slaton asked.

"Nothing. Ten seconds. Remember the position—spine straight, look forward."

"Got it."

"And by the way . . . best of luck, Killer."

"Thanks. And thanks for getting me this far."

Slaton reached down, gripped the yellow handle between his thighs.

"Two . . . one . . . *go!*"

To eject from a fighter jet is an act of controlled desperation. A last-ditch roll of the dice when the only alternative is death. Yet in spite of its desperate nature and apparent chaos, ejection actually relies on engineering of the highest order.

The entire process is governed by an electronic timer, an unseen internal clock which allots milliseconds to various components in a graduated sequence. It begins sedately as the occupant's harness and leg restraints retract, locking limbs into place—necessary to prevent flailing injuries during high-speed ejections. An emergency beacon is activated next along with an oxygen supply, and airspeed-sensing pitot tubes deploy on the seat's frame. Only then does the real journey begin. The hundred-pound aircraft canopy is blown clear by an explosive charge. Fractions of a second later, gas pressure catapults the seat upward on a telescoping rail. Only at that point, once clear of the cockpit, do squibs fire the seat's rocket motor.

After a programmed delay to clear the aircraft, the emphatically unaerodynamic seat-pilot package is stabilized, and then separated from one another, using a combination of a drogue and standard parachute. The end result, assuming all goes well, is an aviator hanging from a parachute, and beneath him a survival kit attached by a lanyard. The seat, having done its duty, falls spent to the earth.

David Slaton never knew any of that. He only knew that if he pulled the yellow handle, his family had a chance. So there was never any hesitation. Already sitting ramrod straight, just as he'd been told, he held his breath as he pulled the handle.

It all happened in a blur. Sensory overload like nothing he'd ever experienced. The seat seemed to seize him. Explosions above and below. What felt like being shot vertically out of a cannon. A two-hundred-mile-an-hour wind striking him in the face. There was an impression of weightlessness and tumbling, no sense of up or down. Darkness all around.

Then, oddly . . . peace.

The next sensation was one of pain. And reassuringly familiar.

His parachute opened, the harness digging hard into his legs and chest. That physical discomfort put him back on familiar ground. Slaton looked up, and in the dim light he saw a full canopy. Looking forward, he found the horizon. All good. He'd gotten a full chute, and was right where he wanted to be. On enemy ground, with a loose idea of where to go.

He scanned all around, and over his right shoulder he saw a cluster of lights. They were grouped on the side of a hill, perhaps three hundred yards distant. It had to be the place. Rhea had told Slaton he'd be bailing out at roughly three thousand feet—that gave little time to maneuver. He looked down. The first thing he saw was his survival kit hanging by a cord. The ground was barely visible in the darkness, a handful of muted shadows. Picking out a favorable landing zone was hopeless. He was headed for the trees, and very soon.

His parachute was a basic canopy, nothing designed to be flown or steered. All the same, he reached up for the risers—a round chute gave almost no forward motion, but in the best case one could rotate and face into the wind. Right before punching out, he'd checked the GPS-computed wind display on the navigation panel—at last look, ten knots from the east. He combined that now with the orientation of the moon and a particularly bright planet—the kind of celestial reference whose military value far predated Super Hornets. He decided a ninety-degree twist to his left might help.

Slaton pulled down on that riser. He'd not yet completed the move when he crashed into the treetops.

The ejection from Fast Eagle Two took but seconds to register in the White House Situation Room. They were already monitoring the jet's every move, and one of the consequences of any ejection—unless disabled during preflight for missions into combat zones—is the activation of an emergency locator transmitter. The JCS chairman rushed to a phone to inquire about the situation. His call lasted two minutes, and by the look of surprise on his face there was more to come.

The president asked, "Well? Has our jet been shot down?"

"Not exactly," the four-star hedged. "The Navy just got a radio call from the pilot, Commander Rhea. There was some difficulty in understanding him due to the wind noise, but apparently Slaton has bailed out of the back seat leaving Rhea in the Hornet. The commander is flying back to the border as we speak, although at an unusually low speed since he no longer has a canopy on his airplane. Barring any engagement by SAMs or triple-A, he should cross the DMZ any minute."

There was an interlude of silence, before someone asked, "Did we take down North Korean air defenses in that sector as well?"

"We did," the DNI replied.

The president spoke again, his eyes on CIA director Coltrane. "So just to be clear—this jet just deposited your Israeli friend on top of Park's compound. Which we estimate will become a hornet's nest of activity in . . ."

An army colonel filled in the blank. "The inbound convoy of North Korean regulars should arrive in thirty-four minutes."

As tree landings went, it could have been worse. Slaton kept his legs together and used his arms to protect the vital arteries around his neck. This was the primary risk of landing in trees—lacerations from sharp branches. The second most common setback was getting suspended by your harness fifty feet in the air. Here Slaton caught a break, although he didn't know it right away.

He pinballed down through countless limbs until his parachute finally caught on something. At that point things stabilized, and Slaton opened his eyes knowing he was hanging in midair. When he looked down, he was relieved to see the ground little more than ten feet below.

He performed a quick self-assessment, and everything seemed to work. Having survived the most violent part of the ordeal—at least to this point—it was time to get moving. He reckoned that somewhere in his survival vest there was a line he could attach to the risers and use to lower himself from the snagged harness. Not knowing where it was, or having the time to find out, he cleared the shadowed area below, assumed a safe posture, and pulled both harness releases.

Slaton dropped like a stone. He rolled on impact and ended up lying on his side in thick underbrush. He removed his helmet and went to the next critical step, already practiced during his time in the Hornet—he knew exactly where the flashlight on his vest was located. With the light in hand, he quickly located the seat-mounted survival kit that had been attached to his harness by a lanyard. He opened it and made a quick series of decisions. He discarded sea dye markers, a life raft, food rations, and bandages. Into his pockets went an IR strobe light, flares, survival knife, and compass. The flashlight and gun were a given.

He then took in hand his most important asset: a survival radio. With the aid of the flashlight, Slaton found the power switch. As soon as he turned it on he heard a high-pitched warble from the speaker. He changed settings until the emergency signal was silenced. He checked the selected emergency frequency and poised his thumb over the transmit button. Then he hesitated. The radio was tuned to 243.0 MHz, the UHF emergency frequency. But who would be more likely to hear him—North Koreans or a U.S. military outpost? That question was answered as he stood pondering it.

"*Fast Eagle Two Bravo, do you copy?*" came a male voice over the speaker.

Slaton saw a pair of earbuds and quickly plugged them in—he didn't know exactly how close to the compound he'd ended up.

"Two Bravo backseater is here," he said in a hushed voice.

A pause.

"*Two Bravo, this is Anna.*"

Slaton felt a lift. The voice hadn't changed, still male. It was obviously not Sorensen. But the meaning was clear—whoever he was talking to was legit.

"Anna" kept talking. "*Two Bravo, be advised this channel is not secure. Are you harmed?*"

"I'm good."

"*Are you mobile?*"

"Affirmative. I could use a vector if you have my present position."

Five seconds, then, "*Your objective is southwest, one point five nautical.*"

"Any change in the situation there?"

"*Not yet. But we expect big changes in twenty-six mikes.*"

"Okay, I'm outbound."

"*Suggest you power down for comm-sec. Check back at intervals.*"

Slaton turned off the radio. He checked his compass once, then set off through the darkness on a trot.

The general's open palm pounded down on the table three times in succession. The JCS chairman was livid. "He put one of our jets in harm's way! And now he's assaulting an armed compound single-handedly! This guy is nuts, I tell you—he's trying to take on North Korea single-handed!"

The president looked around the table. Only one other voice ventured to rise.

"No," CIA Director Coltrane said. "What he's doing makes perfect sense. Slaton is forcing our hand."

EIGHTY-THREE

When the compound came into view, Slaton froze in his tracks. He drifted behind a tree, and bent one knee to the knuckled, snow-encrusted trunk. He found himself staring at the main house. After so many days of searching, traveling halfway around the world, his wife and son were no more than two hundred yards away.

But a difficult two hundred yards it was.

As Slaton stood breathing in frigid night air, his eyes stepped between a half-dozen windows glowing with warm amber light. *Which one?* he wondered. *Where are you?* Any hope for a response to his sixth-sense inquiry was shattered in the next moments.

He heard the engines first, followed by a sweeping glare of headlights. Two large SUVs hurtled up the drive. They skidded to a stop in front of the main portico. Men began piling out and dispersing—so fast that Slaton lost count. Thirteen, fourteen. All had either machine pistols or handguns at the ready. The only positive was that he saw no bulkiness to imply body armor.

His first thought: he was looking at Kwon's response to the failed coup. Yet according to the CIA,

Dear Leader had dispatched a battalion-sized army unit, hundreds of regulars. This was far too small a unit, and they wore tactical clothing, not uniforms. Slaton finally understood when he saw one of the new men coordinating with the guards at the main entrance.

His very bad day had just gotten worse.

These men weren't here to arrest Park—they were his reinforcements, here to protect the head of SSD. Perhaps he kept a unit of loyalists nearby, or maybe this detachment hadn't gotten word of the attempted coup. Kwon might control the army, the rest of North Korea, but this remained Park's territory. His refuge—for at least another fifteen minutes.

Slaton remained motionless behind the tree. It seemed yet another insurmountable obstacle. He watched the new men string out a perimeter defense. He'd been expecting to encounter a force of between ten and fifteen men—terrible odds, but with surprise and some luck, he might at least have gotten inside. Might have been able to spirit Christine and Davy into the woods where they stood a chance. Now he was facing a force twice that size, all of whom were well armed. Presumably, the sharpest troops in Park's personal army. On top of that, in roughly fifteen minutes, Chairman Kwon's force would arrive . . . and the bloodbath would commence.

His family squarely in the crossfire.

Slaton's tactical lobe went into overdrive.

He looked hopefully at his silenced radio. But what good was it? He knew the situation here better than anyone in Washington. Knew it was nothing short of dismal. Any conceivable plan would be rushed and incomplete. And with no plan at all, he was facing impossible numbers. Slaton wondered if his emotions were getting the better of him. Pushing him into mistakes he wouldn't otherwise make.

Of course they are, he thought.

But there was never any choice. If he didn't go in now, in the next sixty seconds, he never would. And that was something he couldn't live with.

In the end, he decided his greatest assets remained speed and surprise. Catch them before they organized.

He began moving to his right.

"There he is," said the technician in the White House Situation Room.

On a large central screen they all saw the real-time image—Slaton was circling the main house where, by their best estimate, thirty-one guards were taking up defensive positions.

"He can't be thinking of going in alone," said the director of national intelligence.

"Can we reach him?" the president asked.

"No, sir. His radio is powered down."

"Where are Kwon's troops?" asked Coltrane.

A map appeared on a secondary monitor, and everyone saw an "ETA" clock counting down in one corner. *00:18:45.*

"Is that enough time?" the president asked, looking pointedly at the JCS chairman.

"Maybe," the general responded.

The weapons at Slaton's disposal were hardly ideal. One Sig P228, twelve rounds remaining, not suppressed for sound. Even in Slaton's expert hand, the gun had a realistic range of no more than a hundred yards. Far less when things went to hell and he had to start moving. The knife in his pocket would have been more useful had it been a combat blade. Unfortunately, it was little more than a survival tool—more suited to shucking oysters than cutting carotids.

Slaton did, however, have one other weapon—which wasn't really a weapon at all. He pulled out the two cylindrical survival flares. They were identical dual-use items. One side was pyrotechnic, filled with red phosphorous for getting the attention of rescuers at night. The other side was for daytime use and would generate a dense cloud of orange smoke.

He maneuvered as far west as his cover allowed, until he had a view of the side of the residence where it joined the hill. There, on the back corner, two guards stood between the main residence and an attached garage. The garage was big enough to hold four or five vehicles. Directly behind the guards, on a slab abutting the house, was a fuel tank the size of a car. Slaton could only guess what it held. Fuel for vehicles? Low-grade oil for the furnace? *Or perhaps nothing at all,* he thought dismally.

He counted four men on the roof, double the number in the surveillance photo in his pocket. They looked ridiculous standing between pleasant gingerbread peaks, but would be no less lethal for it. At least five men had moved to the front side of the house. Slaton noticed a door on the corner of the residence, with a path leading to the garage. A service entrance to the house. It seemed the softest point of entry. Slaton readied the Sig. The nearest two men on the roof, roughly sixty yards distant, had a commanding view of the driveway. They had to be first in line. Slaton settled into a good stance and took careful aim. No more than one round per target was mandatory.

He fired, the report of the shot violating the cool night air. Even before the man dropped, Slaton was settling his sight on the second target. The first man went down, disappearing behind the roofline. The second spun from the impact, clutching his throat, and fell from the roof. Slaton popped one of the flares, the daytime side, and threw it toward the top of the driveway—the area of highest threat. The flare skittered across the gravel and came to rest spewing thick smoke that went ochre in the half light.

He sprinted into the open, making for the garage. He heard shouting all around him. Everything to his left was obscured by smoke. At the corner of the garage was a chest-high woodpile that continued twenty feet in a line with the building's front edge. Slaton vaulted the woodpile to reach the garage, then threw his back against the side wall. He waited one beat, then led with the Sig around the corner. The two guards near the side entrance hadn't moved—their guns were drawn, but they were looking at the smoke. Slaton splurged for two rounds. Both went right past them and hit the tank. He backed away around the corner, but he knew he'd been spotted when the two responded with heavy fire. The weatherboard at the corner of the garage shredded like it was going through a wood chipper.

Slaton forced himself to wait—ten seconds, twenty. The return fire paused—time for new magazines. He popped the pyro flare, glanced around the corner for one good look, then threw it skidding beneath the ruptured fuel tank. He spun back into cover, waiting for an explosion. *Hoping* for an explosion. Nothing happened. He feared the tank might be empty after all. Or that his rounds might have struck too high on a half-full tank.

He needn't have worried.

Had Slaton ventured a look, he would have seen a puddle of fuel on the ground light off under the 1,600-degree-Fahrenheit torrent of phosphorus. At first the rising conflagration only surrounded the tank, enveloping it like a giant log thrown on a fire. Then, finally, the tank blew.

The explosion rocked the hillside. If anybody didn't yet know the compound was under attack . . . they knew now.

"Mommy!" Davy yelled, running into her arms.

"It's only thunder," Christine said, holding him tight.

"I don't like thunder."

"I know baby . . . I know."

"I hear fireworks too," he said. "Is it Fourth of July?"

"No, it's just—" She didn't know what to say, so she just held him. She had done her best to insulate her son. Done her best to not relay the fear she herself felt. It was no longer possible. His tiny hands clung to her sweatpants.

Christine saw only two guards at the door now. The others had run off moments ago, and the two still in place had their weapons drawn. She looked around the room. The most heavy-duty piece of furniture was the large hardwood desk. She carried Davy behind it, kneeled down. Christine pulled back a roller chair and together they crawled into the well.

EIGHTY-FOUR

The woodpile was getting obliterated. Amid the cacophony, Slaton discerned voices behind him. He spun and saw two men rounding the back corner of the garage, one with a machine pistol, the other with a handgun. Slaton sent a round toward the more heavily armed man. He jerked once, but remained standing and sprayed a wild stream of fire. Completely exposed, Slaton threw himself to the right as bullets laced the frozen ground. He felt a stab of pain in his right foot. From a prone position it took four more rounds to put both men down.

He crawled closer to the wood stack, bullets still raining in—now coming from both the roof and the front driveway. The smoke flare was dying out, only a few orange wisps fluttering in the breeze. The fuel tank was a smoldering mass of twisted steel, but little fire remained. He was certain the two men who'd been standing near it were dead. The door of the house was thirty feet away, but he could never get that far over open ground.

With the heaviest fire coming from the roof, he shifted right behind the log stack, then rose. He saw two men, sent one round toward each. He didn't wait to see the results. The instant his head came back down a grenade exploded beside the woodpile. Most of the blast was absorbed, but this time he felt pain in his left leg. He looked down, saw blood and torn fabric. Still, everything seemed to be working. *But for how long?*

If he didn't move he was doomed.

And if he *did* move?

Same result, only quicker.

He needed ammo. Needed a better weapon.

Slaton looked toward the rear of the garage, saw a machine pistol next to one of the bodies. It seemed his best chance. He was quite sure he had one round left, but didn't want to bet his life on it—not given the chaos of the last minute. He did a quick press check, saw glistening brass.

One round.

He felt like he was facing an army. Bullets were pinging in. He suddenly realized rounds were now chipping at the stone garage wall. Someone was trying to flank the woodpile. Slaton rose to one knee, preparing to dash for the distant machine pistol. Then a flash of motion caught his eye.

Twenty feet away on the driveway.

He whipped the Sig toward two shadowed shapes and fired his last round. The man on the left fell. The Sig's slide locked back—as Slaton knew it would.

Empty.

The other man had him cold, his short-barreled weapon directed low toward Slaton's feet. At that range, with a clear view of his target, all he had to do was raise the gun slightly to seal the deal. In that moment Slaton should never have hesitated. He should have rushed the man, hoping to absorb the first rounds in some non-vital organ. For reasons he couldn't quantify, he didn't.

The man remained motionless. *No*, he thought, *he looks like he's made of stone.* Slaton wondered if he was suffering a manifestation of "time standing still." The last moment of his life being prolonged through some primal mental process.

Then the man shuddered ever so slightly. He fell in two distinct phases—first onto his knees, and then a face-plant into the gravel. He lay perfectly still.

Slaton's first thought: he was a victim of friendly fire. But then he realized the logs around him were no longer being ground to pulp. He still heard shots, but a second type of weapon had entered the fray. A sharp, muted clatter. Audible mechanical action. This sound he knew very well—someone employing high-end, sound-suppressed weapons.

Then he saw four heavy shapes emerge from the treeline, crouched and firing on the move. Tightly spaced, disciplined fire. Perfect spacing between elements. The barrage that had begun five minutes ago was dying fast. Slaton watched two bodies crumple near the house. Another seemed to take flight off the roof. Park's men, falling like rain.

Slaton's next thought was more logical—Chairman Kwon's battalion had arrived. Yet these were not North Korean conscripts.

Four more shapes emerged from the darkness, playing Reaper to Park's fast-fading defenses. The gunfire died down abruptly. Only an occasional burst now, and exclusively from the new arrivals. Slaton had no doubt he was watching professionals—a point finalized when a black man built like a mountain jogged toward him. He stopped three steps away, his breath going to vapor like a train at the top of a hill.

"Mr. Slaton?" he asked in a deep baritone.

A nod.

"Commander Marcus Danford, SEAL Team Five. You look like you could use some help."

When a bullet had come through the window minutes earlier, Christine was thankful she'd bundled Davy under the big desk. It protected them on three sides.

The pair of guards at the door had disappeared when the gunfire broke out. A tremendous battle had been raging outside, but it seemed to be dying down. Not knowing the implications of it, she decided staying where they were was the safest option.

A rush of footsteps echoed from the main room. That was followed by the only two voices Christine would have recognized here: Park and Khang. The two men's words were in Korean, but their tones could be read. Khang was in charge, Park compliant.

The footsteps came closer.

"Mommy—"

"Shh!" she responded, putting an index finger to her lips.

Davy frowned, but seemed to sense the importance of what she was telling him.

They came into the room, and she saw shadows beneath the desk's front panel, moving toward the wall on the left. Then she heard an odd sound, like a heavy door creaking on old hinges.

Park said something, the fear in his voice not needing translation. That was followed immediately by a heavy blow and a grunt.

More squeaking, then silence.

Christine realized her hand was over Davy's mouth. He looked frightened. After a minute of silence, she softly removed her hand and tried to smile. He half smiled back.

A minute later she heard a second group of footfalls from the main room—at least three or four this time, heavier and intermittent. No voices at all. Christine bent lower, trying to get a look beneath the low gap of the desk's façade. She saw two pairs of boots pause at the study's entrance. Davy suddenly mirrored her move, falling on his belly to peek beneath the one-foot gap.

She reached to pull him away, but he squealed and wriggled free.

"Davy, no! Get back—"

He squirmed underneath and disappeared. Christine's heart seemed to stop. The next sound she heard was her son's voice. "Daddy!"

She backed out and cleared the desk just in time to see Davy leaping into his father's arms. Relief swept through her like a wave—the fear, the tension, all purged in an instant. Christine locked eyes with David, embracing him from afar as their son clung to his chest. Two men stood next to David, both soldiers. Neither looked Korean.

She walked slowly toward them.

David looked like a battle-weary warrior. There was blood and dirt on his face. His hair was a grimy mess. He was wearing a uniform of some kind, parts of which looked like they'd gone through a shredder. None of that mattered.

His arms remained locked around his son. His eyes never left hers.

Only when she was closer did Christine see the rest. Something she had never before seen.

There were tears streaming down her husband's face.

EIGHTY-FIVE

As much as Slaton wanted to take a moment with his family, he knew they weren't out of harm's way. So he had no complaint when Danford declared, "We need to get the hell out of here! Inbound regulars are getting close!"

"Where are your Black Hawks?" Slaton asked.

"We put down in a clearing about a klick out. The house is secure now, so I'm bringing them in closer—the parking lot outside is a decent LZ."

No sooner had Danford said it than Slaton heard the low-frequency *whoop whoop* of rotors.

They left the house as a group, Slaton carrying Davy, Christine right behind him. The two SEALs outriggered on either side. The chopper was waiting like a rented limo, the side door open, alert team members standing on either side.

As Slaton was lifting Davy into the helo, a pair of SEALs rushed up to Danford. "Sir, we can't find Park," the lead man said.

Danford began coordinating on his tactical mic.

Christine pulled Slaton aside. "They're looking for Park?" she asked.

"Long story, but yeah. They want to bring him out as a defector."

"I think I know where he is . . ."

A minute later Christine was in the Black Hawk seated next to Davy. Four SEALs were inside with them.

The second of the three Black Hawks was landing behind them, more of the team ready to board up. Danford was still coordinating on his comm unit. A man began waving Slaton into the Black Hawk with Christine and Davy.

Slaton hesitated.

He knew that if they didn't get Park out, the Korean was as good as dead. Given that the man had ordered the kidnapping of his family, Slaton wouldn't lose any sleep over it. But there was another consideration. One he couldn't shake away.

He sided up to Danford. "I've got something for you."

"Make it quick," Danford said.

Slaton relayed what his wife had just told him.

The big man eyed him. "You sure about this?"

"If my wife said it, it's solid. And it makes sense. You've searched the entire house and come up empty—but Park couldn't have gone far."

Danford looked at his watch. "Can you show me where?"

Slaton looked at Christine, then Danford. "You saved my life—and my family. What goes around comes around."

"Okay, let's do it."

"I need two quick things."

Slaton got them both. Danford went to the nearest Black Hawk and requisitioned an MP5 from one of his departing men. He handed it to Slaton, then looked at the pilot in the left seat and spun a finger in the air. The Black Hawk's engine began spooling up.

Slaton looked at Christine. At first she looked uncertain, and reached out a hand pleadingly.

He backed clear of the rotor wash and tried to shout, "It's okay, I'm on the next one."

His words were drowned out by the noise.

Danford had his platoon organized quickly. After the second Black Hawk took off, the third landed in its spot. He assigned two of the team to stay with the helo, then led the way back into the house. Slaton and Danford were joined by two other men. On the fly, Danford introduced them as Cutter and Snipe. Slaton doubted those were the names on their birth certificates, but he hardly cared. He was sure they were among the most capable men on a very capable team.

They moved quickly to the study, everyone on alert—they couldn't be sure every hostile had been dealt with. According to Christine, Park and another man had gone through a door in the southern wall of the room—a door that had to be concealed. She'd also described to Slaton the man who'd apparently forced Park inside—she said it was the same one who'd abducted her and Davy from Mallorca. Based on that description, Slaton asked if the man had an injured leg. His wife had looked at him like he was a mind reader. He didn't take the time to explain.

The wall in question was roughly twenty feet in length, and it didn't take long to find the hidden entry. Rapping on panels and fingering gaps, Danford was the one who hit paydirt. He beckoned Slaton and pointed to a false panel.

The commander cautiously cracked it open an inch, trying to peer through the gap. "Looks like a tunnel," he said.

"Booby traps?" suggested the stocky man who went by Cutter.

"No way to tell," Danford said.

"No time to find out," said Slaton. "We go now or we don't go."

Danford looked at his men, got two nods. Slaton echoed the sentiment.

From that point hand signals took over. Danford, apparently, had validated Slaton as an operator of some kind. Or perhaps he'd been briefed on his background. Either way, he did what any good commander would do—he paired himself with the new guy.

Flashlights and weapons were readied. Danford pulled the door open slowly, cautious for the least resistance. It opened with little more than a few creaks on the hinges. Cutter and Snipe moved through and began clearing.

It was indeed a tunnel, and flashlights weren't necessary. A strip of lights lined one wall—dim, but enough to see the passageway. The tunnel was cut through rock, uneven edges over a dirt floor.

With the other pair established inside, Slaton and Danford leapfrogged, moving ten steps ahead, then taking cover in recesses along the ragged wall. They went through two more iterations, trying to keep a balance between speed and recklessness.

At that point, with his shoulder against the cut rock wall, Slaton could see thirty feet ahead. Beyond that, the passage seemed to widen and eventually terminate in a flat wall. It was either a junction where the tunnel branched, or possibly a terminus ... which meant a room of some sort. He looked to Danford, who was preparing to signal another advance, when the silence was shattered by gunfire.

Bullets tore into the walls, chipping stone and shattering one of the overhead lights.

Everyone backed into cover as best they could, and Slaton and Danford immediately returned fire. It was dense counter-fire, and soon the two men in back had positioned themselves to add to the response. There was a quick signal from Danford, and seconds later Cutter threw a grenade into the opening ahead. Slaton knew it had to be a flashbang—they wanted Park alive—so he averted his eyes. Even from thirty feet away, the sound was deafening inside the tunnel. For anyone at the junction it would have been disabling—which, of course, was the point.

Cutter and Snipe vaulted ahead on Danford's signal. Slaton waited, his MP5 ready to lay down fire. His ears were ringing mightily.

Seconds later, Cutter shouted down the tunnel, "All clear!"

Slaton followed Danford's big frame to the end. He rounded the corner. It was indeed a room.

The man who had to be Park was rolling on the ground holding the sides of his head. He was moaning and looked bewildered as Cutter searched him. The other man was slumped against the back wall. Slaton of course recognized Scarhead—a man he'd last seen stumbling out of Paul Mordechai's flat.

Snipe approached him cautiously, and with Danford covering, he bent down to make sure the Korean wasn't armed. Scarhead looked catatonic, his eyes glassy. He'd taken at least two hits from their return fire—one in his chest, the other in what would have been his good leg. The chest wound was bleeding badly.

Slaton held steady. Before him were the two men who'd abducted his family. One had placed the order, the other carried it out. He also remembered what Scarhead had done to Mordechai. The hammer, the knife.

Snipe stood, and said, "He's clean. This guy's gonna bleed out."

"Can't be our problem," Danford said. "We need to move!"

Cutter and Snipe each took one of Park's arms and lifted him. They began carrying him toward the study, his feet dragging in the dirt between them.

Slaton bent down and looked at Scarhead. His gray eyes probed, and soon he saw recognition. The Korean looked angry at first, tried to move. A hand began to rise, but Slaton blocked it effortlessly. The man tried to speak, but was unable to generate any sound. Whatever surge of adrenaline had come faded just as quickly. Slaton looked at the chest wound. Snipe was right—without attention very soon, he was done for.

"Come on!" Danford said, backing out toward the tunnel. Slaton stood, his MP5 poised across his chest. He turned and ran down the tunnel.

As they reached the door to the study, Danford leapt through. Slaton slid to a stop in the dirt just short of the entrance.

"What the hell are you doing?" Danford said. "Kwon's force is less than a klick up the road!"

Slaton looked down the tunnel. He saw five lights remaining on the side wall. He trained the MP5 and took careful aim. Beginning with the farthest he took each one out. Five lights, five shots. The tunnel fell to complete darkness. He stepped out into the study, then very carefully closed the door. Properly closed, it was an artfully crafted panel—no hint whatsoever of the passageway behind.

He turned to see Danford staring at him. Without comment, the big man turned and ran with stunning speed. Slaton could barely keep up. They were out the front doors seconds later, pitching themselves through the helo's side door.

The last Black Hawk rose quickly, throwing a massive cloud of dust, and soon faded into the night sky.

EIGHTY-SIX

Spring had come early to Montana. The hills remained tawny and the distant mountains were capped in snow, yet tendrils of green had begun to emerge. Sprouting from highway overpasses, budding beneath stones, clawing from melting snow banks. According to local prognosticators, it was probably all for naught—a late cold front was on the way. Even so, after the long winter, even false starts were welcome.

Sorensen drove her rented Nissan along a winding mountain road. She could barely take her eyes off the scenery. The desolation was as absolute as it was inviting. They called it Big Sky country, and she could see why. The blue dome above seemed cast through a fish-eye lens, the high popcorn clouds untouchable. Altogether, a scene light-years removed from where she'd started her day—the Washington Beltway. An early-morning commercial flight had taken her to Denver, and a connection to Missoula put her in the right neighborhood. But a big neighborhood it was.

She'd been driving for two hours, long enough to understand why speed limits here were effectively optional. Sorensen followed the directions as best she could—the signal on her phone was spotty, and she'd already missed one turn in a place called Paradise.

Paradise, Montana, she thought. *How perfect is that?*

The final turn point wasn't a road but a landmark—a rust-brown barn fronted by a pond on the far side of mile marker 119. She found it, or so she thought, and was stunned to have to give way to another car for the left turn. It was the first traffic she'd seen in twenty miles. The road turned out to be unimproved, but it was in decent shape with a raised bed and a recently groomed surface. She'd been warned it might degrade farther on, but four-wheel drive wasn't required—as long as the weather held.

Five miles on, she came to a fork in the road. This too had been briefed—she steered left. There Sorensen's directions ended. Assuming she hadn't taken any wrong turns, there would be but one residence at the end. The road paralleled a stream for a time. To the left were high hills, to the right a broad plain fed to the distant Rockies. Five minutes later she came to a fence and a cattle guard. She eased the Nissan over, rattling across the grate, and accelerated up an easy rise. At the top of the next hill the house came into view.

It was a modest one-story ranch—of course—with a multi-peaked roof that cradled snow in the shingled valleys. To one side she saw a big wooden playground—the kind that came with extensive directions and got delivered by a lumber truck. Assembled by a dad. A faint swirl of smoke climbed from the chimney. She saw one vehicle on the wide parking apron—a standard pickup truck, not new, not old.

Sorensen pulled in behind the truck and killed the

engine. She got out and paused on the gravel drive. She stood and listened for a time, stunned by the silence. Then the sensation came again—the same one she'd had standing between twin fountains at Frankfurt's Alte Oper.

"Is that like a personal challenge for you or something?" she asked blindly. Sorensen turned to find Slaton standing casually five steps away. How he could have approached so silently over the gravel she had no idea.

"How are you, Anna?"

"I'm good. And you?"

"Never better."

She smiled, and thought he probably meant it. Slaton looked good—far better than the last time she'd seen him. That had been in a hospital at Osan Air Base. He'd had multiple shrapnel wounds and a bullet graze on one foot—he probably would have been admitted if his wife wasn't a physician. Today he was wearing cargo pants, a light jacket, and trail boots. The five-day shadow she remembered was gone. He'd even gotten a haircut.

"So is it really forty acres?" she asked, casting her gaze across the hills.

"That's what the lot diagram says, but I never bothered to measure it. Doesn't matter, really. There's national forest on two sides, and my neighbor has about eight thousand acres—his place is three miles up the other fork in the road."

She nodded thoughtfully. "That's a lot of ground to watch over. The offer still stands—I can give you a security detail."

Slaton shook his head. "I tried to talk Christine into that, but she wanted no part of it. She said it would make her feel like a prisoner. She wants a normal life. She wants to get out and work, have a social life for her and Davy—maybe even one for me."

Sorensen smirked. "I'm having a vision of you joining the Elks club."

"Maybe I will. Anyway, a big security contingent . . . that can be a flag in itself. I keep a close eye on my family—as close as Christine will allow. But I have to admit, the way things are now—we're relying pretty heavily on the identities you gave us."

Sorensen looked at the noticeable bump beneath his jacket. "But not completely."

He grinned. "If there's one way to stand out up here, it's to *not* carry."

"Makes sense. So no problems with what NROC put together?" The National Resettlement Operations Center was the CIA's protection program for agents and officers thought to be at risk—like the FBI's Witness Protection Program, but on steroids.

"Seems to be working so far. Thankfully, our legends kept our first names in line—it'd be hard to explain to Davy otherwise."

"How's he doing?"

"He's good. There were a couple of awkward questions, a few bad dreams. But at his age . . . I don't think he'll remember much."

"And Christine is working?"

"Yeah, she's there now."

"Out of your sight?"

"Yeah, I know . . . with what we've been through and all. But she refuses to go through life looking over her shoulder. She does a half shift four days a week at the local clinic. Usually takes Davy with her—the PA lives across the street and has a girl the same age. Her husband stays with them."

"A play date with a girl?"

"They have a trampoline."

"Ah. Sounds like a pretty good gig for everyone."

"Christine didn't have any trouble finding work. Small communities in these parts are starved for primary care physicians. The group that hired her offered to pay off her student loans—unfortunately, she didn't have any."

Sorensen laughed. "Speaking of money, *Sirius* sold. I made sure the proceeds were routed very quietly to your new account—no way the funds could ever be traced."

His eyes went to the horizon.

"Will you miss it?" she asked.

"The sailing?"

"The running."

He regarded her thoughtfully. Instead of answering, he said, "Come for a walk with me."

Slaton led up a well-worn path that rounded a stand of trees, then turned up a steep hill. The air was getting cooler in the late afternoon, and Sorensen turned up the collar of her jacket.

"Have you been following the news?" she asked.

"A few things trickle through up here—but I find my interest in world events waning. Has the crisis in North Korea abated?"

"For the most part. The Kwon regime is damaged, but still in place. They took some serious heat for what happened on Midway."

"Let me guess—they weren't the only ones to get blamed?"

"Park figured it perfectly. The waters were just muddy enough to spread the outrage—some of the uranium was sourced from elsewhere, then there was a Thai fishing boat. The IAEA had its share of internal failures. Of course, ISIS laid claim to the attack, but we've shot that down pretty effectively for political reasons."

"Not hard to do when you're running the investigation."

"True enough. The bottom line—there's a lot of finger-pointing going on around the world, but nothing much has changed."

"Imagine that. And the CIA will never admit they knew it was coming all along."

She looked at him sharply.

"Sorry," he said, "cheap shot. I know Park put you in a bad spot. Are his debriefings proving productive?"

"I can't say too much . . . but yes, he's been very helpful. We wouldn't have gotten him out without your help."

"I wouldn't have gotten my family out without Danford and Team Five. All the same, if you end up giving Park his own forty acres, make it in a swamp somewhere."

"I can promise it won't be here."

"That would be best for his sake," Slaton said.

"Midway Atoll is getting cleaned up. It's going to take time, but it could have been far worse."

Slaton paused and looked at her directly. "Yeah, you and I did okay." He veered onto a secondary path, more a deer trail than anything manmade. The vegetation suddenly gave way to a broad clearing.

Sorensen stopped in her tracks. "Wow."

She looked once at him, then back at the scene in front of her. Laid out along a long swale between hills was a comprehensive shooting range. There were pop-up targets, fixed targets, all at a wide variety of ranges, along with multiple shooting stands. Upright plywood walls stood randomly around the basin, different heights and widths. There was a wood-framed room with four walls and a door. An obstacle course ran the length of one side.

"I lost a step on the boat," he said. "Perishable skills. I won't let that happen again."

Having seen Slaton work on three missions now, she wanted to argue the point. What she said was, "So this is what you wanted to show me?"

"No."

He turned and led back to the trail. They kept going on the path, climbing a gradual rise. After a few minutes they reached the crest of the highest hill in sight.

"This was what I wanted to show you."

Sorensen looked out over a breathtaking view. A broad wintering plain was cut by a fast-running stream, all of yearning to burst to life with the new season. The great mountains in the distance shone amber in the fading light.

They both stood still for a long time, just watching and listening. Breathing the mountain air.

"Someday you're going to call me, aren't you?" he finally said.

She turned and looked at him directly. "Not anytime soon. But you do have a unique skill set, David. And I promise, if we do call, it won't be for anything that can't be done by your rules."

His eyes flickered with humor. "You shouldn't put it that way."

"Why not?"

"Because what I'm trained to do—there are no rules."

They both looked back out across the valley, reveling in the peace.

"There is one thing you could do for me, Anna."

"What's that?" she said.

"Bring in a team next week to watch over Christine and Davy for a couple of days. I've got something I need to take care of."

"Okay . . . I can do that."

He turned back toward her. "They're going to be home soon. I know they'd like to see you. I've got some soup simmering on the stove—you should stay for dinner."

Sorensen smiled. "Yeah . . . I'd like that very much."

Eight days later, at the church of St. Nikolaus and Holy Spirit in Rosenheim, Sister Magda was exiting the weekly choir meeting when the deacon approached her.

"Sister," he said, "a man has come to see you."

"Who is it?"

"I'm not sure. He speaks only English and mine is not very good. But he was insistent—it is you he came to see."

"Very well."

She went into the cathedral and found him near the entrance. A tall man in work clothes standing with practiced patience. He was holding a bag of tools in one hand, a heavy bag in the other. Because she hadn't scheduled any work to be done that day, and perhaps because the prescription on her glasses needed updating, Sister Magda didn't recognize him until she was very close. It was the man she had spoken to some months earlier—the one she'd allowed to use the computer to contact his family. She recalled now that he had left a very kind note of thanks.

When she stopped in front of him, he smiled engagingly, his gray eyes alive with life. "Good morning, Sister. I trust you remember me?"

"I do, my son."

"Good. And I haven't forgotten you. Now, about that window casing . . ."

ACKNOWLEDGMENTS

I am deeply indebted to those who helped create *Assassin's Revenge*. To my longtime editor, Bob Gleason, your sharp eye and creative input is always appreciated. To Elayne Becker and the staff at TOR/FORGE, you are the best in the business—thank you one and all. Debbie Friedman, your faultless copyediting and recommendations were spot-on.

Much appreciation to my agent, Susan Gleason, for your advice, encouragement, and of course the wine. Captain Brian Fitting was of particular help in detailing the ejection system on the F/A-18 Super Hornet.

And finally, thanks as ever to my family. Your support and input are never less than essential.

Read on for a preview of

ASSASSIN'S STRIKE

WARD LARSEN

Forthcoming from
Tom Doherty Associates

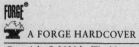

ONE

Few people presume to whisper into the ears of presidents. Fewer still are duty bound to do precisely that.

Ludmilla Kravchuk sat with practiced calm in a straight-back Louis Quinze chair. She wore a heavy skirt that, even when seated, fell demurely below her dimpled knees. Her shapeless blouse was cast in neutral beige, not by chance blending seamlessly into the curtained backdrop. Her earrings were modest, small cultured pearls in a gold claw setting. Her only other accessory of note was an ordinary wristwatch, this shifted above the cuff on her right wrist. It was conceivable she might be asked the time, but to be seen checking it of her own accord would be a grievous faux pas.

Ever so discreetly, Ludmilla reached down and slipped a finger into the heel of her right shoe. Sensible flats, battleship gray, the shoes had been furnished specifically for this occasion, chosen so as to not clash with anything worn by the two main actors of today's show. Unfortunately, the shoes proved to be a size too small. No doubt, she would be rewarded with a blister by the end of the day.

Ludmilla would be situated at President Petrov's

right shoulder, her chair perfectly placed in the staged meeting area. The two larger and more comfortable sitting chairs were situated at a perfectly diplomatic slant, the armrests canted toward one another at a thirty-degree angle. Anything less might appear aloof. Anything more confrontational. This would be President Petrov's first summit with the newly elected Iranian president, Ahmed Rahmani, and it was not to be mishandled. Or as the adage went in diplomatic circles, *If everyone does their job, a completely forgettable event.*

As if to keep the world off-balance, the meeting was taking place in Damascus. The Syrian regime was desperate to put the war behind it, and playing neutral host to its two greatest benefactors—or coconspirators, some might say—was a baby step back onto the world stage. In a notable snub, however, the Syrian president would not take part. He had been left behind near a tray of scones at the breakfast table while the two principals pursued the world's real business.

They were presently standing at the head of the meeting room, the presidents of Russia and Iran, posing and smiling for a band of official photographers—three Russian, one Iranian—who were capturing a series of wooden smiles and handshakes to be beamed over news wires later that day. Under a backdrop of whirring and clicking, the two men approached the upholstered chairs with a decorum that would have sufficed in any house of worship. Once comfortably seated, there were more handshakes and strobes until, all at once, the presidential smiles blanked like a pair of lights being switched off. The photographers took their cue and were ushered from the room. Next to go were two small contingents of support staff, followed at the end by the respective security details, two clusters of serious men, one Slavic, the other Persian, who eyed one another with that mix of suspicion and bravado invariably reared into the type. When the great double doors finally closed, a disconcerting silence fell across the room.

Ludmilla took a deep breath. The meeting today would be among the most unusual between heads of state, a pure one-on-one: no whispering advisors or busy stenographers. Had the two men shared a language, even in the most rudimentary sense, Ludmilla was certain that she and her Iranian counterpart would not be in attendance. As it was, the specter of misunderstanding demanded their inclusion.

Her eyes connected briefly with those of the attractive young Persian woman seated to the left of the Iranian president. Ludmilla thought she looked nervous. There had been no words between them since arriving in the room, although they'd met earlier at the hotel, as interpreters often did, to establish a few ground rules. Her name was Sofia Aryan, and she had admitted tautly to Ludmilla that she was nervous about the meeting: this was but her second occasion interpreting for the new Iranian president.

Ludmilla harbored no such insecurities. She had studied Mideast languages at the prestigious Lomonosov Moscow State University, and later honed her linguistic skills at the special language academy of the Ministry of Foreign Affairs. Mastering both Farsi and Arabic, she had thereafter served in various embassies across the Middle East: Iran, Jordan, Oman, and most recently two postings to Syria. It was this, her experience in both Tehran and Damascus, that had put her at the president's side for this summit. She would be his linguistic filter, expected to catch every verbal nuance and colloquialism, to neither editorialize nor embellish, and to present herself with paramount dignity. More subtly, but no less important: she had to do it all as a chameleon, blending into the surroundings.

In the three weeks since learning of the assignment, Ludmilla had committed herself fully. She'd memorized the name and location of every military base in Iran, and could cite employment statistics from the most recent government economic report. She knew the Iranian president's extended family tree, his relationship with the ayatollahs, his penchant for European football, and that he enjoyed fishing for trout. Ludmilla would of course never steer a conversation toward any of these subjects, but if they arose naturally she would be comfortable with the vernacular in every case.

She waited patiently for one of the two men to break the ice. Russia's ties to the Iranian regime went back to the revolution, and the war in Syria had brought the nations closer yet—an alliance of convenience by any measure. Now the two heads of state were meeting in the heart of the killing grounds.

Not surprisingly, it was Petrov who began.

"I am glad we could meet," he said in Russian.

Ludmilla listened closely to Aryan's translation—not so much for content, which was basic enough, but to get a feel for her pacing and volume. At this level, interpreters were expected to operate with carefully governed modulation, the volume subtly loud enough for their counterpart to double-check, and the interval not stepping on the other principal's reply. Aryan seemed on task, if a bit measured.

"As am I," Rahmani responded.

"I hope we can someday meet in the new villa you are building. The pictures I have seen are inspiring."

The Iranian smiled, but a trace of discomfort shone through. Construction of the villa—the word *palace* carried uncomfortable connotations, regardless of how apt—was supposed to be a closely held secret, a necessary accommodation in a country whose economy had been suffering for years. The president of Russia, who began his career as a KGB officer, had made his first point: on matters of intelligence, Rahmani would be at a disadvantage.

With alpha status established, Petrov meandered to a bit of small talk about families and acquaintances. It was the usual banter of two leaders getting to know one another. Then, after some off-color humor about the American president, Petrov induced a sudden shift.

"My people have swept this room thoroughly," he said, waving a hand through the air. "We can speak freely."

The Iranian gave the slightest of nods.

"It is best to not be obtuse," Petrov continued. "You know what I have come to discuss."

Ludmilla felt Rahmani's eyes hold her for a moment, before he said, "Of course. The new capability you have offered us."

Petrov said, "I am convinced the transfer of this technology will help stabilize the region."

"Yes, a bit of stability is always welcome in our corner of the world."

"Indeed. Iran is surrounded by Sunnis, and Israeli strike aircraft are never more than a few hours away. Then, of course, you have the Americans blundering about as ever."

"I am happy you recognize our dilemma," said Rahmani.

Petrov might have smiled.

Ludmilla was keeping up well.

Petrov said, "The logistics on our end are in place. The delivery will take place in the coming days. As you can understand, we must be extremely careful about such transactions."

"And this is why you've selected such a remote location?"

"It is. Tell your people that the timing will be rather fluid. Expect a window of a few days for the transfer to take place. I can also tell you that the man making the delivery is not provably Russian. He comes more from your part of the world than mine."

"But clearly you trust him."

"As much as I trust anyone," said Petrov with a stone face.

Ludmilla's ears reached for Aryan's translation, making sure she did not editorialize these words.

"I am glad we have earned your confidence," Rahmani replied. "We accept what you are offering with a due sense of responsibility. We of course have our own program in this area, but Russia has always been on the leading edge."

Ludmilla stuck to her task as the conversation deepened, yet soon it veered onto ground that had not been in her briefing guide. Ground she never would have imagined in her preparations. It was the kind of thing, she supposed, that heads of state might discuss with trusted military advisors. Yet such an open dialogue with a foreign leader seemed acutely misplaced. She tried to maintain focus, and saw Aryan struggling as well.

This was long the conundrum faced by interpreters—try as they might to detach themselves during work, they were in the end humans. Individuals with sentiments and opinions and souls. And as Ludmilla knew all too well, what was heard could never be unheard.

She did her best to stay on task, concentrating on verbiage and tone and detail. Trying not to be distracted by the bigger picture. After ten minutes, the essence of the meeting was inescapably clear. Five after that, Petrov abruptly declared the meeting complete. The president of Russia stood, headed for the door.

Rahmani followed.

Ludmilla remained frozen in her seat. Only her eyes tracked the two presidents as they neared the door. It was Iran's leader who turned and glanced at her. His gaze then shifted to Sofia Aryan. He gently took Petrov's elbow and whispered into his ear—the first direct, unfiltered words between the two. She wondered what language they shared. Broken English? Whatever it was, Rahmani's words seemed to register with Petrov. He, too, looked at Ludmilla and Aryan, as if recognizing their presence for the first time. He gave a slight nod, and the two men disappeared into the hallway.

The room fell uncomfortably still. Ludmilla heard the gentle rush of air from a vent, a door closing down the hall. The welcome return of the ordinary.

Her thoughts still spinning, she stood slowly, deliberately. She absently smoothed her perfectly pressed skirt. Aryan rose, and they exchanged an uncomfortable look. Still cordial, but newly laced with suspicion. A wariness born of the words of others. Words they had both been forced to hear and speak.

"That was . . . unusual," Aryan said, her flawless Russian faltering.

Ludmilla didn't respond.

"What do you think they said as they were leaving . . . when they looked back at us?"

"I'm not sure what you mean," Ludmilla said unconvincingly.

Aryan gave her a plaintive look. "What they were discussing—"

"*What* they were discussing is no business of ours!" Ludmilla interjected. "We are paid for our language skills, not our opinions."

"Of course, you are right. It is just that . . . certain things are difficult to forget."

"Perhaps, but forget we must. That is our duty." Ludmilla hoped the conviction in her words belied what she felt. She had interpreted for many important meetings. Never had she come away with her thoughts in such disarray. She was confident her translations had been accurate, but she also knew she'd hesitated distinctly on realizing what the two men were proposing. Aryan's unease was understandable. Even so, Ludmilla would not fuel it further.

"The Four Seasons is a very nice place," Aryan ventured. "How long will you be staying?"

In a tone that held no regret, Ludmilla said, "Regrettably, I am scheduled to leave tomorrow."

"Too bad. Perhaps we could have met for coffee."

Ludmilla recoiled. Such contact would be blatantly unprofessional. Still, she found herself thinking about it. By pure chance the two of them, a Russian and an Iranian who would likely never meet again, had been bonded by circumstances. Tied by a secret neither could share with anyone else on earth.

"No," Ludmilla said decisively, "that would not be possible."

Aryan nodded to say she understood. She seemed suddenly smaller, her pretty face gone pale. She looked like a woman being pushed to sea alone in a lifeboat. It occurred to Ludmilla that she would have to report this conversation. A part of her—the old Soviet part of her youth—imagined that the exchange they'd just overheard was only some convoluted test. An assessment of her loyalty. Could Petrov really have sunk to that kind of thing?

Aryan walked toward her, still at sea, and offered a hesitant handshake.

Ludmilla gave her that much.

With a tortured smile, and in a shuffle of crisp polyester, Sofia Aryan turned toward the door and disappeared.

TWO

Situated centrally in Damascus, on the northern bank of the Barada River, the Four Seasons was as close to a luxury hotel as remained in Syria. As with the rest of the country, a decade of war had taken its toll. The pool was closed, the hot water intermittent, and half the items on the room service menu were no longer on offer. A letter squared on the writing desk, immaculately scripted in the general manager's hand, offered his personal apologies for these running inconveniences, and asked guests for their "forbearance in light of our nation's ongoing troubles."

It was all of little concern to Ludmilla Kravchuk. As she stared distractedly down from her twelfth-floor window to the empty pool and vacant deck, there was no room in her mind for regrets about not having the opportunity to sunbathe. She turned into her spacious suite, her thoughts no less a maelstrom now than when she'd returned from the palace two hours ago.

The meeting remained stuck in her head, segments of disjointed conversation looping time and again. She'd had misgivings after meetings in the past, but they had mostly centered on her performance. Had she used the right words? Captured accurately the principals' tones? Today was different. In that unique affliction suffered by interpreters, every word arrived in her head with an echo—in this case, once in Farsi and again in Russian. She searched for faults in her translation. Prayed for them even. Try as she might, there were none. Her work had been unerring. The problem was the subject matter.

Ludmilla's meandering ended near the nightstand. She stood stock-still in front of the full-length dressing mirror. She thought she looked suddenly older, her face weary. The subtle lines in her forehead had gone to grooves, and her shoulders drooped as if she were hauling heavy bags. She had been working for the foreign ministry for twenty-two years, long enough to draw a modest pension. And what more did she need given her situation?

Ludmilla had married young and impulsively, and for a time it had worked. Then Grishka had lost his job at the tractor factory, and soon after she began a series of foreign postings. He had left her ten years ago for a woman half his age. Two years after that he'd been found dead in a ditch on a sub-zero January morning, an empty vodka bottle by his side. They'd never had children, which was probably just as well. Aside from a sister in Murmansk she hadn't spoken to in years, Ludmilla had no immediate family.

Perhaps it's time, she thought. *A small cottage near the Black Sea.*

She turned away from the mirror, not liking its company. She strove to regain her interpreter's composure. Subject matter aside, Ludmilla had sensed something unusual today in the current of Petrov's words. His constructions had seemed crafted with inordinate care, almost as if rehearsed. Conversely, she'd sensed caution, even mild surprise in Rahmani's responses—an impression she would include in her after-action report. *If I could only collect myself long enough to write one.*

A knock on the door rattled her back to the present.

Ludmilla edged toward the peephole and peered through. What felt like a shot of stray voltage coursed through her spine. The face in the fish-eyed lens was painfully familiar. Close-cropped black beard, heavy brow, fearsome eyes of coal. Cinderblock head on crossbeam shoulders. It was Oleg Vasiliev, the head of Petrov's security detail.

She hesitated, wondering if she might call out that she was in the shower. Of course she knew better. Ludmilla was a product of the new Russia, and a near-confidant of its czar. She strongly suspected they'd wired her room. It was a discomforting thought, but one she'd grown accustomed to—one of the prices paid for the privileges she enjoyed. As a more practical matter, Ludmilla recalled what she'd been told in her arrival briefing. The Russian delegation had taken over the hotel's two highest floors in their entirety. She was on the penultimate level, directly beneath the presidential suite, and as head of security, Vasiliev had in his possession a key that would open any room on either floor. An accommodation made by the Four Seasons, she supposed, for the security chiefs of visiting heads of state.

After a bracing inhalation, she pulled open the door.

Vasiliev barged inside. "Your shoes," he demanded.

"I beg your pardon?"

"My man brought you a pair of shoes last night—

you wore them at today's meeting. They must be returned."

Ludmilla blinked. It was not uncommon for interpreters to be issued wardrobes, particularly for head-of-state summits. Indeed, her closet at home displayed an entire rack of grain-sack-cut skirts and neutral blouses, issued like so many uniforms to a diplomatic corporal. As far as she could remember, this was the first time she'd ever been asked to return anything.

She set out toward the closet, feeling Vasiliev's eyes on her. It was more a watchdog's gaze than anything leering. This Ludmilla knew all too well. She had not been chosen as the president's interpreter based solely on her language skills. Solid as they were, a dozen men and women in the foreign ministry were every bit as proficient. What set her apart were her physical attributes—or, more bluntly, her lack thereof. Her peasant's jowls and thick build had been with her since childhood. So too, her stern facial set and officious manner. Yet what had proved a social handicap as a young woman she'd turned to an advantage amid her small community of interpreters. At the apex of Russia's male-dominated pyramid of power, she had claimed a niche with her plain, undistracting appearance. Payback of sorts, she told herself, for a lifetime of doors not being opened and catcalls missed.

She went to the closet and saw the shoes in back.

As an interpreter, Ludmilla was something of a professional listener, an expert in the nuanced details of spoken phrases. That being the case, she recalled precisely what Vasiliev had just said: *a pair of shoes.*

Singular.

His minion had yesterday delivered the dress she'd worn to the meeting, along with *two* identical pairs of shoes—two, she'd been told, because they had been unsure of her size. It seemed rather wasteful, but Ludmilla thought little of it at the time. This morning she'd slipped on the larger pair. They were tight—her mother's side of the family was cursed with big feet—yet by the end of the day the shoes had broken in nicely. She also thought them rather stylish, at least more so than the chock-heeled black wedges that dominated her closet back home.

In a decision any Russian would understand—and one that would soon change her life forever—Ludmilla retrieved the smaller pair she'd never worn and handed them to Vasiliev.

He took them in his hairy hand and was out the door.